SILENCED

THE FORGOTTEN BOYS: ONE

SERENA AKEROYD

Photograph: Daniel Jaems

Model: Aaron O'Connell

FOREWORD & TRIGGER WARNINGS

DARLINGS!

Welcome to a brand new mafia series from me.

SILENCED is book one of The Forgotten Boys and while there are Easter Eggs for fans of my Five Points' Mob Collection, SILENCED is a *complete standalone* and requires no other reading to enjoy this story.

Triggers:

Graphic Violence

Dubious Consent

A heroine who has been a victim of domestic violence, including physical aggression and substance poisoning

Stockholm syndrome

Please note, we're dealing with Russian characters who, while I am their puppeteer, there is no denying that in their culture, certain beliefs are set into stone and certain practices do go ahead in their social services that would horrify us.

The spectrum simply does not exist over there.

Our standards of care are not the same.

Don't forget when **SILENCED** reaches 500 reviews, head to my Diva reader group for a bonus scene! www.facebook.com/groups/ SerenaAkeroydsDivas

Much love and happy reading,
Serena
xo

PLAYLIST

If you'd like to hear a curated soundtrack, with songs that are featured in the book, as well as songs that inspired it, then here's the link:

https://open.spotify.com/playlist/3jYiUcjkQcGLySfjR67y8b?si=2e6ca51b157e4bd9&pt=db1205412d1c45e13d9b86630d45c191

"THE DARKER THE NIGHT, THE BRIGHTER THE STARS. THE DEEPER THE GRIEF, THE CLOSER IS GOD."

FYODOR DOSTOEVSKY

1

WHERE IT BEGINS...

*NIKOLAI IS *a speaker of sign language. Please, unless otherwise specified, whenever you read his dialogue, assume that he is signing, not verbally speaking the words. This will make for a much more enjoyable reading experience. As for any other language, sign language uses the same dialogue tags as any verbal variety.*

Daylight - David Kushner

"DO YOU THINK SHE'S DEAD?"

It's a good question.

Through the dusty glass panes of a window that saw better days a decade ago, I can barely make out the still form lying on the shady motel room's vomit-yellow, flower-splotched carpet.

Cassiopeia Rundel *could* be dead.

From this distance, and with the terrible visibility, I can't answer for certain.

Dmitri Turgenev, my second-in-command, nudges me at my lack of response. "Well?"

I grunt.

He scrubs his floppy blond hair out of his eyes, muttering, "The men are in the car. You can talk."

My brow furrows as I shoot him an impatient look and sign, "You need a haircut."

He smirks. "I might head to the barbers if you *told* me to."

"When do I ever talk?" I dismiss.

He mumbles something beneath his breath then switches to Russian: "You'd think I'd get used to you being a mute after eighteen years of knowing you, wouldn't you?"

With a pointed stare, I nod.

"Why is it you can talk to Misha? I mean, five words are five words. Why do I get zero?"

This time, his petulance has me rolling my eyes even as I wipe at the glass to try to clean it.

I need to know if the woman is dead or not because there's no sense in wasting my time on rescuing a corpse.

"I don't care that I sound like I'm pouting. I totally am," Dmitri grumbles, switching back to English and breaking into my thoughts with the precision of an ice pick through the surface of a frozen lake.

Then, he huffs when I remain silent and don't bother signing a reply.

Why he huffs when I'm always silent is between him and God.

"If I asked you to cross the country to go and rescue a stranger from her husband, would you?" he peppers.

Breaking off from my attempts to clean the filthy panes of glass, I heave an irritated sigh but, again, I nod.

Not that Louisville is across the country from Miami…

Still, he proves that geography never was his strongest subject in school and that he's twenty-four going on four by perking up at that.

Not for the first time, I regret bringing him to the US when he was a teenager because that impacted his personality and made him, God help me, *exuberant.*

I decide to deflate his bubble and gesture at the SUV that's parked behind us.

"No way," he argues.

It's these things that irritate the living hell out of me.

"No way."

When there is a way.

"*Totally.*"

A horrific adverb.

"Like."

Always surrounded by, "like," commas.

"*Whatever.*"

Without a question mark.

Americans somehow utter a thousand words without meaning any of them, and because he's spent most of his formative years in the States, he sounds like them, acts like them, *and* talks like them.

As much as I prefer my adopted home to the motherland, the depth of his integration is horrific.

Last week, he was even talking about going to fucking therapy because of what his father put him through when he was a boy.

A Bratva soldier. In therapy. Save me now.

I point at the SUV.

"It could be an ambush!" he argues.

I scowl and sign, "Ambush?"

Who the fuck would dare ambush me?

"I don't care if three-quarters of Miami is terrified of you," he retorts, his gaze skimming over my fingers and apparently dismissing my scorn. "I've got your back! Always!"

The trouble with having a second-in-command who's a son to you?

Who says things that lower your defenses?

You let him get away with shit.

But he can only test my patience so far.

Eyes flashing a warning, I slice a hand through the air to halt his whining.

He swallows at the sight, knowing that my patience has worn thin.

Instinctively, he tips his throat, exposing the Oskal—a tiger with bared fangs—inked there.

The submissive move is one I've trained him and the rest of my men to make, but it stings worse when I pull these stunts with him.

Dmitri may not be my blood, but he's my son nonetheless.

He should know not to test me.

He just forgets his place sometimes.

Discipline is vital in my life, not just my ranks, and he knows that better than anyone. So when I point at the SUV for the third and final time, twice more than I'd allow any of my other men, he slouches his shoulders and trudges over to our ride without further complaint.

The healthy dose of fear and respect I inspire in my men is why I'm in the position of Pakhan; it's a mindset I've spent a decade cultivating.

Now that he's stopped chattering in my ear, I revisit the gruesome scene in the bedroom.

Squinting through the murky glass, I examine the motionless form lying on the rug—my reason for being in this godforsaken town on the outskirts of Louisville.

She hasn't moved once since we arrived at this motel that makes a crack house look homey.

My frown deepens as I study her.

She's in a bra and panties, so almost every part of her is on display, and through the filthy windows, she isn't a blurred mass of purple and red from bruises and blood as I'd anticipated finding.

I thought she'd be like my mother—a battered wife beaten to death by her fucker of a husband.

The comparison was subconsciously made. But even though I've gone through worse since the day I found her body and am no longer affected by the memory, I can't help but remember how *she* was as still as Cassiopeia currently is.

My fingers clench with remembered hatred for the man who spawned me.

My first kill.

Fond memories of his death allow me to return to the matter at hand.

Is she dead, then?

As I reach for my lock-picking kit, deciding that she's worth the effort of breaking and entering, I hear the sound of footsteps on the sidewalk in front of the building.

Turning at the annoying whistle that accompanies the stranger's presence, I study the designer 'beat-up' leather jacket, faded jeans, expensive cowboy boots, and cigarette dangling from his bottom lip, and immediately catalog him as a set of 'fists.'

Though I can't deny that he's an unusual one. His outfit looks rough and worn but each item is expensive.

Too expensive.

Curious.

When he sees which room I'm standing outside of, his stroll speeds up into a lackluster jog as he bellows, "Who the fuck are you?"

In answer, I simply angle my head to the side and, dismissing him, peer into the bedroom again to see if the woman reacted to his shout.

No dice.

Is this Rundel?

Is he the reason why the woman is lying as still as a corpse on that disgusting rug?

"Well?" he demands as he comes to a halt outside room fourteen. "You'd better not be here for Harvey Rundel. My boss owns—"

So, not Cassiopeia's husband, then.

Before he can finish that sentence, I grab him by the throat and slam him against the wall as, with my other fist, I punch him in the solar plexus. Once, twice. He might not be Rundel, but fuck if I don't need to let off some steam anyway.

Goddamn wife beaters—they all belong in Hell.

As he struggles for air, I tighten my grip around his throat, squeezing at him like the stress ball his windpipe is to me.

I snag the knife from my alligator-skin holster and press it into the softness of his stomach before dragging it down his abdomen in a line that scores his shirt and leaves a cut in his skin behind.

When he realizes my intent, his eyes widen to a comical degree and his fingers cease scrabbling at mine for possession of his throat as he hesitates over his decision—to protect the family jewels or his airway...

Hobson's choice.

"Who the fuck's he?"

Well accustomed to Dmitri's timely interruptions, especially with questions he knows are rhetorical, I remain silent as the stranger chokes out, "I-I'll leave!" He gasps as I burrow the edge of my knife into his dick. The imminent threat to his manhood has him squealing, "Lem-me g-go!"

As my 'translator,' Dmitri pops up beside me while I hold the stranger in place.

"Who are you?" Dmitri demands.

"Who are *you*?" the guy sputters, his face bright pink. As my grip tightens again, he quickly barks, "I work for Çela. I'm here for Rundel."

The Albanian Mob?

My brows lift in surprise but I dig the knife's edge into him some more.

Albanian trash.

How the fuck did Harvey Rundel get involved with them?

Luckily for me, years spent together means that Dmitri is not only my translator, he's also my radar—he always knows which questions I want to ask.

"How the hell did Rundel get involved with the Albanians?" he demands, his own shock clear.

"That's my boss's business."

Dmitri's grin is like his Oskal's—*feral.* "You ever heard of Nikolai Veles?"

"'Mute?'" The prick's eyes bulge as he stares at me, dread filtering into his expression. "Y-Yeah, I've heard of M-Mute."

I don't bother stiffening at the combination of title/insult/instiller of fear that is 'Mute.'

I'm too fucking old to care what my contemporaries think about me.

All that matters is they fear me, and between my alligators, my twitchy trigger finger, and a penchant for twisting the knife when I stab someone, my rep has long been established.

Dmitri looms between us and chuckles when he finds what he's looking for. "Guess who's got you by the balls?"

I dig the edge of my blade deeper into his crotch, the threat of spearing his cock with my knife ever-present. I almost smile when the stranger yowls like a cat in heat.

"My boss is Adrianu Kadare," he splutters around a panting breath as he tries to squirm away from me.

The Çelas deal predominantly with gambling, but Kadare is their man on the streets for anything narcotic—prescription or recreational.

In these parts, Kadare's God.

Dmitri, as if he read my mind, states, "Rundel's into drugs?"

"Likes little blue pills but don't wanna pay for 'em," he wheezes.

My brow furrows.

Rundel stole Viagra from the Albanians after he imprisoned his wife in this shithole?

I glance through the window over the shoulder of this specimen of pond life but still come up with nothing—she's as motionless as ever.

My jaw works with the desire for this asshole to be Rundel.

The justice I'd mete out would be medieval—that's a promise I'd gladly make to the potential corpse twenty feet away.

Dmitri questions, "Why are you here?"

When the fucker sniffs, I know he intends for that to be his answer. Then he yelps when I remind him *why* 'Mute' instills fear into the hearts of most men in the Bible Belt.

"He tried to steal Viagra from one of our guys!" he shrieks. "I'm here for payment in kind."

Payment in kind?

I speak better English than most Americans so there's no translation issue, but this piece of shit is definitely talking in another language.

Equally as confused, Dmitri, frowning, retorts, "You know who 'Mute' is, fuckface. Stop speaking in code before he slices your dick off and feeds it to the gators."

'Fuckface' whimpers as my knife burrows ever deeper into his crotch. A little more and I'll slice into the denim. "Rundel couldn't afford the price of his fix. Beat the crap out of our man. We caught him in the act. Now, my boss wants payment. Only fair."

My grip tightens automatically around his throat. As he gasps for air, his face turning purple, I turn to Dmitri who nods at my prompt and asks, "How did you know about the wife?"

Fuckface groans as I let go of him long enough for him to speak: "We got ways."

Torture.

Still, the husband of a battered wife wouldn't sell his property without a fight...

"Rundel's dead?" Dmitri asks.

Fuckface shakes his head and croaks, "Not yet."

Shame.

"What are you waiting for?"

"Make a good drug mule," is the hoarse reply.

After stroking a hand through his messy hair, Dmitri peers at his signet ring. "There's one business 'Mute' doesn't get involved in."

Fuckface closes his eyes as he garbles, "Hookers."

That's when I grab ahold of his hair.

"Please," he pleads, but I don't listen.

I tip his head back, on the brink of snapping it, then I spy something from the corner of my eye.

Cassiopeia's foot moved.

Distracted, I twist him around and snag the piece of shit in a hold that sees him crumpling to the dirt-strewn ground as I deny his brain oxygen for fifteen seconds.

"Why didn't you kill him?" Dmitri exclaims once fuckface drops to the dust bowl that's masquerading as the sidewalk outside this dump.

I don't bother answering him, just squint through the window again, trying to see if she's awake or if I was imagining things.

"I know, I know," he says with a sigh as he kneels beside fuckface and starts going through his pockets. "Mr. Strong and Silent won't tell me dick. What I'd do for one of those voice modulators.

"Hey, I might get you one for your birthday. Why the fuck didn't we think of that years ago? I'm a goddamn genius, I swear. Still don't get why this guy is breathing, though."

Unable to see much through the window, I roll my eyes at him and then, pointedly, kick Fuckface between the legs.

"You're right," Dmitri agrees as if I spoke to him. "He *was* way too happy to be picking up some random woman. Doesn't mean he was going to—"

I kick the bastard between the legs again. He turns his regard onto me as I sign, "Since when do these fuckers not sample the merchandise first?"

Grimacing, Dmitri mutters, "If this *is* Çela turf then Misha's gotten you into more trouble than he let on."

He's right but I ignore that.

Misha, my reason for being in this dump, and Dmitri are the banes of my fucking existence.

One's like my son, the other like my baby brother—both are more trouble than they're worth.

Hell if Maxim Lyanov isn't as well. But he's the middle child, capable of more havoc than both Misha and Dmitri combined.

Luckily for me, he's pouting right now so all's quiet on the northern front.

"What are we going to do with him?" Dmitri inquires. At my sniff, he sighs again. "We just bought that plane and you want to besmirch it with Kentuckian Albanian asswipes? You know he'll piss himself when he wakes up. That smell is hard to get out—"

My dour stare is unimpressed and he knows it because he angles his head to the side for the second time since our arrival, just barely gracing me with a hint of the Oskal's fangs.

When fuckface's ID is in his hand, Dmitri grabs him in a loose hold before swinging the sack of bones onto his shoulders so he's wearing him like a scarf.

My men scamper out of the SUV to help while I ponder Cassiopeia's potential cadaver.

Inexplicably annoyed, I take a step back from the path in front of the motel and beyond, into the lot.

A glance around the shitheap confirms there's no CCTV anywhere, not as far as I can see.

Hell, there isn't even a visible alarm system on the walls, never mind anything that could be used against me...

Technically, I've only defended myself.

Until things morphed into abduction, that is.

Scratching my chin with the edge of the knife I've yet to stash in my shoulder holster, I determine this place is either safe because it's under Çela protection *or* it's that decrepit no one steals from the poor fuckers who have to stay here *or* it's a known den of vice where people keep to themselves...

"Shit, Niko," Dmitri grumbles, swiping his hair out of his face as I approach the SUV. "He's only a fucking Çela too. Igor, tell him what you just told me."

Igor hands me the ID. "Marku—he's Çela's sister's kid. The heir to the whole of Kentucky once Çela croaks."

Pursing my lips with interest, I cast a glance at the ID and then at the knot of limbs Dmitri has stuffed into the trunk with Igor's and Boris's help.

Altin Marku.

Thirty-six years old.

Reading the rest of the driver's license, I listen as Dmitri orders Boris and Igor to get back into the SUV.

As their doors slam closed, Dmitri drawls, "You always did hate the Albanians. You regretting not snapping his neck now?"

He's right—I hate the Albanians because I don't like chaos, and the Albanians are exactly that.

Each one of their gangs in the US is autonomous so you have to deal with them on an individual basis. That's a pain in the ass when I'd prefer to confer with a higher power.

And I'm not talking about God.

"You've got that look on your face."

Despite myself, my lips quirk at the corners. "Why is Çela's nephew, *his heir*, being used as a courier?" I sign.

The Albanians are hereditary and it's common knowledge that Çela never managed to spawn a male heir of his own; that's why the son of a sister is the potential next-in-line to his throne.

His brows lift at my question. "You know Çela, don't you?"

I nod.

"Think he kept quiet about his ID so we wouldn't extort money out of the family?"

"He probably knows 'Mute' has beef with his uncle," I sign.

"Never did understand why you don't like him."

I grunt.

"They're into horse racing. Our business paths don't exactly cross."

That's when I rasp, "Daughter."

Dmitri takes a step nearer to me. "Çela's daughter... you know her?"

I sign, "Long ago."

Disappointed, Dmitri's shoulders sag as if he knows I've used up the number of words I'll utter in a day. "Who is she?"

Who was Elena Çela?

I almost chuckle to myself.

Elena Çela's the reason I have a scar practically bisecting my eye.

"Do you like her?"

I nod.

"Huh." He frowns. "But her father can chew cyanide pills?"

I grunt.

He rubs the bridge of his nose. "You want to stick it to him?"

That has me grinning.

He whistles. "Words, a smile, *and* a grin? Fuck, how badly do you hate this guy?"

I don't answer that, just stride over to the SUV.

Whether or not Cassiopeia is alive doesn't matter anymore.

I'll save her if she's on the brink of death, and if we're too late— well, I've got Marku. I'll riddle the motel room with enough Albanian

Mob DNA to make even the bent cops in this shithole town sit up and act...

In fact, no.

If she's dead, then we'll make a real spectacle out of it.

I won't just stick it to the Albanians—I'll tear their house of cards down and use it to set fire to their bodies while they're still breathing.

Why?

Because I fucking can.

Eyes alight with glee, I pop the trunk and retrieve a set of gloves from the inside pocket of my sports coat.

After sliding them on, I yank off some of Marku's hair. He groans so I punch him in the face until he's knocked out again, then accidentally on purpose catch his head with the trunk lid as I slam it closed.

Dmitri, acting like my shadow as usual, appears with a small plastic baggie in his hand.

Tucking the strands inside it, I watch as he seals the bag.

He'll need to open it sooner rather than later, but I don't bother stopping him.

Then, I'm back on track.

This time, I don't bother with the lock-picking kit, I just slam my shoulder once, *twice* into the door and break through the opening.

I click my fingers at Dmitri who scurries forward. I point at two places on the doorjamb and motion at the baggie. "Make sure his DNA leaves a mark on this place."

With that task delegated, I make my way over to Cassiopeia.

That's when I get my first glimpse at her.

And I freeze to a halt.

She's fucking beautiful.

More than that, she's *stunning*.

With so much blonde hair that my gloved hands ball into fists as the desire to feel that tangible golden silk between my fingers overtakes me.

She has a heart-shaped face with high cheekbones. Her eyelashes, long and thick, rest atop the crown of her cheeks, but there are shadows beneath them, and a frown puckers her mouth as if she's in discomfort even as she's unconscious.

Her lips are doll-like, her skin too—porcelain. A dainty nose, softly sloping golden brows…

My God, she's the most enchanting creature I've ever seen and *that fucking hair.*

Blyad.

It makes her seem as if she's glowing.

Amid the filth of this tawdry motel room, on a floor that was clean the last time Reagan was in office, she's like the sun peering through the shadows.

But she's still—not even my breaking down the door roused her. This near, I *can* see the faintest of movements as her chest rises and falls with stuttered breaths…

Alive.

The relief I feel is unnerving. Especially as her corpse would serve me better in fucking with the Albanians, but she's…

Solnyshko.

The term of endearment slips into my thoughts.

'Little sun.'

She's untouched, free from bruises aside from at her ankle where she's cuffed and her hands appear to be grazed. Otherwise, she's utterly serene in her stillness…

Persephone on a bed of miserable flowers just waiting for Hades to save her.

"Look at that hair," Dmitri mutters behind me, jerking my attention from her and directing it onto him. "Is she Russian? She has to be. Man, it's been years since I've seen hair that blon—"

I have no fucking clue why, but his appreciation has me spinning on my heel and grabbing him by the throat.

Pinning him to the nearest wall, I loom over him, my broken voice unlocking long enough to roar, "Mine."

My fingers tighten around his windpipe as his eyes widen in bewilderment and his Adam's apple bobs beneath my palm.

Immediately, he raises his hands in surrender, croaking out his agreement of: "Yours, Niko. *Yours.*"

I release the breath I didn't know I was holding, then still pinning him in place, I turn to face my *solnyshko* once more.

She should repel me.

A man who lives in the shadows? Who made them his home?

She's the antithesis of that.

The antithesis of *me*.

But that just makes the craving stronger.

The urge to touch her is unreal.

To be bathed in that light, to be coated in a warmth I've been denied since the day I was pushed out into this cold, unforgiving world...

Dmitri presses his hand to my arm. "Nikolai, do you know her?"

Aggravated, I skewer him with a look I know he can't decipher. Which, for my 'radar,' has to be disconcerting. But I don't understand this so how can he translate the uninterpretable?

As his brow puckers, I release him and turn away.

Striding to her side, I take note of the fact that she hasn't moved an inch even *after* the noise I made strangling my son over her.

Drugs?

Some kind of internal bruising that shows only on her back, perhaps?

Whatever Rundel's done to her, if he's killed my little sun before I have the chance to bask in her warmth, then what Kadare put him through will seem like a walk in the park—I'll make exploding condoms full of heroin in his small intestine look like a good time once I'm through with him.

As I study her stillness, I absorb a singular truth—she has a face worthy of starting a war. One worthy of ending it too.

Possessiveness spikes inside me, which is when her eyes flutter open.

She's dazed for a handful of seconds, her pupils like pinpricks, the irises flooded with the warmest amber. She tenses as she spies me looming over her. Her breathing quickens and her nostrils flare as if she knows she's walked into a bear's den and has to hide but her body isn't cooperating.

No other part of her moves.

Paralyzed with fear? Or drugs?

She *has* walked into the den of a man many believe to be heartless, to be a beast, but I see her.

She cannot hide from me, and she will not.

Solnyshko.

Mine.

Her eyes widen as if she knows I've come to an internal decision, the sensation of paranoia undoubtedly flooding her because of her position.

As I kneel in front of her, kneeling for her when I kneel for no man, my hands reaching for the cuffs that bind her to the disgusting footboard of the bed, I know she's watching me.

So, she's feeling brave…

Our gazes meet.

Hold.

Fear has been replaced by surprise.

Something deadly, toxic—*wild*—pummels at my insides, demanding to be released.

Mine.

I don't even realize that my lips form the word and that I noiselessly utter it out loud. I just see her face pinch and blanch.

I've saved her.

Mine.

I will keep her.

MINE.

I *will* protect her.

M.I.N.E.

No one will hurt her.

Ever.

Again.

And that's when she vomits.

2

CASSIE

Space Cowgirl - Tanerelle

THE FIRST TIME I STIR, the only thing I know is that my head is throbbing.

My ex-husband has drugged me on enough occasions that I know this is the start of the comedown from hell.

Because of that, I get a sense of danger as he looms over me. The panic only makes my heart pound harder and has me retreating into myself where no one can hurt me.

Where no one can touch me.

Then, my head naturally tumbles to the side, leading to a pain knifing through my temples like no other. Swiftly, I'm drawn to the brink of unconsciousness.

Nausea swirls inside me even then, and I lean onto my side so that I can be sick.

I don't care that Harvey slaps me when I puke, I *have* to vomit. I just have to.

Anticipating the bitter discomfort that stirs at being backhanded, instead, I hear the softest of grunts.

Then, the fingers I expected to feel marking my cheek smooth over my jaw and up to my hair. Even in this state, I expect Harvey to grab me by the ponytail he's made with his hand and to yank me across the room to the bathroom, but he doesn't.

No, he…

That's when I realize this isn't Harvey.

It can't be.

It might have been the man I married, but he hasn't been that elusive gentleman since our first year of wedded 'bliss.'

I can't smell disinfectant so I know I'm not in a hospital—I've been in enough to recognize that inherent scent—nor can I feel the motion of an ambulance beneath me.

If anything, I can smell cologne and, against my back, I can feel carpet.

His scent is expensive, *rich*, but it contrasts with the dirt from the rug, the smell of sweat and *feet*. Dirty feet. And rat urine. *God.*

I groan as it makes me puke again, which is when I get confirmation—this. Is. Not. Harvey.

As the stranger gently turns me over, his finger pops into my mouth. It makes me gag more but he tucks my tongue down as if he's concerned I'll choke on it…

I force myself to focus and through the so-called high of the drugs, I can see the blurred edges of a face that belongs to a fallen angel.

"Am I dying?" I slur between bouts of retching.

I have to be.

An angel has come to save me, and just like Harvey promised, I'm going to Hell.

The notion doesn't scare me. If anything, it seems a better option than dealing with my ex-husband anymore.

I'm used to being tortured.

Maybe I'll be lucky and there'll be nothing *after.*

Damn, I can't even describe the welter of relief that floods me at the thought.

Death would be a release.

Freedom.

I sigh at the idea and sink into unconsciousness, uncaring if I choke on my vomit, just hoping that this is the last of it.

The end of me.

3

CASSIE

Toll - So Below

MY HEAD FALLS BACK.

Again.

Not unlike before, it drags me awake but the nausea from earlier isn't as strong. The pain is though. It's worse. Five times worse.

I can feel tears leaking from my eyes as I'm jostled, then I realize that I'm covered. My semi-nudity is shielded by something *thin*.

I blink my tired, crusty, stinging eyes open and see a yellowed sheet covering me. Before I can tip my head forward, a hand is there, supporting it. That's when I find the fallen angel from earlier staring at me, his eyes…

I swallow.

My mouth tastes gross, but that's irrelevant right now.

Why is he looking at me like that?

As if I'm his.

I'm nobody's.

A no one.

A sudden, blinding light has me sobbing with the pain of it.

The hands holding me with a surprising amount of kindness scoop me closer to his chest and encourage me to hide my face there.

He smells good and I suck that scent down, trying to use that as a distraction, but the next thing I know, I can hear the sounds of people talking in a language I don't understand but one that's oddly familiar too.

Nuzzling my face into him to hide from the light, I can feel the vibrations of his steps against—

He's climbing stairs.

Metal ones?

"Where..." I pause, because *motherfuckerouchdamngodhellshit-OUCH,* and, gathering my strength, slur, "Takin'. Me?"

The angel doesn't answer.

Don't fallen angels talk?

Rude.

I force myself to open my eyes, refusing to allow the pain to suck me under again as I take in my surroundings.

That's when I know I'm dreaming.

Apparently, rides to Hell happen in a private jet.

That's the last I know before unconsciousness tugs at me once more.

Maybe the next time I wake up, I'll no longer be Harvey's toy, just the Devil's.

He can't be much worse, can he?

4

NIKOLAI

I'm Only A Fool For You - Dybbukk Covers, Domingo Morales

"WHAT ARE you going to do with her?"

I continue to ignore Dmitri much like I've been doing since I decided I'd be taking my little sun home with me.

His disapproval is more than evident. He's been watching me dress her ankle which has a minor contusion and a faint graze from where her skin rubbed against the cuff—it should be fine in a couple days.

There are scratches on her arms, though.

A long cut around her wrist looks sore, but I doubt it will need stitches.

Both her palms have matching lacerations as if she tried to defend herself against a knife—those might take longer to heal. As for her fingers, the right pointer looks as if it requires a splint, and her left thumb has a deep cut down its center.

Each slice into her skin makes my blood boil with the need to deliver justice to Harvey fucking Rundel.

Seating myself in one of the bucket seats, I reach for my cell phone and check my messages, finding that Grigoriy, our doctor, will be waiting when we land in Miami in two hours.

When I show Dmitri the screen, he grunts. "She's not our responsibility."

I arch a brow as I pound my chest with the flat of my hand—*mine.*

The truth throbs through my fucking soul.

She.

Is.

Mine.

"How can she be yours?" he whisper-hisses, surreptitiously glancing between Igor up front, who's watching Marku, and Cassiopeia who is draped across the sofa opposite me.

Not once has she left my line of sight since I first looked at her.

She's angled so that if she vomits, gravity will help her until I can intervene. She's already got some in her hair and droplets of it coat her skin, but I don't care.

The man who demands his mistresses be showered and waiting in bed for his arrival doesn't give a damn about her less-than-clean scent.

If anything, I'm just glad she got the drugs out of her system.

I finger the bottle we found on a nightstand in my hand, rattling the pills remaining in there.

Rohypnol.

If Rundel survives the night, he won't survive the year.

As I make that vow to myself, and after returning the bottle to my pocket, I sign to Dmitri, "Do I answer to you?"

His Adam's apple bobs. "No, but you just got us into shit with the Albanians. I have to be able to justify this to Pavel."

My lips twitch.

Justify.

More like he's a nosy little shit.

"As if Pavel will care."

I don't answer to him either.

"Only because he got shot last month," Dmitri retorts. Then, his mouth twists into a sulky pout that might have worked when he was fourteen but stopped when his voice broke. "He's the only one who can talk any sense into you when you get like this."

I grunt at those home truths and send Maria, the wife of my Obschak, a message. Not because Dmitri's right, but because I should check in.

> Me: Is Pavel well enough for a phone call?

> Maria: No.

As always, Maria is short and not so sweet.

> Maria: Any updates on who did this to him?

> Me: It's under control.

She leaves our conversation on 'read'—the only person in the Bible Belt with the balls to do so.

She isn't to know that before I swept into Kentucky to save my *solnyshko* from her fucker of a husband at Misha's behest, I was handling two of the B4K gangbangers behind Pavel's shooting.

Safe to say, their bodies will be feeding my alligators tonight.

Nor is she to know that I discovered there'll be an armed robbery soon. One that the Bratva will definitely be 'policing.'

Turning my screen for Dmitri to glance at, knowing her sass will cheer the miserable little shit up, I watch him smirk. "The rest of those B4K pushers who shot Pavel were asking for trouble by targeting him...

"In fact, you should just set her on them. She's almost as terrifying as 'Mute.' What she could do with a pair of heels is probably worse than anything the KGB could come up with."

Huffing because I can't deny *that*, I return my focus to my phone.

> Semion: Those B4K pushers you left alive started squawking. They confirm that the warehouse was where they stored their recent shipment of coke, Pakhan.

> Me: How's the blaze?

> Semion: Firefighters are still trying to contain it. Three million dollars' worth of cocaine is apparently fueling it.

Dmitri, spying the text exchange, cackles. "Serves the fuckers right."

I nod my agreement then text:

> Me: Feed them to Vasily.

> Semion: You don't want to talk to them, Pakhan?

My gaze flickers to my little sun.

Earlier, the pushers were my priority.

Now?

Jaw working, I come to a split decision. "Deal with them tomorrow, Dmitri."

His brows lift. "You sure?"

"Why wouldn't I be?"

> Me: Dmitri will handle them tomorrow.

> Semion: Da, Pakhan.

"Not like you to delegate."

I sniff but don't answer my brat of a son.

Instead, I tuck my phone away and study my *solnyshko*.

Immediately, the strangest urges itch beneath my skin.

She's filthy.

Vomit-speckled, even.

But fuck if she isn't the most beautiful thing I've ever seen.

Surrounded by disgusting cotton sheets that aren't worthy of her and unconscious, she's better than any of my mistresses.

Mine.

The word rumbles through me again and I know it's *that* that's confusing Dmitri.

I don't lay claim to anyone or anything.

Ever.

But I've claimed her.

I've covered her in soiled sheets so my men can't see her lack of clothing, and Dmitri is lucky that I love him like a son or I'd have gouged out his eyes for looking upon her nudity how he did.

These feelings are overwhelming.

Alien.

I don't feel. Period.

I stopped wasting energy on emotions a long time ago.

But I'm feeling now.

And it's… crazed.

Chaotic.

With them roaring through my veins as much as the blaze I started in Miami earlier, I turn to Dmitri and sign, "Make sure Klara and Beatriz vacate their apartments by the end of the month."

Dmitri's brows lift again. But before he can shove his foot in his mouth, he closes it, stares at my *solnyshko*—correctly guessing why I made the request—then shakes his head as he retrieves his cell phone to evict my mistresses.

As he enacts my order, I study Cassiopeia.

Even her name is of the sky...

But she doesn't belong to the heavens.

She belongs to me.

Mine.

She isn't ready for what she's stirred to life by simply existing.

Neither, I fear, am I.

5

NIKOLAI

I Feel Like I'm Drowning - Two Feet

"HOW CAN I treat her if I can't uncover her, Dmitri?"

I hear our official doctor's hissed complaint from outside the ambulance and listen to my son's response: "You do what you can. Just don't get him mad, Grigoriy. The repercussions aren't worth it. I'm telling you he's not in his right mind where she's concerned."

The hand I placed on Cassiopeia's forearm tightens slightly.

Dmitri had dragged Grigoriy out of the vehicle after he'd attempted to tug on the sheet covering her not once, but twice.

Dmitri, fearing for the safety of our doctor's carotid, had been swift to explain the lay of the land.

Grigoriy must have more of a death wish than usual because he demands, "What's he going to do? Stick that fucking knife of his in my neck? I think he needs me more—"

"He doesn't. If you touch what belongs to him, you'll regret it," Dmitri states, tone grim. "You've been warned."

Grigoriy grunts but stomps back to the ambulance that's parked beside the jet on my privately owned airfield.

As he climbs aboard and shuts the door behind him, he frowns at me. "This is irregular, Pakhan."

I arch a brow at him and press myself deeper into the corner beside her head so that I'm as out-of-the-way as a man my size can be within these small confines.

He sniffs at the sight but takes that for the answer it is and starts to check her over.

When his stethoscope begins to nudge the sheet aside, I growl.

"Sir!" he complains.

I merely narrow my eyes at him, snag the chest piece from the stethoscope, then carefully raise the sheet so he can't see skin that belongs to me and place it above the swell of her breast.

Though his gaze effectively transmits his belief that I'm insane, he doesn't say anything, just shifts his focus onto Cassiopeia, where it should be.

Then, he sighs. "I need to check her pupils."

Pleased that he's finally started to fucking listen, I gently lift her left eyelid as he flashes a light into her eye, then I do the same with the right once he gestures with his hand that he's done.

Which is how the rest of the checkup goes.

When he's about to touch her, he explains where and how, and he lets me move his equipment so that he never comes into contact with her.

It's not the first time I've played nurse, nor is it the first time my actions matter, but this is different.

This is her.

This is my little sun, and *her* light is *mine*.

To shield, to protect. To care for, to defend.

All mine.

"Without running a full bloodwork panel, I can't confirm—"

I shove the bottle of drugs we found at him. "Rundel wouldn't waste money he doesn't have on these if he wasn't going to use them. She's been drifting in and out of consciousness since we found her and she's dazed and disoriented whenever she awakens, which is only for a few moments at a time."

"Dmitri said that her..." He clears his throat. "...husband—"

Rage surges through me. "Do not use that label again."

"Did he r—" As my eyes narrow, he quickly corrects, "—sexually assault her?"

If Rundel had to leave his captive to go and buy Viagra, then I'm going to assume that erectile dysfunction is an issue with him.

"I doubt he penetrated her." Just signing the words has fury filtering through me.

"Could he have used something else? His fingers? A dildo?"

Wrath, as intoxicating as heroin, pummels my system. Trying to keep my cool when my little sun might have been harmed is next to impossible when I'm seeing red.

Sucking down a breath, I shuffle around the doctor in the tight confines and drag the sheet away from her. Carefully, I move her leg aside, all the while making sure Grigoriy can't see her.

Once I've taken in the state of her inner thighs and the crotch of her panties, I cover her up again.

"There's no blood on her underwear. Would there be if he penetrated her?"

"It's likely." His frown darkens. "If you won't let me check, then —" He chokes on his words as I glower at him. "It's too late for activated charcoal to counteract the Rohypnol, but we can give her an emetic."

"She's already thrown up several times," I sign.

"Without bloodwork, I can't do much more for her. If I dose her with flumazenil, which is an antidote, it helps but it can lead to withdrawal symptoms or seizures, and she'd require monitoring if that's the case. When do you estimate she was drugged?"

Unable to answer, I open the ambulance doors and don't have far to look to come across Dmitri. Upon seeing me, he lopes over, a silent question in his expression.

"Bring Marku to me. I need to know when Rundel approached the Albanians so we can guesstimate how long she's been drugged."

Dmitri frowns but nods.

As he makes his retreat, I turn back and see Grigoriy staring at me over his glasses.

"What?" I demand, spreading my hands.

He shrugs. "Never seen you so verbose before."

He isn't wrong. Sign language is something I learned out of necessity, but I rarely use it.

In this instance, however, my little sun needs the best care I can provide her.

I squeeze my fists at the thought—am I doing her a disservice by not having him check for assault? Is that more of an intrusion, *an invasion*, than what she's endured?

She's already been violated. An examination by a trained medical professional shouldn't put me on edge, but it feels like more of the same—something else being forced upon her by a man.

With a displeased scowl at my own uncertainty—indecisiveness can get you killed—I move over to the gurney and carefully lift the sheet to expose her ankle and remove the bandages I put there earlier.

Until she's aware enough to consent to a vaginal exam, I won't force that upon her, but there are plenty of other wounds that need treatment—

"For God's sake, Pakhan. If you can't handle me seeing her ankles, then—"

I glower at him as I drop the sheet. "Don't try my patience, Grigoriy. You know what happens if you do."

Though he bares the Oskal on his throat, he mutters under his breath in French, *"What is this? 1843?"*

"Where she's concerned, yes," I retort, fingers snapping the words at him.

Cheeks blanching when he realizes I understood him, he hunches his shoulders but peers at the tender skin that's been grazed by the cuffs.

"Looks like mild friction burns. Rope?"

"Cuffs. Police-grade."

His chin dips in understanding but he doses the sore skin with some peroxide, then antibiotic cream, and follows that with some fresh bandages. A process he repeats for both feet.

By the time I've tucked her ankles away, he's treating her hands and wrists.

"These need to remain dry," he informs me as he places dissolvable stitches on the tender skin and sets her finger into a splint.

Dmitri isn't known for his good timing, but in this instance, it couldn't be more perfect. Marku, yowling like a Siamese cat, is dumped in front of the doors of the ambulance just as Grigoriy is finishing up.

Before I jump down, I grab his arm and tug him onto the asphalt with me.

He doesn't protest though I'm sure he wants to—he isn't dumb enough to let his annoyance show.

As my feet collide with the tarmac, Marku spies me and immediately, his eyes widen.

Lifting his bound hands in surrender, he sobs, "I didn't do nothing! Just let me go home. I won't tell my uncle. I won't say anything about what you've done, I swear."

"Just had to name-drop your uncle, huh?" Dmitri sneers. "We know who you are, Marku, and if you think we give a fuck then you're mistaken."

"I don't wanna die, man. I don't wanna fucking die," he mumbles before he starts sniffling like a baby. "I'll do anything you want. Just ask! I'm important. I can get my uncle to do whatev—"

I snag him by the ear and lift him to his feet with that single hold. As he screams in pain and tries to stand, I let him fall to the ground before he can get his feet under him. His head collides with the tarmac, and I slam my boot against his throat to pin him in place.

I flick Dmitri a pointed glance who rumbles, "When did Rundel attack your dealer?"

"You're gonna kill me," he slurs. "Why should... I... help you?"

"Because there are many ways to die," Dmitri says pleasantly. "Having your cock sliced off and stuffed into your mouth before you become a gator appetizer isn't the nicest method."

I can feel Marku's throat bob as he gulps. "Ten PM."

Checking his Rolex, Grigoriy mutters, "Seven hours ago. It should be working out of her system soon, Pakhan.

"There's little else we can do if she's already vomited. She isn't showing signs of overdose or a bad reaction to the Rohypnol so just let her sleep it off."

Nodding, I release Marku and head toward the ambulance again.

Dmitri calls out, "You want him gone, Niko?"

I shake my head—I have plans for him.

Just not tonight.

Tonight is about Cassiopeia, not her wannabe tormentors.

6

CASSIE

THE PAIN in my temples is weaker the next time I awaken.

That I remember the agony from before tells me how bad it was.

Harvey's been dosing me higher on each occasion he's drugged me unconscious, and my body knows it.

Where is *Harvey?*

The thought has my eyes popping open where it registers that I'm alone in the shadowed backseat of a car, lying supine on the leather cushions, the scent of which overwhelms the space around me.

Slightly nauseated by it, I inhale deeply in an attempt to settle my stomach. Once that's calmed some, I draw the sides of the sheet that's covering me apart and check my body.

I can't feel any internal pain, but that doesn't stop me from getting confirmation. I touch my inner thighs for the remnants of cum but find none. Seeing as I only feel skin, I have to assume there's no blood there either.

A sigh of relief escapes me but it swiftly morphs into a sob.

I've never been more grateful that Harvey's impotent, but it's his issues that destroyed our marriage. That wrecked my husband and turned him into the monster who...

"How is this my life?" I whisper as I cover my face with my hands, jolting when I feel bandages where skin should be.

Still, it's too late to care.

I allow the tears to fall.

My shoulders heave with emotion, and I'm lost in the whirlwind of fear and self-disgust and shame, so it's only luck that has me hearing the creaking of the leather.

Pain sends lightning bolts across my skull as I jerk in surprise when I realize I'm not alone. Immediately, I lower my hands to check out the rest of the car.

This time, it registers that I'm in a limo.

Before I left the upper East Coast to run from Harvey, I had savings and a functioning business and was affluent enough to support us. Even so, I'd never been able to afford a limo outside of on the night of my bachelorette party, where women Harvey was jealous of attended, women I no longer speak to.

The isolation is... horrifying.

I feel it now. Clawing at me.

No one cares if you live or die, Cassie. No one. And it's all your fault.

Staring around the luxurious vehicle, trying not to trigger a panic attack, keeping my head as immobile as possible, I rasp, "Who's there?"

Silence.

The leather creaks again, and that's when I realize my still-aching eyes are failing me in the dark cocoon of the backseat—but, that smell... I recognize it first before, finally, I see him.

The fallen angel who never delivered me to Hell.

"You," I whisper, aware that it's an accusation.

He doesn't respond, but he's not ignoring me because the next thing I know is that I'm being lifted.

Scrabbling against the inexorable hold, I find myself on his lap anyway.

It's as if it doesn't register that I'm fighting him—his hand settles on the back of my head and just as I fear he's about to force me to do something I'm in no state to handle, I'm stunned when he presses my face to his throat.

It takes me a beat to understand what's happening.

He's trying to comfort me.

My mouth works with questions I need the answers to, but I don't voice them.

I can't.

I have no idea who he is, how I'm here, or why he's trying to soothe me, and right now, I don't particularly care.

Instead, I let the tears fall into the vast wasteland of despair that I didn't know I needed to shed in a stranger's arms.

I let loose my sorrow and grief and fear.

As I cry on a stranger's lap, into his throat, in a limo that I have no idea how I ended up in, on the road to someplace I don't know, I've never been in a more precarious position.

So why do I feel safe?

7

NIKOLAI

Baby - Elvis Drew, Avivian

IT TAKES an hour to reach *Nav*, so-called because Dmitri thought 'Underworld' was a funny name when I bought the parcel of land on his fifteenth birthday and gifted him with one of the alligators that live here.

Still, I've passed worse nights in my life than having a little sun huddled on my lap.

She doesn't understand the importance of me drawing her onto my knees as I have. Not only because I've never given enough of a shit to hold a woman as she cried, but because I'm *in* the backseat.

No one drives me. Ever. Yet here I am, holding her, trusting one of my soldiers to transport me to *Nav* when I trust no one behind the wheel...

For her, I trusted.

For her, I opted to use one of my limos when I only ever drive my Porsches.

For her.

I nuzzle my nose against her hairline where the liquid gold of her sunlight forms a halo around her head.

The scent of vomit is prevalent. Sour and bitter, it's a reminder I didn't need about how I found her.

My temper is already at its limits, but I can feel the blistering urge to rain hell on those who dared hurt her drawing me to the outer edges of sanity.

But, for now, everything is under control.

Boris is still in Kentucky under orders not to return until he's brought me Rundel—alive.

If he kills him, he'll feel my wrath, and no one wants to experience that.

Marku... well, he'll suffer.

Soon.

When Cassiopeia sighs against my throat, the sound contented, I stroke my fingers over her hair, aware that she fell asleep a half hour ago. There's a distinct difference between her passing out and her resting, and I'm relieved that the drug is starting to fade from her system.

That bastard will sob harder than she did earlier when I get my hands on him. My fingers fucking ache with the need to reap vengeance upon him.

Nostrils flaring, I spy the lights of *Nav* in the distance and, without jostling her, reach into my pants pocket for my phone.

The first message from my butler has me grunting in satisfaction.

> Nikita: Your orders are in effect, Pakhan.

Then, I switch to the next conversation.

> Dmitri: You owe me, Nikolai. Marku puked all over my brand fucking new Velascas.

I roll my eyes as I type an answer:

> Me: Pussy.

> Dmitri: Grigoriy says that blow to the back of his head when he fell on the tarmac gave Marku a concussion.

Me: It took a doctor to figure that out?

> Dmitri: Just passing on the message. You want Grigoriy to treat him?

Me: No. Let him suffer. He won't be alive long enough to worry about a little headache.

> Dmitri: Want me to bring him to Nav tomorrow?

Me: Da. Once you secure him, get some rest. Be at Nav at eight AM.

> Dmitri: I get to sleep in?

My lips twitch.

Me: The Lord giveth and he can taketh away...

> Dmitri: Now you've got a God complex. Great. 8 AM is fine. Until tomorrow.

Me: Sleep. No hookers. Not tonight. And make it nine AM so you can get a goddamn haircut.

> Dmitri: Da, Otets. Fucking wet blanket.

Smirking at the term of endearment, 'Father,' I tuck my phone back into the pocket of my pants just as the limo brakes and idles outside *Nav's* gates. When they shift inwards, the driveway lights up as we roll forward onto my estate.

Five minutes later, Karl delivers us to the front entrance.

She doesn't stir until he opens the car door for me, and I twist in the seat with her in my hold, carefully straightening up, making sure that I don't knock her head in the process.

As I cross the courtyard, she shifts against me with wakefulness but doesn't fight me. If anything, she studies me as I walk her past the line of staff awaiting my arrival.

Ignoring them all as they respectfully bow their heads and murmur a polite 'welcome' in Russian when I pass, I head upstairs to my suite.

"Who are you?"

I don't look at her.

I can't.

Fuck, if I do, I'll…

Blyad, I don't even know what I'll do.

What happens to the shadows when the sun touches them?

They fade to nothing.

Disintegrate like they were never there in the first place—

"You're Russian. Maybe you don't understand me?" she mutters, more to herself than to me. Then, she almost makes me smile when, in broken Russian, she asks the opposite: "I don't understand you?"

As I requested of Nikita, the only one with the key when I'm away from *Nav*, the door to my suite is open when I arrive on the third floor. Everything, I take note, is arranged how I wanted.

I've been thinking on the fly, reacting with never-before-triggered instincts, but the journey back to Miami gave me the breather I needed to figure out what I have to do next.

She will only know safety from this point on—my vow is silent but struck nonetheless.

I know Dmitri thinks I'm crazy, and he can continue thinking that as long as he never looks at her again.

I tighten my arms around her fragile form as the urge to hide her away from the world mushrooms.

The need to keep her safe has grown exponentially.

The number of those who'd wish her harm now that she's mine will have expanded beyond an abusive ex-husband and a bunch of Albanians who are baying for her blood in payment of a debt.

Ignoring the sourness of the vomit in her hair, I press a kiss to her temple. She jolts but remains passive in my hold.

"Who are you?" she mumbles.

Kicking the door closed behind me, I head over to the bathroom in the master suite.

"Why am I here?"

The bathroom entry is an open layout with no doors which serves my purpose more than the architect could ever have imagined. The passage is shielded by a wall that can be accessed on either side—no doors.

No locks.

No escape.

As I walk inside, she sighs as I carefully sit her on the vanity.

Shoulders rounding, she stares at me, exhaustion lining her expression, fatigue seeming to draw her deeper into a slouch.

"I don't think I have the energy to shower," she admits wistfully.

Of course, she doesn't—she's been drugged and abused but she's covered in vomit.

I tug at the knot of my necktie, enough that I can draw it over my head. Her brow furrows as she watches me drop my suit jacket to the floor, her confusion deepening when I work on the shoulder holster which houses my knife. Placing that on the opposite side of the vanity, on a shelf that's too high for her to reach, I start unbuttoning my Oxford.

"What are you doing?" she whispers, her eyes widening as I let the silk fall to the tiles too.

It's when I start on my belt buckle that she both amazes me *and* educates me—she's a runner.

With a nimble spryness I didn't anticipate because of her fragility, one that can only be born of an adrenaline rush, she jumps down to the floor, lets go of the sheet that swaddles her, ducks to grab my suit jacket, and takes off out of the bathroom.

She manages to slide the sports coat onto her shoulders, but as her hand closes around the doorknob, it's too late for her.

It was too late the minute I closed it.

It's self-locking.

Unusual for a bedroom door, but not for a Pakhan with more enemies than friends.

Chest heaving as her energy abates, she presses her forehead to the glossy ash and starts tugging on the knob as if trying enough times will make the mechanism work for her.

It won't.

With a snarl that does things to my dick, which has no business reacting right now, she twists to face me and shoves her back against the aperture.

Dressed only in my suit jacket and her underwear, rage streaking through her eyes like Lichtenberg figures, the power reminiscent of the burning fires of Hell, she is the most beautiful woman I've ever seen.

Stamping down the urges she's in no position to handle, I tip my head to the side as I study her.

Then, I hold out a hand for her in silent invitation.

Her gaze flickers to it, eyes dancing over the scars and nicks from years of fighting, before she hisses, "Who are you?"

My hand remains outstretched.

She ignores it to demand in broken Russian, "Debt has Harvey?"

When I don't reply, she weakly stomps her foot. It's ridiculously endearing until her legs give out from under her.

When she sags onto the floor, my sports coat puddling around her, the dark silk offsetting her bright gold hair, every part of me lights up in response. Not to her weakness, but to her *existence*.

She's shrouded in my clothes, in a room that belongs to me, under a roof that I possess—I've successfully caged sunlight.

I own it.

Own *her*.

Now, to protect what's mine. To care for what's mine. To cherish what's mine.

Even if she fights me every step of the way.

Making my approach, I watch her, enjoying how she watches me in turn. For someone so exhausted, for someone still feeling the aftereffects of drugs in her system, she is unexpectedly alert.

And yet, why would that come as a surprise?

My own father taught me better street smarts about how to watch my back than the first year of living rough ever did.

She's the same as I was as a child—vulnerable.

But I'm here now.

I will protect her and keep her safe from the world.

Whether she wants me to or not.

8

CASSIE

I KNOW there's nothing in his jacket pockets that could help me in any way, but as he pulls me into his arms, I have to try.

I have to.

Even if his hands are gentler than Harvey's ever were.

Even if he tries to swing me against his chest with a care I've never been shown before.

It doesn't matter.

The only problem is that I don't know how I got to the door under my own steam, and it's clear that my brain isn't firing on all cylinders yet because getting to an exit, *any exit would suffice,* was only phase one of an escape strategy that I fucked up.

God, stupid, so stupid.

So. Fucking. Stupid.

I want to scream at my own idiocy.

How many times have I planned an escape from Harvey? This isn't my first rodeo! I should have known better than to react on instinct when a man like him will only…

Shit. Shit. Shit.

I've just put him on red alert.

The urge to scream is strong, and though I want to slam my hand into his throat with as much force as I can, with as much power as I learned I can harness in my self-defense classes, I know that's not the smartest move to make when the door's locked and I have no idea where the key is.

It kills me to be obedient.

I've spent so many goddamn years being that, playing that role, and I'm tired of it. *Exhausted* by it, more so than any drugs could ever make me.

Utterly drained, I close my eyes as he tucks me against his chest with a tenderness I ignore in the face of the inexorability of his hold.

No, his touch isn't cruel.

But it's inevitable.

Those fingers of his are more effective than any cuffs Harvey's used on me.

My husband's dangerous—a part of me accepted long ago that he'd be the reason I died young. But this man is different. Red flags pop up around him like his own personal fireworks, but the sparks don't touch me. The flags never brush my skin…

My read on him has me swallowing my nerves while he returns us to the bathroom.

This time, there's no sheet between us. The jacket covers my top half but not the bottom, so his forearms and the faint hair dusting them brush against the surprisingly sensitive backs of my thighs.

How he holds me is unnerving.

It's obvious he means to keep me here against my will—why else would he lock the door? Why else would he strip in front of me?

His embrace, however, is discordant.

There's no escape here, granted, but I know violence and aggression. They became Harvey's love language, after all. He stopped holding me with any tenderness years ago, but it doesn't mean I've forgotten it, doesn't mean that I don't know how it should be between a man and a woman.

And this, bizarrely enough, *is* kind.

"Who are you?" I demand, but it's weaker than I'd like. The words crackle with my exhaustion and the remnants of the drugs Harvey forced down my throat.

Again, he doesn't answer. He doesn't even flinch as—

A 'eureka' moment backhands me.

When he places me on the vanity again, I stare at him and sign, "Who are you?"

Or, at least, I try to.

The bandages are unwieldy and the flexibility of my fingers is diminished because Harvey got me into his trunk at knifepoint and my palms bear signs of my defense.

Fuck, those cuts hurt.

Still, the pain is worth it—progress. His brows lift as he studies the words I sign. *He understands.*

Oh, thank fuck.

So, he's hard of hearing?

Calling on a childhood spent communicating with ASL, a language I stopped using years ago, I request, "Please, tell me who you are." He just stares at me blankly until I continue, "I'm scared."

His nostrils flare. "You're safe here."

I almost sag with the relief that swells at our first bout of communication, my eyes stinging as I roughly translate the movements of his fingers.

"I want to go home," I reply.

Of course, that's when the thought strikes me—I don't have a home anymore.

"Too dangerous."

Swallowing, I demand, "I want to leave."

"Not safe."

"It's my choice!"

That's when he stops answering because his hands are busy with his fly.

Gulping, I watch as he opens the zipper. My attention is immediately caught on the scars I can see on his lower hip—they're nasty. Deep and still puckered, I can tell they're old. There's one on his face which is, at least, cleanly healed—a knife, probably. Maybe a serrated blade? I've been around the kitchen enough to know my scars and the eyebrow one is nasty and uneven, though I can tell it was stitched. The other on his hip speaks of a run-in with fire.

The thought has me biting my lip in sympathy considering the extent of the burn and how badly the flesh…

Didn't he have a skin graft?

Surely that's standard practice in Russia too, especially for a man this wealthy.

Completely in the dark as to where my mind has gone, the stranger draws the expensive fabric down his hips as he simultaneously toes off his shoes.

I don't know where to look and, this time, it has nothing to do with scar tissue. Hell, that'd be easier to study than—

A breath hisses from between my teeth.

It's the first time I've seen an erection in years because as Harvey's situation worsened, he wouldn't let me see his penis. But that this stranger has an erection, period, means…

"Are you going to rape me?"

His frown makes an appearance at my words. "I will never hurt you."

Ha.

A likely story.

"Why are you getting undressed?"

"Nudity isn't dangerous."

"There's no need to get naked at all!"

He doesn't listen.

While I know he can't hear me, I scream and start to sign, "Don't ignore me!"

Christ if I haven't signed those words so many times in my goddamn life. My father was deaf and he was like talking to a wall sometimes, and that had everything to do with his imperious attitude and nothing to do with his perforated ear drums from a workplace accident.

Then, my captor is naked and memories of my beloved father fade to nothing.

Still, that's when he signs, "I'm not ignoring you."

I grit my teeth, refusing to peer below his neck, until he moves nearer to me, snagging his knife along the way.

My breath hitches in my lungs as he draws the blade nearer and, eyes wide with fear, I back into the vanity, pressing my spine to the mirror, pleading, "Don't hurt me."

His hand swipes down in the universal ASL for 'never,' but that goddamn knife comes closer, closer...

That's when the strap of my bra pings as he slices it in two.

I swallow in response.

"You are soaked in vomit."

Well, that's rude.

My scowl is inconsequential to him. "I can undress myself!"

"You smell and need to shower and you can *not* do it yourself."

I shove my balled fists at his shoulders. The burst of energy I experienced earlier depleted my meager reserves, but I have to try even if the move hurts my hands more than it hurts him.

Only, my weak resistance is batted away like I'm as inconsequential as a moth butting heads with a lightbulb.

He ignores the fists I press to his shoulders, too, because he's clearly an asshole.

Not only that, he's massive, bulky with muscles that even in the peak of health, I wouldn't be able to fight.

Harvey's not muscular, but he's taller than me, stocky with the weight he gained once depression took him in a chokehold. I can never win in a fight against him, never mind *this* guy who makes Harvey look like a sapling and who hauls me around as if I'm featherlight, which I'm definitely not.

"You are too weak to clean yourself. I will clean you."

"I don't want you to."

His hands settle on those stacked hips of his. He has those hard rolls that only sports guys and models have. Hades belt? *Ha.* Something like that. And I should not be noticing—

"Your hands have to remain dry." Apparently, he can tell I'm about to argue because he continues, "You are safe but you are filthy and these rags need to go into the trash."

"These are *not* rags," I grumble.

But again, he ignores me, and I only release a squeak this time as he slices through the band at the sides of my breasts, leaving me to grow tense in preparation of the tip of the blade scoring my flesh—

Except...

It doesn't.

The bra puddles around my hips in various strips of stained, cheap cotton that are undeniably speckled with vomit.

Lifting my arms, I automatically cover my breasts from his sight, nonplussed when he allows me to.

Next comes my panties, which he slashes at the hip. Again, the knife doesn't touch me, but the most bewildering flutter of vanity drifts through me—I'm not thin.

With my panties gone, my hips are *there*.

On display.

What a time to be body conscious.

Not that I'm allowed that feminine triviality for long—he gives me mouthwash and, after returning the knife to the shelf that's too high for me to reach, watches me expectantly until I've completed that task.

Once I have, he snatches hold of me, then he picks me up like I don't weigh two hundred pounds on a good day and carries me behind a glass shower screen.

That's when I realize there's a kind of shelf or seat, I guess, on the wall which he sets me on.

My cheeks immediately flush as its purpose hits home.

The water sprays on as I'm trying to think of why a man who captures women and holds them hostage would need a shower seat at this height that makes it easy for him to go down on them...

Cheeks red, I sign, "I can clean myself."

But he's back to silence.

I jerk when he grabs my wrist and turns my hand over. His grip on me is firm, unwavering, but not painful. If anyone knows the difference, it's me.

He moves them away from the spray and shoots me a knowing glance that has me gritting my teeth. Then, I growl when he collects the soap.

He doesn't use a washcloth, just pours the liquid soap straight onto his palm and starts to smooth it over my shoulders and my arms. He coats my breasts in it but doesn't fondle them or molest me in any way.

With every stroke of his hands, I can't deny it's more clinical than I expected.

Like a caretaker washing a patient.

The notion makes me uncomfortable and is only amplified when he trails his fingers through the lather he makes, scrubbing at my sweat-stained, vomit-speckled chest and arms.

There's no denying I needed help bathing, but this is just too much.

It's intimate yet not.

Clinical, sure, but too close for comfort.

Just like his goddamn erection.

There's no evading it from this angle and the sight does strange things to me. Things I shouldn't be thinking at a time like this.

No, I should be punching him instead of staring at something that I've been repeatedly told I'm incapable of triggering in a man...

As annoyance goes to war with my worry, which battles my insecurities, he confuses me further by shampooing and rinsing my hair *twice* before applying conditioner to nourish it.

The products are for women—who do they belong to?

Does he have a wife who's okay with her husband bringing strange women into his home to shower?

Maybe she's like me.

If Harvey had brought a sex slave into our home, I wouldn't have been able to do anything about it. I like to think I'd have contacted the cops, but I don't know if I'd have been able to.

Fear is the worst type of chokehold a man can have on you.

Especially at the start of the abuse.

Back then, I cared if I lived or died.

After years of enduring it, years of isolation from anyone who had ever loved me, I often contemplated suicide to escape my life, then a random meeting with an old friend in the city made me realize what I'd become.

Something Harvey compounded a week later when I smiled at a delivery guy. He tied me to the bed and either went out for more of the Viagra that had stopped working on him years ago or tools to kill me with—I still don't know which for sure. Knowing him, it could be either…

That's when the friend I'd dumped at Harvey's demand, a friend I didn't deserve, came to my rescue.

As the memory from earlier this year plagues me, that's when I have another 'eureka' moment.

Before Harvey had held a hand over my nose and mouth to force me to swallow the drugs he'd shoved between my teeth in the motel room he'd taken me to, I'd managed to get in touch with that friend again, Savannah Daniels, and had asked her for help.

Is this stranger the cavalry she sent?

Is my friend waiting somewhere for news on my status?

Quickly, I sign, "Do you know Savannah Daniels?"

No response.

I suck in an impatient breath.

"I asked her for help with my husband—"

A growl escapes him, and with snappish movements of his fingers, he signs, "You are not *his*."

If a man could sign in italics, then he'd just done that.

It's his turn to suck in a breath, but this time, I can see he's seeking calm.

He snatches one of *six* detachable shower heads and starts to stream it over my hair, taking me aback with how gentle his touch is as he rinses it again.

Wordlessly, he returns to his earlier task.

Only this time, it's worse.

He settles on his knees and he moves my legs around as if they're his to control, not mine.

He's there—right there.

Pussy height.

He can see it if he looks.

But he doesn't.

At least, it's not obvious if he *is* ogling my sex. To be fair, he's doing a better job than I am of ignoring his cock.

Instead, disregarding my blazing hot embarrassment that has me kicking out and trying to get him in the face, he moves his hands over my thighs and calves as if I'm a doll, going so far as to massage my feet. He proceeds to hold them hostage before I can attempt to kick him again, then he stands once more.

But my humiliation isn't over yet.

Now, he rubs my shoulders, moving soap to my nape where he gently palpates the skin, robbing me of the tension that had gathered there.

When he cleanses my face too, I blink up at him as he makes circles at my temples.

Overwhelmed, I sag against the wall, trying not to enjoy his tender ministrations which help with the intensity of the migraine that's plaguing me. A migraine that's undoubtedly worse than ever because I overexerted myself.

I almost moan with disappointment when he finishes and helps me get to my feet. That's when shame filters through me.

Mortification as well.

Here I am, being showered against my goddamn will, and I'm moaning when the bastard stops!

Pride makes me refuse to lean into him, but the heat and steam from the extensive shower has made me lightheaded so I press a hand to his chest to prop me up.

That's when he stuns the ever-living crap out of me.

Those long, lean, slender fingers aren't finished—he slides them between my thighs.

Yelping, I dart backward, wincing as that 'shelf' digs into my ass cheeks, but he moves nearer to me, entering my space and looming over me, seemingly uncaring that I don't want his help with *this*.

It's bizarre but I'm not scared, more angry by his presumptuous-ness. I know what a man looks like in the heat of rage, know when I'm at the epicenter of a storm that'll see me being backhanded or kicked or punched in the stomach.

This stranger shows none of those signs.

Still, I shove at his shoulders, uncaring that I'm feeling woozy, and when he moves deeper into my periphery, I try to knee him in the balls.

That's when a flicker of *something* flashes over his expression, snagging the scar that's sliced through one eye, marring what I can't deny is the perfection of his face.

His fingers retreat.

He doesn't give me time to sigh in relief as he signs, "It's likely that you haven't showered in days. You are safe. I will not hurt you."

Before I can even think to respond, and in less than a minute, I've been twisted around, held firmly against his body, his dick prodding my butt cheeks, one of his thighs positioned between my legs, his calf settling over mine with his foot holding me in line.

One of his hands captures both of my wrists and glues them to my waist while the other carries on as if I did *nothing*.

His fingers move between the folds of my sex, rubbing soap here and there with a thoroughness that I don't think I've ever graced my pussy with in a lifetime.

And yet, it's not sexual.

At all.

He doesn't focus on my clit.

He might as well be washing my hair again.

Still, I feel awkward. The last time someone cleaned me like this, I was a child, and I'm not a kid and he's definitely not one of my parents.

I know I should be struggling against his hold, but I'm trapped and, even though my heart is pounding, the fear that was prevalent every time I came into contact with my—with Harvey—in the past is notably absent.

That terror has shadowed every experience with him to the point that I almost choked on it whenever he came within a foot of me, but it's not a part of *this* interaction.

That doesn't mean I'm not relieved when the man's almost finished.

Until, that is, he reaches for the detachable shower head again and flashes it over my sex.

Which is when the most disconcerting pulse of, *God*, pleasure throbs through me.

Eyes wide, cheeks hot with mortification, I tilt my face to the side so he can't see my features and read between lines I don't want him to see at all.

Once he's satisfied I'm clean, the shower cuts off, and he releases his tangled hold on me before carrying me back over to the vanity.

I can't deny that it's good to be clean, especially when I know I've vomited over myself, but with that seat in the shower, I could have handled that alone.

I don't care how weak I feel; I would have goddamn managed.

Huffing when he peels a bathrobe from one of the hooks on the wall, I ignore the fact that it smells of him as he wraps me in it.

"I'm not a doll," I sign at him.

No response.

Frustration has me gritting my teeth so fiercely that I'm going to need to visit a dentist soon.

He presses down on the toweling, patting me dry with the bathrobe. Just as I tuck myself within its voluminous folds, huddling into it, grateful for the covering, he's dragging it off me and tossing the admittedly drenched fabric on the floor.

"What are you doing?" I sign at him, shrieking the words too.

Either way, he ignores me, picks up another towel, and starts to dry my hair.

Then, he withdraws a hairdryer and hits the 'on' button.

As the motor whines to life, I hover there, butt naked, in front of a guy who would be out of Gigi Hadid's league, and he's drying my fucking hair.

It's then that I have to concede I wouldn't have had the energy to do any of this.

Just standing here is tough.

The drugs and the pain in my head are making me sway on my feet, and when he draws me closer, I lean against him even though it galls me.

When he picks me back up, I'm actually past caring that I'm fat and naked and every un-supermodel inch of me is on display.

He hefts me onto the vanity and snags my leg in his hand.

"Can't you stop prodding me?" I snap, grabbing his shoulder when he ignores me so that I can sign in his face.

In comparison to the fierceness of my grip, his hold is tender as he lifts my foot.

The strangest notion drifts into my head—*is he going to suck my freakin' toe?*

Then, I'm almost relieved to spy the bandage on my ankle.

He peels that off and douses it with rubbing alcohol and antibiotic cream he finds in a drawer from the vanity along with a bandage he uses to cover the wounds.

All the while, I don't even bother wincing because though it stings, I've been through worse.

He tends to my hands, which hurt more. Those cuts are deep, and my thumb feels like it could fall off, never mind the splint that's digging into my finger, but afterward, that's when he surprises me yet again—he cups my chin. Gently. He smoothes his alcohol-scented thumb over my jaw.

When I study him in turn, his face bears no expression but his eyes are loaded down with…

Too much.

Much too much.

Confusion whispers through me.

How many times would I have killed for Harvey to look at me that way?

With my world shaking beneath my feet, the stranger carries me to the bed and rests me on top of the comforter, and it's almost with relief that I settle amid the luxurious pillows and sheets that smell too good for my senses to handle.

That's when he finally deigns to sign, "Sleep. You are safe now."

When he doesn't make for the door but for the bathroom, I quickly grab his arm, ignoring the jolt of pain as my thumb protests, so that he can see me reply, "You're a stranger! I have no idea who you are. How am I supposed to sleep if you're—"

But he isn't around long enough to read the message I impart with my hands. Hands that are *hurting* with everything that I sign. This is the finger equivalent of talking with laryngitis. Every fucking word is precious but he dismisses me with a waft of his fingers then turns his back on me.

I refuse to look at his ass.

Re. Fuse.

A couple moments later, the shower powers on again.

Suddenly, my adrenaline soars and with it, some gumption. I sit up and start the hunt for another exit.

A quick scan of the bedroom reveals little.

It's big, cavernous almost, but more than anything, it's empty of any tchotchkes, possessing only the bare minimum of furniture, like the nightstands and a table that could either be a desk or for a woman to do her makeup at. There's a wall of shelves that could be for books, but its emptiness is all the more jarring.

On the side wall, there's another opening, much like there is with the bathroom, so ignoring the pain in my head and hands, I clamber to my feet and haul the comforter off the bed, swaddle myself in it, then groan with how much fabric there is as I nearly fall flat on my face.

The bed is as huge as he is, and the comforter is larger. Bulky, too.

Dragging the deadweight, I hurry over there as quickly as I can. Which, disconcertingly enough, is when I find what has to be a walk-in closet but the racks are empty, the drawers too. There's not so much as a pair of boxers in here.

"Is this a guest suite?" I ask myself, perturbed by the barrenness of the space. "If it is, then how goddamn big is the master suite and why does everything smell of him?"

The shower's still running, so I head back into the bedroom and move over to the shuttered windows.

I tug on one, trying to open it, pulling so hard that I almost knock over the chair that's in front of the maybe-vanity, but it doesn't budge. Nor do the other five.

My heart's starting to pound again when claustrophobia settles in.

Desperate, I run to the door and try the handle a final time.

No dice.

Still locked.

It's a massive room, beautifully appointed if barren, but it might as well be a five-by-five cell.

Mouth trembling, I stare at the blank canvas surrounding me and swallow down a bout of nausea that has nothing to do with the drugs Harvey fed me and everything to do with fear.

How did I leap from the frying pan into the fire?

Shakily, adrenaline petering out, I stagger to the bed when the shower cuts.

Feeling more lightheaded than ever, I snap out the comforter so it covers the mattress again, hoping he won't realize I explored the space. As fatigued as I am, that's a difficult task.

With some relief, I switch off the lights and duck beneath the covers, hiking them high so that I'm swaddled entirely, muscles trembling in exertion.

After preparing myself for another round with him, he spoils my plans when he doesn't immediately return to the bedroom. If anything, he's in there for so long that I start to feel drowsy.

Maybe it's the lingering fatigue from the drugs, maybe it's the repeated adrenaline crashes, or maybe it's a combination of *everything* that has my eyes closing now that I'm beneath the covers and my head is cushioned by one of the softest pillows I've ever slept on...

Whichever reason it is, I don't let the 'whys' linger as I escape my present and tumble into slumber.

And if that slight glimpse of his ass is the last mental image of the night, that's between me and the sandman.

9

NIKOLAI

Hayling - JC Kahuna

TEMPTATION IS something I rarely experience.

I take what I want when I want it.

Whether it's a car or a Patek Phillippe, a Monet or turf that belongs to another faction, if I want it, I procure it.

But I never *want* a woman.

I want to come. I want to burn off some energy. I want to fuck. I want a pussy.

The creature in possession of the pussy isn't something I particularly desire.

Fucking is an act that relieves tension, much like a heavy workout in the gym does.

But at this moment, I'm tempted.

Pure sunlight is lying atop my bed.

In my bedroom.

Under my roof.

The notion makes me breathe heavily as I allow the rainfall shower to pound my nape while I fight the craving to jack off.

Desire plagues me, urges crawling down my spine that the water won't wash away.

Ordinarily, I wouldn't bother fighting my inclinations.

But she's not only my *solnyshko*, she's been drugged.

That changes things.

I cut off the water.

Not tonight, I tell myself.

I'm not my father.

I. Am. Not.

With a growl, I place my hands on the shower wall as I try not to think about what happened between us a mere half hour ago.

That golden silk in my hands, her burning chestnut eyes as they lasered a hole into me...

The feel of her tits in my palms, her pussy against my fingers...

My nostrils flare at those last two memories.

Softness.

Blyad, she's so soft. Everything about her is round and curvy instead of the harsh lines I'm used to.

My life is tough. Brittle.

She's the opposite.

I stare at my cock, which is already leaking pre-cum now that the water isn't there to wash it away.

Gritting my teeth, I shove off the wall and then ball my hands into fists as I head out of the walk-in shower.

There's only a small hand towel remaining on the stack, but I was in the fucking stall staring at my dick for so goddamn long that I'm practically dry anyway.

Luckily, I've spent enough time inside that the lack of a towel doesn't matter. You'd never imagine that one of the most complicated parts of prison life is getting your fucking towel dry so it doesn't grow mildew. It's a luxury people who've never served time don't understand.

Sloughing the droplets that remain on my shoulders off with my fingers, I study myself in the vanity.

Nothing's changed about my appearance since the last time I was at *Nav* a week ago, yet somehow, nothing is the same either.

Scraping a hand through my hair, I duck down. After picking out my cell and the keys to the door from my pants pocket, I toss the keys on the shelf with my knife and stare blankly at my phone.

It's an unexpected boon that she knows sign language. Her variant is unusual. It's mostly standard ASL with a few odd signs thrown in that I don't understand.

That makes her skill even more curious and worthy of further investigation.

My blank stare sharpens when my phone screen lights up.

There are a couple of updates from Boris which I read with interest.

> Boris: The Albanians are on red alert. Marku's absence has been noted.

AN HOUR LATER

> Boris: Either they let go of Rundel or he slipped out of their hands.

He's a slippery fucker, then, because it's unlikely they released him —who'd be that generous?

As I ponder my next moves, I ultimately decide to check something off my to-do list.

> Me: I have Cassiopeia.

> Misha: Expected to hear from you hours ago.

> Me: There have been some complications.

> Misha: With Cassiopeia?

> Me: Yes, but she's well.

I purse my lips as I consider whether or not to tell him I have her under my roof.

Misha Babanin is not my blood, but he *is* my brother.

As is Maxim Lyanov.

We were three orphans subsisting in a Muscovian orphanage before I hit fifteen when my arsonist brother started a fire there, making the hellhole a literal one.

In the aftermath, we ran away together and took to the streets, which were more of a home than the slum we left behind.

They'd been with me in Florida for years until Maxim and I had an argument when I'd been named Pakhan—the youngest in the brotherhood's history at the time—and he lit out to New York, taking Misha with him.

My relationship with Maxim has yet to recover.

Not because he was a jealous fool over my promotion, but because I picked Pavel Oborin as my Obschak and not him.

The distance between Maxim and me is one of the few things I actually regret. It's also why, when Misha asks for help, I tend to offer it without argument. Something that floods Dmitri with envy...

Sometimes, I feel like a father to them all. I certainly deal with their tantrums enough.

> Misha: And? I have to tell the Irish what happened to her. Give me more than 'she's well,' Niko, please.

Ah, yes.

Rescuing Cassiopeia was technically a favor for the Irish Mob with whom Misha has become entangled...

Stranger things have happened in our lives, but this is infinitely more bizarre than usual.

Misha is somehow dating the sister-in-law of the head of the Irish Mob in New York City, and yet he still breathes.

Bizarre is an understatement.

> Me: What were the terms of the offer of rescue?

> Misha: Are we being recorded for a deposition?

My lips quirk.

> Me: No. I just want to know the parameters of the offer.

> Misha: You're a piece of work, Niko.

> Misha: I just said I'd send you to help save her from her husband. Savannah, Aidan O'Donnelly's wife, believed that Cassiopeia's ex would hurt her.

She wasn't wrong.

> Me: And that was it? No promises of Rundel's death?

> Misha: Nyet.

I hum.

Savannah O'Donnelly likely expects to hear from Cassiopeia, however, which is a kink in my plan.

Fucking with the Albanians is one thing. They're a two-bit gang with no wider ties. The Irish, on the other hand, not only rule over the northeast but are certifiable.

Aidan O'Donnelly Sr., the one-time leader of Manhattan's Five Points' Mob, might be dead, but that doesn't mean his version of insanity has fallen far from the tree with his sons.

I've no desire to poke that particular bear, not when Maxim's position as Pakhan of the New York Bratva is still precarious and my actions could lead to instability on his home turf.

Tapping the corner of my phone to my chin, I extrapolate the various options available to me and eventually come to a decision.

That's when I see Misha has already replied.

> Misha: She's safe from her ex, then?

Me: You can inform Savannah O'Donnelly of that, yes. But when I rescued Cassiopeia, Rundel wasn't there. He'd tied her to the bed but he wasn't present.

Then, for the first time in my life, I lie to Misha.

Me: I took her to an airport and gave her money.

> Misha: Do you know where she went?

Me: No. She has no belongings so I doubt she'll be in contact with Savannah O'Donnelly soon.

That isn't a lie.

The motel had nothing in it aside from Rundel's paraphernalia and the shredded jeans, tee, and sneakers she'd been wearing when he kidnapped her.

> Misha: Damn. Savannah is worried.

Me: There's always a pay phone if she chooses to get in touch, but you can reassure Savannah that her friend is safe.

> Misha: Doubtful... What with her ex on the loose.

Me: Do you doubt me, brother?

> Misha: You're going to kill him?

Me: Of course.

> Misha: There's no, 'of course,' about it. Why would you do that for free when I haven't asked you to?

Me: You didn't see the state of her.

Misha: Since when do you care?

Me: Since she reminded me of my mother.

It isn't a lie. Even if Cassiopeia does not look in any way, shape, or form like my *mamushka*.

Misha: Ah, fuck. Sorry, Niko.

Me: Hmm. Happy Thanksgiving, Misha.

Misha: Lol. You're the gift that keeps on giving, brat moy.

I narrow my eyes at the endearment—*brother mine.*

Me: You owe me.

Misha: I know :)

Me: Just so you remember. Before you go, how's Maxim?

Misha: Pain in the ass as always.

Me: Good to know. Secure, though?

Misha: Da. It's almost funny. He has no right to his seat as Pakhan, but because he's treating the men fairly, he's popular.

Misha: Plus, we just uncovered an interesting income stream that the old guard didn't loop us in on. Good thing—fair wages come at a high price.

Me: Oh? What income stream?

Misha: Diamond smuggling via Atlantic fishing hauls.

Me: Fascinating. I might have use for that at some point.

> Misha: You'll have to speak with him.

That has me sighing.

> Me: I'll consider that repayment of the favor you owe me.

> Misha: Fuck. You never make it easy, do you?

> Me: Nyet.

> Me: I've heard he's spending time in Moskva?

> Misha: Da. Trying to please the Krestniy Otets.

My top lip curls.

The Krestniy Otets is the head of the Bratva brotherhood. Pakhans lead individual brotherhoods. I, for example, reign over the Floridian branch. The Krestniy Otets sits above me in the hierarchy. Our current Krestniy Otets makes Aidan O'Donnelly Sr. look sane.

> Me: How's that going?

> Misha: Poorly. The K.O. is pissed about Maxim's power grab.

That has me grimacing.

> Me: I warned Maxim.

> Misha: Say, 'I told you so,' and you'll never get in on this smuggling business.

> Me: He needs to grow up. I've managed to rule over Miami for a decade without any mutiny, Misha. He should listen to me but taking my advice is too much for the big fucking baby.

> Misha: He's a dangerous one...

I grunt.

> Me: Not if the K.O. decides to take his ass out. It's easier to kill him than it is to work with him. Especially if he doesn't drop the attitude.

> Me: Even more so if he brings fucking communism to the lower ranks.

Podonok.

I rub my eyes at the thought.

There are many ways to be fair to the foot soldiers without pissing off the rest of the Bratva. I pay my men better than most, but I do it in different ways: bonuses, investment opportunities made on their behalf, gifts in gold bullion.

As always, my brother is a fucking headache by working to the beat of his own drum.

> Me: Fuck off and don't cause me any more work.

> Misha: *salutes in Russian*

> Me: *rolls eyes in Russian*

With a mental note made that Savannah O'Donnelly will need to be contacted at some point, I switch over to another text conversation and type:

> Me: Dmitri, if Misha asks... Cassiopeia got on a flight and we watched her go.

Barely a second passes before he's replying:

> Dmitri: Misha and I barely talk, but if we do, it's never about business.

> Dmitri: Why do you want me to lie to him?

Little shit.

> **Me:** This wasn't an invitation for question time. Just do as I say.

> **Dmitri:** Da.

With a grunt, I switch to yet another text conversation.

I can feel the fatigue of the very long day beginning to work away at my focus, but this is important.

> **Me:** You know Altin?

Unsurprisingly, the 'read' ticks are immediate.

Elena Çela is the most paranoid woman I've ever met in my life. And with my past, that's saying fucking something.

Before *Solnyshko*, I thought she was the most beautiful woman I'd ever met too. Ironically, that was how she'd earned her nickname—Troy. Short for *Helen* of Troy.

But I've met the real Helen of Troy now, and she's lying on my bed...

That doesn't help my hard-on.

> **Troy:** You mean my dipshit cousin?

> **Me:** Da.

> **Troy:** Of course, I know him then, kretin.

My lips quirk into a smirk.

She's the only person with big enough balls to call me that. Not even Dmitri, Misha, or Maxim would fucking dare.

> **Me:** How well?

> **Troy:** I wouldn't attend his funeral if he were dead.

> **Troy:** Is he?

Troy: Feel free to make my night.

My brows lift.

Me: He's not dead.

Me: Yet.

Troy: So there's hope?

Me: Da.

Troy: What's he done this time?

Me: What did he do to you?

Troy: I see how this is going... information for information. I'd call if you didn't have that little voice box issue. You still can't talk?

Me: I can talk.

Troy: Ha. I've never heard you utter a word. Never known anyone who's heard you speak either.

I sigh.

Me: Why is everyone so fucking fascinated with my voice?

Troy: Ah, well, you're weird. And dangerous. What others would perceive as a weakness, what others could use against you, ISN'T your downfall.

Troy: People prey on weaknesses like yours and yet, with you, it's almost a strength.

Troy: You don't fit the pattern.

Me: How fascinating that you've given it some thought.

> Troy: Don't get ahead of yourself.

> Troy: Anyway… Altin used to have a little problem with strangling his hookers.

Anger filters through me.

> Troy: My darling papa covered those murders up though.

> Troy: That enough to kill him?

> Me: Is it true? Or are you just baiting me?

> Troy: You know what IS fascinating?

> Me: What?

> Troy: How the Russian mobster has a conscience where his hookers are concerned.

> Troy: I know about your mother…

> Me: I'd expect no less.

> Troy: Is she why you only have a small stable of prostitutes in your retinue? Because your father whored her out?

Just one of the reasons.

But I refuse to get angry tonight.

Not when my 'little sun' is piercing the darkness of my world.

I loathe prostitution but… it's expected of me, so, I keep my answer clinical:

> Me: Prostitution is a short-term investment. Women aren't machines.

> Troy: That's why your girls all cost twenty K a night?

Me: For someone I haven't spoken to in five years, you've made sure you're up to date about me, haven't you?

Troy: Don't get a big head. I do this with everyone.

Me: Hmm, if you say so.

Troy: What's Altin done? They use him as fists if my latest intel hasn't failed me. He's too volatile for anything else.

Me: Still your father's heir?

Troy: Yes, but he's not happy about it.

Me: You've spoken to him?

Troy: Nyet, comrade. He used to tell me when he'd beat on me for being a girl that it was my fault he needed Altin when he was a POS.

Troy: Trust me, if Daddy dearest thinks he's an asshole, you can take that to the bank.

Me: Want me to kill him?

Troy: Awwwww, is that a declaration of love?

Troy: Anyway, nah, but thank you! I've let Father live this long. I'm waiting for a special occasion.

Me: Special occasion? Let me know so I can take advantage?

Troy: *snorts* Since when are you interested in Kentucky as turf?

Me: I'm interested in everything.

Troy: If you say so.

Me: I appreciate the intel.

> Troy: It's surprisingly good to hear from you. How's the scar?

With a quick glance at the line of puckered flesh that bisects my eye, I type:

Me: Healed.

> Troy: I almost regretted marring the perfection of your face, but you were too pretty anyway.

> Troy: I credit myself for making you as terrifying as you are now.

> Troy: I hear rumors about 'Mute.'

Me: Rumors never stop.

> Troy: No, they don't. Not when you're trying to make a name for yourself, which you've done. Never thought you would.

> Troy: Glad you proved me wrong.

Me: I am too.

> Troy: Does my father know you took Altin?

Me: Who said I did?

> Troy: :P You're talking to someone who can read you like a book.

Me: One night in Minsk over a decade ago doesn't mean you're the 'Mute whisperer.'

> Troy: You can trust me.

Me: I'd be a fool to.

Me: But nyet, your father is unaware of his nephew's current location.

Me: I doubt you'll loop him into that intel...

Troy: You're right. I won't.

I already knew she liked me, but that's just confirmation from the horse's mouth.

Me: Want me to make it hurt if I DO dispose of Marku?

Troy: Please. And... if you do, I'll owe you.

Me: You owe me nothing.

Troy: NO. I would owe you, Nikolai. It's a token freely offered. Understood?

I understand that she's not telling me the whole truth if she's offering me a token, but I'm not going to turn it down twice.

Me: Fine.

With that, I switch back to the conversation with Boris.

Me: Do the Albanians know we're involved?

Boris: Nyet. Not at all.

Me: You're sure?

Boris: 100%. I'm in one of their strip joints listening to Kadare bitch about Marku being 'incapable' of doing the simplest of tasks.

Me: So, no love lost?

Boris: No, Pakhan. Definitely not.

Me: Stick to him.

Boris: Da. Of course.

Scratching a hand over my stubbled jaw, I return to my chat with Troy, aware that I missed something in that conversation.

For her to offer me a token...

Scanning the chat, I piece *something* together.

> Me: Igor, how powerful is Kadare?

It takes a few minutes for the foot soldier I sent on a reconnaissance mission to Kentucky last year to reply.

> Igor: He's a thorn in Çela's side. Has the loyalty of his men and earns the Albanians a fortune.

> Me: Is he related to Çela?

> Igor: No, he's one of the few Komandants who isn't.

I smile.

There.

With Marku dead, Troy's father will either have to spawn another child from some poor female—a feat he hasn't managed since Troy's birth—or name someone else as his heir.

The Albanians are about to have a power struggle—that's why Troy says she'll owe me a token.

And does she but know it, Cassiopeia triggered it.

Somehow, that makes my cock pound harder than ever.

There's no way I'll be able to sleep like this.

10

CASSIE

Often - The Weeknd

THE BEDROOM IS SO PITCH black that I don't know why I wake up. There are no sounds in here either, and I don't need to use the bathroom even though…

A few memories drift into my mind.

He woke me, lifting me by the shoulders until I was sitting, pouring water into my mouth, and offering me pills from bottles of acetaminophen and ibuprofen every now and then.

The sting of rubbing alcohol on my ankles and hands disturbed me from my slumber—he must have changed the bandages.

I remember him guiding me to the bathroom on the various occasions he tended to me.

Discomfited by the memories of his care while I was at my most vulnerable, I hike myself higher in the bed, aware that the pounding in my temples is so much better than the last time I was conscious.

Still there, but not entirely.

Mostly, it's my hands that hurt. The skin is raw and sore. My fingers ache, the splinted one throbs dully, and my thumb still feels weak.

For a few minutes, I stare into the darkness, but the longer I stare, the more my heart begins to slam against my ribcage and the harder my panic stirs to life, forming wings that has me scrabbling out of bed, seeking the light switch.

As my fingers discover the cool plastic, I flick the switch and jolt when a different light flows around the ceiling, flooding a recess I didn't spot before.

Dragging the comforter off the bed, I cuddle into it as I shuffle over to what I decide *is* a vanity and plunk my butt on the seat and glance at the bedroom from this angle.

Last night, I'd mostly been trying to find an escape route. Now, I just take in the barren space.

It's bizarre.

Oddly ornate yet modern too.

As I stare at the bed, I break the cloistering silence by muttering to myself, "It's like the queen's *chambre* in Versailles."

A canopy of curtains falls dramatically from the high ceiling which is then secured to the wall with fancy fastenings above small night-stands on either side of the bed. The canopy is old-fashioned in premise, but the lines are modern and the drapes are a rich cyan velvet —not exactly antique.

It gives a grandeur to the space that speaks of wealth.

Extreme wealth.

Especially as the bed itself is the size of a California king and a half, and there are over a dozen pillows that act as an unofficial headboard.

Then…

I gasp as I climb back onto the bed and study the painting above it which is tucked safely behind glass.

"Climate controlled," I whisper as I peer at the canvas.

Art history classes come to my aid in helping me recognize the artist—Clyfford Still.

I even recognize the work—*PH-144*.

It had been featured in an article a couple of years ago because the original owners had passed away and Sotheby's had secured twenty pieces from their collection.

If my memory's right, then I'm looking at thirty million dollars.

Literally *looking at it*.

I slept beneath it.

It's stupid, but that doubles down on my panic from earlier.

How rich is this bastard if he can have that hanging above his bed?

And it's not like he stole it. This was a legitimate sale, for God's sake.

As I sink onto my heels, I stare at the canvas, wondering how it escaped my attention last night.

On a background of textured white/cream, larger 'puddles' of black, gray, and red dominate the canvas. It reminds me of those Rorschach inkblot pictures where you have to explain to a therapist what you see amid those blotches of black paint.

This has more direction, more of a purpose, but the red and the black almost makes me want to drown in grief while, on the upper right quadrant, the sharpest, brightest patch of yellow oversees it all.

It's like the sun.

Rays of light beam through the shadows.

Without knowing why, I shudder at the sight and huddle into the comforter then jump when the sound of a lock clicking ricochets around the cavernous space.

Turning to the doorway, I swallow when I see the man walk through it.

He takes me in with a single glance, managing to appear utterly calm when I'm the opposite.

It's stupid when he's the one who put me in this goddamn room, but seeing *his* calm enables me to inhale with more ease and to release the exhalation without feeling as if my lungs are constricted.

I twist on the bed and watch him step inside, only now taking note of the tray in his hands. My stomach rumbles with an aching need but I ignore it. I'm used to it. It's either my PCOS or just bad genes that means months on the run without regular meals have made me drop only a handful of pounds while keeping most of my 'bulk.'

Fucking hormones.

In the silence I'm coming to associate with him, he moves over to a wall beside the bathroom recess, then he places his hand against *something* and a panel pops up. He taps in a few numbers and a door slides back, revealing an opening.

Blinking, I watch as he steps inside.

"That wasn't weird," I mumble. "Or faintly *Star Trek*-esque."

I stay on the bed, wondering what he's doing and *why* he's doing it in here.

Then, because I can't confirm my stupidity quickly enough, I clamber off the mattress, recognizing that the bed could do with one of those steps to hike onto it, and pad over to the opening.

I don't walk straight through, just peep around the corner and…

"Wow," I exclaim.

It's a living room. Sort of. With a dining area. Sort of. It's modern and filled with the furniture the bedroom isn't. There's a TV and knick-knacks and even photo frames with pictures of either three boys huddled together or a single teenager with sparkling eyes…

Why do I remember his face?

That teen is different from the others who, despite posing for photos, are serious. Somber.

They're actually quite ghoulish.

With the soft features of childhood, the ancient souls that peer back at me through ageless eyes are disconcerting.

By comparison, the one on his own is either grinning at me from beneath a Yankees' cap that, along with a mop of bright blond hair, covers half his features or is dressed in a varsity jacket from high school with a cocky smirk he aims at the camera.

He couldn't be more different than those three boys who stare at me with a fierceness I haven't seen on a kid's face before.

The sensation plagues me as I check out the rest of the space. My gaze continually darts over to those pictures even as I take in the warm brown leather of the couch and the art that dots the walls as well as the massive bookcases in here—sheltering what has to be over a thousand books.

It's quieter too, I note.

Even more so than it is in his bedroom.

That is until a soft hum sounds in the space.

Air regulation.

"Is this a safe room?" I sign, aiming the words at him from his place at the dining table.

I'm stunned when he nods.

The notion is both disturbing and reassuring.

The man has a thirty-million-dollar painting above his bed so it's fitting he'd have an emergency solution to a home invasion, but somehow, I get the feeling the home invaders would have to be insane to break into *his* house.

I bite my lip. "Will you lock me in here?"

This time, he doesn't look at me as he shakes his head and, instead, retrieves something from the tray—a napkin. One that was shielding a plate of breakfast foods.

My stomach gurgles and I press an embarrassed hand to it as I peek at the dish in front of him with an eagerness I can't hide.

He tilts back in his chair, spreads his legs slightly, then pats his knee.

My mouth gapes.

Is he for real?

I retreat a step, simultaneously snarling and signing, "I'm not that hungry."

His eyes narrow and, with angry flicks of his hands, he retorts, "If you want to eat, you will sit here and let me feed you."

It gets worse.

"I'm a grown woman! I don't need you to feed me!" I spit then, with an annoyed hiss, remember that he can't understand me so I sign that to him.

He just looks at me.

And that sense of inexorability plagues me again…

There's a timelessness about him.

It's as if he can wait a thousand lifetimes without losing patience.

Well, I don't have the patience of Hades, dammit.

I suck in a breath and spin on my heel before storming out of the safe room. Much like before, he follows me, but as I crawl onto the bed, he's there. The comforter is dragged from my shrieking self and I'm hauled into his arms.

As I hit out, hands slamming into his chest, fists pummeling his shoulders in a way my battered fingers will regret later, he ignores me like I'm a mosquito buzzing around his head while he sleeps and carries me into the safe room.

That's when I notice something I hadn't spotted earlier.

From over his shoulder, I can see the side of the bed I didn't sleep on—there are indentations and ripples in the sheets.

Did he sleep there too?

The fuck!

When he takes a seat, plunking me onto his lap, he informs me, "You lost the right to a covering."

Though I gape at him, I'm swift to react—I shift and try to knee him in the balls at the same time. He grabs a firmer hold of me, catching my knee at the last moment and twisting me around even more.

How he maneuvers me is worse than if I'm a puppet. His strength leaches into the air as he manipulates *my* body so that I'm no longer sitting on his lap, I'm straddling him.

And my pussy is right over his dick.

He has an erection.

Yet again.

Over a decade without them and now I've had to deal with two in as many days.

I shudder at the realization. "Why are you doing this?"

His eyes drop to my lips but this time, he doesn't answer me. Instead, his hand moves to the dish where I realize there's fruit in a crystal bowl and then a plate with bacon on it as well as strips of pancake and scrambled eggs too.

I can't imagine this guy cooking so his personal freakin' chef must have cut the pancake into slices and the eggs into medium, bite-sized chunks for me.

Someone knows I'm here and hasn't called the cops…

Antagonized, I sign, "How do I know you haven't drugged the food?"

The only time I've seen him truly angry with me was when I called Harvey 'my husband.' That same whisper of rage flares to life in his usually impassive features.

Rather than reply, he places a strip of pancake on his tongue and as he chews, my brain shifts off the topic of wondering whether he's dosed the food and shuffles onto *him.*

I still don't know his name, still have no idea who he is or why he's taken me, but… did he have to be so beautiful?

I hate myself for thinking that. For associating this asshole with *beauty.* But I won't be one of those women who could forgive a man his treatment thanks to his good looks. After Harvey, I know better, but *after Harvey*, I can't help but think that's why this stranger has such an impact—not because of his attractiveness, but because of his response to me.

Harvey's a solid four. On a good day.

Back when we'd first gotten together, I hadn't seen that though.

When I informed my mom that I was marrying him, she actually told me that I was settling. We'd fought about it, and I'd almost considered not inviting her to the engagement party. Ultimately, she'd refused to attend the wedding.

But this man is *not* a four.

Solid or otherwise.

With a suit on, he's a twelve.

Naked?

He's a fifteen.

And, to be honest, I'm probably scoring down because of the whole 'being taken against my will and not being allowed to leave or wear clothes' thing.

Whether or not I settled on my husband, I'm no way near a seven, never mind a twelve or a fifteen.

That erection of his… I don't understand it.

I know better than anyone that dicks don't lie. Even Viagra can't fix the unfixable.

I study his features, trying to read into what he's thinking, but his impassiveness is as frustrating as his inability to speak. Something that has nothing to do with his need for ASL but his inability to communicate. Period.

He *chooses* to be silent.

Jerk.

So instead of succumbing to that pretty face, I try to rationalize his beauty.

The scar that should have spoiled his looks somehow enhances the other perfect parts of him.

He has a wide forehead which leads to stark brows that shield hazel-brown eyes which glitter in the light. They're usually expressionless if I ask him a question, then, somehow, they'll shift.

Heat up.

Gleam…

Whenever he looks at me.

Huh.

There's a word for it, but it scares me—*reverence.*

Stopping *that* train of thought, because no one reveres someone like me, I study his nose.

That's safe, right?

Except, *no.*

Even that's attractive, for God's sake.

It's strong but thin, and it sits above pert lips which belong to a mouth that's the opposite of mobile.

Silence categorically defines him. Characterizes him.

His features are as still as he is.

His jaw clenches and releases as he eats, drawing my attention to the stubble on his chin and above his Cupid's bow.

As for his hair, it's a rich chocolate brown that's tousled. Neatly. That's an oxymoron. How can something be neatly tousled? But it is.

He is.

He reminds me of that Clyfford Still painting above his bed.

Evocative.

Beautiful.

Inherently untouchable.

Yet here I am, perched on his lap, *touching him.*

And somehow, the exercise that was supposed to dissect his masculine beauty so that it didn't hold any power over me backfires.

Extraordinarily.

When he finishes chewing the pancake and swallows it, he arches a brow as he picks up a piece of bacon for me.

A part of me expected him to force me to eat, but he doesn't. He just holds it aloft. Patiently.

"I can feed myself."

That brow arches higher, making his scar ruffle, puckering that half of his face in a way that should've been ugly, but nothing about him could ever be that.

Nothing.

Opening my mouth, I accept his offering. The bacon's salty and rich and it makes my mouth water. My eyes close of their own volition as I savor food after what feels like a week without it. My stomach twinges as I swallow.

Upon opening my eyes, I find him watching me.

That glitter's back.

No longer are they expressionless...

He wants me.

I've seen that look too often on Harvey's face not to understand it.

Want.

Arousal.

But, in my experience, that 'want' soon shifts into hatred.

Loathing.

Still, this stranger doesn't have an issue with arousal, does he? After all, I can feel his dick against my most intimate self even if he isn't shoving it against me.

Confused by my reaction to his erection when I should be repulsed, I sign, "Why are you doing this?"

Unsurprisingly, he doesn't answer *that*. Rather, he stuns me by asking a question, "Did Rundel sexually assault you?"

"Why do you care?" I retort, gaze locked on his hands before I scowl at him. "Aren't you going to do that to me?"

I can feel his sudden surge in tension. "You are safe."

A denial? Or a nonanswer?

My scowl deepens as I motion over my naked form. "I really feel safe." I only wish it were possible to imbue sarcasm with my fingers— I have to hope my expression says it all.

His jaw works but he stays silent, just snags a piece of pancake and presses that to my mouth. I get the feeling that he's trying to shut me up.

Ha.

Not gonna happen.

As I eat, I sign, "Tell me your name, at least."

His gaze drifts along my very naked curves as he takes in my statement, then he spells out, "Nikolai."

I have a name, at least.

Step one in humanizing him is complete.

My throat feels tight as I swallow the pancake and manage that feat without choking.

Onto step two—understanding the trouble I'm in.

Slowly, I inhale.

I can do this.

Calmly, I exhale.

"Did Harvey owe you money?" I ask. "Is that why I'm here?"

He doesn't reply to that, just studies my lips before he presses a piece of egg to them. I accept it, wishing like hell that I wasn't so hungry; otherwise, I'd spit it in his face.

While I'm busy chewing, he's studying me, and it's difficult to adjust to his very avid attention.

I've never been comfortable naked, especially after Harvey would accuse me of being the reason why he couldn't get it up—because I was fat, because I needed to diet, because I didn't look like a pornstar...

Always my fault, never his.

Nikolai, however, doesn't appear to be disgusted by my shape.

His eyes are heavy-lidded with want.

I swallow the egg and, after that, eat everything he places on my tongue until the dish is empty. Then comes fruit. Apple, crisp and fresh. Orange, tart and sweet. Fig, chewy and flavorful. Pomegranate, bitter and juicy.

At least this is confirmation that my unwanted host won't starve me.

When I'm done, and he still hasn't answered me, that's when he taps my bottom lip with his finger. "Now, a reward for eating every bite."

My brows lift. "You're letting me go?"

His hand drops, lower, lower, then his fingers are riffling through the soft hair at the apex of my thighs.

Eyes widening, I jerk higher onto my knees when I understand his intention, but his other hand clamps onto the softness of my ass to hold me in place.

Expecting him to drag down his zipper, I find myself stunned when, instead, his fingers remain on course and they aim between my legs.

Before he can touch me *there*, my hand slides around his wrist, nails digging into him as I rasp, "What are you doing?"

I can hear my pulse in my ears. Only, it isn't because I'm scared. Fear should be at the center of this interaction, but it isn't.

"Well?" I demand huskily.

I know he can't hear me, but our fingers are too busy for signing and I figure the claws in his forearm kind of give the game away…

His gaze is back to being heavy-lidded, the amber-like irises primed with a heat that I swear I can feel deep in my core.

Fuck, how he looks at me—I could get used to that.

Having never experienced it before in my life, having never been looked upon as if I'm the most beautiful woman alive, it's shockingly heady stuff. Too shocking. Too heady.

Because apparently, it's turned me into a lunatic as *that* is the moment when I confirm my insanity—I move his hand.

I don't know why I do it—

Lies!

A man like this looking at a woman like me with the intention of giving me pleasure?

A man like him looking at a woman like me as if *I'm* the goddess? As if *I'm* a pornstar? As if *I'm* perfection?

Swallowing thickly, oddly nervous yet excited too, I maneuver his fingers until they're close to my mouth.

I have no idea what the hell I'm thinking as I let my tongue flutter around the tips, but his groan encourages me to continue.

Heart pounding so hard a cardiac arrest might be in my near future, I make sure they're nice and wet, his amped-up breathing giving me the confidence I need to return him to his original trajectory.

There's only expectation here. Only want. Only need.

And it's bewildering and nuts and insanity and lunacy, but I'm only human and after the last few days I've had, I think an orgasm is a human right.

When he finds my clit with the precision of a heat-seeking missile —and trust me, I figured it was the eighth lost wonder of the world with how impossible it was for Harvey to uncover the myth that is my clitoris—I release a shaky sigh and grind into him when he flickers those dexterous fingertips over the sensitive nub.

My eyes shutter into slits as I release a moan and experience a full-body shiver.

His expression shifts.

His gaze grows fierce. *Focused.*

It jerks me into awareness. I'm at the very center of this man's attention and I have no idea what to do with myself.

Uncertainly, I hover in place, my thighs quivering as he carries on rubbing my clit with an experienced touch.

Not too fast, not too forceful.

No clumsiness.

Just a delicious amount of skill that has chills surging up and down my nerve endings, sending sensation to every corner of my deprived self.

I start to forget my discomfort, focusing only on how damn good this feels.

My head suddenly is too heavy and it rolls on my neck as he continues to touch me, to *pleasure* me.

The strangest of desires whispers along my nerve endings—I earned this.

I deserve to be pleasured.

I'm awake, aware, free from drugs, in total possession of my wits, and have a full stomach.

Why shouldn't I accept this? Why shouldn't I enjoy it?

Does it matter that I don't know who this psycho is when he's giving me something no one else has in years?

Does it matter that I didn't think to ask for it?

It wasn't like he gave me a breakfast menu with 'orgasm' as an option to be checked...

My hips begin to rock, knees digging into his outer thighs on the chair as the fingers that had clutched at my ass move, trailing upward with a delicate touch I wouldn't expect this man to be capable of. When he finds my nipple, he tweaks it softly.

Very softly.

No pain.

None at all.

Then there's a pinch—sharp enough to make me moan and for my pussy to clench around air.

He speeds up, his fingertips trailing to my channel, getting wet with me. The butt of his hand nudges my clit as he teases me with more, more... He stops. Pinches my nipple again. My pussy clutches at nothing *again*.

As I groan in hungry disappointment, his eyes burn with a fire that should scald me but, instead, douses me in an overwhelming heat that makes up for the gaping emptiness deep inside.

My nostrils flare as his slick fingers return to my clit. It's sloppier now, and he can move faster. There's no friction. Just an easy glide that he takes full advantage of to steal my breath away from me.

Mouth rounding, hips rolling, one arm surging high, the back of my hand pressing against my forehead in a show of sheer feminine need, the other flails against my chest as I struggle to figure out what to do with it.

That's when I stare down, for the first time looking at myself sitting naked on his lap, and I see *us*.

His hand, my pussy.

The calluses on his fingers. The nicks and grooves.

My pinkness, my *wetness* filling in those gaps that time and experience have left on him.

The sight, the sound of *us*—it's exhilarating.

Yet, this is about me, *for* me.

Not him.

Me.

My reward.

Mine.

For a split second, he pauses. Then, he gently pats my softness. My clit reacts as if he just started tongue-fucking it. He pats me again, harder this time. A spank, more than a tap.

Shuddering, I jerk onto my knees, a keening cry escaping me.

"Oh, God," I moan as he slides his fingers over the entirety of my pussy, slipping them from side to side so fast that I can't help but release an expectant sob as I approach the pinnacle of my desire.

"Close, so close," I mutter to myself, unable to recognize my voice, the need, the heat, the lust, the hunger.

That's me.

Me.

My hips roll faster.

Pleasure is there—so close.

So near.

"Fuck, fuck," I breathe. "More, please. More. I need—"

He stops.

My empty pussy continues clutching at nothing.

I let loose a choked cry, but my hands know exactly what to do—they grab his shoulders and dig in.

The urge to drag him against my chest, to feel those lips on my nipple is real and raw and unexpected. My nails claw at him, but he ignores my unspoken demand and simply stares at me with eyes that fan the flames of my want because he's back to looking at me like I'm a goddess.

I've never been a goddess.

Until this man.

And it could get addictive.

With digits slick with my arousal, an arousal *he* built, he sticks one of his fingers in his mouth.

The groan he releases—oh. Fuck.

His tongue smoothes over the tip and he sucks one deeper before he sticks the other one in too, scooping up the juices that have dripped onto his knuckles.

My pussy throbs with emptiness.

I'm so fucking empty.

I didn't anticipate that being a problem twenty minutes ago, but now it is.

I haven't had a decent orgasm that wasn't self-donated to the cause since Britney's hair grew back.

When I shudder, he returns those spatulate, callused, slender tormentors to my clit.

I'm too busy shivering and quaking to register his next moves until he makes them—he thrusts those two digits he wet into me and scissors them wide.

The spasms that rush through my muscles make me wonder if I need a doctor because this has to be a seizure.

How my head fills with white noise, the way that buzz zips along my nerve endings—I'm about to pass out.

No doubt about it.

My head falls backward as he rocks his hand, widening his fingers, twisting them inside me, making me feel full for the first time since I met Harvey.

Shuddering, I look down at us.

Strong and supple, his work-worn hand is tanned against the soft pinkness of my pussy. Unfamiliar, yet welcome. The visceral display has my breath hitching in my chest as, with that sight bombarding me, full of *him*, I come.

It's simple and easy and soughs from me like a sigh would.

Until the sigh forms a hurricane as he picks up the pace, that is. Hand bucking, thumb caressing my clit, fingertips pinching my nipple until I feel the bite of his teeth replace them.

Pleasure/pain—God, they said in the magazines that it felt good, but I never expected *this*.

My eyes close with the release as it gains ground, storming through my veins, making my heart pound, my lungs burn, and my skin prickle with its ferocity.

As I sob with the power of it, my nails dig into the muscles at his shoulders once more, fingers clenching as fiercely as my cunt while I fly through my orgasm.

I want to ride that high for as long as I can, but like always, fabulous things come to an end.

It's at that time that I realize my legs are literally shaking with the strength of my climax.

Dazedly, I study my thighs then peer at him and find him licking his fingers clean again.

His hum makes me bite my lip—honestly, I've seen people slurp down strawberry syrup on a sundae with less enjoyment than him doing *this*.

Then, he signs, "Better than ambrosia." And he smirks when I blush.

Cheeks hotter than ever, even after everything he just did to me, I accept that there's no standing, never mind an escape attempt, until my legs stop with the shaking thing—that has *never* happened before.

What the hell?

A part of me is embarrassed by what I let him do to me, and another part wants, as a token gesture, to try to knee him in the balls again, but mostly, that fades away when the cocktail of unease, annoyance, ecstasy, and calm hits my bloodstream.

When he stops savoring my pussy juices, he maneuvers me on his lap so that I'm leaning against him, my legs settling over the side of the chair.

That's when his hands, one of which is still slick with me, because *I freakin' came*, smoothes along my thighs and calves in a gentle massage that feels really good with how badly the muscles were seizing.

The beginnings of cramps ease immediately at his petting.

That's when the most ridiculous sensation whispers through my veins, gentle but filling me with warmth. Making me feel, insanely enough, safe.

Like he said I am.

Especially when he cups the back of my head and presses it to his shoulder, much as he did last night in the car.

I sag into him, my body accepting what my brain can't yet.

Then, my cheeks turn bright pink as it registers what that thing is that's digging into my butt—his cock.

And it's big.

I mean, I saw it in the shower, but it's another thing to experience it *in situ* as it were.

His fingers were big enough... Harvey didn't prepare me for anything other than average and nothing about this guy is average.

Nothing.

So, we sit there, his cock a brand against my ass until, finally, he decides to move.

That's when he takes me to the bathroom and washes me.

This time, once he's done cleaning me with discomfiting thoroughness, he moisturizes me, sliding the cream over every inch of my skin with an ease that Harvey never had with me.

Ever.

All the while, he's back to looking at me as if I'm special. As if I'm one of the pornstars Harvey accused me of not being.

Any body conscientiousness has faded into dust and it's too freeing.

I could get used to this.

But that doesn't take away from what's happening here.

I have questions with no answers in sight, and I'm not sure I'm going to get them when Nikolai's intent is to tend to me with his odd acts of service while locking me away from the world.

I fought too hard to escape Harvey to let someone else imprison me against my will.

I need to figure out his motives.

Because it can't simply be that he wants me.

That's just not logical.

NIKOLAI

AN HOUR EARLIER

Savior - Rise Against

FROM THE CORNER of the screen, I can see that my expression is blank.

As always.

Only someone who knows me would discern that I'm annoyed.

Very fucking annoyed.

But then, video calls with my brothers always tend to veer toward irritating, especially when I have to get information about them from a goddamn blog.

I told you so...

BLOG

Rumors abound about Maxim Lyanov's absence in NYC.
Contacts assure me that he's actually in the motherland,
   sucking up to the Krestniy Otets who *isn't* happy about his
   'takeover' of New York.
I've yet to determine if his continued presence in Moscow is
   related to business *or* to a certain woman who's been seen
   dripping off his arm at recent social events.
Are there Bratva-shaped wedding bells in the future?
I'd always believed that Maxim Lyanov would make a play for
   Victoria Vasov, the daughter of the late lamented Pakhan
   whose shoes Lyanov's currently trying to fill.
Whatever his reasons for staying in Russia, whether or not a

marriage announcement is in the making, follow me for updates.

You know they'll be here first.

When you're out of the loop, don't let me say... *I told you so.*

"I DON'T HAVE time for a conversation with the silent man," Maxim snarls, drawing my attention away from the blog.

Most of its contents I was already aware of, but that this blogger is so well-informed is worrisome.

"Screw you," Dmitri retorts immediately. "You're lucky he gives a fuck about you, you arrogant piece of shit."

I almost smile—he's always my first line of defense.

"He's right, Maxim. Stop being an asshole," Misha wades in.

For once, he's on my side of an argument, which acts like a backhand to Maxim's face—a backhand he needs.

Unluckily for me, the dipshit is in Moskva so he's too far away to feel it.

"How is he right? I *have* to be here. I have to suck up to the Krestniy Otets," Maxim counters. "You think I want to lick that bastard's ass? Of course, I don't. What alternative do I have?" That has me heaving a sigh, which Maxim immediately jumps on. "Don't you dare say 'I told you so.' New York is mine. It wouldn't have been if I'd listened to you."

"I didn't say a thing," I sign, the words ironic enough that Dmitri chuckles as he shoves his hair out of his face—the little fucker didn't get it cut.

Maxim grits his teeth. "I don't need this."

"I'm not saying you do. You've made your bed and now you have to lie in it, but don't bullshit me by telling me that you're still there for the Krestniy Otets. You think I don't have ears to the ground?"

"You're spying on me?"

I sniff. "I'm spying on everyone. If you're not, then you're a fool."

Maxim flushes, but I ignore his embarrassment to continue, "Who's the woman?"

My brother scowls. "What woman?"

So, it's going to be like that.

With a roll of my eyes, I sign, "I've heard you've been asking about Kuznetsov."

Dmitri shudders. "What the hell are you doing getting involved with him, Maxim?"

The Kuznetsovs are as integral to Russian culture as the Kremlin.

Two parts ghoul, one part imagination, one part boogeyman.

The average Russian doesn't know if they exist or not, but they know to never whisper that name.

It's like an American teenager not daring to utter Bloody Mary out loud.

Except, in this instance, it's the grown-ass adults who are scared, not pubescent, zit-pocked kids.

For good reason.

"I said I'd help someone," Maxim mutters.

"You?" Dmitri retorts. "Since when do you offer to help *anyone?*"

"Dmitri!" Misha barks. "Know your fucking place!"

"What place?" he argues. "I'm Nikolai's right-hand man. That puts me at a higher goddamn rank than *you*, Misha, seeing as Maxim didn't make you his Sovietnik."

Neither of us knows why Maxim chose Kirill and Tima for his officers. Not when Misha has had Maxim's back since he was a small boy or Maxim's issue with my choosing an Obschak that wasn't him all those years ago.

It's clear, however, that it's a point of contention when Misha grows red-faced and Maxim ducks his gaze from the screen.

It might only have been for a handful of seconds, but that's enough for me to know there's trouble in paradise.

Angling my head to the side, I place a hand on Dmitri's shoulder before signing, "Infighting will get us nowhere. This isn't a pissing contest or a popularity competition. Each of you is my family.

"Whether you choose to listen to me or not, I will always want what's best for you, do you understand?"

Though Maxim is sulking like a child, even he hunches his shoulders at my words.

Dmitri might be the only one I consider a son, but Misha and Maxim aren't far off. Maxim is nine years younger than me, after all, and I looked after him when he was small—those kinds of bonds are difficult to forget.

Even if Maxim wishes he could…

"Why is Kuznetsov of interest to you, Maxim?"

"I owe a debt to someone."

Well, that was a lie.

They forget I know them better than they know themselves.

I heave yet another sigh. "Whatever reason has you sniffing around danger, you need to watch yourself and you need to get back to New York. *That* is your turf. You snatched it out of rightful hands and have already had to deal with several mutinies.

"Moskva will never accept you as its Pakhan, but that doesn't mean you can't hold it." I flicker a look at Misha. "I've been informed that you have the support of the men."

Maxim tilts his chin up. "I do."

"Then that's all you need, isn't it?" When he frowns at me, I warn, "If you bring communism to the Bratva, you need to be prepared for another fallout. You can't do that if you're overseas."

He grunts. "Any news on Pavel?"

I shrug. "Maria is still guarding him like a momma bear."

"How did you let him get shot by B4K?"

Thousands of miles may part us, but the tension that springs to life at his words ping pong between us as if we're in the same room.

"Maxim," Misha warns.

"Pavel shouldn't have been outside that club," Dmitri counters. "Not without guards. He's the goddamn Obschak. He knows that. We can't make him listen to us."

"Is B4K still giving you trouble?" Misha inquires, aiming that question at me, clearly trying to defuse the conversation.

Jaw working, I shake my head. "They were."

"But they're not a problem anymore?"

Having spent yesterday morning feeding what's left of the B4K pushers we took hostage to Vasily, my favorite alligator, Dmitri snorts. "He set fire to their main warehouse in retaliation before we rescued that chick. Ya know, the one on Albanian Mob territory? Where *you* sent *us* without warning?" Uneasily, Misha shifts in his seat, but my kid's on a roll: "How did you even figure out where she was?"

"One of the O'Donnellys is a hacker," Misha mumbles. "He triangulated her location from the cell she used to contact Savannah O'Donnelly for help."

"You sure the Irish weren't trying to fuck us over?"

"I trust him," Misha snaps. "I wouldn't have—"

"Sent us into dangerous turf?" Dmitri mocks.

I grab his shoulder to stop the argument from escalating then sign, "This is getting us nowhere."

He's right and Misha's wrong, but it's in the past and I found a little sun for myself so I'm more than satisfied with how the situation panned out.

Dmitri huffs but picks up from where he left off: "Anyway, we took B4K prisoners who assured us that three million dollars' worth of cocaine was destroyed in the blaze."

Maxim flinches but immediately covers it—he's hated fire since our final days at the orphanage. That ended what was becoming a problem—his pyromania.

Misha, on the other hand, doesn't remember the inferno Maxim left our orphanage in, so he chuckles. "Bet that was a fireworks display worthy of the 4th of July."

"Better than that. They'd taken the coke on sale or return."

Misha hoots. "You're fucking with me?"

"Nah." Dmitri cackles. "It was a recent shipment. The Colombians are calling in the debt too."

"Also thanks to 'Mute?'" Maxim inquires, tone droll.

"The Colombians had a problem with ICE in Arizona. Nikolai

eased the strain." Though Dmitri's grinning, it starts to fade as he clears his throat. "Have you seen Sofia?"

Some of Maxim's tension disperses as he rolls his eyes. "I'm not going to discuss your infantile crush."

Misha grins. "Come on, Maxim. It's worth it to see him blush."

"Fuck you," Dmitri grumbles.

"How is she?" I demand in his stead, knowing that his ties with Sofia, the daughter of the Krestniy Otets, run deeper than Maxim or Misha could possibly understand.

"She's still not wearing an engagement ring," is Maxim's disinterested answer.

Taking note of Dmitri's barely noticeable sigh of relief, I ask, "But her well-being?"

"No bruises," is his short reply. "Not for a while."

Dmitri grimaces. "I hate him."

"We all do," Misha mutters.

"The Krestniy Otets doesn't seek our friendship, just our servitude," I sign though I can't help but agree with them.

"He needs taking off his perch," Maxim grouses. "Maybe he'll stop thinking he's the next Tsar of Russia, then."

Misha whistles. "Treason, Maxim?"

"Why not? We did it in New York."

"You're a big-headed asshole," Dmitri retorts.

"Don't be Icarus, Maxim," I agree. "Flying too close to the sun won't serve you well."

My words have unintentional amusement drifting through me.

I, on the other hand, can *be Icarus when Cassiopeia is my little sun...*

"Jesus, is he smiling, Dmitri?" Misha demands, eyes wide in surprise.

"He's being weird."

"Weirder than usual?" Maxim asks with a snort.

He clears his throat. "Yeah."

Maxim's regard is intense. "Think about it, Nikolai."

"Think about what?"

"A takeover. If anyone could do it, it's you." His stare remains unusually direct. Maybe he thinks he can hypnotize me into agreeing to take part in his madcap schemes? "You have the loyalty of a lot of the men. They trust you. *Respect you.*"

"Fear him, more like," Dmitri argues.

"That as well," Misha inserts with another chuckle. "The trifecta of leadership—trust, respect, and terror."

"Stabbing first, twisting the knife, then feeding the body to your gators later earns you quite the reputation," Maxim concurs.

"If anyone even knew we were talking about this, we'd get our asses killed," Dmitri remarks.

"This is a secure line," Maxim insists. "No one can get into this channel, but it's important. The Krestniy Otets is the one who's flying too close to the sun. And we know what his Obschak and Sovietnik are like…"

Dmitri stiffens.

Why wouldn't he when his father is the Krestniy Otets's Sovietnik?

Again, I rest a hand on his shoulder. He relaxes, *minutely*, but it's better than his tension from before.

"Careful, Maxim," Misha rumbles, astutely reading between the lines.

Misha is a wild card. On the regular, he makes Maxim look Type A, except I can't help but notice how he's changed since he took up with his new squeeze—Page 6 darling Aspen Daniels.

A relationship I definitely do not approve of.

Maxim grunts. "Dancing around the subject does him a disservice. We all know what that piece of shit put Dmitri through. How is it fucking right that he gets to lord it over everyone?"

"Might is right," I sign.

"And that's my point! We take away their fucking might. They're nothing. Old pieces of shit who can be slain in their beds if we get together—"

"Moskva isn't NYC," Dmitri argues. "None of you understand the hierarchy like I do. None of you were raised eating, breathing, and shitting it like I was.

"It's not as easy as you think it is to pull off a takeover.

"Whether he's liked or not, he owns Russia. Hell, the Baltics, even. The US is different."

Misha rocks back in his chair. "What do you mean?"

"I mean that the US is different from Russia," is his flat retort. "The links over there are entrenched. It's like a hydra—you cut off one head and seven more shoot up.

"Plus, you take out the K.O., then my father will snatch his position, and if not him, Petrov." The Obschak. "There'll always be someone waiting to jump onto his throne, someone older and, because of that, with more connections than all four of us put together.

"These alliances were made when Niko was still wearing diapers; that's how they remain in power. That's why you're not popular with the old guard, Maxim—you broke the cycle.

"Despite that, it's different in the US. *Younger*. They own it through their Pakhans. It's their Pakhans who have the ties, the influence. Not the lords in their palaces in Moskva."

Exasperated, I pinch the bridge of my nose. "This wasn't why I started our call. I just wanted to know what game you were playing over there."

Misha jeers, "Sedition."

I narrow my eyes at him. "If he dies because you can't save his ass from NYC, that's on you and not me seeing as you're encouraging *this* where I'm not."

"That's not fucking fair," Misha snarls, his good humor instantly fading.

"Misha can't be here," Maxim inserts calmly. "I need him in the city."

"Why?" Dmitri inquires before mocking, "Can't you leave Silk without a keeper?"

Silk is one of Tribeca's hottest clubs and it's Misha's baby.

"Hush, Dmitri," I chide. "Silk makes the New York branch a fortune."

When silence falls on the video call, each of our gazes darting from one to the other, Maxim breaks it first with a grumbled, "I have a traitor in my ranks."

"You have several," Dmitri retorts. "What's the difference now?"

"Someone close to him," Misha mutters. "I'm monitoring things."

Concerned, I sign, "Do you need help? Extra men?"

"They'd be loyal to you, not me," Maxim points out.

"And *I* am loyal to you, Maxim."

The simplicity of my statement has his shoulders slouching as he sinks back into the sofa. I don't know where he's staying, but I can imagine it's Bratva-owned. If he hasn't swept the place for bugs...

God, these *podonoks* are going to turn me prematurely gray.

"I'll never understand how the two of you can fight so much when Nikolai barely says a word," Misha complains, but a smile is dancing around his lips as he takes in Maxim's reaction to my statement.

"If you need me," I sign, ignoring Misha. "I can be there. Whether that's in the flesh or whether it's with trustworthy manpower." My cell buzzes, drawing my attention to it from its position on my desk. Seeing Boris's name, I continue, "I have to go. Don't lock me out, you two. Keep me in the loop."

Before they can argue, I cut the call, but as I reach for my phone, Dmitri sniffs. "Why you put up with them is beyond me."

"You think I don't put up with you too?" I counter, smirking when he scowls at me.

Grabbing my phone, I scan the messages. My smirk dies shortly after.

"What is it?"

I tilt the screen at him.

> Boris: The Albanians are on the hunt for Rundel but they can't find him.

> Boris: He's a slippery motherfucker. I broke into the motel's office to see if he'd paid cash or on credit, but though he paid by card, it wasn't under Rundel.

Boris: It was under Turgenev. Does Dmitri know of a family branch over here?

"I don't, and you know how rare a surname it is. What didn't die out in the First World War, the rest almost faded with Stalin's purges. That's why the remainder aligned with the Bratva—safety." When I nod my agreement, Dmitri inquires, "You think Rundel's got a Russian background, or is it a stolen ID?"

I ponder the question and answer it with one of my own: "Can you get into the Social Security Administration still?"

He nods and drags his laptop over to him. "Give me five."

"Sure."

Three minutes later, he pushes his computer my way and I type into the search feature of the database: Cassiopeia Turgenev.

I get a hit.

"He's using her maiden name," Dmitri exclaims. "I said she had to be Russian with that hair."

I elbow him in the side, hard enough to wind him.

"Yeah, yeah," he grouses, spluttering around a cough. "She's yours." Because I didn't raise a fool, he's quick to change the subject. "So, there *is* a branch of Turgenevs over here. I wonder how that happened."

"Immigration," I drawl.

But he shakes his head. "My great-great-grandfather would never have allowed that. Ever since we aligned with the Bratva, we remained true to the brotherhood and its wiles or got our throats cut."

I can hear the belief dripping from every word—family lore that's as bred into him as his dirty-blond hair.

"Can you get me her birth certificate?" I sign.

"Yup."

As he seeks that out, I flick on the app that enables me to access the cameras in my bedroom.

She's still sleeping.

That's thirty-six hours now...

I consulted Grigoriy yesterday, and he said not to wake her but to get her to drink fluids and if she slept in between bathroom breaks to let her rest.

If she sleeps much longer, I'll contact him again.

"Here you go," Dmitri says, drawing my attention to him. "And the twilight zone expandeth."

When I read all the data on her birth certificate, I see why. "You know who that is?" I ask, pointing to her father's name.

"Aside from a relative I've never heard of before? Nope."

"Only in your line do you learn your family tree as if it's the gospel."

He snorts. "Not by choice, Niko. Not mine, at any rate."

Though I grunt, I sign, "Ever heard of Peshnya?"

He blinks. "The KGB assassin? Sure."

I tap on Peshnya's real name—Mikhail. "The man himself. I just never put the pieces together before now. You must be related."

"Peshnya's family?" he half-croaks, gaping at Cassiopeia's birth certificate like it holds all the answers.

Unfortunately, neither it nor I have them.

"Wouldn't your father have claimed a familial tie with Peshnya if he could've?"

Dmitri purses his lips. "Unless Peshnya threatened him to keep quiet…"

I hum. "Interesting."

"Confusing, more like," he rumbles before he turns still.

At his hesitation, I ask, "What is it?"

"Peshnya was loyal to the KGB, the *Kremlin*. Not the Bratva."

"Maybe that's why you don't know his name. Your great-grandfather exiled him?"

He frowns. "Maybe."

"I never heard any rumors of him defecting," I sign, amazed to find that Mikhail Turgenev was in the US at all. Never mind long enough to marry and spawn a daughter.

"That alone might explain why he'd have been burned off the family tree. Defection—he's lucky he made it out of Russia alive." He whistles. "I can't believe *Peshnya* is a Turgenev. How didn't I know that?"

"I don't believe in coincidences," I muse.

"You think this is one?"

"Perhaps."

"Peshnya retired, didn't he?"

"They say he got caught up in that explosion in St. Petersburg—the church blast? Lost his hearing."

That would explain why her ASL had strange inflections that I couldn't interpret. Didn't explain why her spoken Russian was dire, though, when her father was a born and bred native.

"He's dead now, isn't he?" Dmitri asks.

"Have to think he is or Rundel would be insane to piss off Peshnya." My lips curve. "Almost wish he were alive just so I could see him carve his name into Rundel's brains with an ice pick."

Dmitri chuckles. "That would be a sight to behold for sure."

"Confirm if he's dead or not."

Nodding, Dmitri gets to work then shows me a death certificate. "Accidental death."

Nonplussed, I sign, "I have to think that's an understatement."

"For a man with a reputation like Peshnya, I can't disagree," Dmitri retorts with a chuckle. "Think he had enemies?"

"No. He didn't change his identity."

"Arrogance?"

My lips flatline. "Maybe. But it's one thing to put yourself in danger, another to fail to protect your family."

"True."

"Check his death out. And while you're at it, make sure her mother isn't approached by Rundel."

"Why?"

I scowl at him. "Because I asked you to."

"Who is this chick to you?" he grumbles. "Why do you even care? Did you know she was Peshnya's daughter or something?"

"I told you—she's mine. That's what matters."

"She's not a watch, Niko. Or a Porsche."

"I'm aware of that."

He nudges me slightly. "Nikita says you haven't let her out of your bedroom."

"She's been asleep since she arrived," I counter, even though I wouldn't have let her out if she *had* been awake.

Dmitri grunts like he already knows what I didn't speak out loud. "What are you going to do with her?"

"Keep her."

"Against her will," he says flatly, his disapproval apparent.

I blink at him. "It won't be against her will forever."

"I'm not sure I want to know."

"Then don't ask."

He returns his attention to the computer screen, muttering, "She's family, Nikolai. Don't hurt her."

Damn Turgenevs—you can take the man out of Moskva, but you can't take the Turgenev out of the man. "I have no intention of hurting her. She is safe with me."

He sniffs but, instead of commenting, mumbles, "They say Peshnya inspired Ilya Levin."

"'Inspired?' More like he stole Turgenev's MO. Either that or his ice pick."

"Is it true what they say about—"

I arch a brow. "Him being a virgin?"

Dmitri shoots me a sharp grin. "Impossible, right?"

My shoulder hitches. "You've never met him in person, have you?"

"No."

"He's... *odd*."

"Odd."

I nod. "Odd. He's a watcher."

"Like, a voyeur?"

"Worse."

"Worse?"

I think about the hookers Ilya keeps in his stable who fuck each other for his entertainment, whose sole purpose is that, then after I flick

Dmitri a glance, I dismiss the memory and slap my palm against the desk before reaching for my cell.

Ilya is unusual. Americans would say he's on the spectrum. In Russia, where things are less politically correct than they are here, he's treated like a freak.

Of course, once Americans realize Ilya has killed more people than Ted Bundy, I think their sympathy would lessen.

> Me: Keep to the hunt. I want Rundel brought to me.

> Boris: Might need help, Pakhan.

Dmitri swipes his floppy hair aside. "He has a point. If I were Rundel, I'd be getting my ass out of Kentucky fast."

"If he knows the Albanians didn't get Cassiopeia, then he'll want her back." Just saying the words makes me want to tear Rundel apart.

I blow out a breath and promise myself *soon*.

Rundel *will* die at my hands.

And maybe, to honor Cassiopeia's father, I'll use an ice pick…

12

CASSIE
THE FOLLOWING MORNING

You're Gonna Go Far, Kid - The Offspring

YESTERDAY WAS, in a word, bewildering.

It's like I've been transported to some weird Narnia place where clothes are forbidden, orgasms are compulsory, and food can only be ingested after a hot guy places it on your tongue.

Surreal.

Maybe that's why, when the window shutters open out of the blue and jerk me from my sleep, I don't scream in fright.

I just roll over and slur, "Asshole," into the pillow.

One day in this madhouse and I'm already starting to acclimate.

Of course, that's more than likely thanks to years of living on my nerves. My stress levels are incapable of surging any higher, not when Nikolai seems to mean it when he says, 'You are safe now.'

Relatively speaking, no one can get to me. Never mind Harvey. Which means Nikolai is correct—technically, I'm safer than I was a week ago.

I *have to* find comfort in that. Technicalities are my friend...

When my arms collide with one of the many pillows on the bed, something oddly smooth and cool connects with my fingers, gaining my attention.

Squinting at the bright light pouring through the windows—maybe him shuttering them has nothing to do with locking me in and everything to do with me getting a good night's sleep—I find an envelope leaning against the indentation on the pillow.

A head-shaped indentation.

Yesterday, I'd noticed the mussed sheets and realized he'd slept there but I'd kind of forgotten in the aftermath of a hand-fed breakfast, orgasm as a reward for eating (not dieting), and a full-on shower experience with a fallen angel who was more than willing to drop to his knees to wash me.

This is starting to drift into the realm of softcore 90s porn-era fantasies.

I'm pretty certain that there'll be a brothel somewhere filled with male escorts who charge top fees for this experience.

And no, I'm not downplaying the fact I have zero say in what's happening here but honestly, I'm better off than I was when I was on the run.

That's the simple, damning, *uncomfortable* truth because what that says about the state of my life is depressing.

Reaching for the envelope, I open the flap once I see my name on the front.

If a lot can be drawn from someone's handwriting, Nikolai's is as stark as his personality. His aggression leaks through into the pressure of his pen which has left indentations on the paper. His letters are sharp and angular but neat to the point of ridiculousness as he spells out my full name—not the abbreviated version, but Cassiopeia and all its many vowels.

Correctly, too.

He gets marks for that.

As I withdraw the piece of paper, it appears to be relatively normal —unless you look deeper, which I am, because I guess I have confirmation that he doesn't just know ASL, he *can* speak English with a good degree of fluency.

Which means he's either ignorant, arrogant, annoying, or all three.

The letters are the same, of course, but they're written differently. A small 't' is shaped like a small cap 'т.' The same goes with the 'в,' 'н,' 'м,' and the 'к.' In fact, the 'Y' is more decorative too, 'У.'

From my Russian classes back in college, I know the Cyrillic letters don't naturally translate with their English counterparts, but it's interesting that he's made a merger with his mother tongue and this learned one.

When I found you in the motel room where Rundel left you, a man was on the brink of stealing you away. Rundel's actions have left you with a bounty on your head—the Albanians see you as nothing more than a currency to repay his debt.

You don't have to believe me, but if you step toward the window, you will see what happens to those who wish you harm…

When I tell you that you are safe with me, I mean every word, solnyshko.

I STUDY THE LETTER, rereading it twice before a scowl settles on my brow.

Yesterday might have been the strangest day of my life, but it looks like today will be even weirder.

And that weirdness has nothing to do with the fact that my ex-husband's actions have once again put me in danger.

Hell, I'm almost surprised he didn't try to sell me like I was a bag of oranges at the market.

Harvey, after all, has never been very good at managing his money, and with the drugs he buys and how he follows me around the country, I know his savings have to be as depleted as mine are.

So, it's not the words on the note that have me frowning or the notion that I'm in more peril than I was before. Not their meaning, either. Well, not the first half, anyway.

You are safe with me.

He told me that again after dinner and my orgasm dessert.

Of course, there's also the fact that Nikolai just confirmed my presence here has nothing to do with my husband.

Which means his reasons for keeping me remain entirely unknown.

Perplexed, I stagger to my feet and draw the comforter from the bed once I'm standing beside the overly high mattress.

Swaddled in the luxurious wrapping, I step over to the window and squint at how bright it is.

God, the sunlight feels good on my face though. Good enough that I don't immediately focus on what's happening in the courtyard.

Instead, I just bask until, eventually, my eyes stop watering and I can look into the distance.

If he meant to reassure me, he hasn't.

This estate is in the middle of nowhere, surrounded by thousands of orange trees that hide the house from the road.

It's also massive.

The courtyard is as big as a soccer pitch, split up into outdoor seating arrangements that, in different circumstances, would be a great place for a family BBQ if the family had five hundred members in it.

While I can also see a pool and a tennis court close by, there's...

I swallow and raise a hand to shield my eyes.

There's a kind of enclosure with a chain-link fence. Even from here, I can see a sign that says: 'Danger: Keep Out.'

And...

"No. Fucking. Way," I whisper, trying to unsee the shadowed illustration of a crocodile.

Or, I guess in these parts, *alligator.*

I don't know where we are, but I know it's sunny as hell in November... We're in the South. And alligators live in the swamps.

As well as private estates.

Estates that belong to Bond villains, maybe?

Then a random factoid hits me—if this *is* Florida, and this *is* the Everglades, crocodiles and alligators coexist because of the blend of lake water from Lake Okeechobee and salt from the Atlantic Ocean.

So, great.

Double the reptiles to gnaw on me if I try to escape.

Yay.

I only stop studying the enclosure when something catches my attention in my peripheral vision.

It's him.

Nikolai.

Like he's walking out onto a stage on Broadway, he crosses the courtyard.

For such a heavyset man, he's incredibly light on his feet.

"I bet he's a great dancer," I mutter to myself, then I cringe and rub my eyes. "It's too early for Stockholm syndrome, Cassie. Get a goddamn grip."

Still, in that suit of his, the delicious tailoring that shields him as if it were poured onto him, it's difficult not to be impressed.

'You are safe now.'

The words ricochet in my brain like a game of ping-pong, a match that only ends when Nikolai steps in front of my window and two men carry what I can only assume is an Albanian who saw me as a debt repayment plan.

When they drop him to the tiled floor before Nikolai's feet, he doesn't even stir.

Death will probably be a relief.

He's so far beyond black and blue that he's on a different color spectrum altogether.

Nikolai leans down and grabs him by both ears. I flinch at the sight and watch as the guy shrieks into consciousness and, with a sob, hustles into whatever position Nikolai wants him to take.

I've been the Albanian.

I've been Nikolai's doll.

He moves me around like I'm a puppet, and the parallel I'm drawing only makes the unease in my stomach turn into a whirlpool.

Nikolai, however, has been silent with me. Not violent.

I'm not a moron—I know what's about to happen.

I should probably turn away, glance into the distance as Nikolai attempts to prove to me that I am in no danger from him, but I don't.

I watch.

Cassie from a year ago might have squirmed away from it, might have cried. Cassie of today doesn't have many tears left. The ones that remain aren't going to be wasted on a piece of trash who wanted to use me like I was merchandise.

Eyes glued to Nikolai, not the Albanian, I see his hand retrieve the knife from the holster I know he wears, and then the blade is pressed to the man's throat.

The torture already happened, but I'm still startled by how easy he makes it on his enemy. He pushes the tip to the juncture between throat and shoulder, pushes it deep as the Albanian cries out in pain then—the cherry on the sundae—he twists the knife.

Twice.

Okay, not so 'easy.'

The twisted features that speak of pain on the Albanian's face morph into a rictus of agony as he tries to get away, but that knife keeps on rotating like a chicken on a spit.

Blood spurts in a colorful arc.

The Albanian drops forward, writhing on the ground in a scarlet puddle until he's still.

Free.

Everyone's so afraid of death, but truly, that's where there's no pain at all. No fear. No worries. No regrets.

The soft, wistful sigh that whispers from me is loud in the otherwise peaceful room.

I can't say I'm jealous. It's not that I *want* to die. I'd just like my life to stop being a minefield, and Nikolai, whether he's trying to prove that I'm safe with him or not, the reasons for which are still unknown, is a massive minefield.

Red flags dotted everywhere.

No Princess Diana in sight to save my butt from him, either.

I half-expect the shutters to close now that the show's over, but they don't. The two men who brought in Nikolai's prop make another appearance and they drag the corpse away, leaving a bloody stain on the ground.

That's when I realize Nikolai has disappeared, but I don't ponder on it for long.

Instead, I study that wash of red, absently wondering if bleach will get rid of it or if they'll need baking soda to brighten the white tiles again. Though, peroxide would probably do the job too.

When the door opens behind me, I know it's him.

I don't turn around.

I don't look at him.

Much as he did twice yesterday, he ignores me, heads to that panel beside the bathroom passage, opens the safe room, and steps inside.

In the time I've been here, I've learned the lay of the land—he controls my day, my food intake, my shower schedule, and if I want something as luxurious as a towel to dry me. Even my sleep is controlled because the power will suddenly switch off out of nowhere.

Yesterday, after dinner, he allowed me to stay in the safe room where there's a TV, but when that cut out, I knew that was his silent prompt for sleep.

With no other form of entertainment, TV and sleep are pretty much the only pastimes open to me.

I guess it makes up for *years* of living on my nerves, hmm?

With a yawn, I walk over to the safe room.

I want to be mad, and I am, but I'm also tired despite sleeping more than I have in months—thirty-six hours according to him.

I guess I'm world-weary.

Apathetic.

Part of that was down to what Harvey did to me, yet the fatalism is new.

Not caring whether I live or die is something that's been developing since I first took off but here, now, the old me is at war with the new one.

Pre-Harvey Cassie would have slapped a man for suggesting she sit on his knee while she ate from his fingers.

New Cassie recognizes that in this room, I actually *am* safe from Harvey. As well as any random mobsters my ex-husband set on my ass by being a moron.

Old Cassie, never mind Pre-Harvey Cassie, wouldn't permit a stranger to touch her pussy.

New Cassie?

She enjoyed the orgasm.

"You are thinking too much."

I translate the words he signs without even realizing I'm doing it. I've grown rusty over years with no use and ASL is definitely not like riding a bike, but I remember enough to get by.

"What can I do when you won't talk to me? When I can't talk to anyone? When I don't have anything to entertain me but my thoughts?"

Seeming to ignore my questions, he tilts his head. "Do you believe me when I tell you you're safe here?"

"I'm not safe from you, though, am I?" I argue, face expressionless as I take a seat on his knee like that's normal.

"That isn't what I asked," he signs.

"I'm safe from Harvey," I agree, weariness making me sit deeper on his lap than I'd like—my hip brushes his abs.

I learned my lesson yesterday, after all. Comply and I only have to sit on his knee. Disobey and I have to straddle him.

"You're safe from everyone." His fingers manipulate that final word, imbuing it with irritation.

My lips tighten as I stare at the tray on the table. Then, I dare ask a question, uncertain if he'll know the answer or if he'll give it to me if he does: "Why did Harvey have a debt with the Albanians?"

"He wanted to buy Viagra from them, but he didn't like the price." He surprises me by replying. "He beat the dealer, got the drugs, but they caught up to him before he could get away and made him regret the day he was born."

That has my brows lifting—Harvey was dealt a taste of his own medicine.

Apparently, my apathy isn't *so* bad. Not if I can enjoy him being handed some karma.

"They still have him?" I ask.

He shakes his head. "He escaped. I have a man looking for him. He won't get to you again."

Because I know Harvey too well, that doesn't fill me with reassurance.

I'm clearly a terrible person because I was hoping the Albanians had killed him.

It takes me a few beats to register that he signed a word I don't recognize.

"What does that mean?" I sign, copying the movements he made before.

"It means 'little sun' in Russian."

My brow furrows as I tug at my hair, muttering, "I wonder where you got the inspiration for that from."

That's when I see him looking at my blonde locks as if they're literal rays of sunlight. Not just bits of keratin. There's a starry-eyed look to him and it's unnerving mostly because I like that.

Damn, 'like' is too much of an understatement.

This is deeper than 'like.'

This is a problem in the making.

When he twines a strand of my hair around his finger, I watch as he strokes his thumb over it. His gaze flickers to my face and he graces me with that same starstruck glance that is beyond delicious.

There's power in how he looks at me.

It tips the balance in my favor, and that balance has never been in my favor. Ever.

That it is with a guy like this is bewildering—and I don't just mean a hunk but a freak who thinks nothing of keeping women in his goddamn bedroom.

My temper stirs.

Long dormant, I don't even recognize what it is as it burns deep in my soul. Flickering from embers into low flames.

With his free hand, he retrieves a strawberry that's been saturated in sugar syrup from a dish I only just noticed and places it against my bottom lip.

I might have meekly accepted the succulent fruit if he hadn't trailed it over my mouth, using it like a strange lipstick.

I know what he's doing—amusing himself.

At my expense.

My nostrils flare as I snag it between my teeth when a drop of syrup falls onto my chest. I chew. He watches me. Then, as my throat starts to bob, he reaches for another piece, but it's while he's distracted that I gather the juices in my mouth and I spit at him.

The moment I do it, I regret it.

He tenses, his limbs turning into ice beneath me as my eyes bolt wide with terror. I jump off his lap and race into the bedroom, almost falling on the train from the comforter as I do so.

That's when my mortification is complete.

There's a small team of women in the bedroom—two dusting and, now that I'm outside of the safe room, what sounds like two in the bathroom.

Did they hear that?

I didn't hear them so, maybe?

My throat bobs as I think about whether or not they overheard me yesterday, but my fear dissipates and is replaced with a wider maw of anger.

Not a single goddamn one of them called the cops overnight.

Not a single goddamn one of them looks at me now.

Not a single goddamn one peers up from their task or even thinks to ask if I'm okay.

I mean, it's obvious that I'm not.

I'm wearing a comforter as a dress, I can *feel* how pale I am because I blanched in fear of Nikolai's retaliation, and I'm running around like a chicken with its head cut off.

Annoyance rolls into anxiety as my captivity is rammed home with the power of Mjölnir to my amygdala, but then aggravation overtakes it.

I. Will. Not. Take. This. Shit. Any. Fucking. *MORE.*

My outrage at an all-time high, my fury giving my feet wings like Hermes himself, I dart toward the door but, goddammit to hell—no dice. It's still locked as I tug on the handle, any lingering desperation fading as wrath booms through me. The door shakes with the force I use, but I don't care how I get through it so long as I do.

When arms grab my waist and haul me against a solid chest, I scream, "FUCK YOU!" as I kick out, trying my best to destabilize him.

My shrieking doesn't even seem to register with the staff, but I'm past caring. I struggle in his hold, doing my damnedest to make this tougher on him, but he's resolute in his stance, his intentions.

The fruit still staining his cheek, he walks me toward the safe room as if I'm no heavier than a freakin' kitten, not a size 20, and this time, he closes the door behind him.

That's when my heart sinks and fear replaces anger.

Freezing in his arms, I swallow hard as the lock clicks.

Heart racing, lungs burning, I sag into him as he props me on the back of the sofa.

That's the first chance I get to study his features and what I see bewilders me.

No irritation, no annoyance.

Impassivity.

Again.

Fuck!

Agitated, I glower at him as he drags the comforter away, baring my nudity to him.

Again with the dumb moves, I slap him, unsurprised when he snags my hand in his. Except, it's not *before* my palm connects with his cheek—it's after.

The bright pink splotch on his face makes me swallow.

Regret personified.

My bottom lip wobbles as I study the mark I left behind, aware that my breathing sounds overly loud in the silence.

His fingers around my wrist don't trigger pain—they just contain my hand.

I stare at it like it doesn't belong to me because it doesn't.

How could I have hit him like that?

Mouth still trembling, I make a fist with my free hand and press it to my chest. Rubbing it in a circle, I both sign and whisper, "I'm sorry."

His gaze flickers to my breasts where my fingers have settled and, slowly, he nods.

His lack of anger is unnerving, but that's a relief because guilt is already eating me up inside.

He's never hurt me.

Sure, he's a fucking weirdo, but he…

I swallow.

'You are safe now.'

Then, he lifts my hand to his mouth and presses a kiss to the inside of my wrist.

When he grabs me by the waist again, I don't fight. He returns us to the table and takes a seat. I can't help but notice in the time it took for me to run off like a lunatic, he moved the tray.

Because he doesn't sit me down on his lap, uneasiness filters through me. Something that's compounded after he lays me on the table instead.

I flick a look at the holstered knife that makes the faintest of bulges through his sports coat, but he doesn't reach for it.

"What are you going to do?" I demand. My actions might be passive but my words aren't. "Stab me? Rape me?"

My words have him freezing in place. Then, in a flurry of movement, he snatches a napkin, dips it into the water glass on the tray, and, as he scrubs at the fruit on his cheek, stares at me all the while.

To be the focus of that weaponized silence is unnerving, but not as much as watching him sign, "You are safe here," when he's done.

Those fucking words—who knew they could be the most annoying ones imaginable?

Temper overtaking my worry, I sneer at him. "This is how safety looks to you?"

I can *feel* his anger surge like I lit a match to a canister of gas, but he doesn't back away, doesn't hit me, doesn't curse at me.

Instead, the only part of him that softens is his eyes.

That reverence has returned.

Fuck, I don't need to see that right now.

I'm angry, *furious*, rightfully so. But it's hard, okay, *impossible,* when he looks at me like I'm some kind of superstar and he's a fanboy.

That's heady shit for a woman who has too many hairs to pluck off her chin every day.

A soft hand trails over my thigh, and I know I could smack it away. Know that I could try to aim for his balls again. But that reverence— it's crack. No, *fentanyl*. More addictive than heroin.

I suck in a breath as he brings a million nerve endings to life with that simple touch, and when he pulls back, *disappointment,* of all things, fills me.

Until he signs, "You might not be hungry, but I am."

Then, with my eyes wider than ever, he takes a seat at the table and spreads my legs.

And I don't think to stop him.

Don't think to kick him so hard that I turn the fucker into a eunuch.

No, I let him.

Maybe because I'm an idiot, or maybe because that fentanyl-coated reverence is something I don't just need to see…

I need to feel it.

13

NIKOLAI

Retrograde - James Blake

AM I ANNOYED?

Of course.

Do I appreciate being spat on?

No.

But…

I'm relieved.

She lives up to her name—*solnyshko.*

What is the sun if not a roiling, boiling mass of fury that pounds down on our heads?

As I part her legs, she doesn't fight me.

I don't think she's scared.

Mostly, I believe she's surprised by her actions and stunned into compliance because she's uncertain of my reaction to her tantrum.

Then, as I draw her farther along the table so her cunt is easier to reach, I see it.

It.

Need.

She might chafe at the restrictions I'm placing on her, but she isn't unresponsive to them.

Her cunt is pulsing, throbbing. The small slit quivers as her juices slip and slide from her, tunneling toward her ass.

Inwardly, I hide a smile as I run my nose along the side of her mons. She yelps, squirming on the table with embarrassment.

I pull back and level her with a look.

She swallows, her gaze darting from my eyes to my mouth. Then, she licks her lips and seals her fate as I move closer to her again, slowly, slowly.

Letting her feel my breath on her slit.

Letting her know that I can scent her with every inhalation.

As my tongue flickers along the line of her crotch where it meets her thigh, a moan whispers from her chest.

That moan is mine. Just as she is.

Every moment of every day she's here with me, I'll deepen the ties that bind us together until she's as locked into *us* as I am.

Pressing a kiss to her pubis, I let my nose nuzzle her slit.

She releases a soft sigh as she grabs a hold of my head. She could shove me away, but she doesn't. She holds me in place, whispering, "Jesus fuck," when I nudge her clit.

The hair is a problem I'll deal with later. But, it amplifies her scent, intensifying it to the point where I could drown in her.

What a way to fucking go.

Closing my eyes, I let my tongue drift out and connect with her pussy.

A shudder roils through me at her taste.

I'd sucked my fingers clean yesterday but that's nothing to savoring her directly from the source.

How the fuck does she taste of the sun?

Why is she so goddamn hot that she burns my tongue?

Gathering reconnaissance as I map her pussy, I quickly seek out and find her hot spots—she has many.

And worse still, she isn't used to them being touched.

That this woman has been denied her rightful pleasure is something that bewilders me.

I'm many things, however a fool isn't one.

Taking advantage of that, I flutter my tongue over her clit then suckle the entire area, knowing she's sensitive there. Her hips buck, rearing up as she shoves her cunt in my face, and, satisfied, I continue in that vein, working her higher and higher until her thighs clench around my head.

And *this* is why she's beautiful.

No hard, muscular lines but soft curves that cushion me as I eat her out.

Thrusting two fingers into her slit, I scissor them as I retreat, fucking her there with none of the care that I use to pleasure her clit.

Fast flicks to the tender nub have her hands clutching at my hair. I never do this with the mistresses I fuck but she can tear it from the roots if she wants.

Growling against her cunt, I slip down, spreading her slit wider so that I can thrust my tongue into her and savor her taste with no resistance.

Her ecstasy-soaked mewls are a soundtrack I could die hearing, *will* die hearing, and I peer at her, finding her watching me with dazed eyes that are loaded with a confusion that's borderline tangible.

She doesn't want to like this, but she does.

She doesn't want to need me, but she does.

I smile against her cunt and suckle one of her pussy lips before I lap at her. Her cheeks burn hotly at the noises we make together—my feasting is *not* silent—but she doesn't break eye contact with me until, overwhelmed, her lashes shutter and close.

Brow furrowing as she writhes against me, I push my face deeper into her pussy and bask in her sunlight.

Bathed for the first time in *her*, I let myself go, devouring her like a man who's been starved his whole life, savoring her heat when I've been locked out in the cold since forever.

When she sobs with her release, I take her through it, edging her higher, higher until she lets loose a scream.

My fingers grip her ass, following her as she writhes because I wouldn't be surprised if she attempts to twist my neck in this chokehold.

I smirk as I lick her clit, gentling her once she shudders through her second orgasm. I don't retreat, however. No, I stay right where I want to be, cushioned by her exquisite softness.

Her scent floods the air, charging every breath I take with her release.

My nostrils flare when I hear her mutter, "This is insane. This is insane. This is insane."

Not only does she think I'm deaf, but I doubt she thought anyone would hear her anyway in that low whisper.

Unfortunately for her, my ears are *very* sensitive.

Inexplicably annoyed, I straighten to my feet. Her eyes widen at the abruptness of my motion then widen farther when my hands find my zipper.

"No," she rasps, sitting up, her fingers shoving at my hips, one of her knees falling into what I'm starting to consider her default position as it automatically lifts to kick me in the balls.

I maneuver deeper between her legs so she can't maim me, swiftly signing, "You. Are. Safe."

They're words I'll repeat until she believes in them like they're gospel-sent.

Not that they provide her with any comfort right now.

She turns to ice beneath me, her owl-like eyes gawking at me as if the Holy Trinity themselves have floated into the safe room.

My movements morph from sharp with irritation to slow, easy ones that would be simple for her to shield against.

Only… she doesn't.

When I pin both her hands together at the wrists with one of my own while the other drops to my dick so I can start to jack off, a shocked gasp escapes her at the first stroke, but our eyes lock as she gapes at me.

She doesn't struggle, though. Doesn't fight me.

Because she believes me?

I don't know.

What I do know is that when she exhales noisily and frowns at me, her gaze trickles toward my cock.

Then, she signs my death knell—*she licks her fucking lips.*

Again.

With her scent perfuming the air and her naked form spread beneath me, I have plenty of inspiration to find a swift orgasm. This is the opposite of an impressive performance, something compounded by the use of my fingers that are still wet with her cunt juices, which I spread over my shaft.

I get myself off with minimal fuss.

This isn't about an orgasm.

This is a claiming.

Just the thought has my head rearing back on my neck as release pounds through my veins, boiling the cum in my balls and making it spurt onto my fist until I direct it at her slit.

She surges upright as my seed dances over her pussy. Her focus is fixed on the bright pink flesh weeping with her own juices, slicker with my semen.

The pure white is obscenely bright against her apex and it has me gritting my teeth with the need to—

I suck in a breath as urges and cravings plague me, ones that I've never experienced before.

I feel like a wild fucking animal as I stand there, crouched over her, fighting my instincts, my very goddamn nature—

I can't stop myself.

I just can't.

I slide my fingers through the mess I've made. Her hand snaps around my wrist, bringing me to a halt. Then, my thumb traces over her clit and she shudders. Her hold on me lessens. Shifting within her grip, I speed up until her nails dig into my wrist harder than before.

Then, my little sun fills me with the warmth I knew she was born to give me.

I let my fingers circle her slit and she doesn't stop me from thrusting my seed inside her as her pussy clutches at me.

With rhythmic pulls, something that's exacerbated when I continue rubbing her clit with my thumb, I work at her again, not stopping until she's wailing with a third orgasm, her legs drawing up to her belly as she rocks from side to side, agony on her face as the ecstasy *I* was born to give *her* pummels her.

Then and only then can I stop.

I blow out the breath I didn't realize I'd been holding as a sense of rightness filters through me.

"You could have gotten me pregnant," she signs a lifetime later, but the shaken whisper packs more of a punch than she could know.

My tongue feels thick in my mouth and, against all odds, my dick starts to harden again.

I could think of nothing better than watching her grow round with my child.

One day…

It's a promise I make to myself.

One. Day.

14

CASSIE

IT'S while I'm having a meltdown over the fact that I allowed him to do *that* to me when I learn he has more to do with his days than annoy me.

The second his cell phone vibrates with an incoming message, he quickly finishes his self-appointed task in the shower, drapes a toweling bathrobe across my shoulders then, while he pats me down, grabs his cell and checks the notification.

The text is in Cyrillic, and I bitterly regret my teenage rebellion of refusing to talk to my father if he spoke to me in Russian because I can't read the message. Not even what I learned in college helps.

His brow furrows for a moment before his expression clears like someone hit the delete button on emotions in his software.

I huff at the sight but don't argue when he races through the rest of my toilette. Still, he takes the time to change my bandages before he lowers me from the vanity as if I couldn't manage the jump myself.

After spitting at him and trying to make him a mezzo-soprano, I half expect to be locked inside the bedroom for the day as a punishment but I'm not.

Maybe the prospect of breeding me has blown his mind, too,

because he just dumps me on the sofa in the safe room, switches on the TV, and heads out the door.

I definitely don't argue when he leaves me in the bathrobe—I get the feeling he forgot about it.

Then, just when I curse my luck, he makes a swift return. Expecting him to snatch my one item of clothing away, he stuns the shit out of me—a feat I thought had happened an hour ago—by ducking down and pressing a kiss to my temple as if we're an old married couple before making a retreat.

Except, Harvey never did anything like that to me.

The unexpected tenderness is…

No.

I refuse to be disarmed.

After that, I'm left to my own devices.

The entire day.

So, of course, I think about nothing other than what occurred between us.

Of the fact I let a stranger do that to me.

Of how ironic it is to be grateful to have PCOS because it means I can't get pregnant.

Of how it'd be even more ironic if I *did* manage the miracle of getting pregnant when it'd be to a stranger after mine and Harvey's various issues never permitted it when I was in a somewhat stable marriage.

As a result, I spend the next few hours in a state of perplexed pouting over the various, terrible life choices I've made that led to this moment.

I know I should enjoy not being pawed at or being his idea of appropriate breakfast food, but I don't. Not particularly.

I guess, and I can't believe the thought crosses my mind… I'm lonely.

The safe room is comfortable and there are plenty of things to watch on his TV, but I find myself heading over to the YouTube channel I created when things had felt so much simpler than they do today.

During darker times, I'd made a career out of food blogging.

Some of New York's eateries were on the map because *I* had put them there.

But when I left the city, I couldn't keep the blog going. Little-known eats in NYC were the backbone of my content—not restaurants in a buttfuck-nowhere town in the Bible Belt.

Watching the long-form videos I created is a special kind of torture. Success was mine, but I didn't even show my face because I wasn't talented enough with makeup to hide the bruises Harvey's temper left behind.

"Definitely had enough practice," I mumble.

Huddled in the damp bathrobe, I remain on the channel I'd made popular, viewing my creation, and decide to check out the blog too just for extra torment.

When I head to the web browser on the TV to see if I can access the internet, I shouldn't be surprised that there isn't one, but I'm still disappointed.

"Jackass," I call out to no one, just in case he's watching *or* listening. I tack on, "Pervert!" for extra clout.

Returning to my channel, I watch nothing but my videos where a sense of pride overcomes my earlier feelings when I uncover the ones that have had ten-plus million views. Never mind the feature on Ellie's Bakery in Hell's Kitchen and their brownies—forty million people watched that.

Forty million.

It still blows my mind.

"You weren't always a wimp," I mutter to myself, staring at the bandages on my palms. "You didn't always take Harvey's shit lying down. It just feels like you did."

It's tough being a survivor of abuse.

People don't understand how you can stay with someone who treats you like shit. But that's the thing—they make you believe you're crap. They make you believe that you're lucky to have them. They make you believe you deserve to be treated that way.

Gaslighting motherfuckers.

I should have realized the truth before we'd gotten engaged—the writing had been on the wall.

It was why my mom had told me I was settling for Harvey.

Looking back, I have to wonder if she saw him for what he was—a monster. Or did she really just think I was settling?

"You can't control that; you can't *change* that. Not anymore," I tell myself an hour later when my brain won't stop racing at 100mph. "And so what, you had three orgasms. Those were well-deserved. Definitely no reason for an identity crisis.

"In years and years of a miserable marriage, Harvey never got you pregnant and, so what, you've got a cum fetish on top of everything else! Take a breath and chill. What will be will be, Cassiopeia. Just like always."

My words do the impossible—they calm me. My inbuilt pragmatism won't let me stress over something I definitely cannot control, so the rest of the day is spent in silence, sticking to the channels I enjoy, not just my own, catching up with things I'd been too scared to watch when I was fighting for my life, aware that Harvey was hunting me like I was an injured doe and he was a rabid wolf.

When I start to relax, I know I'm decompressing, a feat that's only possible because of the cocoon I'm in.

A cocoon that exists because, subconsciously, I trust Niko when he tells me that I'm safe.

Even from him.

Nikolai might be more of a wolf than Harvey could ever be, but I'm no longer a doe.

Injured or otherwise.

15

TEXT CHAT

Troy: I heard that I owe you one.

Nikolai: Why are you messaging in Russian?

Troy: Why not?

Nikolai: You're a piece of work.

Nikolai: And yes, you owe me.

Troy: He's dead? For real.

Nikolai: He is.

Troy: Bahahahaha. RIP, NOT. God, I hated that bastard.

Nikolai: Let's hope, for your sake, he rots in Hell.

Troy: Oh, he will. But knowing my luck, so will I.

Troy: I won't forget this.

Nikolai: Watch out for chaos in Kentucky.

Troy: I'll be watching. Don't you worry about that.

Troy: Let's hope Kadare kills dear old Daddy.

Nikolai: I'll keep my fingers crossed for you.

Troy: Nikolai! WAS THAT A JOKE?

Nikolai: You know me, Troy—I never joke.

Troy: I dunno… sending my father my cousin's teeth was pretty fucking funny. :P

16

NIKOLAI
TWO DAYS LATER

Wicked - Miki Ratsula

SHE'S fast asleep when I walk into my bedroom.

I expected no less at three AM, but the soft sounds of her breathing, the gentle whispers of her limbs moving against the silk sheets, have the tension in my shoulders shifting away, drifting as if I took a Valium.

Solnyshko.

My awareness of her location in the room feels preternatural. She wouldn't have to be in the bed for me to know precisely where she is. Not when I sense her light, her heat.

Walking toward the unshuttered windows, I take a moment to study my domain.

My personal kingdom.

I remember when I was eight years old and had nothing to my name—*blyad*, less than nothing—like it was yesterday.

That's why I do this every night I spend at *Nav*.

The estate cost me a fortune. Me. Not the Bratva. It's mine. Every acre of it.

I strove for this place, killed for it, begged, stole, and borrowed to possess it, and yet, none of that seems as important as it did last week.

Twisting around, I look at her in the puddle of moonlight.

She might be my *solnyshko*, but even here, she glitters like a diamond.

My hands curve into fists as my cock hardens in response to her beauty.

I head over to the safe room to drop off the keys there, then on the return journey to the window, I strip out of my jacket and let it fall onto a chair.

After unbuckling my knife holster, I pull at my shirt, unfastening the buttons and tossing it on top of the sports coat. As I drag off my belt, I walk over to the bed like I've done every night since I brought her here.

She doesn't know how she torments me.

A part of me wishes she did.

Perhaps she wouldn't fight me as much as she does if she knew.

But the other part, the part that knows any weakness can and will be exploited, is aware of the wisdom in her remaining in the dark.

Not that sunlight *can*.

By its very nature, the sun exposes everything... the good, the bad, and the ugly.

The clock is ticking.

With every passing day of the eternity she'll spend by my side, it's only a matter of time until she realizes she has the upper hand simply by existing.

At long last.

I tug on my zipper, silently pulling it down when I reach her bedside, relief swimming inside me at the release in pressure.

I take it as a good sign that she doesn't stir.

Even unknowingly, she registers that she's safe here on my estate.

And so she should.

My reasons for bringing her to *Nav* weren't simply selfish.

Selfishness can be nuanced.

With my cock in my hand, I study the pristine lines of her features.

Awake, her beauty is unrivaled.

Asleep, her glory is merely muted.

I grit my teeth when she shuffles under the sheets—a silent tease as she reveals the upper swells of her breasts to me.

I tip my head back as I start to stroke my length, gripping tighter than usual as a punishment for doing this while she sleeps.

But she's a temptation I can't fight.

That I won't fight.

She brings light to my life even as she struggles against my dictates.

Mine.

She's mine.

She'll learn this over time.

She will.

A breath hisses from between my lips at the thoughts that have plagued me since her fateful words a couple days ago—images of her round with my child, of my ring on her finger, of a baby that would be raised in her sunlight—have haunted me.

Fuck.

The pressure builds, my heart pounds, and I tighten my fist.

Short, hard pumps get me going more than another woman on her knees with her lips around my dick could ever hope to.

My hips buck as need and want and desire coalesce into one fiery ball of flame that forms right in my fucking soul. I release onto her chest, watching as she frowns, grumbling at the disturbance, before she's turning onto her side with a sleepy pout.

Fascinated, I watch her, curious if she'll wake up. Almost wanting her to.

I've surprised myself by finding enjoyment in her reactions. When you reach the position that I have, few will spit in your face without fear of reprisals. Her feistiness is a sharp contrast to how she must have been with Rundel...

Another good sign.

The day's tensions abated, I stroll over to the chair I dumped my jacket on. My mood is practically cheerful thanks to the primitive claiming. My seed trickles between her breasts, loading her down with my scent, a scent she'll smell all night long... What isn't there to appreciate about that?

Humming, I rifle through my discarded clothes for my cell phone.

> Me: Boris, any news on that piece of shit?

> Boris: Nyet, Pakhan. I'm sorry.

> Boris: Truly, I've only stopped for sleep.

My eyes narrow with disappointment so I switch text conversations.

That's the problem with worms like Rundel—they know how to burrow deep and hide out until the heat fades.

Unfortunately for him, he's come to my attention and I don't stop until I get my man.

In this instance, I won't stop until I'm the reason he takes his last breath.

> Me: Dmitri, tomorrow, send more men to Kentucky. I want to find that motherfucker.

Not expecting a reply when I know he's on the way back to Miami and I've warned him about texting while driving, I retrieve my knife from its holster then return to the bed.

Climbing in beside her, I check my other messages before I tuck my cell beneath my pillow with the knife.

Rolling onto my side, I watch her as she rests, finding comfort in that, in her peace.

I have *never* known peace, so to see her rest is to enjoy the serenity that surrounds her.

A serenity I'm providing her.

I close my eyes.

I sleep.

As always, I don't sleep well.

When she has a nightmare, I'm awake before I realize it, knife in hand, ready to attack whatever caused her fear. Then, it registers that I can't kill whatever torments her when she's unconscious—Morpheus owns that world, and not even I can fight his chokehold.

Instead, I fight him with fire of my own.

Skimming over the mattress, I gently tug her into my arms.

Much as she hasn't each night since I brought her here, she doesn't demur, just tucks her face into my throat when I hold her close.

She feels like something I've always been denied—heaven—and smells like *us*.

Perfection.

This time, when I sleep, it's deeper than before but I'm still awake at five AM.

Untangling myself from her is difficult, but I do it because I can't be seen to change my routine, not for a woman my men are clucking about like Siberian hens.

If I alter my routine, it could be construed that I have a weakness to be exploited.

I have no weaknesses.

Only strengths.

And I include her in that mix too.

Retrieving my keys from the safe room that's activated by my palm and a passcode, I leave the bedroom and head next door, where my closet was temporarily moved, and pull on a pair of workout shorts.

Heading downstairs, I train for a couple hours, switching between a reread of Dostoevsky's *White Nights* and the broadsheets over in the UK which I find to be more informative and less US-centric.

Clued in on the world's events, reminded of the value of human life even though it means less to me than I'm sure Dostoevsky would approve of, I tip my chin in greeting when a yawning Dmitri makes an appearance.

"Thought you'd still be in Miami," is all I say.

He shrugs. "Bad night. Woke up, came here early, and had Nicoletta make me blinis before I crashed in my room."

He's been plagued with night terrors since he witnessed his mother's brutal murder on the streets of Moskva.

I clap him on the shoulder before signing, "Did you wipe me out of beluga?"

Sheepishly, he grins at me, and it takes me back to the days of laundering crusty socks and always running out of food because he ate me out of house and home. "Maybe." Patting his abs, he drawls, "Figured I'd get in a workout before our meetings today."

Nodding my understanding, I leave him to burn off his anxiety through exercise like I taught him to and go use the shower in the gym.

Once I've dressed in a suit, I head for my office, scan the emails that have flooded in while I slept, wait for Dmitri to show up and for the early morning meeting to start.

Evidently wanting to flirt with death today, one of my Brigadiers, Pavlivshev, demands, "Why are we meeting at your estate, Pakhan? Why the change in routine?"

In answer, I simply settle my attention on him.

Just like that, he angles his head to the side.

When I see the Oskal's fangs, I glance away and point at Dmitri who, as always, is far too amused when I make my captains submit.

A simple look is all that's required nowadays but that's forged on years of brutal task-mastering.

I've cut out the tongues, chopped off the hands, and sliced the throats of those who don't understand that an order from me might as well come from God himself.

Because I trust the men sitting around my table, I offer them more leeway than the average *boyevik* but that can only be taken so far.

Rocking in my seat, I rest my hands on my abs as Dmitri states, "I got final confirmation in the early hours—every ounce of coke B4K had in the city is now either in our command or destroyed."

The announcement has everyone cheering. I'd call Nikita for vodka but we've barely started.

"The pushers you kidnapped, Pakhan, are dead?"

Pavlivshev again.

"Vasily's purring," is all I sign without deigning to look at him.

"Is that why we're here?"

"Is this Jeopardy and no one told me? This hole sits between two cheeks and wears too much Prada cologne?" Dmitri snarks. "What's with the twenty questions, Pavlivshev?"

Only a year older than Dmitri, Iosif Arsenyev starts cackling then immediately hides his grin when Pavlivshev glowers at him.

"We're not following protocol. Since when did the Sovietnik deal with drug pushers? Things are changing without the Obschak here. Brigadiers have a right to—"

"You have a right to dick," Dmitri retorts. "Whatever *rights* you have, Nikolai bestows them upon you. Nothing more. Now shut your fucking mouth. If I hear from you again, never mind Nikolai, I'll be the one who deals with you."

"Like I'm scared of some two-bit punk—" Immediately, I straighten in my seat. My chair creaks with the abrupt motion. Pavlivshev sinks into his like I cut off his legs and sputters, "I'm sorry, Pakhan. I didn't mean—"

"Too late. You insulted my son, Pavlivshev. Clearly, you're not thinking straight. I'd watch yourself before I start removing teeth for every stupid word you utter." I settle a look on each Brigadier, finding no dissent in their expressions aside from Pavlivshev. Antonin Barkov even bares his Oskal in submission as I sign, "We're a man down and we're dealing with the repercussions of *that* as well as the need to take vengeance for those motherfuckers thinking they can touch one of our own. Never mind someone so high up the food chain.

"Now is the time to band together, not to sow the seeds of discord. Pavel *is* my Obschak. He will return to this table once he is fully healed. Until that point in time, if I hear anything to suggest you're trying to brown-nose me into earning yourself a promotion, it won't be your teeth you'll lose. Do you understand me?"

When twenty heads bob in response, and with that warning in place, everyone, not just Pavlivshev, shuts the fuck up, leaving Dmitri to share the intel we'd gleaned, which sources had corroborated, since we set fire to their main warehouse.

Miami is my center of operations, but I 'manage' the majority of the Bible Belt.

Right now, I share certain areas of my territory with the Indigo Cartel and B4K, but by the end of the decade, I fully intend for the cartel and gang to have gone the way of the dodo.

When the meeting is over, having passed quickly because none of the Brigadiers dared speak, Nikita is waiting by the door with a tray.

Knowing my intention, Dmitri shakes his head at me but retreats to his office and leaves me to my business.

Accepting the tray, I go upstairs to awaken my *solnyshko* as I study the dish of pomegranate seeds and various berries that make up her breakfast.

Each contains nutrients that will...

My jaw works.

Those images of her full of my cum have my dick hardening to a painful degree.

As soon as I open the door, even without checking the cameras, I know she's awake. Mostly because she tosses a bar of soap at my head. Perhaps it's because she realizes I jacked off on her last night or simply because she wants to.

Either notion makes me smile to myself because if she looked, she'd see the pre-cum already filtering through the silk of my fly at her rebelliousness.

Of course, with my reflexes, she misses, but I won't be deterred from my course of action.

I gain entry to the safe room then place the tray on the table. Returning to her side, I grab her in spite of how hard she fights and bring her back with me.

There, I don't stop until I've fed her most of the fruit.

As the seeds in the dish disappear, taking root in her being, something settles inside me.

Something timeless, something *ancient*...

Something worth fighting for.

Something that will trap her by my side—*forever.*

And even that won't be long enough.

17

CASSIE
TWO DAYS LATER

Dreams - The Corrs

"WHERE'S MY CAR?"

He shrugs. "I don't know."

That car contains my *life*. Depressing, considering it's a beat-up piece of junk, but true.

"I don't have much stuff left but what I do have is in there." Scowling, I cut him a look. "I have clothes in the trunk too. I could wear them instead of, you know, bathrobes."

His blank expression has me huffing until he signs, "Could Rundel have taken it?"

"I guess," I mutter, batting his hand aside when he tries to place a slimy piece of potato salad on my bottom lip.

Our obstinate personalities go to war as he refuses to move away until I open up for him but I keep my lips sealed. Triumph roars through me when he grunts and pops the morsel into his mouth instead.

That's when I tell him, "He had his own ride but he might have taken mine."

"Where did you last park it?"

A dull throb starts to beat in my temples when I try to find an answer to his question, but I come up blank.

Shoulders slumping, I mutter, "It's all a blur." Refusing to cry, even if the tears would be born of frustration, not sorrow, I ask, "That man—"

He shoves a piece of potato between my lips.

When did he even pick that up?

The bastard.

With no choice other than to chew, I watch as he signs, "Which man?"

I'm pretty certain captives aren't supposed to be annoyed by their captors, but mostly, that's where I'm at now.

It's difficult to be scared when he isn't scaring me.

Pissing me off?

He's got that down to a fine art.

Fear?

No, that's not what I experience when I'm around him.

And trust me, I'm as freaked out by that as the next woman. How could a powder puff like Harvey scare the everliving crap out of me by breathing, but this Russian Albanian-killing machine doesn't?

It makes no sense.

"The one you killed," I sign with a glower.

"What about him?" he replies as expressionless as ever.

A part of me contemplates trying to break his nose just to see if he *will* react. Another part wonders if he's had Botox *everywhere*.

Studying his features for wrinkles—he has some on his forehead so I know he *can* move the muscles—I ask, "How did you find him?"

"He approached the motel room after we arrived." His gaze remains glued to my mouth. A second later, his thumb smoothes what I assume is some mayonnaise along my bottom lip.

This time, I succeed in batting his hand away. "Why were you there? Did my friend send you?"

I don't know why a wife of the Irish Mob would send a Russian in for help, but who am I to argue with politics and turf?

Hey, I've seen *The Sopranos*. I know how this shit works.

Sort of.

Especially when Savannah thought nothing of sending in a biker to save me from Harvey the first time I asked her for help.

How fitting that the Prince of Darkness saved me then, and the King of Hell has taken over.

Just my freakin' luck.

When he doesn't respond, I state, "Savannah will be worried."

He tilts his head to the side and gives me a nonanswer, "You know it's not safe out there."

I blink at him.

Because… he isn't wrong.

Harvey is still living and breathing, or I assume so. Otherwise, I reckon I'd have witnessed his death in the gargantuan courtyard too.

Even though he had me sold off by accident, that the debt is still wide open and that we're now both in danger from the Albanians won't stop his deluded ass for long.

I'm still his.

At least, in his eyes.

The thought makes me shudder with revulsion.

A soft touch on my shoulder draws my attention to Nikolai. I don't realize it but I turn into his hold, settling deeper onto his lap, seeking a comfort I shouldn't be finding in this man but… I do.

Just being closer to him makes me feel better.

Stronger.

"What is it?"

I stare at his hands, trying to piece together what I want to say.

I don't want this—to be held here, to be denied clothes. No freedom, no escape. But there's no arguing that a week ago, I was okay with dying.

Christ, I was more than okay with it—I'd have welcomed it.

This is better than death.

A definite zero out of ten.

Would not recommend.

I clear my throat and, unsteadily, ask, "Will you ever let me out of here?"

Almost as soon as the words are out there, I want to suck them back in. Hope is too fragile to mess around with—

Before the thought formulates, he stuns me by nodding.

Slowly.

That's promising.

Unexpected, but promising.

With that in mind, as well as his ongoing assurance that I'm safe here—which I am, apart from being overly exposed to semen and orgasms—I ask something I have no right to ask: "You *are* going to kill Harvey, aren't you?"

Again, he nods.

Relief filters through me.

I don't know why he's keeping me here, not when he treats me like a patient whose next breath depends on how many times he can get me to climax, but at that news, I don't care.

The cops never stopped Harvey. If the mob will, I won't complain.

Still, I'm confused about why he's doing any of this so I pepper, "Why?"

"You're not ready to hear the answer to that."

God damn him.

Though my lips purse, I demand, "Does he owe the Russians too?"

Nikolai stills and something flickers in his gaze as he shakes his head.

Once.

More perplexed, I inquire, "Are..." Well, he just killed one so maybe it's past tense. "*Were* the Albanians and Russians allies?"

His top lip quirks. Minutely. I think that means he's amused.

I earn myself another shake of his head.

Okay, so my being here, my continued protection—as weird as it is —has nothing to do with business.

Man, this conversation's been less enlightening than I'd prefer.

Sucking in a breath, I try again: "Will you let me out of here when he's dead?"

The smallest of flickers of his eyelashes lets me know that he's of two minds about how to answer.

Honestly, the fact that I can read his eyelashes is indicative of how little his face ever moves.

My nails dig into my palms as, ignoring the shimmy of pain from the still-healing lacerations there, I await a response.

Just when I'm certain he won't reply and I'll be fed some more goddamn potato salad on a breadstick, I try to encourage him to communicate with me by asking, "Am I still in danger from the Albanians?"

He hitches a shoulder that jostles me—with his heft, he's the male version of the San Andreas Fault. "Technically. They see you as a means of repayment. That repayment is still required... Danger follows you, *solnyshko*. Only I can promise you safety."

Damn if he isn't wrong.

My shoulders hunch inwards. "It isn't my fault—"

"Whether it is or not doesn't matter. The Albanians were wronged by your ex, and they believe you're their property."

Before he can continue, I grind my teeth. "I'm not a commodity."

"To the Albanians, you are."

His perennial lack of expression makes me want to shake him. Instead, I sign, "Why did you kill him?"

He studies me. "You mean the Albanian?"

Who else?

"Yes."

"Why do you want to know?"

"Because."

"You're not ready to hear the answer to that either." His hands glide softly as if he's trying to reassure me. "But you are safe here. Remember?"

Gliding or not, he irritates me with the most annoying words in the English language. "Even I know the Bratva sells sex just like every other two-bit gang. So if safety comes with a price tag, why haven't you fucked me yet?"

That has his eyes narrowing into slits.

Which gives me the answer to the question I was really asking—he *is* Bratva.

And he *can* lip-read because I didn't sign any of that so what the hell that first night was all about, I don't know.

"To me, you are not a commodity."

When he stabbed the Albanian, he twisted the knife in his throat. That's what his words do to me. They twist at something vital in me, tearing me apart as they put something back together.

Like always, he's expressionless, but I believe him.

To him, I'm not a commodity.

So what the hell am I if not that?

The potential acts like a hot knife sealing a cut in my soul.

"What am I then?" I dare to ask, my voice so low it's not even a whisper.

"Something else you are not ready to hear, *solnyshko*. We will revisit this conversation when you are."

Then, he scoops some more potato salad and shoves it into my mouth.

That, it seems, is the end of our chitchat.

For now.

And if I settle deeper onto his lap, that's between me and his knee.

No one else.

18

TEXT CHAT

Nikolai: Cassiopeia was traveling in a car when Rundel snatched her.

Boris: Okay?

Nikolai: Dmitri will forward you the registration. Perhaps Rundel is traveling in that vehicle?

Boris: I'll send it to the state troopers I'm conferring with.

Nikolai: Good.

Nikolai: If he isn't using the vehicle, but you find the car, clear it of her possessions and I'll have someone collect them and bring them to Nav. Understood?

Boris: Da, Pakhan. I'll keep you updated.

19

CASSIE
THE FOLLOWING DAY

"ABSOLUTELY NOT," I snarl, reiterating the words with my fingers, repeating them twice over so he can know that I mean business.

The guy might have found my hot spots and knows how to target them better than radar, and sure, he's working some weird wiles on me, but no way, no how, is he going to shave me down there.

His head tilts to the side in confusion.

Asshole—he totally understands me.

"Absolutely. Not," I repeat, flicking my hand at him.

His expression never changes—of course, it doesn't!

The only time it goddamn does is when I'm orgasming or when he shoves his cum inside my pussy!

Gritting my teeth because I refuse to get turned on at the memories of *those* expressions right now, I try to wriggle off the perch in the shower then huff when pain flashes through me as my thumb collides with the 'shelf', twisting it back.

Immediately, he's there, scowling at me while he grabs my shoulders and pins me to the wall. The razor is tucked between his pinkie and ring finger, angled away from me so it won't cut me.

Peering at the razor then glowering at him as I tuck my stupid hand against my chest, I retort, "I can do it myself."

Over dinner last night, I came to learn he can lip-read, so I say the words again, hoping they'll make an impact.

Naturally, they don't.

When he lets go of me and shuts off the water, my mouth gapes.

Did I win that round?

I watch him in bewilderment as he snags the bathrobe from the wall.

Inwardly, I start to celebrate, fully expecting to have the robe tucked over my shoulders, then…

Fuck.

He drops the robe to the floor and kneels on it.

There goes my covering for the day.

Shit.

That's when I see his dick.

"Do you take Viagra?" I blurt out.

He frowns. "What?"

"You're always hard."

Ignoring me, his hands move to my knees and he pulls them apart, levering himself between my thighs even as I squeeze to keep them together.

Still, after days of seeing various body parts of his down there, I've come to associate his oddities with orgasms.

I'm certain women in similar positions to me are facing worse conditions than this, but it's starting to get ridiculous—climaxes are becoming a right rather than a privilege.

A fact that's confirmed when I can feel the soft hum of expectation in my core.

"With this pretty pussy in front of me, how couldn't I be hard?"

Did it just get ten million degrees hotter in here?

Yeah, I think it did.

His gaze zooms in on my sex and he licks his lips.

Fuck. Fuck. Fuck.

A droplet of pre-cum beads on his shaft.

That's even hotter.

How he studies my pussy was something to blush about on the first day, but now, I realize, I'm just preparing myself for his offensive.

Not that I *am* offended, but I suppose there have to be some advantages to being drawn into the underworld...

His fingers trail over the inner lips of my sex, thumbs spreading me apart to expose the tender pinkness of my channel.

His pupils dilate.

God.

His reactions might be minute, but I'm beginning to adapt to them, so each one is like a siren blaring.

This is my moment to kick him, to try and suffocate him with my legs—hey, I saw that viral video with the watermelon exploding when squeezed between the inner thighs—but... I don't.

I don't do *any* of that.

If anything, my mouth trembles in anticipation of what I *know* is coming next...

A shudder wracks me when his tongue flutters around my clit.

"Jesus Christ," I whimper.

He smacks his lips then trails the tip down my center.

Naturally, because my body has no shame, I'm wet, and it has nothing to do with the shower.

His hum of pleasure at my slick has me staring up at the ceiling to avoid him because I know he'll be staring straight into my eyes.

It's telling, I think, that I still don't try to kick him in the back of the head.

I could.

But I don't.

Getting the drop on him would be satisfying but... not as satisfying as what his mouth does.

His hands, large and strong, palm my ass before they drag my thighs wider apart. When his tongue trickles down my slit, drinking me like I'm his favorite vodka, I allow myself to relax.

That just makes me even dumber when he stops and waits for me to look at him.

At first, I figure he's not going to let me hide from him. Then, his fingers shift and he signs, "Orgasms only if you're shaved."

It's insane that my first retort isn't, '*Good.*'

No, it's indignation.

"That's not fair," I snap.

He smirks.

The sight of his lips actually moving has mine forming a circle.

"I can do it myself," I croak.

His fingers trail toward my asshole where he rubs the puckered flesh. Then, he signs, "Even here?"

I swallow. "Of course."

He shakes his head. "I want to do it."

"You're weird," I mutter, even as I pump my hips in the air as a prompt for him to get back to work.

Okay, so we can add *bossy* to outspoken now.

In the last couple days, I've had some kind of character transplant and I'm not sure how I feel about that. Especially when I've technically never been in more danger in my life but have never felt safer either.

The dichotomy is starting to wear at my reserves.

When his fingers return to my asshole, I don't cringe away as I would have with Harvey.

Instead, I swallow.

Call it perception or call it instinct, but I know that no matter what he does to me, it'll be good.

He'll make *it* feel good.

I release a shuddery breath at the thought of how much trust I have in him when he hasn't particularly earned it through normal interpersonal interactions.

He reaches for some soap that I didn't know was on the floor and he starts to lather it between his palms.

"I can do it myself," I repeat, my voice sterner now.

"Why would you when I can do it?"

I narrow my eyes at him. The desire to have that wicked tongue of his curling around my clit is fierce but... "I'll let you do it if—"

He arches a brow.

It's a strange reminder that I have no power in this relationship, not unless he gives it to me.

Which, by waiting, by listening, by not ignoring me, he technically has.

With that technicality, my needs change. "I want time in the bathroom by myself without you freaking out."

That arched brow furrows. "There are no windows in here."

Ignoring him, I continue, "And I have a list of things that I want but I'd like a woman on your staff to buy them for me."

His frown deepens. "Like what?"

Tweezers.

God, I miss tweezers.

So. Fucking. Much.

My eyebrows are turning into caterpillars.

"If you want to shave me," I say with a sniff, "don't ask questions."

"There are no windows in here," he repeats.

I snap, "I'm not trying to escape—" I blink. Did I just say that? He looks as shell-shocked as I am. "—I just want some treats."

Like *my* shampoo and conditioner. I don't give a damn if the stuff he bought cost a fortune, I want my grocery store shit.

And if I'm being honest, I'd kill for some wax too.

I mean, what I *really* want are clothes but that's a big ask for what I intend to be our first negotiation for my basic human rights.

Softly, softly...

If this is actually happening, if this is my new normal, then it's time I got some kind of worldly pleasure.

Even supermax prisoners get those.

That's when he surprises me—he nods, then with his soap-lathered hands, he smoothes them over my less-than-silky legs.

Flushing with embarrassment because PCOS means I'm hairier than the models I'm sure he normally dates, I watch his eyes lock on mine as he continues spreading the bubbles over my calf.

Wanting the letter of the law carved into freakin' stone, I insist, "Do we have an agreement?"

You have to pin a guy like this down—I've learned that already.

Soapy fingers tell me, "We have an agreement."

About to be satisfied in more ways than one, I take control of this situation and arch my foot then set it on his shoulder. "Go on. I want my orgasm."

His smirk makes my core burn with heat, but I ignore it. Then, I suck in a breath when he presses the razor to my ankle—it doesn't tickle when he starts to shave me, but it's more intimate than I'd expected.

For endless moments, there's silence between us as he works.

Then, once that calf is complete, he continues with the other.

When he's finished, his lips quirk into another smirk—damn, he looks prettier when he smiles. Even if it *is* a smug smile.

"Trust me with your pussy now?"

I have no idea where the demand comes from, but I make it none-theless: "How many orgasms do I get as a reward?"

His brows lift, but the gleam in his eyes makes warmth puddle in my core.

"Two."

Somewhat shakily, I nod my agreement then watch as he goes through the same motions, switching on the water again only so he can create more of a lather.

As he soaps me up, I tremble then freeze when he draws the razor through the bubbles and metal meets sensitive skin.

I've never thought this could be in any way sexual. Couldn't have imagined Harvey wanting to tend to me and, not having done this to myself, it's an entirely new experience all round.

The breath I hold, however, has nothing to do with nerves.

As he works, his fingers smooth over my most intimate self, and my body, confused, reacts as if he intends to tease me, to entice.

I bite down on my lip as I stare above his head, trying to shift my focus, my awareness.

It doesn't work.

I flick a look at him, spying the intensity of his concentration, feeling his desire not to cut me, and a strange whisper of... *something* flutters through me.

Once I'm bare, he scoops water from the detached shower head into his palm and trickles it over my sex.

Shuddering, I watch until he's done, then I groan as he shoves his face into my cunt.

Wait, did I just use *that* word? What the hell is he doing to me?

"Oh, God," I cry, no longer caring about my potty mouth as my back immediately arches, hyper-aware of the fact that I'm ten times more sensitive than I'd been before.

With all of me exposed now, a single stroke of his tongue has me sobbing with relief at the contact.

The orgasm hits me too fast.

It's short and sharp and more of a buzz than a release.

I'm not happy about it, dammit to hell.

Then, I remember I negotiated for two so I sink onto the perch and await my second reward.

Like it's my right.

His fingers slide into my wet cunt and they spread wide, scissoring deep, before hooking upward. He touches a part of me that seems... different. I can't explain how, but it does. Spongy? Is that a thing?

When he rubs it, the shudder that rushes through me feels like it comes from my core. Toes curling, I'm incapable of doing anything other than digging my heels into his shoulders as I drag him closer.

Splinters of electricity shoot along my spine, the source my very center, the bolts of pleasure spreading throughout my body until tears of reaction prickle my eyes.

He presses an open-mouthed kiss to my clit then starts to suckle until I release a sob that I can't hold back.

"Nikolai," I cry, his name breaking into two as he continues to torment me.

He freezes then.

His gaze darts to mine when my eyes pop open in a silent demand to know why he stopped.

Then, locked upon one another, he starts to move again.

But this time, it's faster. Rougher. Less composed. Rawer.

I can't explain it, don't know how else to describe it, but I can tell he's at the outer edges of his control.

And, Lord help me, I love it.

"Nikolai," I whisper again, moaning when he growls into my pussy, finding it even more intense with how we're watching one another.

His fingers pump harder and those electric shocks turn into something else, something more.

As his lips cling to my clit, those digits torturing a part of me that has never been touched before, I can feel myself approach the deep end.

Only, it's a deep end I didn't know existed.

When the orgasm strikes, I scream.

The noise is long and sharp and high and that's exactly what he puts me through—the pleasure seems to be endless, hits with the might of a freight train, and makes me feel like there's no such thing as a comedown.

He keeps me there, hovering, waiting, in a stasis that I'm sure will make me pass out, then with a wet kiss, he releases me and I sag like I'm broken. Like he destroyed me with pleasure.

Maybe he did.

Maybe he ruined me because that was...

God.

It was...

I—

We—

That was everything.

And I don't think I'll ever see sex in the same light again.

CHAPTER TWENTY

I told you so... **BLOG**

A little bird has revealed that the Kentuckian Albanians are experiencing a coup worthy of the end of the Romanov dynasty. The Çelas have reigned over Kentucky for over seven decades, but it seems as if their time is coming to an end.

Sources say that Altin Marku, the heir apparent, has recently gone missing. Without him, Çela is adrift in the face of extinction. With his daughter missing, long presumed dead, and his *fifth* wife still not able to pop out another heir, trouble has been brewing since Elena's disappearance.

Something Adrianu Kadare is willing to exploit.

The Komandant, known for his ability to procure any drug at

the buyer's request so long as the price is right, has set his sights on the leadership position.

From the recent deluge of Albanian corpses in morgues, lines have already been drawn in the sand.

Don't let me say *I told you so* when Kadare takes over...

It'll be the dawn of a new day for Kentucky if that's the case.

The Çelas have always focused on horse racing and gambling. With Kadare at the helm, the Bluegrass State will undoubtedly see a surge in drug use.

The Kentucky police departments should start preparing for the war that's heading their way.

If they don't, well...

21

NIKOLAI

"MYATA CALLED."

Despite myself, I snort.

Dmitri huffs. "You're not the one she calls."

"Because she knows what would happen if she did," I retort, fingers flying with the words as I deride, "You're too soft with the women."

He sniffs. "She's Pavlivshev's daughter."

"So? Pavlivshev serves *me*, not the other way around. It's not my fault she's looking for a wedding ring she'll never get."

"She probably thought she would, seeing as he's the only high-ranking Brigadier with an unwed daughter." He clears his throat. "You're not taking her to the party?"

I never attend with a date.

Ever.

"That was what she wanted to know? If I was going to ask her?"

Dmitri grimaces. "She asked if she should buy a special dress. I told her that if you *did* invite her when you've never invited anyone to one of these parties before, you'd supply the outfit. Because you're a control freak."

That last part is muttered beneath his breath.

My lips dance for a moment. "You know me too well, son."

He sniffs. "Been stuck to your side, God help me, for long enough to know how you work." His gaze darts to the door. "You going to ask her?"

"Myata?" I chuckle. "Fuck no."

"I meant Cassiopeia."

I just smile at him.

His brow furrows. "You're different."

"Unlikely," I counter, gaze dancing over the goddamn blog that has been a pain in my ass for too long. "You've still no idea who is behind *I told you so?*"

"No." He studies me before releasing a sigh. "From the tone and the language, it's a woman, but I've no idea where she's based or how she gathers so much information on so many factions."

"She has a death wish."

He hums. "What are you doing with Cassiopeia?"

"Keeping her safe. Just like Misha requested."

"*Da*, but you're doing something else too because he'd know she was here and wouldn't think you put her on a plane."

"Since when did you start assuming that you could question me?" I don't bother looking at him as I flick the words his way.

"Since we're keeping an innocent, already-traumatized woman hostage in your bedroom.

"Nikita says she hasn't been out of the master suite once, and the maids all say she screams whenever you're in there."

Ignoring him, I switch screens, drifting from today's blog post to yesterday's—a discussion about the writer's belief that the Irish Mob is behind a recent spate of 'accidents' some politicians are experiencing.

It could be dismissed as a conspiracy nut by an average Joe, but the blogger is damn accurate. Too accurate.

With a sigh, I switch onto my YouTube account.

Scanning the history, I find that Cassiopeia has been watching dozens of videos from one channel in particular. A popular one. Millions of subscribers, tens of millions of views.

Dmitri nudges my arm as he turns around and perches on the side of my desk. "Niko?"

Tiredly, I slouch in my desk chair. "What, Dmitri? Do you want to know if I'm torturing her, is that it? I told you that she's mine. What I do with her is my business, not yours."

"I'm not okay with you hurting her. Not after what she's been through!"

I arch a brow. "And what has she been through?"

His shoulders hunch. "I looked into her. That bastard made her life hell. He had her committed—"

"He had her committed?" I demand, outraged and uncertain if I heard him right.

I don't realize that I spoke the words aloud until Dmitri frowns at me. "Are you sure you've never met her before?"

Only in a past life...

In another world.

"I'm sure."

"I don't understand why you're so possessive of her," he complains. "You're never possessive. Of anyone. Myata is hot as fuck but you don't care if she goes to the New Year's party with someone else.

"You drop chicks like they're diseased after a couple fucks. Beatriz and Klara lasted longer than most because you've alternated between seeing them once a week for the past few months and we've been busy.

"I just don't understand why this one is different. Hasn't she been through enough? I think she's earned her peace."

His defense of her is annoying, but it's also... *reassuring.*

He just wants to protect her.

Whether it's because he believes they could be related or simply because I inadvertently raised a good man, I'm okay with that.

"I agree," I sign. "I'm giving her peace. I'm giving her safety. She will never be hurt again. Not under our protection."

"So why are you making her scream?"

I blink at him. "Dmitri, do we have to have the talk again?"

"The talk?" He frowns. "Which talk?"

"*Ptitsy i pchely.*"

"Hummingbirds and the bees...," he mutters as if struggling to translate, then he gapes at me. "Wait, you mean the birds and the bees?! You're *fucking* her?"

"Why else would she be screaming?" I sign with an ease that he isn't feeling.

If anything, he's blushing.

Lips twitching, I study him as he shakes his head. "And she wants you to?"

"I'm not a rapist." When he rubs his brow, I ask, "How bad was her file?"

"Bad." He swallows. "Do you want to read it?"

A part of me does.

Another part, the part that wants to keep her locked in my master suite forever, knows that if I want more from her, she'll have to share this with me on her own terms.

That she'll have to trust me with this information and that my researching her could be construed as a betrayal.

Which matters.

For the first time, someone outside of my brothers and son *matters*.

Rapping my knuckles against the desk in annoyance, I shake my head. "It goes against my instincts, but I'll let her tell me."

"She's been here over two weeks now."

"I can count." And still nothing on Rundel's whereabouts.

"You're going to let her out at some point, right?" He clears his throat. "I mean, she isn't a prisoner, is she?"

I want to reassure him, I do.

I want to say I could let her out—*of course.*

But the very prospect has my other hand balling into a fist.

Other men looking at her?

Other men craving *my little sun*?

She's asked me the same question and I answered in the affirmative so as not to break her—hope is as vital to the spirit as oxygen is to mankind.

But *blyad,* can I let her out?

When danger flutters around her like a swarm of wasps?

Instead of replying because I genuinely don't know what to tell him, I point at my laptop where the channel she'd been binge-watching takes up the screen. "Who's this? *We Cream for Ice Scream.*"

"It's her vlog," Dmitri says, his tone heavy with disappointment.

I want to snarl at him that he has no right to be disappointed in me, that I earned this, *her,* that I deserve to take what I believe belongs to me...

But I don't.

"Her vlog?" I inquire instead.

"She's a food journalist. She visits restaurants, cafes, and bakeries, establishments like that, then highlights a dish of theirs in a video and on her blog. She's put a lot of people in NYC on the map."

I have no idea why his words make me sign, "I'm not Rundel."

He should joke and tell me, 'Of course, you're not, *Otets.*'

He doesn't.

His sigh is heavy, redolent with his unease. "If you say so."

22

CASSIE

LATER THAT AFTERNOON

I KNOW I'm going to regret slipping into the bathroom and starting the bath, so I go for broke and shove a shit ton of products into the water because: "It's go big or go home."

The faint tang of rebelliousness sums me up at the moment, and I have to wonder if the very reason for my unusual behavior presented itself this afternoon at roughly three PM—my period.

Combined with the fact that his doctor said he could release my hands from the bandages today, so I finally have enough freedom of movement to turn the damn faucets, as well as our deal for private time in the bathroom, my desire for a bath was cemented into place.

In fact, with that agreement, this is technically my right and if he wants to argue, then he can stand in front of the vanity and bicker with his reflection.

I'm not in the mood for his shit today.

With a huff once the water level is high enough, I step into the tub.

I can't help but wonder if he's got cameras in the bedroom because the second I'm lying flat in the massive bathtub, the outer door opens. In the quiet, the click of the lock is overly loud and I hate that it makes me flinch.

Still, I remain silent because Nikolai has weaponized it to a fine art, and I'm a quick learner so I wait.

And wait.

And wait…

Then earn myself a grunt.

It's difficult to keep facing the wall in front of me, not to angle my neck back, but I do it and the dumbest thought drifts into my mind:

You're not the boss of me, Niko.

I'm not sure which part is the most moronic because *of course,* he's the boss of me, dammit.

And, Niko?!

When the fuck did I start abbreviating his name in my head?

When he moves toward the bathtub, I'm not surprised that his arms are already outstretched. I think I knew he'd see my act of bathing as a rebellion, so I'm quick to sign:

"You agreed—you shave me and I get private time in here. This is that so leave me in peace to soak."

As I settle amid the bubbles, he grouses, "You could have fallen."

I squint at him in disbelief. "I've never been accident-prone outside of my medical records."

His expression, impossibly, turns more sullen than ever.

"I got my period, too, so you can just walk out the door and leave me in peace."

He pauses.

Heck, it's more than a pause. He's practically frozen in place.

I give him a dose of his own medicine by arching a brow at him. "You know what a period is, right?"

His eyes narrow but he nods.

When he retreats, I'm almost…

"There's no way in hell you're disappointed, Cassiopeia," I mutter to myself, but that strange feeling spreading in my chest can only be that.

What a bitterly short confrontation.

Not even an argument.

I huff as I sit up, waiting for the click of the lock or the slamming of the outer door...

It doesn't come.

My head tilts to the side, expectation rumbling into being as I wonder what his next play is.

With Nikolai, it pays to be prepared, but there's no real preparing yourself for a man as odd as him.

When the outer door closes, I don't even hear him return.

Damn his cat-burglar feet.

Then, he's there and he has a tampon in his hand and a menstrual cup.

"So this is a twenty-first-century bat cave, then?"

His brow furrows.

"You have all the mod cons for your prisoners?"

That has him rolling his eyes and shoving his hands at me as if wordlessly urging me to make a decision.

"The Mooncup."

He blinks.

"That one," I answer, pointing to the cup.

The tampon disappears into his pocket as he takes a seat on the edge of the bathtub. I don't bother rearing up, not even if it would be hilarious to soak him in bubbles. I mean, the hilarity is one thing, but it'd be a travesty to ruin that suit.

Unable to help myself, I study the fine silk, how it clings to his muscles... His attire somehow manages to *up*-play his bulk. It's a bizarre phenomenon because he could appear stocky. Instead, he's a walking wet dream.

When I reach his face, I don't bother blushing when his knowing look registers.

"What?" I retort. "I can gawk as much as you do."

His lips quirk into a smile before he signs, "Do you need a doctor?"

My brows lift. "No. It's just a period." An agonizing uncomfortable period to be sure, but a period nonetheless.

His shoulders wriggle slightly, and I get the sense that—

I grin to myself. "Are you uncomfortable, Nikolai? It's a natural process." One that's sent from God himself to plague all womenkind for original sin.

Hades would never be so ungenerous...

He hitches a shoulder. "Most women I know don't have them."

That has me grumbling, "Because they're on birth control."

"And you're not?"

When I shake my head, I frown at his expression—he looks absurdly pleased.

"Do you run a cult or something?"

His expression fades as he *grumpily* signs, "Excuse me?"

"Why would you be happy that you could get me pregnant when you insist on jacking off over my pussy and stuffing me full of your cum?"

Not that I stop him.

He tilts his head to the side but doesn't answer.

I roll my eyes.

See? Weaponized silence.

His hand trickles into the water, skimming over the top at first then brushing the silken skin of my abdomen.

Because my life has become weirder than ever, I don't stop him. I don't even flinch at the first caress. I just watch his expressionless face, knowing that he knows that I'm watching him.

When his fingers find the top of my mons, I shift a little as the whisper of a tickle rattles my nerve endings. He'd showered and shaved me this morning, and I was still acclimating to how sensitive that made my sex.

Spreading my legs with an eagerness that should shame me, I lift my hips slightly when he slips lower, but his gaze locks on mine, stealing my breath as he seeks my clit. Because it feels good, I release a whimper, then I moan as he circles my slit and thrusts deep.

Most of the blood washes away from the finger he slipped inside me as he retreats from the water, but he studies it with an intensity I don't like.

"Didn't believe me?" I spit, unsure if I'm annoyed by the notion of him testing if I had my period or if it's because he stopped.

He blinks. "This should have been my baby."

I gape at him. "Excuse me?"

When his shoulder hitches, it's the first time I recognize that he *is* disappointed.

My gaping doubles down. "You *wanted* to get me pregnant?"

I mean, I'd read between the lines with the whole 'shoving his cum inside me' thing, but getting it confirmed blows my mind.

When he doesn't reply, I'm starting to wonder if his expressionless expressions happen at certain moments.

Maybe they're something that can be interpreted when you know him well enough.

Just over two weeks, some of that spent unconscious, can't be considered long—not enough to learn about someone. Especially when he leaves me alone for five or more hours in between breakfast and dinner. But I do know he's stubborn, un-PC, powerful, strong, perplexing, and weird.

So, if I extrapolate the data, I can reason that he's…

Man, I have no fucking idea.

Uneasily, I tell him, "You don't know me."

His eyes turn to slits.

"People don't want other people to get pregnant unless they're in a long-term relationship."

His mouth tightens.

"Why would you want to get me pregnant when we're strangers?"

His jaw clenches.

"Man, this *is* a fucking cult, isn't it?"

Apparently, our wires had gotten crossed because here I was, thinking the Russian Mob had snatched me!

When I sit up again, water sloshes, and I smack his arm. "Move out of the way. I want to get out."

He doesn't move.

Instead, he signs, "What's your problem?"

"What's my problem?" I shriek. "If it's not enough that you make me stay naked all day, don't let me out of this room, probably won't allow me to leave the estate if you *did* let me out of the room, insist on hand-feeding me, get me off all the time, won't let me shower alone, barter over shaving me—" I suck in a breath as I gather steam. "—now you want to impregnate me! I feel like I've landed in some kind of TV show! I just don't know if it's a crossover of *The Sopranos* and *The Handmaid's Tale* or *Game of Thrones* meets *Girls*!"

He blinks. "I'm Russian. Not Italian. And you need to watch your hands."

Said hands slap against the water—I don't give a damn anymore if his pretty suit gets wet. "*That* is what you take from my outburst?" I growl as I fold my arms against my chest because clearly, he isn't going to let me out of the tub, and while I want to shove him on his ass, it'll get me nowhere.

Well, it'll probably get me an orgasm and I don't know if a period is a barrier.

I used to love it when I got my irregular periods. Sure, they're painful as fuck. *But* Harvey would leave me alone. That made them almost worthwhile.

I already know that Nikolai is a different kind of beast from my ex.

"It's highly likely that I can't have children, anyway," I mutter with a sniff, sticking my nose in the air.

"Why not?"

"I have PCOS."

"What's that?"

"Wiki it," I grouse, knowing that he won't. I punctuate that with a dismissive flick of my hand, bubbly foam surging high and landing on his expensive pants.

The pleasure I take in that is asinine and ridiculously childish.

So, I do it again for good measure.

Ignoring my tantrum, seeming not to give a damn that I may have ruined his pants, he gets out his phone and starts reading.

He. Starts. Reading.

Mouth gaping harder than ever, I watch as his fingers fly on the screen. The way it's angled down, I can see him shift between Wiki-pedia and move on to articles. But he's not skimming. I watch the flickering of his eyes as he moves from left to right.

Speed reading?

God, I tried to explain how painful a period could be to Harvey and he zoned out within a second. He sure as fuck didn't study an article from the University of Cambridge on PCOS to understand my symptoms.

Once he's done, he peers at me. "Rundel suffered with impotence issues?"

For a moment, I hesitate.

I've been conditioned to believe that those impotence issues are a *me* problem.

My mouth works for a handful of seconds as I try to figure out how to reply to him.

Rationally, I know Harvey's full of shit.

But when that shit is pounded into you with fists, it's difficult to break the habit of a decade.

Nikolai waves a hand in my face.

Blinking, I slouch under the water again, oddly enough feeling the need to hide beneath the bubbles.

"We had issues," is what I settle on as an answer.

"He left you in that motel room to go and get Viagra."

My cheeks flush with mortification. "He could never... We... I..." I close my eyes. "Can we go back to me being mad at you, please?"

A soft sound escapes him, one that has my eyes popping open.

And I'm gaping again.

It's hard and croaky. Husky and hoarse. But that was *definitely* a laugh.

Amusement makes his beautiful eyes gleam with a light I've not experienced before and out of nowhere, the urge to make that light appear more often assimilates in my chest.

I need to pull that apart later when I'm alone, especially as his amusement fades.

Which is when I find that I miss it.

He's always so impossible to draw a reaction from that whenever he *does* react, my catalog of his responses grows.

Then, he stuns me again by breaching the water's surface with his hand. I brace myself for his touch, but those fingers of his grab mine, and, wet or not, he places them over his crotch.

Face burning with heat, I know there's no denying what that thick bulge means. No misinterpreting what he's trying to say.

When he lets go of my hand, he signs, "You're a beautiful woman."

I'm not—I'm fat and PCOS means that losing the weight is impossible. It also means that I'm a little hairy. One of my boobs is wonky, too, while the other is smaller. Unsymmetrical.

On top of the fertility issues, I have other health problems that a man like him would be freaked out by when he only knows zombie females who don't get things like periods and zits...

But his dick says he's not lying.

I've seen it in the flesh every time we shower. I've felt it digging into me when I eat. I've watched him jack off over my pussy.

He has erectile dysfunction in the sense that it's always working.

Because of me?

It seems unlikely, but this game of 'show and tell' speaks louder than words.

After dealing with a faulty one for years, I'm not sure I trust that his isn't broken too.

Harvey's never worked properly; the Viagra stopped being effective after a short run even if he keeps hoping one day it'll work again. On the other hand, Nikolai's never fails to rise to the occasion—why must everything I've got to deal with be polar opposites?

Huffing at the thought, I take note of the thick shaft as my fingers struggle to curve around him entirely.

I could try to crush it in my hand. Make him pay for holding me here in his master suite. Have him suffer for the promise he gives me with a dick that is always erect around my fat ass. Instead, I swallow and shape it through his fly.

Like an alien has taken over me, I sit up soon after. This time, both hands move to his crotch and I pull down the zipper so that I can dig between the tines and free him.

He's thicker than Harvey. Enough that, after years of only fucking my ex, I know he'd be a tight fit.

He's longer too—nine inches, maybe?

Harvey was barely six.

Maybe it's the hot water, but I'm flushed and overheated and kind of enchanted by his response to *me*.

When I touch his shaft, he shudders and angles himself so that I can get better access. His features lock: jaw clenching, nostrils flaring, and eyes narrowing into slits.

All of that intensity is aimed at me.

It's mine—*I did that.*

A heady feeling of success roars through me.

Harvey took that away from me. He stole the innate feminine power that a woman has when she gets her man hard. His issues didn't do that—I understand how the body can work against you. That's exactly what PCOS is, after all. But he vilified me when it was *his* issue, not mine.

He made me feel lesser than.

He made me feel ugly.

The triumph I experience as I shape Nikolai's dick with my fingers has any nerves fading. I've never done this before with him. It's always him touching me, him stroking me, him getting *me* off.

I blow out a breath as I let my other hand find his balls.

They're hot and heavy in my palm. Throbbing, almost. Filled with *life.*

The back of my hand brushes the pulsing vein that runs along the underside and I know it's wrong to crave my captor, but I want to feel that.

It's mine.

It belongs to me.

I did it.

I made him hard.

No one else.

Feeling overheated, I start to jack him off while I twist and fondle his balls. The time for breaking his cock has gone. Why would I want to destroy something that reveres me so?

Shuddering, it takes me a moment to recognize that Nikolai has tipped his head back.

God, I could do so many things right now.

He's probably got a key somewhere on him. I could snatch his cell phone. I could try to grab the knife he always has holstered on his shoulder.

But I don't do any of that.

I just stroke him with long pulls as I tighten my fist, exploring him for once. Pre-cum makes the journey easier. My mouth gapes at how much of it there is. It leaks out, seeping free with abandon, making my palm slick...

God, that's not the only part of me that is either.

My thighs rub together as I try to ease the internal ache that's spiked into being in my core.

I twist and flick my hand like I'd learned to do from the first guy I'd been with until he grabs a hold of my wrist and shows me what *he* likes.

Somehow, it's not embarrassing. He doesn't make me feel like a failure for doing it wrong. If anything, the groans he releases when he makes me grip him more fiercely, clamping down harder than I'd ever be comfortable with, has my pussy throbbing.

My hips rock of their own volition as the emptiness deep inside makes me feel hungrier than ever, especially when he starts grunting.

He's always silent. Always. But today, I have him making noises and it's *glorious*.

I can feel myself blushing all over at the sounds.

They're guttural and raw and wild and I'm in love because he's making them for *me*.

I angle upward, sitting higher in the water, and I let go of him which has his eyes popping open—yeah, he closed them.

But when I shift onto my knees, he frowns then realizes what I'm doing.

One minute, he's sitting there.

The next, he's on his feet.

A cry of disappointment escapes me when I think he's departing, then I realize that's not his intention at all.

His jacket flies to the floor, his shirt next. Pants are discarded after his shoes are toed off.

From one moment to the next, he goes from dressed to nudity and I. Am. Here. For. *That.*

Shuddering at the sight of him, I half expect him to drag me out of the water and to try to fuck me or something. But he doesn't. He slips one foot into the tub and then sits down where he was before.

As I take in the sheer majesty of this man with no clothes on, I can't help but skim over the scars on his hip. They're brutal but old. I want to know their backstory as much as I want to touch him...

Apparently, we share the same train of thought.

His hand reaches for mine again and he curls it around his dick, reminding me with a soft squeeze of how much pressure he prefers. That he takes care to only place that pressure on my fingertips makes something clutch in my chest at his care.

Cheeks still hot with the impromptu strip show, I take in again just how much pre-cum he releases. I mean, it's not like I haven't seen or felt his cum after breakfast and dinner, but this is different.

I'm the protagonist here, not him.

The very idea has me wanting to rub my clit, but I don't. Not yet.

Instead, I think about how it'd feel if he were coming inside me and if all that cum was flooding my womb.

Jesus, why do I feel lightheaded?

Breathless with excitement when his hips rock as I jack him off, I pump him faster, wanting to see him explode. Needing it. Almost as much as I want to come.

He's officially made me as weird as he is. Or maybe it was always there and he's just brought it out of me.

I shiver when he starts making soft, thrusting motions with his ass, his head angled back slightly even though I know his eyes are locked on me.

Again, I'm flooded with the realization that I did this. I'm doing this. Me. I'm making him hot and bothered. I'm the reason he's hard.

I'm behind that pre-cum that oozes down his shaft like he provides his own bottle of lubricant with every hand job.

I grab his balls again, palming them, twisting them gently, urging him to come, wanting it with every fiber of my being.

Then, a strange whisper of *something* hits me.

And I act on it—I snag the end of my braided hair and curl it around his shaft.

When he realizes what I've done, his guttural groan feels like it comes from Hell itself. His eyes flare wide, *wild,* as I wrap him up and jack him off with what fascinates him so much.

I barely get four or five strokes in when his hand grips my shoulder and he's dragging me through the water toward him.

My mind freezes.

Any joy I was finding in this starts to fade.

Harvey would do this.

He'd shove my face in his crotch.

Would force me to suck him—

Before I can freak out, Nikolai is making broken grunts as his hips pump the air and his cum is suddenly splashing all over me.

My breasts, my throat, my belly. Higher—my face. Cheeks, nose.

It pours out of him for what feels like forever.

The heat of him stains my skin as he ekes out every second of pleasure with rough growls that make me want to melt.

When he's done, his heavy breathing sounds overly loud in the quiet space. I'm used to his silence, but I much prefer this.

He watches me with eyes that are slitted and it comes as no surprise when he starts to rub his cum into my skin—moisturizer it isn't but I don't tell him that, not when his touch has me jerking in astonishment at my level of enjoyment.

Then, much as he always does, he drifts down, down, down.

Falling backward into the water, I prop my heels under my ass. It's difficult not to slip, but I want this as much as he does. The move angles my hips higher and lets me spread my legs wider.

When his fingers find my slit, I shudder as, more gently than he usually does, he rims my entrance and thrusts inside me.

As he retreats, he pets my clit on the way out.

A soft whimper escapes me as he rubs me there, fast little circles with his slippery fingertips that have the water rocking and splashing as I uncover a hot, hard orgasm that quenches the ache deep inside.

A moment later, as I'm still panting from my own release, he slides into the bathtub, startling me by drawing me onto his lap.

It's one of those basins that have no faucet at either end, ya know, *expensive*, but I don't complain. Nor do I argue when he smoothes his arms around my waist and adjusts me so that I'm sitting on his lap.

Then, he grunts and, because the bath is so damn big, he shifts me sideways so that I'm sitting between his thighs, my legs resting over one of his.

Flushing, thinking he had to do that because I'm too heavy for him, I start to maneuver away but swiftly realize he positioned me like that so we can communicate and he can still have me close.

The notion makes me feel all kinds of messed up inside.

"You are the most beautiful woman I've ever seen, *solnyshko*. That Rundel made you believe otherwise is a crime against nature itself."

The way he signs, his fingers flying, the motions short and sharp, I know he's angry at my perceived treatment.

I bite my lip as I relax against him, aware that I hadn't given him any of my weight just in case.

"Thank you," I sign back, hoping that how I relaxed *shows* him my appreciation.

"You suffer with your periods?"

It's easier to talk about this stuff when I can turn my face away from him.

"Yes. They're painful but irregular, thank God."

His fingers start toying with the end of my braid. Maybe it's more by luck than management that most of his cum ended up on me rather than there.

When he stops, I almost pout until he signs, "What happened with Rundel, *solnyshko*? The Viagra?"

Tension rushes through me, but it calms when he moves his arm, lowering it to my waist and tugging me tighter into him.

The embrace is exactly what I didn't know I needed.

It gives me the balls to sign, "Harvey and I... we wanted to start a family. He blamed me, at first. Said I was the reason we couldn't have children but he wanted a baby badly enough that he insisted we go through IVF. They tested both of us." I bite my lip at the memories of the night *after* the doctor's appointment where we'd received the results. "The doctor suggested we use donor sperm instead of Harvey's. It was..."

When he holds me tighter than ever before, hugging me harder, it registers how much I'd tensed up. I hate that I began trembling too.

Soft lips brush the side of my cheek, making me more dazed by that than the memories. It takes me a few minutes to reply, "Things got really bad after that."

He lets go of me to sign, "He was the sole problem."

Not a question.

And damn, I miss his arms around me.

"Yes." The wave of shame over how my body has backfired against me has me gritting my teeth. Then, I force myself to bite out, "My odds are abysmal, but there is a chance that I *could* have a child. He could *not*. At all. H-He had issues getting erect before. After that appointment, it was impossible.

"A part of me always wondered if, without those issues, he'd have been a good husband—"

Nikolai squeezes me. "My father was violent toward my mother." As I process the fact he's sharing that with me, he continues, "He killed her in the end. That kind of violence is in someone from birth."

"I don't want to believe that." Because if I do, then I was totally, utterly blind about Harvey.

"You don't live in the world I do."

I blink. "You brought me into it."

He shakes his head. "I didn't. You landed here, and I'm keeping you safe."

His logic isn't particularly sound but there's no denying he's actually right.

He *could* let me go, though.

Like he knows I'm thinking that, he holds me tighter.

I don't push it, just sign, "I'm sorry about your mother." I punctuate it by cupping his cheek in an apology he can feel, not simply read.

He angles his head into my hold. "It was a long time ago."

"Grief doesn't stop. It just gets easier to handle," I counter, not signing since he can read my lips. "How old were you?"

He doesn't answer, which is an answer in itself.

Not wanting the conversation to end just yet after days of continued silence, I pepper, "Where did you get your scars from? Your father?"

His expression doesn't grow tense, but his lips purse in irritation. "After their deaths—" Hold up. *Their* deaths? "—I was placed in an orphanage. I was there until a fire tore through the building. It definitely would have failed the building code in the States. Hell, it probably *did* fail the local code as well," he grouses, the motions of his hands brisk as if this is an old annoyance. "It's so corrupt over there that nothing would have changed even if it had failed."

"You got caught in the fire?"

His eyes shutter. "In a sense."

I don't understand why, but I *have* to know more. I just have to. I need to get a better read on this man who's brought me here, who does the things he does, who says the things he says.

Maybe he sees the plea in my expression because he heaves a sigh. "One of my brothers was caught in the blaze. I saved him."

That has me sputtering, "You saved him? And..." I frown. "You have a brother?"

He dips his chin. "Not by blood, but yes. Two. I took them from the orphanage and raised them." His lips twitch at the ends—my God, is that a smile? "They're listed as dead in Russia."

"The officials think they died in the fire?" I screech.

"Yes."

"Damn," I mumble. "Are your brothers still over there?"

Slowly, he shakes his head. "They live in New York."

"Are they in the same business as you?"

As if he senses my hesitation over that choice of word, 'business,' the curve of his lips deepens. "Yes."

"Are you close?"

When he doesn't reply, and knowing I've pushed his conversational abilities as far as they're likely to go, I don't press him about that. Instead, I trail a finger over the scar on his face. He doesn't flinch, just stares at me.

"How did you get this one?"

"From a CIA operative."

My brows lift. "Who won?"

His smirk turns surprisingly cocky. Well, surprising for Nikolai. "I'm here and not in jail, aren't I?"

"True. What happened?" I ask, not expecting him to answer.

"She was trying to stop a shipment of drugs from leaving a port in Antwerp."

"And she failed?"

He shrugs. "No. The drugs didn't leave Antwerp, but I did. At that point, I was just grateful not to be hauled into a black site. We didn't expect the drugs to be tracked by the CIA, just local law enforcement."

He signs the words so easily, but they're terrifying to a boring civilian like me.

"Your life is like something from a TV show," I mutter, unease dripping from every word.

He snorts. "More glamorous."

Though I smile, I'm still a little freaked out. I don't know what I expected when I asked about his scars, which was undoubtedly naive of me, but I got more than I bargained for.

Maybe he can sense that he scared me because he starts toying with my hair again, which simultaneously puts his hands out of action for signing and calms me down.

For the rest of our time in the bathtub, we don't talk. It's both relaxing and odd to be this at ease with my captor.

Until we get out of the water and he insists on inserting the menstrual cup, that is.

For a moment, I'm sure he's kidding. Then, I sputter, "Are you for real?"

He angles his head to the side in a gesture that I'm coming to know means, 'Of course, I'm for real.'

With a growl, I stomp my foot. "There's no way you can put that in me. Sometimes even I can't get it in right!"

He shrugs and retrieves the tampon from his pants.

That's when I gape at him.

Of course, I gape the hardest when he signs, "There should be nothing between a man and his woman."

His woman?

When did *that* happen?

Unsure if I'm about to start hyperventilating or hysterically laughing, I don't even argue when he nudges me toward the partition where there's a separate toilet.

Though he's blowing my mind with this Neanderthal display, a spark hits me between the eyes when we're halfway there.

It's enough to make me tug on his hand, and though I could remind him of our agreement, instead, I demand, "What do I get as a reward?"

Negotiating—it's something I know he'll permit.

He stills, studies my face for *whatever*, then, after letting go of his hold on me, purses his lips as he signs, "What do you want?"

The word 'freedom' could and should spill off my lips.

But I don't think to ask for that.

Not only because I don't think he's that generous, but because, fuck a duck, I don't particularly want to leave.

Harvey's out there.

Albanians are out there.

These walls might be closing in, but...

"To go into the garden."

He straightens; maybe he thought I'd ask for something else too? But slowly, he nods.

Which is how, five minutes later, he's the one inserting a goddamn tampon into my cooch.

"When did this become my life?" I mutter to myself in a daze.

Yet, somehow, the promise of going outside is worth it.

23

CASSIE

I WASN'T sure what I expected when I woke up the following day.

Let's face it, anything could happen in this madhouse.

So, I'm not altogether surprised to find that my period has further changed things when I see Nikolai is still sleeping beside me.

Before bed last night, he let me put the cup in—scowling all the while—and I know that's why I woke up.

Sneaking off isn't as difficult as it should be, not when you're sharing nine feet of space.

Not wanting him to try to insert another tampon even if he's willing to negotiate, I shuffle over to the bathroom and do my business.

Of course, when I return, he's awake, one arm behind his head in a way that makes his bicep bulge, and he's watching me.

Either he's *that* aware of me or my movements did disturb him.

Somehow, from his grumpy expression, I think he's aware of me.

Again, feeling like I've gone down the rabbit hole where a guy this hot is annoyed I changed out of my menstrual cup without his help, I ignore him and clamber back into bed.

He turns onto his side as I do.

Across the mattress's expanse, we study one another.

Then, he shifts so he can sign, "We're going outside today."

Gaping at him, I jerk upright. "Seriously?" I squeak, shuttling over to his half of the bed in excitement. "I thought you'd make me wait a lifetime."

His mouth quirks at the corners. "Seriously. I'm going to show you around the estate."

I shriek in glee. "That means I get clothes, right?"

"Of course. No one will ever see you naked again, *solnyshko*." The air chokes in my lungs at the ominous words. But he spies the swiftly surging panic by clucking his tongue.

Before he can continue, I rasp, "Let me guess, you're going to say that I'm safe with you?"

He nods but the smallest of smiles curves his lips and, for some insane reason, that eases my panic some.

Exhaling, I try to recover my earlier excitement and find it didn't drift too far away. Clothes, a trip out of this goddamn bedroom, and a tour of this massive estate? I just won the lottery!

Of course, he has to spoil it.

Again.

"I can't wear that," I exclaim a half-hour later when I stare at the outfit that was laid out on the bed after our shower and the house-keeping fairies made an appearance.

The routine has changed again—no breakfast in the safe room.

Before I saw the clothes he wants me to wear, I was excited about getting to eat in an actual dining room. Now, I almost wish nothing had changed.

His brows lift as he studies the dress on the bed. "What's wrong with it?"

"It's small."

Just looking at it, I know it cost a fortune.

He huffs out a sigh, grabs the plissé-crepe de chine as if it's cheap polyester, then snags a hold of my arm.

The next thing I know, he's dragging it over my head and settling it on me.

My cheeks flush when he zips up the side but it fits without pinching.

Then, he shuffles me over to the empty walk-in closet.

Only... it's not empty anymore.

I blink at how full it is, not just of his stuff but things that are very feminine—for me?

Before I can even ask what the hell's going on, I'm in front of a mirror and he's signing, "You need to see what I see."

His hips rock into me, letting me feel his erection.

I hate that that gives me the confidence to peek at myself in the mirror.

What I see is...

Startling.

In a good way.

The maxi dress is floaty and bohemian with a floral print on the cotton voile. The bodice is ruched, making my wonky boobs look phenomenal, and the slim straps with the sweetheart neckline only enhance them. It tumbles into a tiered, ruffled skirt. It could make me seem frou-frou, but no, it's elegant yet pretty informal too.

"I'd never in a million years have picked this," I whisper, more to myself than to him.

His hands settle on my hips as he draws me deeper into his hold— there's no evading his erection.

Not that I want to.

God strike me down for that admission.

I'm disappointed when he lets go of me to sign, "You're so fucking beautiful that I'm reconsidering letting you go outside."

Knowing he's capable of that, my eyes flare wide as I twist in his hold, grab his lapels, and, squeezing, declare, "You can't renege!"

"I can't," he agrees, his expression more grumpy than annoyed.

Resigned.

I'm okay with that and it has me beaming a smile at him.

He turns me back around then trails a hand over my chest. The move is possessive and I like that too.

Jeez.

With that one finger causing havoc, I can feel my breath turning shaky as he draws those nerve endings to life.

Then, he pulls back and I let him until he signs, "I'm a jealous man, *solnyshko*. I am not, however, Harvey Rundel. I won't hurt you. I will never bruise this beautiful skin…" He pauses to cup my cheek. "…but I will kill anyone who touches you. Do you understand?"

With a marriage like mine, his words are a total red flag.

So why does my heart flutter?

Why do they make me feel cherished?

I lean into him, wanting to maintain contact between us before I tell him, "Harvey used to time me going to the store."

"I have staff for that."

That has me huffing. "I didn't mean that." I have no idea why I do it, but I flick his nose in annoyance. Both of us stare at one another in bewilderment, his eyes silently saying, 'Did she just do that?' where I'm thinking, 'Did I just freakin' do that?'

I choke out, "Sorry."

He rolls said eyes then makes a 'continue' motion with his hand.

"He wanted to control every moment of every day. He hated when men looked at me. He hated if they touched me. I was his. I belonged to him. I was a possession, but he didn't want me. By the end, he loathed me but no one else could have me."

The more I share, the deeper the recognition hits that Nikolai is like Harvey.

A mirror reflection, perhaps, but a reflection nonetheless.

I see him accept that burden of truth, much as the Earth itself settled on Atlas's shoulders.

"I am not him," he shares, "but I mean that in more ways than one. I won't beat *you* if a man touches you. I'll beat him. My world is not Rundel's. If a man touches you, he means to disrespect me. I can't let that go unchallenged."

"I-I understand that." And I do.

"I told you yesterday that my father beat my mother." At my sorrowful nod, his gaze trips over my face. "I will never hurt you like that. I am not my father. I am not Rundel. Do you understand?"

I want to.

My mouth works before I whisper, "I'm willing to let you show me you're not."

Satisfaction etches lines into his expression. "The world outside these doors is dangerous, *solnyshko*. I understand that you could believe my measures extreme—"

"Ya think?"

He heaves a sigh at my wide eyes. "You are wanted by the Albanians, Cassiopeia. You are a payment. If they weren't otherwise engaged, they'd be hunting you just like Rundel undoubtedly is.

"Before I came into your life, you were in more danger than you've ever been in. Now, once you step outside on my arm, that danger intensifies by a hundred." Not allowing me to say a word in argument, he continues, "No one will touch you again. No one will hurt you; no one will use you."

"No one but you," I point out, but my tone isn't bitter.

An expression flickers over his face, one that I'd like to think is hurt. "You are safe with me," is his reply.

I know what he's offering me, and yes, it's an offer.

I can stay inside these walls and no one will know that I'm here.

The Albanians will still want me, and so will Harvey. The danger *has* doubled, but if I leave, I won't be free either.

It's clear to me what he's saying, but I repeat it out loud anyway, "You won't let me go, will you?"

His gaze shutters but he raises a hand *gently*, so as not to startle me. The backs of his knuckles trickle down my cheeks, skimming along my chin, over my lips and throat—places he marked as his yesterday.

Then, he lifts his hand higher still, to his eye height. It makes a curving motion as he slices it downward.

It doesn't take someone fluent in ASL to interpret what he just said. *Never.*

24

NIKOLAI

HER NERVES IMMEDIATELY SPIKE.

I can't blame her. It's an unnerving answer, after all, but it's the truth.

It's time she knows it.

Does it dampen her time spent in the courtyard?

Da.

But when I show her the garden that's littered with herbs of all varieties, she grows cheerier than before. Even starts smiling when she finds the patches where roses, crocuses, violets, begonias, and lark-spurs gather.

"But it's not even spring yet," she says like that makes sense.

To a gardener, perhaps it does.

Mostly, I watch her explore and experience a strange warmth that I don't think I've known for years.

Happiness?

Surely not.

She loves flowers and herbs. Her hands, delicate in their touch, smooth over leaves and petals as if she receives sustenance from their beauty.

A part of me wonders if she has a green thumb…

And it's then that I accept keeping her here won't work if I don't give her what she wants.

What she needs.

What feeds her soul.

I'm not Harvey Rundel.

I want to give her the goddamn world. I just don't want anyone else to look upon her beauty. It's mine. *She's* mine. But it's one thing to make that claim, and it's another for her to feel it.

For it to be imprinted on her. Branded into her soul.

That's the only kind of claim that works—one she accepts too.

I made this first step today, agreed to her condition, because of Dmitri and his judgmental and disappointed looks. But now, seeing her here, enjoying her appreciation of a home I didn't realize I'd built for her until I got the chance to watch her walk around it, I recognize I need to make her happy too.

When we approach the pool which is surrounded by a terrace that's on higher ground than the house, she shields her eyes to scan the rest of the estate. "The sign... Do you have alligators?"

"We're in the Everglades," is all I tell her, my mind still focused on *how* to make her happy within the confines of what I can cope with.

After all, it's not just my control freak nature that needs to keep Cassiopeia locked up in *Nav*—the danger to her is real.

Worse men than me would steal her away and hurt her. Do things to her that makes me want to wrap her in cotton and drag her back to our master suite.

"That doesn't mean you need to have reptiles for pets. In fact...," she signs, her face lined with disapproval as she draws me away from my dark thoughts. "...no one should have such creatures as pets. They're not meant for domestication."

"I never said they were domesticated. They'd be no use to me if they were."

She frowns. "I don't understand."

Such naivety.

Blyad, is it any wonder that she calls to me like a magnet to metal?

"Perhaps it's best that you don't," is all I say, assuming (incorrectly) that that would make her drop the subject.

She tugs on my hand as I start to walk over to the pool. It's a surprisingly warm day, even for Florida, and it's pitifully hot in my suit. A dip in the water would be refreshing, even more so if I got to see her swimming—

Before the idea can bear fruit, she asks, "What are they for? It's not as if they're pretty to look at."

"Depends on your idea of what's pretty," I counter, raising a hand so that I can trail my fingers over her jaw. Her blush is beautiful, and because her skin is like porcelain, the rosy hue dances over her throat and down her chest. "You don't think you're beautiful, do you? Whereas I do."

Though a breath escapes her, she mutters, "Are you comparing me to an alligator?"

That has me smirking. "I could compare you to a summer's day if you prefer."

"You've read Shakespeare?"

"Criminals can read."

Her brow furrows. "I didn't mean to imply that you couldn't. Just didn't think it'd be at the top of your TBR."

"TBR?"

"'To be read' list," she explains, her gaze tripping over my face to stare at the enclosure again. "What do you do with them?"

"Protect them from hunters. Feed them. Make sure they breed."

"And you're *all* about the breeding," she drawls. "Anyway, what do they eat? Chicken?"

"I'm sure cannibals might think that humans taste like chicken, but having never partaken, I don't know for sure."

Her mouth trembles. "You feed bodies to them?"

"It's all protein and fat."

She sucks in her bottom lip. "Will Harvey end up there?"

"Just like Marku and anyone else who harms you."

Her nod, when it comes, is slow. Though I can sense her unease, I can also see that something else lingers in the depths of her eyes...

Satisfaction.

I hide my smile before it can rise to the surface.

As someone who has been denied justice for her entire married life, she deserves it.

I just can't imagine that she ever believed it would be found between an alligator's jaws.

25

NIKOLAI
A FEW DAYS LATER

"WHY HAVEN'T you kissed me yet?"

I tilt my head to the side in a silent question. My fingers tighten on her thigh as I direct the shower spray over her pussy with my other hand.

My gaze locked on hers, I watch as the constant pressure on her clit has her hips rolling.

Breathlessly, she reassures me, "I wouldn't bite your tongue."

I have to grin.

"Wow. You look so different when you grin." Her thighs clench as she shuffles closer to the spray. "I'm starting to get used to your smile. But this is different." Her head rocks back and she moans. "That feels good. Why do you make everything better? I've done this myself, but God, it's nothing to what you—"

When her words falter as she releases a sharp cry, I rub my fingers over her slit and slip inside her. Her cunt muscles clamp around me and she lets loose a yelp as she finds a soft release.

Quickly switching off the water, I dart forward and press my face into her softness. She shudders when my lips find her clit and I focus in on her again. Her hands immediately scrape over my scalp—not pushing me away but urging me nearer.

Fuck, that feels good.

She wants me.

My *solnyshko* wants me.

I groan as I flicker my tongue over the button again and again, wanting more, needing more from her.

When her pussy ripples against my index finger, I make a retreat. My hands go to her ass and she shrieks as I drag her off the bench and onto my lap where I'm kneeling on the floor.

She settles over me, eyes wide, tits heaving as she pants, "What are you doing?"

"Let me inside, *solnyshko*," I sign.

"Why are you asking? You haven't asked for permission for anything else." Her tone is... strange. Not angry, more annoyed. And—

Ah.

Whether she wants to admit it or not, she likes it when I *take*.

She likes it because she doesn't have to decide.

I narrow my eyes at her as I rub my cock over her clit. Watching her shudder and squirm on my lap, I just keep that up, waiting for her hips to roll against me.

The moment she does, I start to jack off.

Her lips form the sweetest of pouts, a pout that I want to be stuffed with my cock.

I wonder if she means it—if she wouldn't bite.

I know she would've before.

It's part of the reason I adore her fire.

She's conceded to me, but with a fight—no one fights me. No one. But my *solnyshko* does. Exactly how it should be.

When my throat arches back as I use her cunt juices to jack off, I'm waiting, waiting, waiting for her response because, in this, she *has* to decide.

When her lips find my throat, I jerk in surprise because that wasn't what I thought she'd do. But when does she ever do what I expect?

Then, she sucks on my pulse in a way that makes my dick buck in my hand. She doesn't let up, lips suckling, tongue flicking, teeth gripping until I know for a fact she's marking me.

Fuck.

My cock pounds in my fist and I know I'm inches away from exploding—

"I hate you for making me choose," she mutters before I feel her fingers, softer than mine, gentler, more delicate, slip over the tip of my shaft.

It bucks again, pre-cum spurting into her palm.

"Why are you always so fucking wet?" she moans even as I release a grunt of my own when I can feel her heat so close to me.

Heaven is within reach.

I tip my head down to watch us, to watch *her*.

She takes over sliding my dick on and around her clit, and as she does, pre-cum soaks her. Her forehead comes to rest on my shoulder as she watches us.

It's the realest, rawest moment I've ever experienced in my fucking life.

Then, with a shiver, she notches the tip into her gate and—

"*Blyad.*"

It's the first time my voice has croaked out a word in days.

She freezes, the thick rim of muscles at her entrance clenching around me in sweet torment as she whispers, "What?"

My eyes flicker open so I can stare into hers. I know I look like I'm being tortured, mostly because I am.

Half in, half out?

This truly is *Nav*—the Underworld.

"You spoke," she rasps. "I know you did."

Of course, even if I wanted to, my fucking voice box wouldn't let me reply. It's locked up and someone else has always owned the key.

Though she's frowning, she shifts to her knees. For a moment, I think she's going to pull away and punish me, but she doesn't. She arches against me, sinking down, drawing me into her heat.

It takes a while.

From her micro-expressions, I can tell it isn't easy for her. I rub her clit, letting her take this at her own pace, not wanting to tear her when this is our first goddamn time together.

After what feels like a century, she takes all of me until I'm brushing her cervix.

A guttural groan escapes me, and when she tips her forehead against mine, I can feel her sigh against my lips in response to our union.

I take a second to concentrate on not ruining a homecoming that's been a lifetime in the making.

Then, I nuzzle into her throat, gracing her with the same treatment as she gifted me. I lick and suck at the tender join between neck and shoulder, nibbling until she starts rocking into me, slowly, slowly.

When I bite, she releases a sharp breath and begins riding me, the motions jerky and anything but smooth as I hold her close with that most brutal of ties—teeth into flesh.

"I need you to fill me, Nikolai," she cries brokenly. "Fill me. Please. Fuck. I've been empty for so long."

The words ricochet inside me like bullets shot wild. I growl because she isn't talking about my dick.

No, she's talking about my fucking seed.

My hands find her hips and I start to grind her onto me, using brute strength to help her ride me faster.

When she finds a rhythm, I release my hold on her then stare into her eyes as I cup her cheeks and draw our mouths together.

A whimper breaks from her as I thrust my tongue between her lips. I swallow it, even as my fingers find her apex.

When I start to rub her clit, this time, I swallow her mewl as I move faster, sliding through the slickness we created together, wanting her pleasure, craving it more than I need my own release.

When her cunt clamps around me, she almost takes me with her but fuck if I don't need this to last longer than ten goddamn minutes.

I'm not ready to leave her yet—I need to bind her to me. Need to make her mine.

Her mouth jerks away as she lets loose a cry as she comes. Fuck, those sounds of hers are almost my undoing.

The cry morphs into a scream as I thrust up into her, not letting her come down, simultaneously rubbing her clit, needing her to associate this, *me*, with pleasure. With ecstasy. With release and relief and bliss.

I only stop when her thighs are quivering, shaking as they clutch at me, seizing and spasming as her hands find my shoulders, nails tearing into the skin as she scrapes over the muscles on either side of my spine.

Shuddering, I find her throat again, this time on the other side. Higher up. I suckle the flesh, wanting her bruised and marked. A claim laid, one that she can't avoid if she looks in the mirror.

"P-Please, s-stop," she sobs. "J-Just for a m-minute."

I want her overwhelmed with pleasure, want to drench her womb in my cum so there's no time to wait, but the break in her voice makes me comply—I stop rubbing her clit, stop urging her to ride me, but I don't stop marking her, biting her, laying the claim that will last longer than this union.

The sound of her breathing is loud in the shower room, but slowly, she comes back to herself.

"I've never felt anything like that before," she whispers.

Pride filters through me, enough that I retreat so I can look into her eyes. Her pupils are shot, the irises flooded with them. I grab her bottom lip between my teeth, tugging at the tender flesh, marking that too. That's when she starts to ride me again.

God, her pussy is so fucking tight, so fucking hot, so fucking perfect.

I wish I could tell her that, wish I could whisper the words, but I can't. My throat is locked, and all I can do is enjoy what she does to me, how she makes me feel.

Her fingers seek and find her clit this time, and I take note of how she rubs them in a circle over the wet nub. Her internal quivers tell me how much she appreciates her touch.

Leaving her to that, I nuzzle my face between her tits, knowing that I'd gladly drown in her soft curves if I could.

She moans when I find her nipple, nipping the tip and then raking my teeth over the tender flesh. When I bite down, fiercer than before, her cunt clamps around me again and she releases a shaky moan. Her other hand is back to digging into my spine, the muscles tensing at her attack.

She moves faster, rocking harder until I know I'm about to let go.

Just when I'm there, so fucking close, almost—

She stops.

Her fingers tug at my hair and she drags my head away from her tits so that she can look straight into my eyes.

"If I let you come inside me, I want you to take me to a restaurant."

The demand has me releasing a growl. She yelps in shock when I twist us over so that I'm on top of her, hovering above her, overwhelming each of her senses with *me*. Until I'm all she sees and hears and feels and smells and tastes.

Fear doesn't leach into her expression. No, *desire* does. I can feel the heat of her eyes as she takes me in, the bunched muscles of my arms and traps.

I don't rock into her.

Instead, with our gazes united, I nod.

A smug, satisfied smile curves her lips.

But we're both winners here.

Negotiations or not, I'll never forget her whimpered plea for my seed.

With a handful of thrusts into her slick heat, I'm coming.

Fuck, it feels like millennia since I last climaxed but it's only because her pussy is perfection.

She is perfection.

Looming over her with one hand, with enough wherewithal to sign a single word, I make a waving motion with my fingers over my face to praise, "Beautiful."

Her cheeks turn pink while I come, and I come, and I come.

As I flood her with my seed, I know she can feel it because her soft moans and the way her pussy clutches and clings to my shaft draws every drop from me.

God, I can almost imagine how overwhelmed her cervix is right now—desperately trying to hold me back, to stop me from getting her pregnant, but there is no stopping fate.

"That's it," she moans breathily. "Give it all to me, Nikolai. Please. *Please.*"

I feel like the top of my head is about to explode from her begging for something I'm desperate to goddamn gift her.

When I'm done, I pull out and spread her thighs wider than before. As my cum starts to soak her slit, the white pooling and slipping and sliding from her cunt, I moan and lower myself so that I can feast.

She squeaks, then sensation overtakes surprise and embarrassment as her hands in my hair draw me into her, not pushing me away but wanting me closer while I lick her clit then thrust my tongue into her. Her moans turn guttural, deep with longing, resonant with need.

The taste of her alone is beautiful, but together, we're nectar from the gods.

When my mouth is flooded with *us*, I surge higher and, without letting her argue, nudge her chin so her mouth opens. Then, with a few inches parting us, I let *us* loose and gently pour what can only be described as ambrosia into her mouth.

Her cheeks burn hotter than ever but she moans.

I know until the day I die, I'll hear that moan on repeat—my brain will never let me forget the first time I took my Cassiopeia and made her my own.

26

CASSIE

"SO, what you're saying is that you want me to lie?"

He arches a brow at me. "I could have just messaged her myself."

While reading his hands, I squirm on his lap because he isn't wrong, and I shouldn't really be questioning my luck. "Why didn't you?"

"Because trust isn't a one-way street and because you're beginning to realize that your position is more endangered than it was when you were striving and failing to avoid Rundel on your own."

"You're an asshole for shoving that in my face," I spit, pushing my fruit salad aside.

Every morning with the fucking pomegranates—I used to love them, but now I'm just sick of them.

Much as I'm getting sick of Russian literature.

Along with the full closet in his suite, his bookshelves are back to being stacked. I don't think he reads anything that wasn't from the nineteenth-century motherland, and bored I may be, but that bored? Nope.

"The truth stings," is all he says, doubling down on his 'I'm an asshat' quota for the day.

Gritting my teeth, I glower around the breakfast room.

His estate is so big that he has several such places for dedicated dining. I've seen them all by this point but got their names from Nikita —his butler—because words like 'brunch nook' and 'lunch den' aren't, I assume, in Nikolai's vocabulary.

But that's the size of this place—a room for every occasion and then some.

Still, it's reassuring that he's let me out of the master suite more than once.

I get the feeling this is phase one, of how many, I've yet to figure out. Along the way, my trip to a restaurant is on his schedule, but fuck knows if that'll happen this year or next.

"I want books for this."

His brows lift. "I have a library."

He does.

A massive one.

"It's full of Russian texts."

His grimace is sheepish. "Write a list."

"That'd require a pen and paper," is my snappish retort.

His eyes roll but he waves a hand. Out of nowhere, a woman appears. These ghost-like wraiths for staff are eerie but damn efficient.

Only when three book titles are written down do I snag the phone from the table where he placed it as soon as we were seated.

Originally, I thought it was him shoving my lack of freedom in my face, never imagining that he wanted me to contact my friend to let her know how I was doing.

Of course, I could always send an SOS to Savannah...

With his request that I tell her I'm okay, though, I finally can let it rest that she's the reason I'm here. Not that I can blame her for my current position. Not when he's right.

Damn him.

If he hadn't gotten there first, I'd be in the hands of the Albanians and I doubt they'd be dressing me in Lanvin and Isabel Marant and force-feeding me pomegranates and orgasms and classic literature that I never wanted to read in college, never mind in my adult life *for fun*.

"You owe me a visit to a restaurant," I decide to remind him, uncaring that I'm pushing my luck.

His lips twitch. "I haven't forgotten."

With another huff, I open a text conversation, aware that he's watching me.

> Me: Savannah? It's me. Cassie.

> **TWO MINUTES LATER**

> Savannah: Oh, thank FUCK! Where the hell have you been?

> Me: I couldn't get my hands on a burner cell.

> Savannah: There are still pay phones somewhere out there, you know? As well as email? Ever heard of that miraculous invention?

> Me: I've heard of it, but I don't know what yours is, lol.

> Savannah: You could have contacted me via my work email. It's at the end of every article I write.

Savannah was a journalist-cum-whistleblower.

> Me: I didn't think to do that.

The lie trips off my fingertips easier than I'd like.

> Savannah: Where are you?

Nikolai's watching me, his gaze locked on my face rather than on the screen as I'd anticipated.

I'm getting used to that focus, even starting to appreciate his intensity in all honesty.

Which probably means I'm as insane as he is.

When it registers that he has my attention, both of us glance away.

> Me: Oregon.

I look back at him and realize he read the message because his brows lift.

I don't blame him.

I can't sense if he's agitated by this conversation, don't know if he's worried or not seeing as, like always, he's expressionless.

Aside from his eyes.

They're glittering like a vein of gold uncovered in a mine.

> Savannah: What the fuck are you doing there?

> Me: I'm thinking about moving to Canada.

> Savannah: Why?

> Me: Maple syrup and ice hockey aren't enough of a reason?

> Savannah: No. I've made Aidan put feelers out for Harvey.

Savannah's husband is the head of the Irish Mob in NYC, which means that Harvey is being sought by three different mafia factions...

Ha.

I can't *not* enjoy that delicious twist of fate even if my mind boggles over how Harvey has managed to stay off their radar for so long.

The guy couldn't pee without getting it everywhere, but somehow he evades the Russians, the Albanians, *and* the Irish?

God is apparently on his side.

Can't be Hades... he's on mine.

> Me: Thank you, Savannah. Truly. You've been a better friend than I've been to you.

> Savannah: Shut up. Like you wouldn't help me if the tables were turned.

> Savannah: Do you need money?

Me: No. Thank you, though. I really
appreciate the offer, but I've found a job.

> Savannah: I could get you into Canada today.

Me: I know, but I'm fine right now. I swear if I
need your help, I'll be in touch.

> Savannah: Sooner rather than later?

Me: Yeah, I'll keep you in the loop.

> Savannah: Preferably before Harvey's got his
> hands on you?

Those words, blasé but loaded with sarcasm, make me shudder.
God, if she only knew…

Me: Yeah. Before he gets within a mile of me.

That has him tensing beneath my lap.

> Savannah: I know we fell out of contact, but
> I'd like it if we could be friends again?

Me: I'd like that too. <3 My shift is about to
start, but I promise, I'll keep in touch.

> Savannah: <3

When I hand him the phone, I study his expressionless expression
which belies the tension in his body.

"What's wrong?"

I don't think I fucked up. I mean, I sold Savannah a bunch of lies
that she appeared to buy…

"He won't get within ten miles of you." His fingers practically bite
out the words. "Never mind a mile."

My lips curve into a soft smile. "Unless he's being eaten by the alligators."

That has him blinking. "Yes."

I nestle deeper into his lap, well aware that what I'm about to ask is heinous, but it doesn't stop me. "Would you feed him to them when he's alive?"

His brows lift. "You'd deny me the right to make him suffer?"

I blink back at him. "Do you know that he had me committed?"

He doesn't reply, but I can see that he knows. I'm starting to read the minute movements of his mouth, brows, and eyes. They speak a language that can only be learned with experience.

"He gaslit me. He had me believing that left was right. He's tried to rape me. He *has* forced me to do things that no woman should ever be forced to do.

"He's made me throw up meals so that I could lose weight. He's had me sobbing with shame over what he's done to me—"

Despite my anger, my fingers tremble as the memories flare to life like they're happening *now,* not in the past. The wounds to my psyche have clearly yet to scar over. Maybe they never will.

His hands gently clasp my quivering ones before he lets go so he can cup my chin. As his eyes lock on mine, he dips forward and presses a kiss to my lips.

I shudder as he does, not in revulsion, just relief.

That's, I assume, a yes.

27

CASSIE

Sweet Disposition - The Temper Trap

I CAN TELL he doesn't want to, but Nikolai spells, "This is Dmitri."

The younger man beams a grin at me as he holds out a hand. When he doesn't shake mine, just raises it to his lips to kiss my knuckles, I get the feeling he knows he's playing a game of Russian roulette—*ha, I'm so fucking funny*—from the twinkle in his eye.

Beneath me, Nikolai is like stone. Every second within Dmitri's proximity has him growing tenser and tenser until the other man lets go of me and flops back in the seat opposite us.

We're sitting in the courtyard beyond the pool with a parasol shading us.

Though I'm wearing yet another sundress that was laid out for me by the housekeeping fairies, the only concession to the unseasonably warm weather from these two is a pair of shades.

Their three-piece suits—they're even wearing vests—have to be miserably hot but they don't look flushed or overheated.

Maybe it's the Russian in them? Ice-cold to their souls...

Still, they might be frigid in nature, but in appearance, I'm the one who needs to be chilled. They do a lot of things wrong over in the motherland, but breeding beautiful men is something they do very, very right.

Dmitri's bright blue eyes dance as, without asking, he pours himself some lemonade from the glass jug that's perspiring on the table, confirming what I already know—they're close.

Most of the people around the estate don't dare make eye contact with Nikolai, never mind pour themselves a drink without invitation.

Is he one of the brothers Nikolai saved from that orphanage fire?

I've seen a few men approach Nikolai and when they do, I imagine it'd be my response to coming face-to-face with one of the alligators that he insists aren't pets.

But, in my opinion, if you name an animal 'Vasily,' they're a pet, no?

"It's nice to meet you. 'Mute' has been all quiet on the western front where you're concerned," Dmitri mocks, his accent purely American.

Not a hint of their home to the words.

Huh.

So, maybe he was born in the US?

Is he...

The kid with the Yankees cap!

Now that I've put a name to the face, I can see it in the smiling eyes and the cocky smirk.

"I don't mean to be rude, but who are you?" *What* are you? That's my real question. Aside from rude, that is.

Who calls a mute person, 'Mute?'

"He's a pain in my ass."

I hide a smile at the words Nikolai signs—I knew it. *Affection.* No anger so that must be a sucky nickname?

"Nikolai is my father."

My brows go for a hike. "You have a son?"

I can't see behind his shades, so I don't know what's going on with his eyes. "You're looking at him."

"You were young when you..." I clear my throat and, spying Dmitri's amusement, mutter, "I mean, you're in your mid-twenties, surely?"

"I am," Dmitri agrees. "Unfortunately, I had a sperm donor before Nikolai."

"Oh!" I glower at him. "Would it have been so difficult to clarify that?"

Nikolai waves a dismissive hand that makes me want to throw the lemonade at his head. "I knew Dmitri would explain."

"Yes, Dmitri's Nikolai's voice box," the man himself mocks, but he peers over his shades as he does so. "I was starting to think he'd never let you out of his bedroom."

"Me too," I mumble, shooting Nikolai a dour look.

Dmitri angles his head and I know he's studying me. I'd say he was checking me out, but it's less creepy and more like a doctor's once-over.

I have no idea why I defend Nikolai by saying, "The only part of me that's bruised is my pride."

Dmitri blinks. "Niko's good at that."

Niko.

Well, my ovaries just fluttered.

Nee-koh.

Yum.

I'm not the only one who abbreviates it, then. Dmitri says it with a slight accent, though, and it's much hotter than my Americanized version.

I'll need to practice the Russian intonation.

"He is?" I ask when I realize my mind definitely went for a walk. "Good at bruising people's pride, I mean?"

Dmitri hums as he takes a sip of lemonade. "I wanted to let you know personally that we've widened the search for your ex-husband—"

Nikolai's hand slams against the table, and quickly, I excuse, "He doesn't like it when you say that."

"Say what?" Dmitri sputters.

"Husband with a possessive pronoun," I offer.

"What would you prefer I call him?" Dmitri questions, his eyes bugging wide.

"How about 'cunt?'"

My lips twitch. "He isn't in possession of one."

Nikolai, *Niko*, grunts. "It's ridiculous how hard he's tunneled down."

"He was a little like you," I admit. "Lost in social services, abandoned by CPS at a really young age."

Scrubbing his floppy hair out of his face, Dmitri mocks, "You Americans think you have it so tough. You don't even want to know what accounts for CPS in Russia."

"I never said it wasn't bad, but bad is bad, especially when it comes to children, isn't it?" I demur, finding myself in the bewildering position of defending my ex.

"What Niko had to endure is something Amnesty International would wade into—"

"Enough," Niko signs with a slice of his hand through the air.

Dmitri, grumbling as he takes another sip of his drink, mutters, "Where was he raised?"

"Connecticut."

Dmitri stills. "His files say Jersey."

"Like I said, they kind of abandoned him. He ran away a lot." Uneasily, I ask, "I doubt he'd head back there. It's not like he has a family. Outside of…" *Me.* But that goes without saying.

I don't have to look at him to know Nikolai is glowering at me for making the unspoken connection.

"He has no reason to think you're in Florida," Dmitri points out.

"True."

"Would he consider Connecticut home?"

"No. Jersey." I shuffle on Niko's lap and, in a wistful tone, confess, "My mom still lives in New Jersey."

"Are you close with her?"

"I used to be." I sigh. "Until my father died and Harvey came along."

They share a look.

"What's her name?"

Why do I feel like Dmitri already knows the answer to that?

Still, I reply, "Dema Turgenev."

"I'll check things out at her place if that's worrying you," he soothes.

Is it worrying me?

I think of the shotgun beneath my papa's bed, one she'd never have tossed out.

I think of my mom's inherent dislike of Harvey, a dislike he was aware of...

"No, I'm not worried about her but having someone check in would be nice."

"Send some guards up there," Nikolai orders, but something in his expression...

Dmitri signs a couple words I don't understand—Russian sign language?—that has Nikolai tipping his chin in agreement.

"It's rude to use another language in front of a nonspeaker," I grumble, but the relief that my mom will be safe goes to war with reality as, uneasily, I say, "You're spending a lot of money on this."

Dmitri beams a charming smile at me that I don't trust. "It doesn't matter."

That smile has me demanding, "Is there something you're not telling me?"

The moment I utter the words, I know what a dumb question that was.

There's plenty they're not telling me.

Still, I freeze when a thought occurs to me. "You don't think the Albanians will go after her, do you?"

Dmitri shakes his head. "Not at all."

Nikolai's fingers fly aggressively as he releases a soft growl.

"We'll make sure she's protected, *solnyshko*. From *him* or the Albanians.

"As for Rundel, he deserves to die for what he put you through. And I made you a promise."

Peering between us, Dmitri asks a question that only someone who considers himself a son to a man like Nikolai would ever say out loud: "What kind of promise?"

My cheeks flush a tad. "That he'd feed Harvey to Vasily alive."

Grinning, Dmitri whistles. "Hardcore. I love it. And you look like Anne of Green Gables in these summery dresses he's got you wearing too." He says something in Russian that has Nikolai flicking his fingers at him in the universal sign of, 'Fuck off.'

Chuckling, Dmitri drawls, "Have you met Vasily yet?"

"No." I grimace at the prospect.

His smile is deceptively angelic. "Don't believe what they say about running in zigzags to get away from gators." If that's meant to be reassuring, he failed. At my scowl, he gets up and salutes me. "I have business to attend and alligator chow to source. It was a pleasure meeting you, Cassiopeia."

"Likewise," I grouse, not bothering to watch the younger man go as I turn to Nikolai. "I don't mean to be such trouble."

He tilts down his shades. "Who said you were?"

"I mean, you've got *men* on this."

How many did he command anyway?

"And? What else would they be doing aside from scratching their asses and waiting for orders?"

When he puts it like that...

His hand settles on my thigh, fingers tipping inward. After weeks of this treatment, I'm getting used to his touches. Can translate them better than I can his Russian.

"What did Dmitri say?"

He merely arches a brow.

I huff. "At the end. He said something in Russian."

Nikolai purses his lips. "You don't want to know."

"I wouldn't have asked if I didn't," I retort.

"You make a pretty Persephone."

"Thank you?"

"No, that's what *he* said."

"Oh." My frown deepens. "Is that a compliment?"

What the hell is that supposed to even mean?

"It wasn't intended to be an insult or he knows I'd have broken his jaw."

I squint at him a second, then I peer at the condensation-covered glass of lemonade in my hand and I do as I wanted to earlier.

I toss it over him, not caring that I get caught in the deluge too.

He sits there in a now-wet, expensive suit, hair sticky and coated in the juice, face drenched, eyes wide, and I merely say, "You deserve that for being…you."

The lack of fear in our byplay doesn't take me aback.

And when he growls and starts to stand, there's still no fear in me as I get up with a shriek, knowing that he'll catch me.

Fully aware that when he does, there'll be no pain.

No hurting.

No, probably just an orgasm.

That's the kind of revenge I can take.

Especially when, twenty-three seconds later, he hauls me over his shoulder and slaps me on the ass.

If this is supposed to be a punishment, his show of strength is anything but…

28

CASSIE

The Beach - The Neighbourhood

WHEN NIKOLAI SURPRISED me with a camera this morning and told me to spend time in the kitchen garden, I didn't take the unusual generosity for granted.

I wasn't even disappointed when I found that he wouldn't be joining me because he was holding a meeting at the estate with something Dmitri called 'his *Brigadiers*' and two goons with the names Vladimir and Oleg would be my shadows.

To be honest, he could have told me Martians were invading tomorrow and I'd have been okay about it because, at long last, I've got my hands on a camera again.

When I ran away from New York, I had to sell my DSLR and photography is one of those hobbies that nourishes my soul. I've always loved it. That and food. It led me to eke out a space for myself as a blogger/vlogger which meant I had a career doing what I loved.

Until Harvey had to wreck things.

Until I *allowed* Harvey to wreck things for me.

With the DSLR around my neck, standing in this beautiful garden that feels like a million miles away from New Jersey, I have to ask myself *why* I didn't leave sooner.

Why I didn't get out before the going got really rough, never mind tough.

I wish I had an answer but I don't.

"It isn't my fault," I whisper to the flowers who can't talk back to me. "I didn't deserve to be treated that way."

My thoughts mar the deliciously warm winter's day, so I force myself to shift focus.

Harvey is my past.

Nikolai will see to that.

I have faith in him that he'll follow through with his promise, which is more faith than I've had in anyone other than Savannah O'Donnelly since the early days of my miserable marriage.

When the undeniable scent of Medovik cake drifts from the kitchen as I zoom in on a hummingbird that's sniffing at some petunias, I'm not shocked when my two shadows, older guys in their fifties, wander inside for some of the sweet treat.

My mom used to make the cake for my dad when it was his birthday. I always hated it—sweetened sour cream isn't my thing. But it was a staple for a lot of people during the Soviet era and nostalgia made it popular with their children.

With the goons gone, it's instinctive for me to glance at the garden to see if there's a way out or a means of escape, but I know there isn't.

Not only are we in the middle of the freakin' Everglades, and for a captor, Nikolai was bemusingly thorough in his guided tour, *but...*

I'm not unhappy here.

In a book, this would be where the heroine would dash into the great beyond, uncaring that the danger from the alligators and cottonmouths was more urgent than an orgasm-obsessed captor.

But I'm no romance book heroine.

I'm just a fat chick from Jersey who has a Russian mobster sniffing at her heels like a psychopathic Prince Charming with an orgasm fetish and a breeding kink.

"Maybe I'm just weak?" I mutter, cringing as I spin around in a cluster of early larkspurs. "I didn't leave Harvey when I should've and I'm not—" I pause. "Nikolai isn't…"

Because there is no way to finish that sentence without seeming certifiable, I duck down and photograph the delicate fronds of the larkspurs as a gust of wind tugs at them and brings them to life.

The scent is far nicer than the Medovik cake, that's for sure.

Allowing the peace of the backyard to fill me, I stare into the distance, spying the acres of orange trees that only amplify how beautiful Nikolai's home is.

"Is it wrong to be rather happy here?" I ask the wind, but, like the flowers, it doesn't answer me either.

I'm not going to bed with an empty stomach. I don't have to worry about where I'm sleeping. I'm not wondering where Harvey is or how far away or close he might be to gaining ground on my location.

I'm safe.

That's a luxury I haven't been afforded in too long and it's as addictive as Nikolai's heavy-lidded glances and lingering touches.

With a sigh, I stroke one of the delicate petals of a crocus, its pollen lingering on my fingertips, decorating them with gold.

I love flowers and adore spending time in gardens in general.

The house I grew up in had a massive backyard and my mom always used to tend to it.

Come rain or shine, spring or summer or fall, she never stopped puttering in ours.

I wonder if she still enjoys the chore?

Does she bake on Thursdays though Papa and I aren't around to eat her treats?

Would she be happy to see me if I managed to show up at her door one day?

Or would she be ashamed of me—

"So, you're the reason why the Pakhan's transferred here, slut."

The words have me jolting as each one lands like a bullet.

Turning around, I find a man standing by the French doors in yet another expensive suit—they're starting to lose their appeal—with a sneer on his aristocratic features.

His accent, never mind his clothes, tells me he's one of Nikolai's men without even knowing that there's a meeting taking place somewhere on the grounds.

Unease hits me when I glance around and spy how alone I am out here.

Vladimir and Oleg's absence suddenly feels less about sweet treats and more about permitting me to be ambushed.

I know enough about aggressive men to recognize that I'm in danger from the expression on this stranger's face alone.

The way his hands are bunched into fists at his sides, that hostile snarl of his lips…

Somehow, I've angered him but I've never seen him before.

"Do I know you?" I ask quietly.

It takes everything in me not to retreat.

The balls I have when I'm with Nikolai fade into nothingness. My heart starts to pound, and I can feel the prickles in my muscles as my flight-or-fight response kicks in.

All of a sudden, I'm back in the kitchen in Jersey.

Cowering against the cupboard, crouched into a ball as Harvey kicks me.

Over and over and over again.

"No, but I know you," the stranger growls, surging forward a few steps. "I saw your marks on him, whore. So close to the gala too. You know he's taken, don't you? Did you do it to humiliate my daughter?"

As terrified as I am, a bark of laughter escapes me. "Nikolai *isn't* taken."

No way, no how.

"*Nikolai?*" His face turns impossibly redder. "You dare say his name. Watch your mouth, slut! He is our Pakhan."

Standing my ground, I swallow. "I'm not a slut."

"You're fucking a man who's engaged to my little girl," he snaps, hands still bunched. "What else does that make you other than a *blyad*?"

I flinch when he storms nearer to me.

Tunnel vision takes over.

My panic is real and raw and there's an internal wail in my head: *Nikolai promised me that I'd be safe.*

Even worse, I believed him.

As I hunch, more distraught at his lie than what's about to happen, as I start to crouch in on myself, I stagger back a step, needing to get away.

Mind darting around what I know of the estate, I figure the quickest place to head is the pool area. If Vladimir and Oleg *are* in on this, then the kitchen won't be a safe space and I already know that the staff might as well be ghosts for all the help they'll offer me.

His hand flies out and I cringe, bracing myself for impact, but... it doesn't land.

If anything, *he* is the one crying out with surprised pain. He drops to his knees as fists pound him, as a hand slams his head into the graveled path, and that's when Nikolai surges into my tunnel vision.

His face, God, his expression...

I know what he's capable of, but I'm so used to seeing that blankness etched into the lines of his features that this is terrifying.

My brain is slow to react.

All I see is a twofold threat.

Then, not even breathing heavily from the exertion, he rumbles in a tone that feels like it's unearthed from Hell itself, "You are safe, *solnyshko*. Just like I promised you," and with that, he brings me back.

His broken voice. Tortured and twisted. More of a snarl than a timbre. It's him.

It is safety.

It's *Nikolai* who's been using the man's head as a basketball, who's about to twist his—

"Nikolai! You can't kill him!" I gasp when I realize he's going to snap the man's neck.

He frowns at me in confusion, but it's Dmitri who steps toward us, his hands spread placatingly wide.

At me. Not Niko.

My brow furrows as I realize I missed Dmitri's approach. "Tell him, Dmitri! You can't let him—"

"He insulted you, Cassiopeia," Dmitri informs me softly. "He made Nikolai break his promise."

That's when Nikolai growls.

It takes me back to the penultimate time Harvey had me in his grasp. Growls and spittle flecking me as he laid into me—

"You're frightening her, Pakhan," Dmitri soothes, his tone calm as he flicks a look at Nikolai.

Niko grits his teeth but manages to grunt, "He called you *slut*."

That he's talking, period, tells me how furious he is. Christ, he's spoken more today than he has in all our time together.

Select mutism? Or just orneriness?

It's only then that it registers he's speaking in English too.

That, however, is a problem for another day.

I suck in a breath. "But I'm not a slut. You know that. I know that—"

Dmitri shakes his head. "He dishonored you."

"*You* dishonored my daughter," the stranger cries, his hands flailing at Niko's hold on him.

The power Nikolai exudes has me flushing.

The brute strength, the raw force—I can't imagine how much his punches must hurt especially after Niko slams the stranger's head into the ground again.

My mouth trembles as Dmitri snaps, "Your daughter is more of a slut than Cassiopeia is."

The stranger tries to break free but it's nothing, *nothing,* to the grip that holds him fast.

"Nikolai courted her—"

"He's broken bread with her—once. You and your wife were in attendance. It was hardly a fucking date," Dmitri retorts. "I've screwed Myata more than Nikolai has even seen her."

Vindicated in the faith I have for him, I whisper, "He said that they were engaged."

Niko utters another growl, sounding more feral than ever, but it's Dmitri who chuckles. "I told Niko that you were fucking stupid, Pavlivshev, but this just confirms it. Put him down, Pakhan. He'll be less trouble dead than alive."

"You can't just kill him," I choke out, but it isn't horror that makes my voice hoarse.

"Why can't he?"

Nikolai and Dmitri both skewer me with their focus, a silent question hovering between us.

My mouth works as I try to put together a reason *why* Niko can't kill this man, then I come up with nothing other than, "Politics?"

Niko grunts, but it's Dmitri who explains, "You were dishonored. Nikolai has claimed you as his own, Cassiopeia. Politics dictate that he returns honor to you."

"What is this? A Regency romance?" I sputter, then I glower at the man in question who must be as nuts as Nikolai because he's only gasping at the chokehold he's in, not pleading for his life. "Sure, he was... *rude,* but you can't kill people because they're rude to me, Niko!"

That's when the overly loud crick of a neck being snapped echoes around the garden.

As the man falls to the ground, a limp tangle of limbs, Niko manages to grind out, "Who says that I can't?"

Which is when I know how deeply I've fallen into his web.

Because he holds out his arms for me, beckoning me toward him to take comfort in him, and I don't run *from* him.

I run *to* him.

Stockholm syndrome or not, his arms, I recognize, are the only place where I truly do feel safe.

Even with, or maybe *because of,* the corpse lying at his feet.

29

NIKOLAI

A WEEK LATER

CASSIOPEIA STRUGGLES on my lap until I slide an arm around her waist and draw her deeper into me. The struggles change, then they shift. She glowers though she has to know it won't work.

"We're in a restaurant," she bites off.

Amused by her orneriness, I ignore her and settle her onto my thigh again when she tries to stand.

Upon the server's arrival, I can see her mortification, but the waitress knows better than to look anywhere other than me.

"Are you ready to order, sir?" she says, tone oozing politesse.

Locking my eyes with Cassiopeia's, I sign our drinks order and point to our selections from the menu.

Once she's faded away, Cassiopeia turns to me with a frown. "Do you own this place?"

My lips quirk; I'm impressed she picked up on the veiled fear in the server's politeness.

She takes that for the confirmation it is. "Do you own everything in Miami?"

"Eighty percent of Miami Beach, forty percent of the outer city," I inform her, mostly because I'm curious about her reaction.

"No way." When I arch a brow at her certainty, confusion puddles into her expression. "But…"

"But?"

"I don't understand."

"What's to understand? Either the Bratva owns it or I do. I've diversified over the years."

She graces me with a single blink then mutters, "I want to sit on a chair."

"No, you don't," I counter calmly. "What's wrong?"

She bites her lip, her focus on my hands. "Nothing."

The server shows up again before I can get her to answer. As she lays out the drinks for us, I study Cassiopeia.

She's been quieter since that unfortunate scene with Pavlivshev, but I haven't pushed her to discuss it.

She needed to learn what I'll do for her, whether she likes it or not.

All I know is that seeing her hunch in on herself, detecting her fear, witnessing her revert into the prey that was hunted by Rundel lit me with a rage so deep it was a wonder the foundations of *Nav* didn't crack beneath my fucking feet.

She will never be prey again.

And Vladimir and Oleg will never return to the privileged ranks they held before either. They're lucky they're not dead and that they have ties to the Krestniy Otets or not even Dmitri's reasoning would have stopped me from putting them down.

"Have you heard…" She fidgets. "Is my mom safe?"

Her question draws me from my grim thoughts. "Yes, *solnyshko*," I soothe, tugging gently on the end of her braid. "I would have told you otherwise."

She flushes a little. "Thank you."

"You don't have to thank me." Not for protecting my future mother-in-law. "She is well. The guards report on her twice daily."

"That's too much."

"That's for me to decide," I say softly, watching as relief makes her eyelashes flutter closed for a second.

She's a strange creature—her relief is tangible, so why she argued in the first place is beyond me.

That's her, though. Difficult.

Take earlier…

Another woman might not want to sit on my lap so that she could try to run. My *solnyshko* is happy on my knee, happy with me—she just fights her natural inclinations.

But I will protect her, even from her own contrariness.

Unaware of my musings and, in a concerted effort to change the subject, she asks, "Do you always have a waiter who can sign?"

"At my establishments, of course."

She studies me, her gaze drifting to my mouth. She keeps doing that since I managed to grate out a couple words. Still, she hasn't asked me *why* I choose to sign over speak.

Nor does she know.

"Do they always want to fuck you?"

Both brows surge high at that—her mind definitely wasn't where I thought it was. "What makes you ask that?"

"The way she was eating you up with her eyes maybe?"

Jealousy.

Fascinating.

I hadn't expected that.

Beyond pleased with this development, I settle back in the booth that's for my use only and, instead of responding, show my appreciation for her possessiveness by kissing the upper swell of her breasts. She squirms on my lap but doesn't try to stop me.

Hiding a smile, I let a finger trail over the ripe curves that peep out from a sweetheart neckline which, combined with two thick straps, frames her tits to perfection.

The dress I have her in today is a cream, soft knit that covers her to the knee then falls into a fringed hem that swishes about her calves.

Combined with a set of tan leather kitten heels that do criminal things to her ass, and a braid that I want wrapped around my fist, she looks like something I want to eat.

I've already established that Cassiopeia isn't comfortable baring so much skin, but I don't understand why.

She's fucking beautiful.

And it's not as if I'm dressing her in short skirts or revealing clothes—why the hell would I want to show those parts off that belong only to me?

Her logic is clearly unsound.

When goose bumps surge over her chest at my touch, she releases a soft moan that deepens as my finger trails along her throat where a mark lingers from the other day. I like the sight of it on her.

Her hand grabs my wrist, though, nails digging in as she complains, "You never answered me."

The server is so irrelevant to me that it takes a minute to remember what she asked.

Ah.

"She might want to fuck me, *solnyshko,* but *I* only want to fuck *you.*"

She bites her lip again so I tug it free from her teeth with my thumb. Then, I slide the tip inside her mouth and, with hungry eyes, press deeper.

Cassiopeia surprises me by swirling her tongue over it.

Blyad, *possessiveness looks good on her.*

Satisfied that our jealousy is a two-way street, I press a kiss to her throat where a mark I left yesterday is starting to fade.

She shivers against me and, over her shoulder, I see the server make an appearance. Her eyes collide with mine and her cheeks turn pink before she looks away, shoulders rounding in on themselves at her approach.

Cassiopeia startles on my lap when the waitress lays our dishes on the table.

I study the other woman and order, "Don't disturb us."

She nods and fades away like the nonentity she is to me.

"I hope you're going to tip her well for being so rude."

Cassiopeia's disapproving tone, in spite of her jealousy, has me hiding a smile as I press a kiss to her lips. "I'll let you calculate it, hmm?"

Though she snorts, her attention soon shifts when a light vibration hums through the seat.

"What is that?" As she twists, her mouth rounds into a perfect circle. "They put up privacy screens."

"You didn't think eating at a restaurant would come without a price?" I taunt.

She whines, "But you ordered food!"

"And I won't make you wait if you come."

Though she pouts, her eyes gleam when I start to drag her skirt up her thighs. "What are you doing?"

Is she being coy?

Not with me.

"You're going to sit on my cock like a good girl, stuffed full with me, taking every inch, and you're going to eat what I feed you while your pussy keeps me nice and warm."

There's no mistaking her response.

Slightly flared nostrils, dilated pupils, heavier breaths... legs parting to give me immediate access.

I'd smile in satisfaction, but in a flurry of movement, she shifts from my lap and straddles me, reaching between us to unfasten my zipper before dragging her skirt higher up her hips.

"Are you moving this fast because you're hungry?"

She grumbles at my teasing. "Hunger can be twofold."

I flick my fingers over her chest so that I can pull down the neckline and expose the upper curves of her tits.

Dropping kisses along the swells, I leave little nips and bites that will stain the pale white skin later.

With my free hand, I spread my fingers in a wave over my face with the sign for: "Beautiful."

Her cheeks pinken. "Thank you," she whispers, but she presses her lips to my throat so she can hide.

Grabbing a hold of her hips, I grind her into me. When her bare pussy rubs over my crotch, she yelps and retreats.

Good—I want to see her face.

"Stop," she cries. "You'll get your pants wet!"

When I arch a brow, her flush deepens, hotter than ever.

"You can't walk out drenched in—"

"I can't?"

"No," she hisses, peering around as if someone can see.

But no one will see her like this.

Ever.

She is mine.

Her pleasure is mine.

Her orgasms are mine.

Her beauty is fucking mine.

I grab her hips again and angle my own upward, further grinding us together. Her eyelids fall to a heavy mast at the pressure, at the sensation of silk against her, but nothing could be as silky as she is.

Nothing is better than *her.*

Nothing.

She groans and starts to rock into me, finding a rhythm that has us both sweating.

When she comes, I smirk, watching the release rob her of tension. It's short, quick. More of a sneeze than an orgasm.

Still, she studies me like I gave her the world, and I'll never tire of seeing that expression.

Plan momentarily awry, I hitch her onto the table and she twists around to move the drinks out of the way so she can fall back on her elbows. Her legs spread wider without my suggestion, and she rests her heels on the table so she can lever them farther apart.

All of this is done with eagerness.

For me.

For what she knows I, and I alone, can give her.

A growl escapes me, one that doubles when I look at the meal in front of me, and I unfasten the now-slick silk of my fly then free my shaft.

As she licks her lips, I can feel pre-cum leak at the tip in preparation for what's to come and I use it to jack off.

No one gets me hotter than my Cassiopeia.

Leaning down, my tongue flutters over her clit, teasing her then dropping to thrust into her slit. I savor her for a moment, enjoying her moans as I slip and slide through her folds.

When she coats my tongue, I surge upright and settle over her. My mouth falls onto hers and I thrust in deep, wanting her to taste herself, wanting her to know how goddamn delicious she is, wanting her to understand why I'm a willing addict.

My cock finds her slit and as I fuck her mouth, I slot myself into her entrance.

She's so fucking tight that her cunt practically chokes me. I can feel the muscles tightening and releasing in internal panic as she concedes to the slow, possessive thrust that claims her as my own.

Every inch is a battle, every inch is hard won, but fuck, if I don't love feeling her stranglehold around me.

Those soft gasps she releases, the heavy breaths that whisper in my ear—they're better than music.

As she clings to me, I tug her deeper into my hold, surrounding her with me, blanketing her with all that I am.

She releases a soft sob at the pressure, and then as I finally slide home, filling her full, I drag her backward, making her yelp as I draw her onto my lap.

With her dazed eyes locked onto me, I shuffle the maki toward us, and with her stuffed full of my dick as promised, I feed her one loaded with avocado.

Like I'd wanted to do all those days ago, I gather tidbits I know she'll enjoy and feed her, feed *my woman*, while her cunt clings to me, clutching and teasing and keeping me hard as she adjusts on my knee and eats every bite I give her.

One of her arms rests on my shoulder for support, then she rocks forward and presses her forehead against mine as if even that's too much for her.

"Why do you feel so good?" she mewls.

I press a quick kiss to her lips as a reward then I retreat and start to pop a maki into my mouth. Before I can, she nips it away and takes it for herself.

The move is confident, at odds with her timidity...

She's a study in contrasts—deliciously multifaceted.

Never boring.

Perhaps she can see my delight in her rebelliousness because when I circle her lips with my finger, she sucks the tip and then slides her mouth down the length.

Slowly, she starts to roll her hips and I prove myself to be a weak, weak man because I don't stop her.

The dual assault of my cock being cosseted by her cunt and how she sucks on my finger drains my IQ by at least forty points.

When she rides me, slowly, torturously, *exquisitely,* I'm not surprised when she stops just before I come. Nor am I surprised why.

Negotiation.

Blyad, this woman.

The suction she had on the digit releases with a faint popping sound as she lets go of it and rasps, "I want to cook for you tomorrow."

I blink at her.

"If I let you come inside me..."

There is no contest.

No need for negotiation.

I'll give her the Underworld itself for that offering.

My hands find her waist as I nod.

Together, we buck until I groan out my release.

As I flood her, I arch my head back, resting it against the booth. She grinds into me again because she's greedy, gluttonous for pleasure after weeks of being given what her body needs. I only touch her when my cum puddles around the base of my dick. Then, I smooth my seed into her, using it as lube when I find her clit.

The tug of her inner muscles keeps me hard enough for her use.

With one hand, I rub her clit, and with the other, I slide it through the mess we made together.

Thrusting those fingers into her mouth, I watch as she licks them clean, her eyes darkening with enjoyment of *us.*

When she bursts again, I shudder in response, savoring the molten heat of her cunt, the only sanctuary I've ever known... until I'm forced to leave it.

As she sags into me, both of us are panting, utterly wrecked.

She's the only woman I've ever been in who comes so fiercely that it makes her shake. So for endless moments, we stay like that until her legs stop spasming, which is when, spying those pearls of cum dripping from her cunt, my fingers slide through the slick. Then, I thrust them into her, making sure that she's full of me even when my dick is left to suffer out in the cold.

Her hips rock and she bites her lip in reaction, but she doesn't complain or argue.

If anything, I can see what it does to her—those pupils of hers are fat with arousal.

My sticky fingers make a retreat and I place a hand on her belly and silently will my seed to bear fruit.

Cassiopeia stares down at it but makes no comment as she circles my mouth with a finger until... "Why don't you have guards?"

"I do," I reply, nonplussed enough by the question to answer.

"I don't see them."

"That's because they're good."

She tilts her head to the side. "Are they in here?"

Scornfully, I snort.

"I'll take that as a no, then," she mumbles before asking, "Did you have them before I came into your life?"

"*Nyet*."

"Why not?"

I almost scoff. "Because I can handle myself." *As any decent Pakhan should.*

"So why do you need guards now?"

"Because I promised you'd always be safe."

When she nods, I get the feeling I've missed something.

She presses a kiss to my lips. "Thank you."

I shrug. "It's nothing."

"No, it's not *nothing*," she snipes. "Are we going to celebrate Christmas on the 6th?"

"Yes." I sigh, annoyed with myself for forgetting she was raised American. I can't deny that learning of her heritage has made her Russian in my eyes. "I should have asked if you celebrate on the 25th…"

"My father was Russian Orthodox. We celebrated on January 6th and I only ever stopped because of Harvey." Her chin tips up. "I don't have to do that anymore, do I?"

I growl at her mentioning *his* name while her cunt is full of my cum. "No."

She hums. "I want to cook."

"Whatever you want. But… first…" As she takes note of my hesitation, I shrug. "There's a gala on New Year's. Will you be my date?"

Her eyes are as round as gold drachmas. "I'm surprised you're asking."

"It goes against my inclinations," I agree.

"So, why… ask?"

"Because I want you there of your own volition. I want to have you dripping in gold and jewels and my cum—"

"Cum?" she squeaks.

I nod then repeat with brisk flicks of my fingers, *"Dripping* in it." When she bites her lip, I rear up and do it for her and only stop when the soft, pink flesh is bruised. "Will you come with me?" Before she can answer, I manage to rasp, "As my woman?"

"Why do you sign when you can speak? I thought you were deaf, but you're not hard of hearing at all, are you?"

There's no point in lying to her. "I have no hearing issues."

"Just speaking ones?"

I nod.

"Since when?"

"Since I found my mother's body." When her eyes flare wide, I quickly sign, "I don't say that for sympathy."

"Of course, you don't," she snaps. "I just didn't realize… But, trauma." She grimaces, and the haunted look in her eyes triggers a feral wrath in me—one that vows she will never be prey again. "It affects us all."

"I thought you'd be angry," I reason.

"I could be, but you didn't lie to me," she retorts, her tone droll before mocking, "'Assuming makes an ass out of you and me.'" Her hand is gentle as she cups my chin. "I like your voice."

Something unlocks inside me.

I release a breath.

She studies me with kind eyes.

I take another breath.

And manage to grind out, "I'm glad."

Her smile is so luminous it could light up the whole restaurant for weeks.

"Thank you," she murmurs, smoothing her knuckles over my jaw before gracing me with a soft kiss.

I fade into that kiss, sinking and drowning in her.

"I'll come with you," she promises.

I grab the end of her braid and tilt her head back. "As my woman?"

Her eyes flare wide at my roughly spoken demand. With a sigh, she whispers, "Yes, plea— I mean, yes. I'll come."

That answer deserves a smirk.

And a fourth round with my fingers...

30

CASSIE

A Case Of You - Joni Mitchell, Ana Moura

WHEN HE TAKES a bite of the Stroganoff I made, one I could easily have poisoned but didn't want to, his groan is beyond satisfying. More so than the dish that's one of my favorites as well as one of my specialties.

Harvey used to tell me that he kept me around because of my cooking, and it's actually something I'd consider to be a talent.

I hate that he taints this too, but Nikolai's genuine enjoyment soothes my unease.

As does the fact that this is a dish I never made for Harvey.

He didn't deserve something so delectable.

I can even remember the time before we married when I almost made it for him, but we had an argument so I prepared risotto instead.

"This is delicious," Nikolai signs.

Happy he's enjoying it, I smile at him as he uses his fork to shovel some onto a spoon that he places against my lips.

Humming my agreement, we savor the meal in silence until I share, "It was my father's favorite dish and it was one of the first my mom taught me how to cook."

His arm slides around my waist because while I might have been allowed out of the house, might have been given access to the kitchen, I still have to sit on his knee at mealtimes. "You don't speak of them."

"You don't speak of yours either," I retort.

"Mine are dead," he dismisses, but the scar on his eye ruches in a quick twitch that tells me he feels more than he's showing.

"My father passed away a long time ago." It's an internal wound that's never healed. "I was a daddy's girl. I think grief led me to make a lot of dumb mistakes I might not have otherwise made."

"The darker the night, the brighter the stars. The deeper the grief, the closer is God."

My brows lift. "Heavy."

"Dostoevsky. True, no?"

"I-I guess."

I press a hand to my heart where the ache of loss is still raw. Warmth starts to thaw the deep chill in my soul when he leans down and bestows a kiss on my knuckles.

I could have expected him to treat my grief dismissively, much as Harvey used to, but Nikolai *isn't* Harvey.

He keeps on proving that mirror reflections aren't wholly accurate.

"It's supposed to hurt," he signs with a heavy sigh.

"Is it?" I ask wistfully. "For so long?"

"Losing love will never be painless. Take the pain and embrace it. Trust me, *solnyshko,* it is better to have that than nothing at all."

He's right.

And it stuns me that the brutish Bratva Pakhan is the first person to ever broach the subject with me so candidly. So *rawly.*

But then, he's more than a brute around me, isn't he?

I've seen that side of him in the flesh after what happened to Pavlivshev, but with me, he's kind. Tender. A man I can believe in because he backs up his words with action.

I *am* safe with him.

"It's funny you should say that," I rasp.

"What do you mean?"

"How it's better to have the pain of losing someone you love than nothing at all."

His brows arch. "I expected you to upend the bowl over my head for that."

My lips twitch because I can see he means it. "I'd never waste Stroganoff."

"Reassuring." A twinkle gleams in his eyes. "Explain."

"Why I'd never waste Stroganoff...?" I snort at his glower. "Hey, that's a part of it."

"Explain," he demands again.

"When Pavlivshev threatened me," I say, feeling him tense beneath me. "I was aware of the woman I used to be around Harvey and I was even *more* aware that I'm not that woman with you."

He blinks.

Then, the spoon scrapes against the dish and it's presented to me.

As I take it into my mouth, I sigh in delight as the rich sauce graces my taste buds and the beef falls apart at the slightest pressure from my teeth.

He watches me eat. "This pleases me." He waits for me to finish then presses a kiss to my chin. "I want this on the 6th."

I don't know why, but that makes me smile. "Is that what you want as your gift?"

Then, he amazes me by rasping in that broken, hoarse, creaky voice of his, "No, that's you."

It takes me a moment to piece together his meaning because I'm so unused to his voice that it always jars me. But I wasn't lying when I told him I liked it. It's loaded with strain, almost as if his larynx is being put through a boot camp workout, but whenever he manages to gift me with words, it's when he's saying something that makes my heart melt.

Something that tips me down a path that proves I've lost my mind.

That's when his words actually register.

'That's you.'

Wait, I'm *his Christmas gift?*

Touched that he said the words as well as meant them, I give him a kiss. It was supposed to be a peck on the lips, a soft brush. Instead, it turns hot. Heavy. His tongue thrusts against mine, stirring a hunger to life that only he has ever created in me, one that only he can assuage.

With a groan, I tumble deeper into his lap, my hands pressing against his chest for support.

For the first time since he gave me a wardrobe, I resent the clothes that separate us.

Then, he pulls back and signs, "Feed me, Cassiopeia. I don't want your gift to go to waste."

This time, I know my smile beams from me.

He means that.

My gift.

Not just a talent, but a present that I made for him.

One that he values.

Even more than sex.

Because he *values* me.

31

NIKOLAI

"NO MEN IN THE STORE?"

"None. All female staff. I checked the payroll."

I grunt.

"God, you're such a caveman," Dmitri chides, but I can sense his amusement.

"You are," Cassiopeia agrees, then she gives a shocked gasp. "God forbid, they might even be into me."

Both of us gape at her.

"Never mind," she snipes. "Do they all want to fuck you?"

Dmitri blinks at her question. "Who, me?"

"No," Cassiopeia grumbles, then she jerks her thumb at me. "Him."

Smugly, I smile at him. She's back to being jealous but mostly, she's grouchy because she seems to think none of the dresses for the gala will fit.

Not that she told me that, but she's easy to read.

"What a pair. I don't think they want to fuck him. They're too scared. Nor do I think they're gay. Do I have to vet for this now?" he complains, making me chuckle which has his eyes widening.

Rolling my own, I grab her hand and help her alight from the town car once we pull up outside the dressmaker's.

Before I settle my fingers at her hip, I tell her, "This is an exclusive dress shop. They'll either design you something new if you want or they'll adjust one of their prêt-a-porter lines."

She tilts her head to the side. "For the New Year's party?"

"Yes."

"What date is it?"

Dmitri snorts. "You haven't missed the new year. Today's the 28th."

"Helpful," she snaps, making me hide another smile. "But we're cutting it close."

Arrogantly, I inform her, "They wouldn't dare anger me, *solnyshko*. If I asked them twenty minutes before the gala, they'd find a way to make it happen."

She sniffs her disapproval.

Dmitri's brows lift but he shoots me a grin—he likes her.

The like is growing.

As we head to the doors, I step closer to her and slide my hand around her hip so that it rests on her belly. With ease, she settles into my slowed step as if this is a dance we've been in for decades, not just weeks.

Today, in preparation for this appointment, I've put her in a halter-top dress that falls to a pleated skirt. It's a little-known designer, one I'd never heard of until I'd personally ordered her wardrobe, but I know Tatiana will treat her with more respect if she's wearing quality.

I will not have Cassiopeia feeling like she's Julia Roberts in *Pretty Woman*.

And yes, I've seen that goddamn movie.

Dmitri can be blamed for that travesty. I truly have spoiled him far too much.

As we step inside the storefront, an attendant moves toward us with a tray of champagne. I shake my head at the sight, tugging Cassiopeia back into me when she makes to take one.

In response, Dmitri surges forward with a bottle of champagne from my cellars.

"Where the hell was he hiding that?" she mutters to herself. "Up his damn ass?"

My lips curve slightly as Dmitri makes arrangements with the confused attendant for us to drink from this bottle only.

Cassiopeia peers at me. "You think theirs might have been poisoned?"

I shrug.

"Better to be safe than sorry?"

I nod.

She hums, and that fucking hum shuttles through my system in a way that makes me wish we'd never left the estate.

Still, this is important—the gala matters.

We have few official gatherings throughout the year, ordinarily on New Year's which, since the Soviet Union era, has become our most important holiday. Sometimes, we switch it up with the May holidays.

We don't paint a symbol on our heads for the FBI for no reason, but New Year's and May holidays are different.

Symbolic.

No reneging on making an appearance—even for me. And I'd prefer to eat glass than attend.

Dmitri sets Igor on 'champagne watch,' while I let Cassiopeia wander around the front room of the store, a flute in hand as she peruses the dresses on display.

My hands settle behind my back as I wait.

And wait.

And wait.

Every minute that passes, my annoyance grows.

Then, Tatiana steps out of her office and her eyes catch mine. Immediately, her mouth rounds in bemusement at my presence, and she storms over to the assistant who flinches at her boss's annoyance.

Even Cassiopeia catches onto Tatiana's hissed words as she turns to watch the assistant be dressed down with a tut.

As angry as I am at being made to wait, I already know this is going to be the first and last time Cassiopeia will come to this store.

Which, to be honest, is annoying seeing as I hold shares in the goddamn place.

But that tut...

It's in defense of the underdog.

No way will she get along with Tatiana.

Sometimes, it's hard to believe that she's a survivor of abuse.

With me, she's outspoken and difficult, unafraid to drench me in lemonade or to state her opinion. The latter being something I wholeheartedly approve of even if it will cost me a cut in the profits of this store.

She *should* know her place—at my side. My queen.

Unaware that she's already lost my patronage, Tatiana obsequiously greets, "Pakhan," as she strides over on stilettos that are as sharp as the knife holstered to my shoulder. "I wasn't made aware that you were visiting today. My sincerest apologies."

Her surgically enhanced face is tight and shiny as she beams a smile at me before gracing my cheeks with kisses I do not want.

Well, I didn't.

Until I see that Cassiopeia's glower has merely deepened.

Satisfaction thrums through me as I enjoy the mutual madness that being together has triggered. Still, I dislodge myself from Tatiana's squid-like embrace with an arched brow as the other woman *knows* I don't appreciate being touched.

The familiarity is perhaps another reason why it's time to terminate my involvement in the business despite it being one of the highest-grossing storefronts in this part of Miami Beach.

Or... hmm.

I wonder if Pavel's wife, Maria, would like to take over.

She loves fashion, after all, and I have a feeling she and Cassiopeia would get along... as much as Maria is capable of getting along with other women, that is.

Unaware I'm making and breaking her role in the business she built from the ground up, Tatiana states, "I also apologize on behalf of my assistant. She's new and doesn't understand the importance of serving her betters."

That last part is hissed and the other woman blanches, her head ducking and shoulders hunching in response to the verbal cut.

"It's our fault," Cassiopeia defends, sliding into my side, her arm coming around my waist in a way I'd permit with no one else.

Never mind another woman.

Tatiana's eyes bug as she watches Cassiopeia settle her hand on my abdomen possessively, mirroring our earlier stance where I held her like this.

The proprietor soon catches herself and demurs, "I'm sure it could never be the Pakhan's fault."

"We asked her to serve us different champagne and Dmitri was flirting with her." She hitches a shoulder. "Hardly her fault when we distracted her."

Tatiana clears her throat. "If you say so, ma'am." She dips her head in a regal salute. "I assume you're here for a gown for the New Year's gala?" At my nod, Tatiana, back on solid ground, takes over, declaring, "Come with me." But I notice that her gaze locks on the way I tangle my fingers with Cassiopeia's before she does so.

Her existence in my life will come as a short, sharp shock for many of my men and their womenfolk who, I know, had hoped I'd find a broodmare among their families.

I doubt Pavlivshev will be the only 'problem' I have to deal with in the upcoming weeks.

As we move into the private room, Cassiopeia follows Tatiana and I shoot Dmitri a look. "When she picks the dresses she'd like to try, escort Tatiana out of the changing area."

He shrugs as he takes a sip of champagne from the flute he snagged. "Fine."

"Make sure there are no cameras in here too."

At that, he nods then sets Semion, Cassiopeia's second guard, to the task.

Knowing that's under control, I make my retreat.

I head over to the changing area, withdraw my phone from my jacket pocket, then take a seat on one of the low armchairs.

With a gimlet stare, I watch the women's interactions as I catch up with business.

> Boris: Rundel is on the move.

Me: He's left the state?

> Boris: The state troopers seem to think he moved into Tennessee.

Me: Is he using Cassiopeia's car?

> Boris: Da. I've given the license to the state troopers. They're tracing it.

Me: Why haven't they stopped him?

> Boris: No cop has come across him yet.

Me: There's an APB out on him?

> Boris: Nyet, Pakhan. Just a BOLO. We don't want to make this official, do we?

That has me gritting my teeth.

I didn't need to be told that, but Rundel's persistent escape from Bratva-shaped justice is starting to piss me off.

> Boris: That's why it's taking more time than we'd like.

Smart man, using *we*.

Me: Likelihood he knows of Cassiopeia's presence in Florida? Why head south instead of north?

> Boris: Have to assume he's just drifting. Plus, there's a heavier Albanian presence in the Carolinas. He'll be avoiding them at all costs.

Boris: It's not as if he'll know the Albanians are individual gangs, and after that turf war last year, EVERYONE knows they made the Carolinas their bitch.

Me: True. Who do we have in Tennessee that'll trace him?

Boris: I'm on it, Pakhan. You can trust me with this. I'll keep you updated.

Me: I'm missing a Brigadier, Boris. Success in this will serve you well.

Boris: I won't let you down, Pakhan. Thank you for the opportunity.

Lips pursed, I prop my cell on the coffee table and start a video call with my Obschak. Pavel got shot a couple months ago; otherwise, I'd have demanded his presence at *Nav* before now.

Pavel's grin is surprisingly cheerful when he connects the call. "Pakhan, I didn't know you cared."

"You look like shit," I sign.

He sniffs. "I almost lost my small intestine. I'm lucky I'm not swimming in shit."

"It's the large intestine that stores feces, not the small."

"Only you'd know that."

"Is it a crime that I read?" I retort, but my lips twitch.

"It's only a crime when you quote Dostivsky at me."

I roll my eyes at the mispronounced name of one of my favorite novelists—Dostoevsky.

But I let it slide.

Pavel is old school. Born on the streets, bred on them, and serves them to this day.

Without me, he'd still be a *boyevik*.

"It's good to see you, old friend," I greet. "Maria didn't let any of us into the ward."

"She's better than an Oskal as a guard dog," he agrees then swivels his cell phone so he can show his hospital room to me. "I'm finally out of the ICU. They only just let me have a cell phone."

"I know. Igor told me. Why do you think I'm calling?" I half mock, but my gaze is picking him apart.

It was a closer call than I want to admit, and despite the shooting taking place a while ago now, he still looks like death.

"Any news on the B4K pushers who did this?"

"Depends on the kind of news you're talking about?"

"Are they alligator food yet?"

His deadpan tone has me hiding a grin. "Not yet. But we have options…"

"We do?"

I nod.

"What are they?" he inquires, sitting up in his bed with a grimace of pain.

"According to my intel—"

"Which is never wrong," he interrupts.

I grace him with another nod. "Exactly."

"Heard about the fire at their warehouse, by the way."

My lips quirk. "You're welcome."

He rubs his hands together. "Three million gone, just like that."

"They're suffering."

"Good. Igor told me the Colombians called in payment early, too. You didn't have anything to do with that either, I assume?"

"Not a damn thing," I mock. "B4K is paying for their actions, but as for the shooters themselves… there's going to be an armed robbery in the Miami Beach branch of Fetch." Peering out the window, I stare at the bank. "It's due to take place within the next hour." And I'll have a front-row seat.

Pavel whistles. "You cut that down to the wire."

"I had plans in place, but now you get to direct things if you want."

It's the least I can do after the disaster that was his shooting. I have a private hospital room at *Nav* but that was no use to Pavel when his shooting took place over in West Park—he had to go to a hospital instead and as a result, Maria had to deal with the cops.

I set my lawyers on the job, but that doesn't diminish the trauma she had to go through.

He snorts then cuts a glance to his left where, I'm assuming, his wife is.

He isn't wrong about Maria having a 'feral' presence worthy of an Oskal.

If I did give her this store, I wonder, would she terrify the clients?

Tone contemplative, Pavel scratches his chin as he inquires, "The shooters are the armed robbers?"

"According to my intel, yes. Not only do they need the cash for the Colombians, *but* Linton is putting their necks on the line as this is their fault."

Linton is the head of B4K.

"It wasn't a sanctioned shooting, then."

"Apparently not." I study him. "What were you doing on their turf anyway?"

He grimaces. Flicks a look at Maria. "I don't remember."

My brow lifts as I sign, "Another woman?"

"That night's fuzzy," is all he says, but his eyes tell me another story.

If he did have a whore on the side, his presence across town would make sense.

Still, if Maria finds out he's cheating, I wouldn't be worrying about my small intestine, just my balls.

She's fiery as hell, beautiful as well as twenty years younger than Pavel... It's not my place to judge my men's decisions when it comes to their personal lives, but he's a dumb fuck for sleeping around on her.

"So, my options?" Pavel queries, unaware of my train of thought.

"We let the robbery go down and facilitate their arrest."

"Or?"

"We let the robbery go down and have cops on our books kill them in jail."

"Or?"

"We let them flee, kill them ourselves, then steal their takings."

Again, he whistles. "I like these options. This your idea of grapes?"

I smirk. "Better than grapes, no?"

"I can't disagree," he concurs, but his gaze turns distant. "Those B4K punks are getting too big for their britches."

"I know. But they're quieter since the fire."

"Happened to overhear that you started a war with the Albanians too," he inserts smoothly. "You've been busy since I got shot."

"You overheard incorrectly. I didn't start shit with them. I triggered a revolution in their ranks."

A snicker escapes him. "It's all in the technicalities with you, Niko."

I hitch a shoulder. "You know it. So, come on. Time to make a decision. We're running out of time to change my plans."

"What would you have done if I didn't answer the phone?"

"Got their asses arrested."

"Why?"

"Because armed robbery will get them twenty-five-plus years in the clink."

"Yeah, it's getting to be you serve less fucking time for murder and more for theft," he grumbles.

"Capitalism at its finest, my friend."

His eyes gleam. "Do I get a cut of their takings if we steal it from them?"

"Less running costs and six percent, it's all yours," I demur, amused by his greed.

That's Pavel for you.

He's the first to give you the shirt off his back, but the first to hold out his hand for a loan when he loses at the tracks.

Again, he whistles. "Fuck letting them rot in a cell. Just let them goddamn die and I'll buy that new Lambo I've had my eyes on."

"You and your cars," I chide. "You certain that's the route you want to take?"

"I am. Make it hurt, *da*?"

"As much as they hurt you, Pavel," I agree.

He graces me with a mock-salute. "It's shit like this that makes you great to work for, Nikolai."

"I'm a good boss. What can I say?"

His grin is weaker than I'd prefer, but it's a relief to see. "I've got another month, maybe two in here, Pakhan."

"I know, Pavel. You are safe. I made sure of it."

He huffs. "Not worried about my safety. Not in here."

"Then what's the problem?"

"Men will be after my position."

"Men?" I scoff. "What makes you think I'd listen?"

"I know for a fact Pavlivshev is interested—"

My brows furrow, not only at his concern but that the news of Pavlivshev's death hasn't made the rounds yet. I'd have thought Igor would have shared that update with him too.

"Pavel," I console eventually, "my inner council consists of men I grew up with. Did Pavlivshev help me when I was on the streets?"

The older man shakes his head. "*Nyet*, Nikolai."

"Your job is secure. Just worry about keeping your ass alive."

"Myata says she's close to getting your ring on her finger."

My brows lift at Maria's catty tone. Pavel, though grimacing, doesn't have much choice about handing over his cell when his wife snatches it from him. "Please tell me that you have better taste than to marry that bitch, Nikolai?"

"Is this what happens behind my back? The women gossip about who I'll marry?"

"It should be impossible how naive you are, but it's not." She squints at me. "You're crazy if you don't think that's all the ovaries talk about."

"Including you," Pavel teases his wife.

"Hey, it's fascinating what they make up about him. You can't blame me for watching that train wreck as it happens."

"What do they make up about me?"

"Oh, things about your beautiful eyes. They wonder if you'll talk to them in bed. Polina told them that you only talk to the people who matter to you. Of course, *she* heard your voice. According to her, you have the rumble of a tiger."

Pavel starts cackling, then he immediately groans and clutches at his abdomen. "Don't make me laugh! Please, God!"

I scowl at them both. "A tiger?" Then, my scowl only darkens as I ask, "Who's Polina?"

A gleam appears in my Obschak's wife's eyes. "Thank you for that ammunition, Niko. I'll enjoy telling her that she's so unforgettable."

"Stop shit stirring," Pavel sputters, still holding his torso.

"But it's so much fun," she mocks, drawing the cell phone with her as she pops a kiss on his cheek. "And I deserve to have fun after this past month or so."

I grimace—she isn't wrong. "We're working on securing you justice, Maria."

"I heard. Apparently, I have a new Lamborghini in my future." She tuts. "My husband is a big kid."

"Hey!" the big kid argues.

With a huff, I inform them, "Anyway, Pavlivshev's dead. So Myata can—"

A flurry of movement draws my attention away from their reaction to my news to the corner where Cassiopeia appears to be seconds away from tearing Tatiana's hair out over a dress.

I click my fingers at Dmitri, who's watching the spat unfold from a safe distance.

"Liquid courage," he mocks, downing his champagne before he strolls toward the catfight-in-the-making. "Tatiana, I think it's unwise to piss off the Pakhan's woman."

Tatiana flashes me a look and sees that I'm watching her. Her throat bobs but she releases her hold on the gown she's clutching.

Cassiopeia, bright red and flushed with anger, storms over to my side. Beneath the anger, however, I can see the sparkle of tears in her eyes.

"I have to go," I sign to my old friends without waiting for a reply from them, then I shoot off a text to Igor.

Me: Set plan three into motion.

As I surge to my feet, he sends:

Igor: Got it, Pakhan.

But my interest in the situation with B4K has faded.

Swiftly cutting off Cassiopeia's attempts to evade me, I snag a hold of her, not letting go when she struggles and tries to break free, then chuck her under the chin to gain eye contact with her.

"I don't want to talk about it," she declares, but that she came to me for protection says everything.

I cast a glare at Tatiana, whose mouth puckers like she's swallowed a lemon, but she stares at the floor rather than at me.

My muteness has long since ceased being an issue for me. It is what it is and I deal with it. My men deal with it, too, or lose their hands for not learning sign language. They know it's not a weakness and it's not something they exploit.

But right now, the way my throat freezes sends a wash of anger through me.

My woman is upset and I can't fucking ask her what that bitch said to distress her.

Because I can't speak, because the words won't come, I sigh and, leaning down, press a soft kiss to her lips.

It's not good enough, but I hope it shows her what I feel.

When I pull back, she peers at me from under her lashes. That's when she gives me hope because the tender kiss appears to unravel her enough for Cassiopeia to mutter, "She said I was too fat for any of the dresses and that she didn't have enough time to get them adapted to my size. She also recommended a diet plan that's *just perfect, darling* for obese women."

Nostrils flaring, I snap my gaze to Tatiana's and click my fingers at her. Not that she has much of a choice—Dmitri grabs her arm and hauls her toward me.

A quick glance at my face has her mumbling, "You can't kill her too." But it's her soft sniffle that seals Tatiana's fate more than anything else ever could. "I don't need you to kill everyone who's mean to me, Nikolai."

The growl that rumbles from me has a soft flush dancing over her cheeks—that's better than the sorrow from mere seconds ago.

And like that, my voice unlocks. "Your assistance will no longer be needed, Tatiana."

Shock flashes in her eyes at the fact I'm speaking, but she purses her lips. "I'll leave you with the dresses I think could work—"

"No. You misunderstand. Clear out your things. You're no longer welcome in this establishment."

She gapes at me then cries, "It's *my* store."

"Nikolai owns sixty-five percent of it," Dmitri corrects, taking over as my mouthpiece much as he always does. His tone turns mocking. "That means he owns more than you."

"But it's mine!" she cries, her face pinching and turning white. "You can't kick me out of my own business!"

"Just. Watch. Me," I growl. "Escort her outside, Dmitri."

As Tatiana blusters and curses at me, Dmitri drags her from the changing area, leaving me with Cassiopeia.

Just before the doors close, he looks back at me and I grace him with a single nod.

"You spoke."

Her soft whisper has my attention returning to her.

When I don't answer, she chides, "Don't freeze up now." Her hand settles on my chest, the tips digging in slightly.

Warmth permeates from the connection, spreading through my limbs, and I bask in her sunlight. In her attention. In the soft cast of her eyes. In the way she presses close.

In her trust.

"You are perfect." It's all I can think to say and color blossoms in her cheeks. "She had no right," I snipe, my voice hoarse and ugly, "to tell you otherwise."

"I've always had a weight problem," she mutters.

"I see no problem," I sign, falling back on ASL.

Her gaze trips off my hands, then she leans on her tiptoes to kiss my cheek. "Would you like to see her suggestions?"

Grateful for the reprieve, I nod, aware of how much courage she has and how much faith she's showing in me by making that offer.

Honored, I take a seat in the armchair, settling in for what I assume will take a while, then I see the 'options' Tatiana gave my *solnyshko*.

Two.

Both are more appropriate for a woman in her seventies than a beautiful creature like Cassiopeia.

As she tries the first on, I frown at the frumpy style that covers every inch of her. I'm a possessive motherfucker—I admit it—but Jesus Christ, I've seen nuns show more skin than this horrific gown bares.

"Why the hell does she have that in stock?"

She sniffs. "For pregnant women."

I frown in bewilderment, but I don't have to wait long to see the next monstrosity.

That's all it takes for me to surge to my feet and to move around the dresses that are on the racks as well as on mannequins.

I find three, each one with a soft flow that I know will suit her. She isn't made for those clinging gowns, the ones that are like bandages, but gentler styles. Not because of her curves—which are glorious—but because of her nature.

When she returns to the changing area, her shoulders hunched with embarrassment, I'm waiting for her.

I shove the three gowns at her. "Try these on," I rasp. Her courage deserves an attempt at speech.

She picks them up, studies each one, then she nods.

I can tell she doesn't want to though.

The first one doesn't suit her—we both know it. It gapes at the back where she can't fasten it. The second one does, but it's not special enough for the gala. Its golden tone is pretty but the lines are more semiformal than formal. It's perfect for her though, and the sparkle in her eyes says she knows it.

"We'll take this one home and get it fitted for you," I sign and smile at her happy nod.

It's the last one that's perfect.

It drapes off her shoulder in a swirl of fabric that swags and swathes on her, clinging to her tits, smoothing over her belly, flowing along the lines of her hips and legs.

She looks like a goddess.

"It's a toga," she chuckles softly as she turns on her heel when I move my hand in a circle.

"I suppose it is. Maybe that's why it suits you," I tease her. "We can have this fitted for you if you like it?"

She nods. "It's beautiful."

"*You* are beautiful," I growl.

That gorgeous blush makes another appearance. "Thank you."

"I had nothing to do with it," I sign with a smile as I get to my feet and approach her. Fingers trailing over the single strap, I trace the line of her décolletage. "I have the perfect necklace for this."

She blinks up at me, all innocence and temptation in one fell swoop. "You do?"

I nod.

Pressing a kiss to her lips, I dance my mouth along her jawline and, in her ear, whisper, "You are a goddess."

Her chuckle is shy. "Hush."

I nip her earlobe. "Say it."

Not unsurprisingly, she doesn't obey, but she goes one better by nuzzling her nose against me in a tender display of affection.

Fuck, she can't know what that does to me when I've been deprived of anything tender my whole life.

It's no wonder my craving for her is only increasing with time.

She's about to speak when an alarm sounds in the distance—the armed robbery, no doubt. Uninterested in that and knowing Igor has set Pavel's choice in motion, I bring her back to the moment by nipping her earlobe again.

In a soft, breathy whisper, she concedes, "I'm a goddess."

"*My* goddess," I amend, pleased by her concession.

She swallows—I can hear it. I half expect to have to force those words from her via an orgasm, but, cheeks a vicious pink, and with words that are more of a croak than anything else, she gives me the greatest gift in the world: "*Your* goddess."

32

CASSIE

Gold - Kiiara

"OH, FUCK," I cry as I rub my clit while he jacks off over me.

His eyes gleam like fiery coals as he stares at me, one hand on his shaft, the other on his balls.

I thought he'd fuck me after we showered, but Niko, I'm learning, always does things the hard way.

Instead, we're fully dressed on the ride to wherever this gala is being held, and now is apparently the perfect time for him to soak me in his cum.

He finds release faster than I do, the visual taking him under swiftly. But when his seed drenches my pussy, my fingers slip and slide with him, and all of a sudden, I'm *there*.

As I cry out with the sheer delicious agony of it, he moves closer to me.

We'd been seated along the length of the limo, on the bench seats directly opposite one another, but he hauls me onto his lap as he touches me under my skirt.

Not to entice, just to pet.

I'd burrow my face in his throat, but I'm already worried about the wet spot, never mind the mess I'd make of my makeup, so instead, I just tilt my head back against his shoulder and let him play.

I'm overheated and tired, and the night's event hasn't even commenced yet.

We'd argued earlier because I'd learned I'll have four guards following me around the house as of today. Not just Igor and Semion, faces I'd adapted to recently, but two other guys—Victor and Sergei—as well.

Calling it an argument was, I'll admit, a bit of a stretch.

I'd shouted at him, and he'd blinked at me.

I can't decide if he's selectively mute or if, in moments of passion or where he feels deeply, that's when he can talk.

Either way, he decided not to today. He just stood there, watching me as I told him he was insane when, in truth, I should have expected it.

It doesn't take a genius to figure out that my presence at tonight's gala is a claiming.

Which means the danger I'm in is exacerbated greatly—not just from Harvey and the Albanians but his enemies too.

Still, understanding the necessity is one thing. Him just having me shadowed by four men without warning me is another.

Annoyed enough to be drawn from my orgasm-induced good mood, I mutter, "You're such a jerk."

"A jerk you trust," he rumbles in my ear, evidently not insulted.

That croak—it shouldn't be hot.

It *shouldn't*.

But it is.

Seeing as I literally let the man get away with murder, I press a kiss on his cheek. "So long as you know you're a jerk, I'll consider that today's win."

His hum tells me he'll let me think whatever I want—I'll still have four guards tomorrow.

"Thank you for the necklace."

"Only fitting for you... *and*," he tacks on begrudgingly, "that dress."

He might be an asshole, but he's crazy good for my confidence.

The pearls are raw, not the smooth beads that I'm accustomed to. These are free-form. Craggy. But they gleam with a multitude of colors. Some are gray, others champagne, a few pink. Either way, each one is separated by a diamond.

I don't even want to know what this necklace cost. I know it's exquisite and he just told me as well as showed me that he thinks *I'm* more beautiful than it is.

"The gala is more than simply about New Year's, isn't it?"

He hitches a disinterested shoulder. "It's the most important event in the calendar year, you know that."

I did. My father hadn't really put much stock in Christmas, be it the American one or the Russian. Now, on New Year's, he'd pull out all the stops. We'd feasted like kings and Mom had been stuck in the kitchen for days in the build-up to it because the holiday season for Russians lasts over a week.

"Yes, but it's more than about New Year's," I press.

"What do you want me to say, Cassiopeia?"

"Why do you always call me that?"

"Because it's your name."

"Yes, but people call me Cassie." I snicker. "Of course, you're *not* people..."

His chuckle is raw and rough, unused. "You're Cassiopeia. It's the name of a queen—"

"A vain queen. When I found out what it meant, I was insulted."

"It's magnificent. Just like you."

My lips twist into a shy smile. "I'd never have imagined it but you're quite the charmer when you want to be, aren't you?"

"Hardly," he derides. "You're right about tonight. People will see you on my arm and it will tell them what you are—"

"Yours?" I interrupt with an arched brow.

His expression isn't blank for once. It's laced with satisfaction. "Exactly." I roll my eyes as he tugs on my necklace. "Dressed as befits a queen too."

"You said I'd be in more danger once people knew I was yours," I mutter, surprised that it's not overly difficult to get those words out.

I've spent years fighting Harvey's possessive grip on me, but Niko's doesn't feel like a cage.

Not only that but I'm different around him—I like *me* when I'm with Niko.

Thankfully unaware of my thoughts as he's already too smug for his own good, he shrugs. "You saw how Pavlivshev reacted. As well as Tatiana."

Speaking of...

"Will Pavlivshev's daughter attend?"

A gleam appears in his eyes. "Very likely."

"Great," I huff.

"You should remember that you are mine, Cassiopeia."

His statement has me studying him. "Is tonight a test?"

He shakes his head. "Not at all."

"Then why did you say that?"

"No reason."

Why don't I believe him?

We arrive at a fancy hotel before I can pepper him with more questions. The entire building glitters like a candle factory as we alight from the limo beneath a canopy that I can tell was for this event only as it stretches along the driveway, diminishing the visibility of the reception.

Either that's because he doesn't want the police to see who gets out of their cars or enemies.

With Niko, it's fifty-fifty.

When we're in the lobby that'd make Catherine the Great sob with delight, all Imperial Russia antiques and expensive classical portraiture, a manager surges from out of nowhere, hands outstretched to take Nikolai's.

Meanwhile, he's babbling away in rapid Russian. Whether he's trying to impress Niko or just kiss ass, I'm unsure.

As always, Niko makes a statue look emotive.

The manager takes us down a grand hallway where there's a massive staircase. A part of me wonders if this hotel was a stately home transplanted from the motherland and rebuilt here because it's totally unfitting for Miami, but who am I to judge?

We walk up the stairs and the manager bows in front of us before heading over to a man standing at a double-door entranceway.

Our names are called out for everyone to hear, and that's when we pass through those doors and find ourselves in a massive ballroom.

There are over a thousand people here, minimum, and each of them has their eyes on us.

When we step inside, the chatter stops, and only the soft music from the orchestra plays in the background.

I'm not sure whether this is the most embarrassing moment of my life or the most empowering.

Either way, I'm glad Niko's arm is supportively tucked around my back as he takes us toward the staircase that'll lead into the ballroom itself.

Once we're there, the crowd parts like magic and Nikolai guides us through the man-made passageway toward a seat that, I swear to God, is a freakin' throne.

And he seats me at his side.

Then seats himself.

While everyone's eyes are on me.

Then, there's organized chaos in the procession of guests who approach us.

Dmitri is first, even though I saw him ninety minutes ago at the estate. He winks at me as he bows over my hand and kisses the back of it.

Nikolai growls, which makes Dmitri shoot me a quick grin before he fades away. Then, there's a woman. She's beautiful. All black hair and stunning green eyes. She's younger than me by a few years, and she carries herself with a grace that I could only dream of emulating.

"Thank you for coming tonight, Maria," Nikolai signs. "How's Pavel?"

I've recently learned that Pavel is his third-in-command and he was shot before I found myself a part of this world.

God, how has it only been a month since I've known this man?

"He's better," Maria replies with a tight smile that doesn't hit her eyes. "Much better. And he's thankful for the Lamborghini."

"No less than he deserves," Niko signs.

Maria studies me, her gaze drifting over my dress and the pearls around my neck. I half-expect her to be a bitch and for her to shoot me a death stare like the hundreds of other women attending this gala, but if anything, I can sense... approval.

She leans over, presses a kiss to my cheek, and murmurs, "If you hurt him, I'll kill you."

I blink. "If you hurt me, he'll kill you."

That has her winking. "At least he'll make it fast."

And with that, she drifts away.

Niko arches a brow at me, but I merely smile and prepare myself for the audience we're about to hold.

I'm not entirely sure how this is my life, how men are kissing the backs of my knuckles and how women are literally curtsying at Niko as if he's the last tsar and trying to hide their bemusement and their jealousy when they're forced to greet me afterward.

It'd make more sense for this production to be for a movie or some-thing, but nope.

It's legit.

When a woman, eyes glittering with fire, approaches, Dmitri suddenly appears from wherever he tucked tail and ran to.

Then, I hear him utter her name as he tugs on her arm. "Myata."

The daughter.

What continues is a flood of Russian that I can't understand but each word packs a punch because her already-erect spine turns even straighter.

She nods at him, though, without looking at him, and drifts forward.

You'd think that her anger would be aimed at Nikolai, but nope, she clearly has no sense because it's all aimed at me.

Every last ounce of it.

Heaving a sigh, I brace myself for impact because I don't think Dmitri's words have done anything other than bake her anger to soufflé-esque proportions.

But she stuns me by curtsying.

Nikolai signs, "I didn't think you'd be in attendance tonight, Myata. Your father was recently buried, wasn't he?"

Shocked that he's prodding her, I cut him a look and, for the first time, spy something other than apathy in his gaze.

She replies in Russian.

Nikolai signs, "Don't be rude, Myata. Speak English."

Nostrils flaring, she snaps, "He was, Pakhan, *da*."

"I'm sorry that I was too busy to attend." He tilts his head to the side. "I'm sure you can understand why I couldn't be there. What with the rumor mill floating around our supposed engagement." His eyes narrow into slits. "I assume that was your doing?"

He rests an elbow on his armrest, the one that's beside mine, and holds out his hand, straight up.

It's too blatant a move for me to fail to understand his intentions.

Gingerly, I mimic him and slide mine against his palm.

Almost immediately, the entire room releases a gasp because it puts our connection on full display.

I can almost feel the women looking for an engagement ring on my finger, but no dice.

Still, it's a power play that has Myata flushing with embarrassment. "I apologize, Pakhan."

Nikolai doesn't make a move to dislodge our connection, nor does he accept her apology.

Her flush deepens but she fades into the crowd after curtsying one final time.

With a huff, I mutter to him, "You just made that worse."

"And her lies made me kill a strong Brigadier, *solnyshko*. She is the reason behind her father's death. No one else.

"You are *mine*. Anyone who tries to hurt you will suffer a similar fate."

The room is still reeling from the aftermath of that 'confrontation,' and that's why everyone hears his words.

His voice is low, a rasp more than anything. It's still broken, the timbre agitated with lack of use.

But because he speaks so little, the crowd at the front hears as if he used a megaphone. His message whispers throughout the assembly like a game of telephone, and everyone, in a wave, turns their back on Myata.

It's like something from *Pride and Prejudice*, but it's fucking cool —I can't deny that.

She stands there, in the middle of the crowd, twisting around in a circle as people turn away from her. She calls out a name, a friend, perhaps? But no one breaks ranks.

No. One.

When she runs sobbing from the room, I bite my lip. "Did you *have* to do that?"

He untangles his fingers from mine, making me immediately miss his comforting warmth as he signs, "This is the first day of the rest of your life in this world, Cassiopeia. The lines have been laid and the laws have been set. It is better this way."

His nod is decisive.

I just can't help but think he made an enemy…

For us both.

33

CASSIE

"HOW ARE YOU, CASSIOPEIA?"

My brows lift at the question. "I'm fine, Dmitri. How are you?"

He shakes his head as he spins me in a circle. "I don't mean that."

"You don't mean, what? You don't care how I am?"

He squints at me. "Why haven't you run?"

His words make me flush with discomfort.

"I didn't realize a dance would come with a critique on correct hostage comportment," I snipe.

"Is this how you keep him on his toes?"

I don't even bother to withhold my snort. "Me? Keep Niko on *his* toes? *Ha.*"

"No, you do. You might not think you do, but trust me, he's..."

"Nikolai. An adjective as well as a noun that belongs in the dictionary." My lips twist. "I mean, all this is a lot but... enough to run away? To dive headfirst into danger?" *To leave the man who reveres me behind?* "No."

"He acts differently around you."

"I should hope so," I say lightly as he guides me around the dance floor. "Or I'd get jealous about the other women he's taken captive over the years."

Dmitri stops. When we brake to a halt, I drag him into moving, but he mutters, "He hasn't done this before."

"Done what? Held a woman captive?" His brow furrows at my surprisingly light tone, enough that my cheeks flush. "I was joking. Bad joke, apparently."

"You see, that's what doesn't make sense to me. How you *can* joke about this."

"Would you prefer for me to cry?"

Even if he did, I don't think I could.

As that strange thought whispers through my mind, he assures me, "I mean, I'd understand if you did."

"I don't need to cry." It's the truth. And it's also the truth that I'm glad I'm Nikolai's first captive.

Man, that's insane.

I'm insane.

Perhaps there's something in the water at *Nav*—

"I love my father."

I blink at his assertion. "I can tell."

"I hope so. He's the reason I'm still alive. He's the reason I am where I am. He's the reason that I'm not insane."

Maybe the water's safe, then?

Or maybe everyone has different definitions of insanity?

Something he confirms by mumbling, "I fed Tatiana to Vasily because she hurt you, Cassiopeia. *He insisted.* For *you.*"

"I didn't ask him to," I argue, but deep in my belly, unease twists and morphs.

It should turn to fear.

Disgust.

Horror.

Instead, I remember how she fucking denigrated me. How she made me feel like I was less of a human because I wasn't a size zero. How she told me she knew of a great diet for 'obese' women like me.

Did she deserve to die for being a rude and mean fat-shamer?

No.

But she wasn't just rude and mean to *me*, nobody Cassie Rundel, was she?

She disrespected the woman Nikolai has claimed as *his*.

That was her mistake.

I'm not Cassie Rundel anymore. Not in Nikolai's eyes, and his are the ones that count in this crazy society he's in charge of.

And *that* is empowering.

"You didn't need to ask him to deal with her," he states, breaking me free from the chokehold of my thoughts before repeating, "I love him."

Because his voice is impassioned, I gently squeeze his arm. "I understand."

"No. You don't. You should ask him sometime about what happened after he left the orphanage with Misha and Maxim." He sucks in a breath. "He might be the leader here, but he was back then too. Nikolai isn't your average man."

"You're not telling me anything new," I counter.

Not that he's to know I just found a logical reason for the murder of a *dressmaker* because of my position in Niko's life...

Having worked in retail, I know it sucks. But working in retail with the Bratva for a boss?

Literal.

Hell.

On.

Earth.

"People think because he's a mute and is capable of... well, what he's capable of, that he's some kind of feral beast," Dmitri admits, his tone turning earnest. "I used to hear the men talking about him before he became their leader.

"They just wrote me off as a kid of some *boyevik* so they didn't watch their words around me and he impressed them then, but they used to think he was weird." His frown is perturbed. "I've never..." In a rush, he blurts, "The only time I've ever thought that was when he locked you up in his room."

"He's let me out since," I point out, finding myself in the disturbing position of defending my captor.

Okay, I'm as mind blown as any twenty-first-century woman.

He squeezes my waist where he's holding me. "If you need to get away, I *will* help you. He's not himself with you. If I need to protect both of you, I will. Do you understand me?"

It takes me a second to realize exactly what he's offering…

On the surface, it's freedom.

But, it's more than that.

He'd potentially damage his relationship with the man he considers his father and he'd hurt Nikolai in the process… to protect *me*.

To safeguard me from Nikolai.

Why would he do that? Why would he make such an offer to someone he doesn't even know?

Studying him, sensing his genuine earnestness, instead of hitting him with a million questions, I rasp, "I don't think I've ever heard a kinder offer, Dmitri. Thank you."

He blinks. "It's not about being kind. It's about doing the right thing. Nikolai's mother was abused by his father. My own wasn't much better off. If he's hurting you—"

I shake my head. "He isn't." When he looks concerned for my sanity, I quickly reassure him, "He's definitely strange. I won't lie about that." Then, a smile dances on my lips as I think about the day at the dress store. "But Nikolai has a way of making me feel special."

His dubious stare remains in full force. "He doesn't frighten you?"

Because I can tell the answer matters to him, I shrug. "Maybe at first, he did. But not now."

"Why not?"

My mouth works as I try to figure out how to reply but it's not easy. Quite fitting seeing as nothing about Nikolai is that.

I settle on: "I'm not sure." When his expression turns impatient, I pull a face. "I guess I like who I am around him."

"And who's that?"

"Just a woman. A woman who isn't afraid all the time. He doesn't make me cower. He doesn't make me feel like I'm a victim. When he looks at me, he just sees…" Cheeks pink, I clear my throat. "His *solnyshko*. I like that. I-I guess I can feel that."

"What? What do you feel?" he demands, his tone urgent—he *needs* to understand. My response matters to him.

"Like I'm his sun." I breathe the words, feeling them in my soul. "Like he pivots around me." *There.* The truth. Nuts but that's my perception of my situation with Dmitri's father. "For a woman who dealt with the opposite for over a decade, that's very empowering."

"You're sure?"

I know I'm probably out of my mind for not snatching at the chance to escape with both hands, but as he turns me about the ballroom, my gaze snags on Nikolai's.

He's not dancing with anyone, and I get the feeling he won't all night. I'm amazed he let Dmitri partner with me, to be honest, though I imagine his son is the only one who'll be given permission to do so.

As the party carries on, and Dmitri's one dance turns into two, Niko stays there, sitting on his throne, watching me. Men talk around him, to him, and his hands work as he signs, but his focus is on me.

Only me.

None of the beautiful women in the room.

No one else.

And *that* is exhilarating.

There are women who could be models attending tonight. They're pristine, *perfect.* Everything I'm not.

But the Cassiopeia in his eyes transcends *them.*

How couldn't I find that addictive?

I smile at him. Long, slow, deep. His brows lift, but I can see the fire banked in them.

A fire that burns for me.

And deep down, right in my core, a core that's coated in his cum, I feel his claim and know that I haven't wanted anything or anyone this badly in my entire life.

As Dmitri turns me again in a spin, I murmur, "I'll never forget the kindness you just showed me, Dmitri."

I can tell he's relieved that I haven't taken him up on the offer. "I love him, but that doesn't mean I think he's perfect."

"Isn't that exactly what love is?" At his frown, I continue, "Loving someone despite them being *im*perfect?"

Though he keeps dancing, he grows oddly still, but then he nods. "You might be right."

I hum.

"I really am surprised you've never tried to run away."

"Farthest I got was the bedroom door at the beginning." I hitch a shoulder. "Now, I just..." My words wane because it's too embarrassing to finish that sentence.

Like being where I am.

That's not PC enough for this world.

"You've settled?"

His gruff words have me shaking my head. "No. He drives me crazy most days, but I've never felt more like myself than when I'm with him." I lick my lips. "Every night, he puts his knife either beneath his pillow or in the vanity dresser in the bedroom. I could have stabbed him by now."

For the first time, I accept that I'm capable of that.

More of Niko's bad influence...

"But you haven't. Or have you? And Grigoriy is keeping things from me?"

"I haven't. I don't need to."

His lips purse, but a few moments later, he drawls, "He almost gave the hotel manager a heart attack for you, did you know that?"

That has me blinking. "What?"

"There's only ever been one throne," he rumbles. "We needed a second one. Fast."

I grin a little. "I knew it was a throne. These people act like he's a tsar or something."

He shrugs. "To us, he is. There is no higher power in our world than him and the three leaders back in Russia."

My gaze darts to his. "Not the US president?"

Dmitri snorts. "No. Not even the Russian one."

My hands tighten on his shoulders. "Yet you'd risk angering him for me?"

He tips his chin up. "That's what family's for, isn't it?"

That he considers me family is more shocking than anything he's already said. Taken aback, I grace him with a slow nod.

Unsure of what to say, however, I try to keep my voice light as I tease, "Now, I'd return me to your father if I were you. He looks like he's going to stampede through the crowd to get to me."

"And that doesn't bother you?"

"There's something special about being in control and having no control," I muse out loud.

"Special? Or crazy?"

"Maybe it's both."

"Maybe *that's* love."

His words have my heart stuttering in my chest.

I don't answer.

I can't.

It's too soon for that.

Right?

Yeah, it is.

Far too soon.

Especially in our situation.

Then, he makes me snort by grinning at me, back to the carefree Dmitri I've come to know, and murmuring, "Come along, *stepmother*. We can't keep Papa waiting."

34

CASSIE

I'VE READ a lot of romances in my life.

Before I married Harvey, I devoured them. During our marriage, however, it was too depressing to dive into a story that contrasted so greatly with my own.

I *knew* what I had with him was toxic, but reading romance and watching Hallmark movies made it so glaringly obvious that it was as if mustard gas drifted into being around my head whenever I was dumb enough to torment myself with the potential of a 'happily ever after.'

For that reason, I know that it's a classic 'other woman' move to stake out the restroom.

The heroine's always taken aback.

The other woman is always a bitch.

The hero either plays down the cutting remarks that are made or swoops in to defend his heroine's honor.

In my case, I know exactly what would happen—Niko would definitely swoop in, but I don't think defending my honor would be his endgame.

Not after seeing him snap one Pavlivshev's neck.

So, when I walk into the restroom, Igor hovering outside like an oversized guard dog, I'm prepared.

But that preparation is ultimately unnecessary.

Here I was, revving myself up for the big showdown, only to find that the restroom is empty.

Until it isn't.

After I use the facilities, there she is, hovering in front of the vanity.

I didn't hear the outer door, only the creaking hinges of one of the stalls, so I know Igor didn't let her in.

She must have been waiting in here for me.

Fun.

"If you lay a hand on me," I warn her, studying my reflection in the gaudy, gilt mirror that would be more comfortable in a palace in France than Miami Beach, "you'll be sharing a grave with your father by the end of the week."

The confidence in my voice is astounding.

Not just because I have complete faith in Nikolai's insanity but because I'm talking about murder here.

Murder.

"He'll tire of you," Myata warns, smoothing some lotion onto her scarlet-tipped hands. "He tires of us all."

"I'm sure he does. The difference is if he tires of me, I won't make a fool of myself and get my father killed along the way by telling lies about a man everyone fears." I turn to stare at her, no longer content with reading her expression from the reflection in the vanity mirror. "I mean, *really*, Myata? You just did the entire female population a disservice with the dumbest move ever.

"How did you expect him to react? Did you think he'd be red-cheeked and hustled down the aisle because your father huffed and puffed and stuck a shotgun up his ass?" I snort at her blush and shake my head, knowing there'll be no sensible answers coming from her. "Now that you've uttered your dire prediction, are we done here?"

She sniffs at me. The pretty curve of her mouth is upturned into a sneer as she spits, "What the fuck does he see in you anyway? You're a fat bitch. You're old. What use are you to him? Can you even have children when you're as ancient as you?"

The sniped words should sting but they don't.

I smile as I remember the intensity on Niko's face when he pumped cum all over my pussy... Who knew our cum kink would be great for my self-esteem?

"I'm not too old, too fat, or too much of a bitch for the man in question," is all I say. "I think you need to grow up, Myata. What are you? Twenty?"

Her sneer deepens. "I'm nineteen."

That has me screwing up my face too. "Dear God, why would you want to be with a man as old as him anyway?"

I mean, Nikolai is gorgeous but he's in his forties. Why would a baby want to be with him? Hell, with a body and face like hers, I'd have targeted Dmitri at her age.

Then, any minute amount of sympathy I might have had for her disintegrates to dust.

"Power," she retorts. "Position. You're taking advantage of both right now, aren't you?"

"I suppose I am, but I'm not a child. Honey, you can't even drink legally—"

That reminder is too much of an insult for Myata—her final straw.

Her hand lifts and begins to soar, but my defense classes weren't totally useless. I grab her wrist before it can connect with my cheek and I twist her arm behind her back. It's a smooth, rolling motion that feels good to enact.

Now, with her arm at an uncomfortable angle, her hand pinned between her shoulder blades, I haul her against me while I snag the other by her thumb.

Dragging it backward until she's crying out in pain, I rasp in her ear, "You're a *kid*. A little girl. You might think you want the big, bad Bratva Pakhan for a husband, but you just lost your father because of your own foolishness. You were just cast out from the only world you know because of your actions.

"Because you're a child, I don't doubt you're about to blame everyone but yourself. You've come in here to try to put me down when Nikolai has clearly staked a claim on me. You're reacting, not thinking." I stare at her reflection. "Nikolai was never yours. He's his own man. You need to accept the consequences of your actions so you can move on.

"This is the end of the road for you in Florida. I don't know if you have a mother or siblings, but your family should move away before you rain down more sorrow on your heads than you already have, *and* you need therapy. Lots and lots and *lots* of therapy."

With that, I let go of her.

Just as the door slams inward, ricocheting off the wall.

Were Nikolai an ordinary man, he'd have been hit by it. Instead, even the door knows not to get in his way.

Nikolai's fury is etched on his face as he glances between us, making me wonder how the hell he knew Myata was in here. She flinches like he backhanded her, but I merely smile and sweep toward him with my arm outstretched.

"What did she say to you?" he signs then takes one of my hands in his.

"Nothing," I lie, smiling brightly at him. "Now, are you going to dance with me?"

That makes his scowl morph into a grimace, but it's the defusing tactic I needed.

"Come sit with me, *solnyshko*," he answers instead, making me hide a chuckle.

Behind him, Igor's frown is concerned as he flicks a look between us all, but I just snag a hold of Niko's fingers and drawl, "My feet are killing me anyway."

As Niko shoots Myata a glower that's a warning shot, I merely arch a brow at her as he tugs me away. It's almost worth it for the darkly possessive hold he tucks me into as we return to the ballroom.

Because I might be everything that Myata claimed I was, I might be barren, old, fat, and a frump, but for whatever reason, I'm Nikolai's *solnyshko*.

And that, I realize, gives me more power than anyone here expects his woman to have.

35

CASSIE
A WEEK LATER

"DO you know who your father was?"

Settling deeper into his lap after I take a sip of my wine, I snort. "Of course. A garnet miner from Warren County with a bad attitude and an obsession with astronomy—hence my terrible name. Why do you ask?"

He studies the expensive merlot in his glass then relaxes deeper into the love seat in the safe room.

I've come to learn that this is his favorite place in the entire house. Maybe that was obvious at the start, but it was more of a gilded cage for me than a 'beloved' comfort zone.

As a result of our location, he's wearing boxer briefs and I'm back to being tucked in a sheet and... I'm okay with that.

Full disclosure: the two orgasms he gave me before we ended up in here *might* have something to do with that though.

While his pecs have caught my attention, I prod him out of curiosity. Why the heck did he bring up my dad?

"You mentioned he was Russian Orthodox."

"Yes. He moved over to the States when he was a small boy."

His brows lift.

"He's why I can sign." Nikolai tilts his head to the side in silent inquiry. "There was a blast at the mine. He lost his hearing. Had to transfer to the offices. Our family was lucky he didn't lose his job. He could have. Can't exactly have a deaf miner underground."

"I suppose not," he signs. "Your mother can sign too?"

"She can."

"Your ASL is unusual."

"It is?"

"Yes. You sometimes use gestures that I can't interpret."

My brows lift. "I didn't know that."

"Probably because you picked it up from your family rather than a book or a class."

"True. The accident happened before I was born so I always had to sign to communicate with him.

"That's why even though I know you can hear me, I tend to use sign language anyway. It's a habit. Though I admit I was rusty at first. How did you learn?"

"I had a variation of sign language that I used to communicate with Misha and Maxim."

"Not RSL?"

"No. The orphanage didn't care enough to teach me. It was a..." His mouth tightens. "You can't raise children in a hellhole and expect them to come out as angels."

A fair point.

He rubs his forehead before continuing, "We had our own way of talking, a patois almost, but then when we came to the US, I was isolated again. ASL was something I picked up fast; Misha and Maxim did too. Then, it spread as my reputation grew."

"What kind of reputation?" I whisper, not even sure that I want to know the answer, but I still ask.

Like he heard me say that out loud, he muses, "Do you want to know?"

Swallowing, I shake my head.

His smile ghosts over his lips and disappears in a heartbeat. "The more power I had, the more anxious people were to learn ASL. Now, only Dmitri, Maxim, and Misha ever use our patois. But you understand that. You have your own."

"I didn't know I did," I say dryly. "Maybe I'm making them up. As I said, ASL isn't like riding a bike. It was difficult to remember at first."

"Your father probably picked up sign language the same as me."

"If I use a sign that you don't understand, tell me so I can clarify in the future?" When he agrees, I ask, "I thought men in the Bratva had to have tattoos."

"That's random."

"Not particularly." Not when I've been meaning to ask after coming across hundreds of inked men at the gala.

Is it *my* fault he swallowed some of his wine and it made his delicious, tattoo-free throat bob and that gorgeous Adam's apple jut?

Technically, that's a 'him' problem.

He smirks, and his gaze is knowing—my fascination was noticed. "They do. They indicate status or their role in the brotherhood."

"Why don't you have any?"

"You wouldn't believe me if I told you."

"I would."

His lips quirk. "I'm allergic to the ink. The red is the worst, and the blue is just as bad."

My eyes widen. "Seriously?" When he nods and raises his arm to show me his tricep, I query, "You had it lasered off?"

"Grigoriy said it would help."

"Did it?"

"It still itches from time to time. Will even swell when the humidity is high."

"You have just the one?"

"I knew something was wrong from the beginning. I never got another one even if it made me stick out among the men."

I trace the blurred edges of the tattoo. "A dog?"

"A bulldog," he corrects. "But it means 'grudge.'"

"Against?"

"The authorities."

"Fitting."

"More than you know."

I bite my lip even as I continue tracing the tattoo's lines. "Why all the questions about my father anyway?"

He hitches a shoulder.

"No." I flick my fingers at him. "You don't get to ask weird stuff about my family and not continue the conversation."

When his jaw clenches, I figure I'm about to be stonewalled whether I like it or not, but he stuns me by answering, "Your father is infamous in my circles."

That has my eyes bugging. "*My* father?" I slow down the patting of my flat hand against my chest to emphasize the 'my.' "How's that possible? Anyway, he's been dead for fifteen years."

"Some say that he was a Bratva assassin. Others insist he was ex-KGB but still on detail to the Kremlin."

I release an awkward chuckle. "You've got the wrong man."

Except... did I really believe that?

My mind flickers back and, for some reason, the memory of him sliding a shotgun beneath his bed hits me.

He'd have killed for his family.

A cliché but not for Papa.

Papa would never have allowed Harvey to treat me how he did.

He'd have stopped him.

But... ex-KGB?

Unaware that I'm reeling, Nikolai purses his lips. "Mikhail Turgenev had a nickname—Peshnya."

"My mom used to call him that!"

He shoots me a knowing look. "Do you know what that means?"

I shake my head. "Love? Darling?"

"Ice pick."

My eyes bug. "What—"

"That was his favorite tool. They say his father killed Leon Trotsky and he taught his son how to..." He shifts on his seat. "... wield it like a weapon."

That has me choking. "You're saying that m-my grandfather killed

Trotsky? *The* Trotsky? Lenin and founding father of the USSR Trotsky?"

Nikolai nods, and that expressionless goddamn face of his just makes his words ram themselves home.

Still, I have to argue, "My dad never bought new socks unless they had holes in the toes. He ate potatoes every single day of his life. His snores were so loud that my mom and I had to wear earplugs. He never missed a day of work at the mine before he retired." I suck in a breath. "There's no way—"

Nikolai presses a hand to my shoulder. "I wouldn't tell you this if I didn't believe it."

More to myself than him, I whisper, "I don't understand."

His hand smoothes over my arm. "Did he ever claim to be a soldier?"

"Sure. He served in Kazakhstan, at the border conflict between Russia and China." I swallow. "That was a lie?"

"I imagine that was in the early days of his service to the Kremlin."

I sag against him. "My father was a Soviet agent? Or did he do work for the Bratva?"

His expression doesn't give me much of an answer. Nor do his next words. "You had no idea?"

"None."

This has *to be a joke.*

"He was ex-KGB. Defected before the crumbling of the USSR." Nikolai's gaze turns distant. "I just don't understand why he didn't change his name."

"Maybe he isn't who you think he is," I reply quickly. "Maybe this is just a coincidence."

"I've seen his ID," he denies, but he pats my arm.

"Why are you telling me this?"

He hitches a shoulder. "I don't want there to be lies between us."

The strange cold that filled me with his revelations about my father fades with the gentle warmth that overtakes it from his words.

I stare at him. "Why have you been looking into my past?"

"I haven't. We're looking for Rundel. It came up during the investigation."

"You're still actively looking for him?"

It's been weeks, after all.

God, more than that.

Time blurs at *Nav* but apparently, the Bratva takes manhunts more seriously than the feds.

He stares at me. "Only when he's lining one of my alligator's stomachs, Cassiopeia, will I stop hunting him. He'll pay for what he did to you." His nostrils flare as he releases a heavy exhalation. "As it stands, I've already let you down—"

Confused, I ask, "How?"

"I vowed he'd be dead by the year's end. He's still breathing," he seethes before pulling out a velvet box from his pocket.

I demur, "That you're going to take care of him is enough. You didn't have to go to all this effort—"

"I did." He hands the offering to me. "It's yours." His gaze is somber. Annoyed. "I've let you down," he repeats.

When I open the box to reveal a set of earrings that match the pearl necklace he gave me for the gala, I rub my thumb over them. Delight fills me. Though I should probably tell him they're too much, I don't.

Nikolai's rich—these earrings are probably pocket change to him.

Plus, you have to train a guy sometimes. If I teach him that I'm fine with him letting me down *now*, well...

I can't speak for the future, but I know I'm sure as hell thinking about it. Nikolai doesn't act like this is a short-term thing, ya know, what with the breeding kink, so why should I?

Screw being polite.

Screw doing what's 'right.'

Nikolai never considers what's right or wrong—I'm going to take a page out of his book.

And, for good or ill, there's nowhere else I'd rather be right now than on his lap.

I immediately put the earrings on and smile at the comforting weight of them.

Feeling like a queen seated on a muscular throne—a surprisingly comfortable one even if it comes with the lump digging into my ass that is par for the course—I offer, "*Spasibo*."

His lips quirk. "Your accent is atrocious."

I scrunch my nose at him. "Charming."

He winks then presses a kiss to my scrunched nose. "We'll get you a tutor. It would be smart if you learn the language."

A strange peace flutters to life inside me as he confirms what I already knew.

A future.

He talks about it so easily.

And I find myself wanting that.

With him.

Despite our unusual beginnings.

I nod. "Fine."

"Fine? I thought you'd argue."

"Papa always wanted me to learn. I refused."

"We all have teenage rebellions."

"I can't see you—"

"I stole two minors from their orphanage, Cassiopeia," he informs me wryly. "I think that's more rebellious than you fighting with your father, no?"

"I suppose." I grimace, but then I realize he gave me the in I've been seeking ever since Dmitri told me I should talk with Niko about his past. "How did that even...?"

"With a lot of corruption and a lack of care from the government." He exhales. "Maxim started the fire at the orphanage."

The one responsible for his scars goes unspoken.

I gasp. "Why?"

"Because one of the workers had his eye on Misha."

Disgusted, I demand, "What happened?"

"Misha didn't tell me at first." He rubs his hand over his lips. "I wish he had. I'd have just taken him away."

"Was it too late?"

"No. Maxim caught it in time but he got trapped in the blaze. You think the scars on my hips are bad. His back is a mess."

"Damn," I whisper, turning into him.

"The bastard died for daring to target Misha. His body burned in the blast. It was set in his office. Maxim hit him over the head with a piece of memorabilia the pervert brought back from serving in WW2." He takes a deep pull on his wine. "The fire was to cover it up. I had to get us away from there fast.

"Then afterward, we had to deal with our injuries and that cost a fortune. There's a national health system in Moscow, but we had to do it off the books, and most of the time, even if it's legitimate, you have to bribe a doctor for what you'd consider standardized healthcare."

"That's terrible!" I squeak.

He smiles at me a little. "Such an idealist."

I huff. "Nobody questioned you? No one asked why a young kid had two boys with him?"

"They didn't care so long as I paid them enough. I used to be a pickpocket. I was lucky that I was good at it. I had enough for the early days of our care—"

"But you were injured too!"

"I had mouths to feed and healthcare to arrange. I survived."

I flinch at the sacrifices he had to make—decisions and choices that no child should ever be faced with.

God, no wonder he's so weird.

"Afterward, we lived on the streets until I was old enough to get us some digs." His mouth tightens. "They were not good times."

"I can't even imagine."

When I think of the crap I gave my dad over his refusal to paint my bedroom black while Nikolai, at the same age, was struggling to feed three mouths…

Guilt hits me.

Sorry, Papa.

"I wouldn't want you to imagine," he signs, the movements of his fingers hard and biting. "I did some terrible things to protect us all."

I stare at him, trying to see past that blank expression to the wall that's between the past and the present.

"It made you who you are today," I say softly.

"*Da.*" He glances away. "I have never been a good man. From a young age, I knew what I'd be." At my questioning look, he answers, "A killer."

"Environment plays a key part in that," I argue. "If you'd been raised on my street, I don't think you'd have turned out that way."

"Are you defending me, *solnyshko?*" he queries, but for the first time since this conversation started, he appears amused.

At my second huff in as many minutes, I retort, "Well, it's true."

"Maybe you're right." His smile fades. "Everything went wrong after Father murdered my mother. He gave her peace though. Instead of beating her and whoring her out when we couldn't make rent..." A breath hisses from him as, staring right at me, he admits, "Still, peace or not, I had to deal with him, Cassiopeia. I'd do it again, too. I am not a good man."

Though I blink, the only thing I can think to say is: "I'm sorry you had to do that. And I'm sorry she had to go through that."

My situation is unnervingly like his mother's...

Interesting how he thinks he isn't a good man when, for the two most important women in his life, he's Nemesis in the flesh.

"Justice is something you take for yourself, something you earn with blood-soaked hands." He shakes his head as if sloughing off the memories. "After we were alone, more came to me."

"What do you mean?"

"Misha and Maxim would make friends and their situations would be just as bad, if not worse. At one point, our two-bedroom shithole had twelve of us living in it."

"Are you kidding me?"

He hitches a shoulder. "What was I supposed to do—turn them away?"

"No. But how did you manage?"

"I didn't have a choice. I made it work."

"Were you with the Bratva then?"

"Not at first," he mutters, and something about his tone has me studying him with more intent than before. "My Obschak now is Pavel. Remember? He's the one who helped me find a place with the Bratva. I owe him a debt for that, never mind the brotherhood."

"He's your third-in-command? Maria's husband, right?"

He nods.

"I mean, isn't that repayment enough? You've given him a lot of power."

His jaw works. "My time on the streets was... dark, Cassiopeia. I can never repay him enough for helping me out of that situation."

Unease filters through me.

It lodges in my heart.

Is he saying what I think he's saying?

How could a boy of fifteen earn money to feed three mouths, never mind twelve, when he lived on the streets? Pickpocketing probably wouldn't have been enough...

My hand grips his, hard enough that it must hurt.

A man like him has his pride, so I don't throw salt onto the wound of his confession.

"How did you find Dmitri?"

His tension shifts.

If I didn't know Dmitri was like a son to him, his clenched jaw, the knuckles that bleed white around the stem of his wine glass—they're telltale signs.

"Dmitri's the son of a high-ranking Bratva brother but Fyodor beat him terribly. One day, he ran away. Maxim found him, and he stuck around until Fyodor came looking. Dmitri didn't give me a choice about fighting for him. He disappeared." He cracks his neck. "Then, when I was about to transfer to the US, Dmitri found me again. We stowed him away in our cabin on the shipping trawler we were brought to the States in."

"Are you serious?" I gape at him.

"Like a heart attack. The first time he came to me, he'd been beaten black and blue. That second time..." He graces me with another shake of his head. "I wasn't about to leave him to get killed by that butcher."

"Didn't his father come looking?"

"Of course, but we were a thousand miles away and I had more money to hide him. The first thing I did when I finally started earning and had some contacts was buy him a different identity so he could go to school here." He sniffs. "How does he repay me? By talking like one of you."

A soft bark of laughter escapes me. "What's that supposed to mean?"

"'Like,' 'whatever,' 'totally.'" He rolls his eyes, but I can see the smile on his lips as he teases me. "He's been talking about therapy for a while now, but I think he honestly means to go. Can you imagine?"

Yeah. I hide my smile. I *totally* can.

"He probably needs it," is all I say though. Hell, Nikolai, Misha, and Maxim sound like they need it too.

As I look at him, I can't help but see how many layers there are to this man.

He's ruthless and cold, a killer with an instinct to match, but he saved two boys from an orphanage and helped countless others along the way.

Because I can sense this conversation is done with, I ask, "Are you sure my papa did... all that?"

He chucks me under the chin. "I wouldn't have told you if I didn't believe what I was saying. I'm just disappointed Peshnya never got to use his ice pick on the man who deserves it most—his son-in-law."

"Papa would..."

He seems to know what I'm saying because he rubs his nose against my temple. "I know, *solnyshko.*"

"I wish he'd killed him," I rasp, my tone fierce. "I wish I'd never married him or met him or been fooled by him or been—"

Nikolai tuts then encourages me to relax into him. I hide my face in his throat even though I can feel the embers of my anger seething in my soul.

Harvey's in the past. He'll be dead soon enough.

As for Papa, he was a murderer.

Nikolai's right—danger *has* been dogging my footsteps for longer than I've known.

It's starting to feel like I'm only safe in Niko's arms.

As if he's reading my mind, *again,* he tightens his embrace.

It's not the first time the thought occurs to me:

I hope he doesn't let go.

But, I chide myself because…

I *know* that he won't.

36

NIKOLAI

Dark Red - Steve Lacy

I ADMIT I stayed out later than usual tonight, working in my office when I'd have preferred to spend time with Cassiopeia.

It's ridiculous to feel vulnerable, but when I'm forced to look toward the past, those memories are tough to hide from.

The shit I did to make a living on the streets repulses even me. I'd do it again, though. Would do anything to make sure that Maxim and Misha had food in their bellies.

Did she know what I was saying—without me having to say it?

Is she revolted? Disgusted?

I don't want to know.

That's why I stayed away.

But I can't stay away for long.

She calls me back to her like a siren. The pull she has on me is something I've never experienced before and now that I know it exists, I refuse to be without it.

To be without *her.*

I know from the cameras that she's asleep as I step inside the bedroom.

Behind me, the door locks, and I start to strip out of my clothes, leaving them over by the vanity where I've watched her primp and preen, stamping her mark, claiming this as *her* space. Making it a home, not just somewhere for me to sleep.

Piling my dirty laundry there for the staff to take in the morning, I drop my knife and cell phone into one of the top drawers, then turn around and stare at her as she sleeps.

Even as she rests, I feel her call and my dick reacts predictably.

As it hardens, I can no more stop myself from walking toward her side of the bed than I can stop my heart from taking its next beat.

Looming over her makes me feel even fucking filthier than I did before, but when did morals ever stop me?

Stroking my cock, I watch her as she sleeps, finding beauty in her stillness. Cupping my balls, I twist them gently.

With my thumb, I smooth the pre-cum gathering at the tip along the length of my shaft to ease the passage of my fist.

A soft grunt escapes me, one I try to contain but I can't.

Even like this, with no part of her touching me, she's the best I've ever had.

I rock my hips, thrusting through the hole I made with my hand, and my eyes shutter, not enough that I can't see her though. Watching her like this is... *blyad,* too good.

I groan as my balls throb, release forming swift and hard because of the stressful day I've had. But just before I can shoot my load, her eyes pop open.

They collide with mine in the low light from the windows.

Her gaze flickers over me, down to my cock, and she freezes.

Then, she sits up.

I half expect her to punch me in the balls—she'd have done that in the early days—but she doesn't.

She stuns me.

She presses a kiss to my bobbing cock and lets the glans flutter along her Cupid's bow.

I can't hold back any longer, so I watch as my cum pelts her open lips, her tongue, and her chin, trailing it onto the tits she exposes as she shoves the blankets away.

When my hips stop thrusting of their own volition, I lean over, let the flat of my tongue slide through the cum on her face until I'm close to her ear and I whisper, "You're too good for me."

Her nails dig into my nape as she grabs my hand. When she slides it between her legs, I find her clit as she whispers back, "Isn't that for me to decide?" When her thighs tighten around my hand, she breathes, "No one makes me feel like you do, Nikolai. No one."

So, it is mutual.

Pride roars through me as does the urge to slide home, to crawl between her thighs, to sink into her, to forget…

When I pump a finger into her, she whimpers, and I can feel my dick start to harden.

Again.

I'm too fucking old for this, but not around her.

I retreat to her mouth, biting at her lips until she opens to me and I can thrust my cum-drenched tongue against hers.

Savoring her mewl of displeasure, I kneel on the bed and slide between her thighs.

"You've done this before, haven't you?" she rasps as I rub my cock over her clit, her knees pinning my hips in place. "You didn't wake me up before though," she answers, seeming to know that I won't.

As I find her slit, a part of me finds it impossible to believe that she's letting me inside her. Not only after waking up to discover me jacking off over her face but because of the day's admissions.

But I've never looked a gift horse in the mouth and I won't start tonight.

I press my hands to either side of her head then lower myself onto her.

The only thing I want from this is her pleasure.

I want to hear her scream as I make love to her.

I need that.

I need to know she wants me.

If she read between the lines, I need to know that I haven't repulsed her with my past.

A soft sob is drawn from her when I *finally* get to slide home. She's not as wet as I'd like, but she takes me. Each inch. Until I'm cosseted on all sides by her heat.

My *solnyshko.*

Beneath me, she shudders. "God, you feel so wonderful, Nikolai. You fill me so right. So perfectly."

My nostrils flare. "You take me like the good girl you are, Cassiopeia. My good girl." When her shudder turns into a low groan that has her nails digging into my spine, I urge the words out, force them when my throat wants to clam up because she deserves to *hear* this. "This pretty little pussy, Cassiopeia, belongs to me. It's mine and I will always look after what's mine."

If anything could come from today's confession, she should know *that.*

I will debase myself to protect her. Commit the wickedest of sins to keep her safe.

She.

Is.

Mine.

The sound of her heavy breathing in my ear is like a wet dream come to life.

I could never have imagined when I was fifteen, jacking off in front of strangers for pay, getting fucked by them to make rent, that when I was in my forties, she'd be here.

My goddess.

My beautiful Cassiopeia.

My reward.

I whisper the words in her ear and feel her cunt clutch at me. My ugly voice, my ugly scars, my ugly nature aren't so repulsive to her. She responds to me like no other ever has or ever will.

Ignoring the rhythmic tugs on my dick, I don't speed up, don't jackhammer into her; this isn't a race. It's a fucking ritual—a claiming.

She's mine.

Always.

Forever.

In this world and the next.

When I breathe the words into her ear, she tightens around me, back bowing, nails scraping over my scalp and shoulders as she holds me tight.

I follow her through her pleasure, continuing to ride her until she's eked out every drop of ecstasy.

Her legs quiver, thighs trembling, then once she's sagged beneath me, clearly tired out, exhausted from being awoken in the middle of the night, I turn us over so that she blankets me.

Softly, I stroke a hand down her spine to comfort us both and when I fall asleep, the nightmares I expect don't follow me into unconsciousness.

Just into tomorrow.

CHAPTER THIRTY-SEVEN

I told you so...
BLOG

There's a rumor that the recent explosion in Petrovsky Park is
Bratva-adjacent.

No one knows for certain, least of all the Muscovian police
force, but that comes as no surprise, not when they're more
corrupt than the NYPD.

Still, the bomb blast *is* a shock. There's been no terrorist action
in Moscow since the Bratva closed ranks and began
policing the streets themselves.

One has to ask who'd have the balls to disrupt this *tranquillitas
ordinis*—peace order.

I have reason to believe that it might be a certain upstart from
New York.

Rumor has it that Maxim Lyanov's reason for spending so
much time in Moscow was *not* to cozy up to the Krestniy
Otets but to plan a revolution.

Only time will tell if this is true or not, but I'll be the first, as
always, with the latest updates.

38

NIKOLAI

Blue and Yellow - The Used

"YOU CAN'T BRING her with us."

Dmitri's retort has me frowning at him. "Dmitri, you're the one who can't come with me."

His eyes round. "Excuse me?"

"I need you here," I sign.

"But my place is with you!"

"You are my Sovietnik." I place a hand on Dmitri's shoulder and squeeze.

Sometimes when I look at him, it's hard to remember that he's an adult now. I still see those eyes flooded with tears, bruised and battered, his face loaded with lacerations from where his father's signet ring tore his cheeks apart.

Whether fifteen years separate him from that moment or fifteen minutes—the last place I want him to be is Moskva. Even if I'd appreciate him having my back in this dogfight.

He swallows. "You need me."

My hand tightens on his shoulder. "Always," I rasp, then I let go of him and sign, "But I need you to hold my territory. The men respect you and with Pavel still in the hospital, I have no choice. Even if he wasn't, I'd prefer you to stay here. I trust you implicitly."

"More than him?"

I have to smile. "Always a competition with you, isn't it?"

Dmitri sniffs. "Not always."

"Just most of the time." I sigh. "And *da*, more than him. You didn't even have to ask that."

Grinding his teeth, he mutters, "If you get your ass killed, I *will* torture Misha and Maxim."

"If I die, it's likely they will too." I didn't want to have this conversation with him, but the situation has come to a head.

He points to the blog post on my computer screen. "You don't even know if that's true."

"We both tried to call Maxim. He didn't answer."

"He doesn't always. You know he's a petulant shit."

Takes one to know one.

The thought drifts into my mind in Cassiopeia's sweet voice.

Barely refraining from chuckling, I sign, "He always calls back. Always. We might have a strained relationship, but he doesn't ignore us."

I just choose not to call him, preferring to have Misha act as a go-between.

That's when I receive a text.

The beep is overly loud as it rings between us once, twice, *three* times. Then three more!

I reach for my cell and grunt.

Passing it to Dmitri, I rumble, "Confirmation."

> Luka: The Krestniy Otets has declared Maxim a traitor.

> Luka: Seems he has footage of Maxim with a small team trying to blast his way into Petrovsky Palace.

> Luka: Which, if you recall, is Kuznetsov territory.

> Luka: Which, if you recall, we have strict orders to avoid.

> Luka: It's pretty much the only place in the city we don't have a free pass to enter.

> Luka: He fucked up big time.

"Jesus, what the hell has he gotten himself involved with?" Dmitri demands. "No way he's working against the Bratva if he's trying to break into Kuznetsov's turf."

"He must know something we don't." Something he didn't share with me.

Suddenly exhausted, I rub my eyes. "This is why Misha hasn't answered us either. He's probably halfway across the Atlantic."

The fact that neither of them trusts me enough to share something as massive as *this* with me hurts.

Fuck, it more than hurts.

I cared for them as children. I saved them, raised them. Made sure they never went hungry even if I starved first.

After yesterday's talk with Cassiopeia, the reminder of the level I sunk to for them stings more than ever.

Yet I'd do it all again in a heartbeat.

"It's not your fault, Nikolai."

Isn't it?

My fingers dig into my fatigued eyes.

"I should never have picked Pavel over Maxim as my Obschak."

"Maxim was young," he retorts.

"And you're not?" I slice my hands through the air. "I betrayed him. I-I didn't see it at the time."

"He wasn't good at listening to orders."

"Dmitri, neither are you. What I forgive in you, I *never* forgave in him. I was hard on him. Too hard. And now, he's gotten himself exiled from the fucking Bratva while in the heart of the homeland." After rubbing my forehead, I sign, "The situation has changed. I *was* going over there on a fact-finding mission. Now, it's to bring his ass back here.

"Arrange for the jet to takeoff in an hour."

Though he nods, he argues, "You can't still intend on taking Cassiopeia with you?"

"You'll have enough on your hands keeping the peace here." I frown at him. "In your opinion, who has the men's loyalty?"

"What kind of question is that?"

"I'm talking about me or the Krestniy Otets."

He blinks. "Oh. Well, that situation with Pavlivshev came out of the blue, but when you claimed Cassiopeia at the gala, that made the situation make sense to most of the men. You have some hardcore supporters like Vladimir and Oleg—"

I waft a hand because I know about them.

"—but for the most part, you. The past ten years have been good and everyone knows that's because of you. The Krestniy Otets didn't make himself popular when he increased the tithe—"

Every Bratva brother had to 'donate' twenty percent of their earnings to the Bratva.

Everyone knew that lined the Krestniy Otets's pockets. When six percent had shot up to twenty, it had pissed many off.

"—and when you ate the cost on their behalf, that amped up the respect they have for you. Another leader wouldn't do that." His lips twist. "You chide Maxim for bringing communism to the Bratva, but I bet he got the idea from you.

"What are you thinking, Nikolai?"

"Aligning myself with Maxim is to unalign myself from the Krestniy Otets." Another reason why I didn't want him there. I grab his shoulder again, squeeze, then let go to sign, "Take control of Miami if I don't make it, Dmitri."

"Shut up."

"I'm being serious. There are no guarantees."

"Then why are you taking Cassiopeia with you!" he snaps.

"Because she'll be safer with me than on her own and you need to hold the city."

"So, you'll take her into enemy territory?"

"The only true ally I have right now is you, son."

"No. Pavel—"

"Is out of commission. The last time we talked a week ago, he fell asleep on the video call."

"Don't fucking go, *Otets*," Dmitri pleads. "Maxim won't thank you for your intervention and you could get hurt!"

"I would go for you. Whether you thanked me or not. It's what a father does."

His mouth tightens, but as the words settle, as their meaning resonates, he graces me with a sharp nod.

This time, I drag him into a hug and it's me who struggles to let go.

With my attention turned onto business here and Cassiopeia, I hadn't even heard about the explosion in Moskva until Dmitri told me it was all over the news a few days ago.

I could never have anticipated that it would be the catalyst for the beginning of the end.

39

CASSIE

Lose My Breath - Rhea Robertson

WHEN NIKO SHOWED up in the bedroom and hurried through our shower without shaving me, I knew something was wrong.

It's weird to use that as a measure, but when your life is out of your control, you find a semblance of it in routine.

When he puts me in a woolen dress, I frown down at it then at the window where the sun is shining brightly. "Do you know something I don't? Is there a hurricane incoming that I didn't hear about in the news?"

We'd had a freak scare right after New Year's, but it had landed in Daytona, not Miami.

"We're going to Russia."

My brows lift. "I beg your pardon?"

"We're going to Russia," he repeats as he starts to drag clothes from both sides of our closet.

"Why?"

"Business."

My eyes narrow. "Why are you taking me with you? I don't even have a passport right now. It's among my things in my car."

"You don't need a passport with me."

My narrowed eyes widen as I roll them, but I stride over to him and tug on his hand. "Tell me what's going on, Nikolai, before you start to frighten me."

He pauses to squeeze my fingers then signs, "You remember I talked about the men who are like my brothers?"

The picture of those young faces with ancient eyes in the safe room rears its ugly head from my memory banks. "Yes. Maxim and Misha."

"Maxim's gotten himself into trouble in Moskva."

"And you're going to help him?" When he nods, I repeat, "Why are you taking me with you, then? Isn't it dangerous?"

Nikolai snaps the necks of men who threaten me. Taking me into scenes of active aggression in a country that isn't exactly friendly with the US seems out of character for him.

"If I side with Maxim, I go against the leaders of the Bratva themselves," he warns. "If that's the case, there could be a rebellion here. If there is, your safety isn't guaranteed. The best way to protect you is for you to be with me." His hand cups my chin. "I had no means of anticipating that this would happen, *solnyshko*." That he speaks the words tells me more than he can know. "I'm sorry."

Studying his expression, seeing the genuine regret etched there when I'm so used to seeing *nothing*, I realize I'm not afraid.

I should be.

But I'm not.

He's just proving what I've already come to believe about him—that he'll walk into Hell itself for the people he loves.

And, even now, he's thinking of me, of my safety, when his mind is on a man who's like a brother to him.

That makes it easy to reassure: "You told me so yourself, Nikolai—I was in danger before you came along."

His mouth twists. "That doesn't make me feel better."

"Didn't say it to make you feel better. The truth hurts." With a deep inhalation, I grab his hand. "I can't help when we're over there, can I?"

"No, but knowing you're safe will be more help than you know." He grinds his teeth then rumbles, "If anything were to happen to you, Cassiopeia..." The words wane as if he can't even verbalize the ramifications of what would happen if I were to be harmed.

That strange warmth gathers in my chest again.

Ever since the dance with Dmitri at the gala, it's started to become more noticeable, but today, it's overwhelming. 'Steals the breath from my lungs' type of overwhelming because while I can't end the world if anything happens to him, that something *could*, that he might be hurt, taken from me...

The pain is worse than anything Harvey put me through.

It's like he's reading my mind because he signs, "I'll make sure that you'll have an escape route if I get—"

My fingers dig into his forearm. "Don't say that," I snarl. "Don't think it either."

He bows his head, but I know he is.

He's too concerned for my well-being when he needs to be focused on his own.

"Nikolai?"

"Yes, *solnyshko*?"

I can tell his mind is elsewhere, probably on the plans he has to make, but all I can think about is him not being here.

Sure, he drives me insane. I want to shake him most of the time, and when he makes me sit on his knee when we eat in restaurants, the urge to smack him is *real*.

And I know it's crazy, probably Stockholm syndrome talking, but I have to say it, "I-I think I love you."

That has his gaze locking with mine. Fire surges into being in his eyes, one that's ferocious in its intensity.

Then, he banks it down and presses a kiss to my mouth. Before I can say another word, he's there, in my ear, with that broken voice of his whispering, "I don't 'think' I love you. I *know* I do."

Swallowing with the momentousness of the occasion, I cling to him as he holds me in a tight embrace.

The prospect of losing this, losing *him*—

No.

Whoever thought to hurt his brother was a fool.

A fire forged him all those years ago, a fire set by the very same brother, which Nikolai used to craft them a new life that led to this orphan becoming a leader.

Nikolai is unstoppable.

I'll go to my grave believing that.

But even so, I tug on his hand and negotiate, "You can't expect me to travel to Russia with nothing to entertain me."

He blinks but his lips curve—that, right there, was my intention.

"I want a notepad. And a pen."

"Whatever you need, *solnyshko*," he signs, pressing a kiss to my forehead.

While I get the feeling I could have held out for a tablet, I don't mind. Instead, I give him a gentle squeeze and murmur, "That's you, Nikolai. You're what I need."

I don't care if it's crazy. The truth often is.

He releases a harsh breath then places a harder kiss on my mouth. "Mine."

Though I nod, because it's the truth, I pull back and, with both hands cupping his cheeks, stare straight into his eyes and make my own claim: "Mine."

His expression flickers between surprise and happiness before settling into smug satisfaction.

When he straightens his shoulders, somehow, I think I've given him the firepower to take down Russia itself, never mind Moscow.

And all I can think is—*good.*

40

NIKOLAI

SHUM - Bo_A

I HATE BEING BACK in Moskva.

Hate my country, period.

The second I stepped foot on US soil was the second that I cauterized my ties with the motherland.

Not once have I had to return.

Until now.

I don't hate it because of the memories or because of what we left behind—my reason for not returning is standing beside the limo on the airfield when we arrive.

Dmitri's father.

I'd expected and planned for a welcome committee, but fuck, why did it have to be *him*?

I've always detested Fyodor, enough that being on the same continent is unwise. Today, it's more unwise than ever. The ties that bind me, that controlled me and kept me in line—they're stretched paper-thin.

"Who's that?" Cassiopeia asks, peering through one of the jet's windows. "You got all tense."

My jaw clenches. "It's Dmitri's father."

"Oh." She knows Dmitri's story now. Her hand slips into mine, smoothing out my balled fist. "Do you have to talk to him?"

"Yes. One day, I'll kill him."

Though her eyes flare wide, she studies me. I can see the intensity of her gaze in my peripheral vision. "Is that day today?"

"It depends."

"On?"

"What he has to say." I flick a glance at her. "His presence changes things."

"Why?"

"I was going to settle you in one of the apartments I own here, but we're running out of time."

"We only just arrived."

"We might already be too late," I sign.

She flinches. "You think Maxim's dead?"

"I think we're running out of time," I repeat.

"What's the plan?"

"Stay on board with Igor. I trust him with my life, *solnyshko*. That means I trust him with yours."

"You think you'll be that fast?"

"I intend to be in and out."

"Okay." She sounds brave, but with how she tightens her fingers around mine, I know she's nervous. "Don't get killed."

I *can't* get killed.

If I do, someone else will take her and make her theirs. She'll be a gift from the Krestniy Otets to whoever kills me.

A prize.

God knows what they'd do to her when they know I've made her mine.

I can't regret the New Year's gala, or staking a claim, but if I die today, then…

Fuck.

I can *not* die.

I raise our entwined hands to my mouth and kiss her knuckles. "It might be a while until I return. Don't worry." Yet.

She glances around the luxuriously appointed jet. "I've waited in worse places."

Though my lips twitch, I get to my feet and release my hold on her fingers. She tugs me back at the last moment and surges to a standing position. When she hurls herself against my chest, I hold her tight.

"Why does it feel like you're saying goodbye?" she mumbles.

"There'll never be a world where I don't come for you, *solnyshko*. Whether it's this one or the next."

"Don't say that," she snaps. "Jesus. That's even worse!"

"It's the truth." And now, she's angry, not worried. "This is just the beginning of our story."

She peers at me but her eyes aren't watery like they could have been. Instead, they're fierce as she stands on her tiptoes and kisses me.

I don't dive into it like I want to, but I savor her, making sure she knows that I don't intend for this to be goodbye.

It takes a lot to kill me, and that was before I had a reason to live.

When she lets go of me, her eyes are still fierce. Once again, I have to reconcile this woman with the one married to that piece of shit who found pleasure in breaking her, and I can only be proud of her strength.

Some people are better together than apart.

I believe that is us.

"If you want only the truth between us," she retorts, tipping her chin up. "…don't make a liar out of yourself."

With a final kiss to her knuckles, a silent promise bestowed, I grab Igor by the shirt on my way to the door and drag him up front.

When we're by the cockpit, I release my hold on him and sign, "You don't let anyone board. If they try to, you get the pilot to fly away. Understood?"

"*Da,* Pakhan."

"The minute I'm on the ground, have Dominik taxi the jet to the hangar. I want it to be far from any potential gunfire."

"*Da*," he agrees, though his eyes light up with inquiry at my order. "You expect gunfire?"

My mouth tightens as I sign, "Whatever his reasons for being here, I won't be leaving with Turgenev no matter how prettily he asks. It's unlikely there won't be some attempts at coercion." When he nods his understanding, I continue, "If we're not back in thirty-six hours, you return to the US. Understood?"

He tenses. "*We*, Pakhan?"

"Maxim, Misha, and I. If I'm not with them, take their orders as if they're from me."

He nods again but doesn't look happy about it.

That makes two of us.

"Whatever you do, you keep her safe. Take her to Savannah O'Donnelly—the wife of the Irish Mob leader in New York."

He gapes at me. "The Irish—?"

"*Da*. The Irish. I'm trusting you, Igor. You, Semion, Viktor, and Sergei." Her guards. "Don't let me down."

"I won't, Pakhan. I swear." He takes ahold of my shoulder before I can leave. "Can't I go with you? I'm better at your side than as a babysitter."

"Anything happens to her, Moskva will burn, Igor. It's in everyone's best interests that she's safe."

Though he sighs, he stares at Cassiopeia who's watching us.

"Are you going to marry her?"

I don't have to answer, but it's important that he understands. "When Boris gets his fucking act together and finds her prick of an ex, yes."

He grabs my hand, shakes it, and that's me done.

I head to the door and run down the steps.

Behind me, the plane starts to taxi away and I release a relieved breath, knowing that no matter what happens, Cassiopeia is out of danger.

Dressed in fur to combat the frigid temperatures, Fyodor Turgenev might look like a wrapped-up teddy bear, but the only similarity is that he's got a rep for mauling enemies.

And sons.

When I move over to him, the car that was waiting for me flashes its headlights. I raise a hand to my friend, Luka, the driver, and turn to Turgenev.

He sneers at me. "The Krestniy Otets wants to see you."

It's hard, so fucking hard, but I know he'll refuse to understand sign language so I have no choice but to rumble, "It'll have to wait."

My throat clutches once the words are out. The strain is unreal.

Turgenev chuckles. "The Krestniy Otets waits for no man."

Heat prickles along my spine as I struggle to bite out, "He'll wait for me. Family calls."

"Family? You call that Lyanov upstart family? That's your first mistake." He grins at me, flashing a set of gold teeth while simultaneously letting me know the Krestniy Otets is well aware of my reason for being here. "He won't like that. Not when he's most wanted number one as they say in the US."

I'm almost relieved because I know we're done talking when he grabs my arm. I react instinctively—slicing my hand against his wrist until I feel the bones buckle beneath the force of my attack.

As he yelps, his guards surge forward, but it doesn't stop me.

I'm already going for broke with Maxim, so the little bastard better not be dead.

Turgenev cradles his broken wrist while trying to punch me with the other. The fucker is out of fighting shape, which makes it easy to twist his arm behind his back until his shoulder dislocates. That's when I kick his knees in so he lands heavily on the joints.

Using him as a human shield, I control him by squeezing his broken wrist as I draw his arm upward. The soft fuck screams in agony but I don't hear his cries for mercy.

I only see his signet ring.

It gleams at me. Taunts me.

Big and brash, clustered with carats of diamonds and emeralds, the old family heirloom has caused *my* son to shed too much fucking blood.

I tug the signet ring higher up his finger, slot my knife beneath it, and I slice through flesh and bone.

As he screams, as blood spurts, his guards surround me. With his digit in one hand, I've got Zub in the other. The tip of which is buried in his throat.

It's an unwise move but...

"This," I rumble, voice straining as I force the words out, "is for Dmitri."

I slice his carotid.

That's when I take a moment to appreciate the fountain of blood that springs forth as it laces the pristine white snow.

Silence fills the air until the click of multiple safeties being disengaged echoes around the clearing.

Men who are loyal to me make an appearance.

See, I'd anticipated the welcome committee, just not with Turgenev as the main dignitary.

As my men deal with Turgenev's, I throw the finger on the snow and pocket the signet ring while I jog toward my car. Luka's waiting with the engine running, so I jump into the driver's side and take off.

"You always know how to kickstart a vacation," Luka cheers, taking in the chaos we're leaving behind with a wide grin. As he turns around to continue watching the show, he informs me, "Maxim's still alive. He's in a hospital in Sakharovo."

That has me groaning. *Shit.* That's almost two hours away from here.

"*Da.* I know. Pain in the ass. But it's why the K.O. hasn't found him yet."

I cast him a look and, controlling the steering with my knees for a brief instant, sign, "What happened?"

"If it weren't for you, he'd be dead," is Luka's grim retort. When my brows lift, he intones, "Men who remember you from the early days helped get him out of the city. Misha's with him. He's claiming they're going to disenfranchise themselves from the Bratva. Is that even possible?"

I shrug. But at the lack of scorn in Luka's voice, I have to assume he's considered it a possibility.

"I always forget how annoying it is to have a conversation with you when you're driving. Why don't you let *me* drive?" He doesn't expect an answer. "*Da, da,* because no one drives you but you." He sniffs his disdain for that and oh, how bewildered he'd be if he knew I have Karl drive me around frequently now when I'm with Cassiopeia.

When we make it off the airfield and are en route to Sakharovo, I know he's right—now is not the time for silence.

Releasing the chokehold on my vocal cords isn't something I can always control—if I could, I'd speak like a regular person—but this is a goddamn emergency so I *have* to try.

I did it with Turgenev so I can do it with an old friend I trust.

My fingers tighten around the steering wheel as I croak, "I appreciate your help, Luka." The words aren't released in a comfortable rhythm—more like staccato gunshots as I struggle to get them out.

When I have, I can feel the sweat gathering at my temples from the effort.

It isn't easy talking to Cassiopeia, far from it, but she unlocks something in me that no one else ever has.

Certainly not fucking Fyodor or Luka.

"I know you do," he exclaims, surprise in his tone at hearing me speak. It's been at least eight years, after all. "Since when do you talk?" He pauses then laughs. "Wait, let me guess—you got yourself a woman, don't you?"

I grunt.

"'Course you do. They can't stand it when you don't talk. Makes it easier, though. Practice makes perfect. You sound like you've been deepthroating a donkey."

"Luka, your way with words," I mutter, the reprimand close to noiseless.

"It's a gift," he chirps, ignoring my glower.

Heaving a sigh, I reply to his earlier question, "Maxim has run out of options." I swallow. Concentrate. "Disenfranchising is his only option for survival."

Luka considers that. "What the hell was he doing?"

I reach for the bottle of water he offers me, well aware of the strain I'm under. "I don't know." The liquid eases the tightness of my throat. "He's been… *distant* since I picked Pavel over him as Obschak."

"Maxim doesn't know what Pavel did for you, does he?" Luka asks carefully.

Luka knows because he was like me—two kids just trying to bring in food for the family they chose.

"*Nyet*," I snap, my answer slipping from me with more ease than before. "And he won't. Understood?"

Luka grumbles, "Understood. You should tell him. It's important."

"It isn't."

"It fucking is if he blows up a part of Petrovksy Palace and you don't know why!" He sniffs. "Not only is that Kuznetsov turf and you know the Krestniy Otets has a hard-on for that old bastard, but we've had that 'no explosive' rule in place for the past five years, Niko. Maxim couldn't have fucked up any worse if he tried.

"Still, he's only new to the game, isn't he? You can tell. Boy's got no place being a Pakhan as inexperienced as he is."

That has me scraping a hand over my face because I know he's right.

There's a reason that the position of Pakhan is granted not taken.

I knew about the 'no explosive' rule, but it's unlikely that Pavel or Dmitri do. Never mind Maxim who was far down the chain prior to snatching the position of Pakhan in New York.

As for anything Kuznetsov-related, the consensus in the brotherhood is to leave well enough alone. Only leaders know how deeply the Krestniy Otets wants to be joined with that old bastard who gives scum-suckers a bad name. It goes deeper than wanting his daughter to marry into that mess.

Luka cracks his knuckles. "You killing Turgenev won't help."

Controlling the wheel with my knees now that we're on a highway,

I sign, "Never thought it would." Relieved that I don't have to talk, I grin. "Still felt fucking good though."

He snickers. "You didn't bring Dmitri with you?"

"Wasn't going to bring him here."

"Sofia would have smoothed things over if you had," he points out.

"They were childhood friends. She doesn't even know him anymore." Not that time or distance has changed *his* feelings for *her*.

"It's your childhood friends who are saving your asses today, Nikolai. Don't discount longtime friendships. All the guys with Maxim are ones from the orphanage or the streets. We don't forget. You know that. Why should Sofia? Especially after what went down before Dmitri ran away."

That has me grimacing. "At least the Krestniy Otets hasn't tried to marry her off since."

Luka hoots. "Probably thinks Dmitri would pop up again to kill the fiancé. You weren't around back then. The top three were mega-embarrassed."

"There the Krestniy Otets was, about to marry off his child bride daughter to one of Kuznetsov's men, and the Sovietnik's spawn kills him."

My lips twitch. "Threw a hairdryer into his bathwater, didn't he?"

Luka nods, but he's chuckling. "Something like that. It was hilarious."

I smile a little but state, "If Maxim, Misha, and I make it out of this, you're welcome to come to New York."

"That where you're going to be heading?"

"Maybe. Might be Florida. Depends on the aftermath. Like you said, killing Turgenev won't make things easier on me."

"You've been waiting for that kill for nearly two decades. I think your patience should be rewarded."

I have to smirk. "Not sure the Krestniy Otets will agree."

"Nah, but he's an asshole so who cares?" He cuts me a look. "You thinking about 'disenfranchising' too?"

"Might not have an alternative. I made my choice in the orphanage."

That has him nodding. "Got a baby on the way. I'd prefer the US, but I'll wait until things are settled, then I'll come over. If you don't mind?"

"Family first," I say softly.

It takes another hour to reach the outer limits of Sakharovo from the airfield. When we make it to the hospital that Luka had input into the GPS, I see the sheer number of vehicles in the parking lot and, bewildered, shake my head.

"You made more of an impact than you remember, Niko."

Clearly.

Not only is the lot packed full but some cars are double-parked.

Luka peers at them then mutters, "I wouldn't be the only one willing to move, Niko. Been fucking shit around here lately."

"I'll bear that in mind," I rasp as I pull up outside the hospital.

"You go. I'll idle until you get back. Misha told me about twenty minutes before you landed that the doctors have him ready to travel."

The news has me grunting as I jump out of the car and find Lev waiting to take over from Luka. He slams into me, dragging me into a hug and murmuring, "Pakhan, good to see you. Maxim's this way."

It's messed up to walk toward Maxim's ward and to see exactly how many men are standing guard over my brother.

There are kids from the orphanage before it burned, then there are the ones who I collected over the years from the streets. Maxim and Misha brought them to me, but I'm the one who fed and sheltered them. Who made sacrifices to keep them safe.

I don't think about those times because they're fucking depressing and to be honest, I've thought about them more in the past couple days than I have in ten years, but it's clear that these guys *do* remember the past. Otherwise, why would they be here?

As men grab me by the hand and shake mine, a few drawing me into hugs, I have to admit that I don't even remember the names of some of them. It makes me feel like a jackass but burying those memories was the only way to stay sane.

I'm pretty sure Cassiopeia would say I'm the opposite of sane, so what I did, I did out of self-preservation and even that wasn't foolproof.

When I'm deposited outside Maxim's ward, I stroll in and find him unconscious. Misha's there though, sitting in a chair, anxiety making him fidget, knee bobbing up and down as he flicks his focus between Maxim and the door.

When he sees me, he surges to his feet. "Thank fuck," he growls before he hooks me by the neck and draws me into a hug. "It's good to see you, Niko."

My brows lift but I suppose, in the circumstances, the manpower we've got will get them out alive. That's bound to make anyone happy.

"Turgenev was waiting for me," I sign.

He nods. "We heard. The Krestniy Otets has men scouring the hospitals for Maxim. That's why we're this far out—they'll be starting close to the center and moving outwards. He wants Maxim."

"Well, he can't have him." Maxim might be a pain in the ass, but he's *my* pain in the ass—my family. Right now, he looks like shit. "How's he doing?"

"Bad. It's not ideal, him traveling, but if we stay here much longer, they'll figure out our location." He studies the men in the doorway. "Never expected this much help."

"No, I didn't either," I admit. "Get him ready for travel. I have some business to deal with."

Misha disappears, obviously seeking the doctors, while I turn to the waiting men. "My jet will hold fourteen more passengers," I sign. "Whoever wants to come with me can fly out today."

Mutters pass among the crowd.

"I'll get more planes chartered too. You won't suffer for helping me."

Lev shakes his head. "We didn't help out for this, Nikolai. And we'll be okay. The K.O. won't know for sure that we were involved."

"Perhaps, but I didn't save you from the streets and keep most of your butts alive until you were sixteen to have them offed now.

"It's up to you. I won't ask again. But if you want to come, you need to make the decision so that I can get things underway."

I have no strategy in mind here. Stealing Bratva men from the Krestniy Otets is asking for trouble, but then, so was killing Turgenev and I didn't think twice about that.

Whatever, our community is going to be unsettled in the upcoming months and I'd prefer to have men who'd save my brothers at my back than over here in Moskva.

Turning aside, I grab Lev by the arm and tug him into the room.

Once I've glanced at Maxim's chart, taking note that he's got burns from the blast as well as some bullet wounds to the chest along with some broken ribs, I sign, "You still have that friend at the airport?"

Lev's brows lift. "Sure, Nikolai. What do you want me to do?"

"See if we can charter another private jet if needed."

He snorts. "That won't be enough. You'll need a commercial airliner. The rats want to leave the sinking ship, Niko. Moskva's been a mess for a while. I swear the Krestniy Otets is losing it."

"Crazy?"

"Delusional."

For a moment, I scratch my chin, but my mind is mostly focused on Maxim.

"You always did cut him too much slack."

I scowl at Lev.

"What?" he mocks. "You do."

The last time I saw Maxim in a hospital bed, he had more burns than these. More burns than *I* did.

I'd stolen a car after the orphanage fire and had driven us to Podolsk, forty minutes from what had once been our home. That was the first time I'd made a legal claim that both he and Misha were my kin after I'd bribed a doctor to tend to us all.

Scrubbing a hand over my head, I mutter, "My brother."

Lev claps me on the shoulder. "I know, Nikolai. I know. I'll see if we can charter a plane. If not today, sometime this week. It's short notice, *da*?"

An hour later, Maxim is in an ambulance and we're heading to the airfield.

There are three cars in front, three at the back. He's sandwiched in the middle.

We're all aware of what's likely going to happen as we approach Moskva itself, but Daniil and Eriks insisted on driving the first two cars and Mikhail jumped behind the wheel of the ambulance without saying a word.

The journey is uneventful until ten minutes from the airfield, an SUV approaches from the other side of the road while a van overtakes from behind and tries to ram into the ambulance.

As metal screeches and the ambulance's brakes scream, Mikhail pulls some insane defensive driving moves to get away from the van, and I growl to Luka, "This is why I drive myself."

I turn hard to the right and fly headfirst toward the van then wait until I'm six feet away to retrieve my gun.

One bullet shatters my windshield, the second breaks his, and the third hits the driver in the forehead. The van careens and overturns on the hard shoulder.

Luka, cackling like a loon and not giving a damn that I'm wrecking his ride, cheers, "You motherfuckers! Fuck you and your granny!"

Smirking, I hit the handbrake hard, drifting for a handful of seconds so the SUV can't drive into me.

Through the smoke that diminishes visibility, one of my men manages to shoot out two of the SUV's tires. It topples over the side of the road. I brake in the middle of the causeway, then jump out, gun in hand.

When the SUV stops moving, I make my way to the driver's door and see he didn't survive the crash. I ensure he can't be resuscitated by blowing out his brains.

Picking his pockets for his cell phone, I retreat to my ride and toss my gun on the dash while I pass the cell to Luka, quickly signing, "Send his Brigadier an update."

"With lies or the truth?"

"Lies." I roll my eyes as I light out of there, relieved to see that the cavalcade of cars didn't stop their trajectory.

Instead, face literally aching from the biting cold pouring in through the blasted windshield, I race ahead and pull in at the front, a scant few feet from Eriks's car.

"You always did have a death wish behind the wheel," Luka shouts, but I can hear the buzz in his voice and shake my head over it.

If I have a death wish behind the wheel, then he's always been an adrenaline junkie.

As my cell rings, I toss it to Luka. "Ilya?" he asks, amazement lacing his tone. When he hangs up a few minutes later, he states, "You sly fucker. You turned the Krestniy Otets's nephew?"

I cast him a look. "I did nothing." Then, I sign, "Our exalted leader did that himself after what happened with Sofia." And after I sheltered Dmitri with me in the US. "What did he want?"

"Says there are more cars incoming but he told his uncle that you were at the airfield in Vidnoye, not Pushkino."

So, Ilya has bought us some time.

I fucking owe him.

"Does he only feed you information?"

"*Nyet.*"

Luka grunts but I can tell he's offended at my nonanswer. "Why don't I believe you?"

"Call ahead and get Dominik to prepare for takeoff," is all I say.

When we make it to the airfield, I can see the jet is where it was after landing.

As I pull up beside the plane, I spot Cassiopeia sitting by one of the windows, staring at me. The relief in her expression is more of a homecoming than she can know.

With my hands finally free, though my fingers feel frozen solid, I give Luka the answer his loyalty deserves, "Ilya came to me."

"What did he want?"

I arch a brow.

"The old man's job?"

"Of course."

"And do you want him there?"

I nod.

Luka purses his lips. "Ilya doesn't even like you. Why do you trust him?"

"The enemy of my enemy is my friend."

"If you say so. Want me to keep an eye on him?"

"No need. He'll do what he'll do. He's only a satellite in these proceedings." I don't wait for him to reply, just get out of the car.

"Igor! You fat fuck!" Luka greets cheerfully, slapping Igor on the back as he hurries forward to deal with me. "It's good to see you."

Igor huffs. "It's not good to see you, Luka. I've dropped at least forty pounds since the last time we met." Then, to me, he states, "Turgenev's men were overpowered—they're all dead. No major casualties on our side, some wounds. Nothing worse than that."

"Any damage to the jet?"

"No. We were in the hangar by the time the shooting started."

My lips twist with relief as I rush over to the ambulance when it finds its way onto the tarmac.

Misha opens the door, shouting, "You're fucking insane."

Luka whoops. "You think it was insane; I think it was better than a ride at Disney. How close *is* Disney to Miami anyway?" He cackles when I glower at him then rubs his chilled hands together. "You haven't lost your touch, Nikolai."

Ignoring him, I sign, "How is he, Misha?"

"He woke up when the van rammed into us but passed out again."

The EMTs, unsurprisingly, appear shaken and are quick to unload Maxim from the ambulance.

As they work fast, I race around the cars, thanking the men for their help, reaffirming the offer to bring them over to the States.

In the end, ten decide to come with me today, enough that we don't need to charter another plane, but Lev might be right about change coming. No one turns me down. They just thank me and slam their fists to their chests in a show of loyalty that's freely offered.

Keyword there being *freely*.

As I'm about to retreat to the jet, my long-awaited greeting with Cassiopeia incoming, I get a text.

Boris: I have Rundel.

With glee pummeling me, I'm about to hit the video call button to speak with him, but before I can, my phone rings with an incoming call.

Brow furrowing when I see Iosif Arsenyev, one of my Brigadiers, on the ID, I pick up and rest my cell on the top of a car roof.

"Pakhan," he greets, his tone grim.

Luka drifts over to me. "Nikolai? What's going on? Dominik is ready to take off."

I raise a hand to him then sign, "What's happening, Iosif?"

"B4K figured out that we were behind their recent troubles. They ambushed one of our offices, ram-raided the storefront, and stormed inside."

Mind racing, the adrenaline fading from the drive as well as the bitter cold making my brain slow, all I can think to sign is, "Where's Dmitri?"

Squeezing my shoulder, Luka asks Iosif, "Why didn't Dmitri call?"

"The office B4K targeted *was* Dmitri's... Grigoriy is with him." Iosif shakes his head. "Pakhan, he doesn't think Dmitri's going to make it."

41

CASSIE

I'VE SEEN Nikolai in a rage, seen him ice cold, seen him act like a king, seen him cut someone with a look and without a single word uttered.

I haven't seen him like this.

When he dropped to his knees on the airfield, I'd nearly kicked Semion in the balls when he wouldn't let me disembark. Unsure if Niko had been hit or if an injury had felled him, all I knew was that I had to get to him.

Semion predicted the threat to his manhood so he starts to open the door to release me before I can make impact, but by the time I'm ready to run to Niko's side, he's there, his face like a storm as he grabs me in a fierce embrace that doesn't last long enough.

When he lets go of me, it's because men are suddenly pouring onto the jet, one on a stretcher, one of them with a face I recognize from the photos in the safe room. There might be a decade or two between then and now, but the lines of his face are, quite frankly, beautiful.

But his handsomeness doesn't hold my interest for long. Mostly, I'm trying to figure out what's going on with Nikolai. He appears unharmed as he heads to the back of the jet, but he dropped to his knees like his world was ending...

I trail after him, needing to understand what's going on. That's when I hear the sound of fists slamming into static objects.

The noise is discomfiting.

A trigger to the past.

I distinctly remember Harvey punching the wall whenever his Viagra didn't work. One time, he even headbutted the door to a kitchen cabinet.

But even if Nikolai is destroying a room, he won't hurt me.

I know that.

Point blank.

So I suck in a breath, hop into my big girl panties, and tap on the door.

As I open it, Dominik, who I met for the first time today, calls out, "Takeoff in four minutes! I have an opening in the air space."

Whether anyone's listening to him is another matter entirely.

Nikolai's growl of rage has me flinching, but I stride forward, pushing past the concern and closing the door behind me.

The damage he's made in less than five minutes is impressive. I glance around the once-pristine bedroom for a split second, but he regains my focus almost immediately.

That's when I see the tears in his eyes.

"What is it? What's happened?" I demand, more scared *for* him than of him.

"Dmitri," he signs, agony etched into his features.

I grab Niko, palms sliding about his jaw to stop him from evading my glance. "What's wrong with Dmitri?"

"He's dying."

"What?!"

I could never have expected him to say *that*.

His mouth works, eyes closing as he shakes his head. When he rocks forward, I have no alternative but to take his weight. His face finds my throat and he hides there.

I have no words, none at all. So I just hold him until Dominik gives the final order for everyone to take their seats.

The bedroom has a couch with seatbelts, so I shuffle us over to it, half-expecting him to stop me.

Only, he doesn't.

He allows me to maneuver him around the destroyed bedroom and doesn't stop me from fastening us into our seats for takeoff. Not even arguing when I don't plunk myself in his lap.

That's when I know my man is broken.

Really, *truly* broken.

I don't talk. I don't have anything to say. Nothing that can make his grief go away.

So I sit there.

I hold his hand.

And he lets me.

That's somehow more terrifying than anything else we've done together.

42

CASSIE

WE REMAIN in the wreckage of the bedroom for the entirety of the trip to the US as we fly to New York.

The original plan was to stay in the city until Maxim was awake and settled into his home in Brighton Beach, but at some point, while I was sleeping, Nikolai must have made alternative arrangements.

Now, we land there. Misha, who I'm introduced to and who is just as shell-shocked as Nikolai at the news from Miami, *doesn't* get off with Maxim.

Instead, the men who made an appearance on the plane after the ambulance showed up at the airfield travel with Maxim as security and Misha joins us on the flight to Florida.

Seeing ten Russians enter the US illegally should have me shaking my head, but in my time with Nikolai, I've learned that to him, laws are like telling a child not to eat the chocolate chip cookies on the baking tray fresh from the oven—an order that's ripe for ignoring.

For the first quarter of the flight to Florida, we stayed in the destroyed bedroom. I worked on my notes in the quiet, and Nikolai mostly stared into space, not saying anything—it's not as if there's much change from the regular. Except this time, it feels different.

Less about being mute, more about being speechless and scared.

I didn't realize how that'd affect me.

Nikolai is endlessly competent. Ceaselessly unflappable. To see him *vulnerable* is both endearing and heart-wrenching. In a strange way, it's almost an honor that he'd let *me* see him like this.

He doesn't exactly decompress, but with an hour to go until we land, he encourages me to stand and, together, we move into the main space on the jet.

Nikolai's men are used to seeing me sit on his knee, but Misha is perturbed by the sight, something he backs up with frequent scowls he aims at me. I've no idea what they're talking about, but I can feel Nikolai's tension as if it were my own.

When he hisses something at Misha then snags my hand in his, raises it to his mouth, and kisses my knuckles, I stop zoning out on the notebook on my lap and tune in.

"What's wrong?"

Nikolai's smile is tight as he signs, "Nothing."

"I asked what the hell Nikolai is doing bringing a gold digger with him to fucking Moskva."

My brows lift. "I assume you don't know our meet/cute?"

Misha blinks. "Excuse me?"

"You heard me," I drawl. "Meet/cute."

With a sigh, Nikolai signs, "My lies are coming back to haunt me."

Misha frowns. "Which lies?"

"Misha, Cassiopeia Rundel did *not* fly away as I told you. She stayed with me."

I snort.

Misha flashes me a look. "*You're* Savannah O'Donnelly's friend?"

I straighten up a little. "You know her?"

"I'm dating her sister."

"Ohh, is that why she got you involved? I wondered why the wife of an Irish mobster would call in the Russians for help."

Though his eyes light up with rage, Misha's tone is relatively calm as he argues, "What the hell are you trying to do, Nikolai? Ruin ties between us and the Irish? I just had one of the O'Donnelly brothers confirm they'd support Maxim as the new leader of the Russians in the city!"

"Hardly new," Nikolai signs. "He's been Pakhan for a while."

"Of the Bratva." Misha tips up his chin. "We're The Forgotten Boys now."

"Is that supposed to sound *Peter Pan*-esque?" I mock, but only because he just called me a gold digger.

"No," he reasons. "It's about a bunch of boys who were fucking forgotten and won't be again."

When Niko's tension surges, I muse, "Is it a wise time to discuss this? We're all just waiting for news on Dmitri."

If I thought he was tense before, that's nothing to how Niko's turned to stone beneath me. "There will be no more news."

"You don't know that! You have to have hope, Niko," I chide, squeezing his fingers as I entwine them further with mine.

"Iosif wouldn't dare give Nikolai hope, and Grigoriy wouldn't misinform Iosif either," Misha snaps, his knuckles cracking as a flash of rage sweeps over his expression. "He's as good as dead."

Nikolai flinches like he's been hit with a bullet, but he doesn't disagree, just turns his face toward the window.

"Why are you here then? Aside from to make things worse?" I spit, feeling Niko's grief as if it were my own.

Misha frowns at me. "Are you sure you are Savannah's friend?"

"What kind of question is that?"

He blurts something in Russian that has Niko, his face still turned away, signing, "Speak in English. It's rude."

Misha grits his teeth. "You are a survivor of abuse, no?"

"Yes." I arch a brow as I figure out what the asshole means. "What? Do you want me to sit here and cower? Is that to be my role for the rest of my life because I picked the wrong man?" I huff. "Well, I'm sorry that I don't fit the part."

More like I'm sorry he typecasted me.

Niko squeezes my fingers as Misha, clearly sensing the error of his ways, rumbles, "Revenge."

"Revenge?" I repeat because that seems a little out of context.

"That's why I'm here. We shouldn't be talking about this in front of her," he snipes at Nikolai.

"You mean aside from already witnessing two murders and the illegal transportation of ten Russians whose only interaction with ICE will be the rocks they have with their vodka tonight... you're concerned I have evidence for the cops?"

Misha's mouth tightens. "Who did you kill, Nikolai?"

"Who didn't he?" I retort airily. "I'm not going to say anything. Why would I?"

It's then, of course, that I realize how strange my words are.

I *have* seen two murders.

Why the hell do I sound so blasé?

It's no wonder that Misha thinks I'm a threat—any normal woman would be.

But I'm not normal.

I *am* a product of an abusive relationship. Justice, I've learned, never comes with much help from the boys in blue.

Tipping up my chin, I intone, "I have no intention of surviving my marriage to Harvey Rundel only to die at the hands of the Bratva for betrayal."

Misha sniffs.

As we approach Miami, turbulence hits, but Nikolai holds me firmer than a seatbelt ever could as Misha and Igor discuss their plan while Nikolai listens in.

But, his part in the discussion is passive. It isn't about *listening*; it's about grieving.

He's in mourning.

Dmitri still lives, but Nikolai is already processing his death.

This is the world I now inhabit, I suppose.

Death, jail, violence, and crime—that's the Bratva way, and as scary as that might be, I've already been living so long with those four criteria that Harvey prepared me for this life without even knowing it.

So, I turn my face into Nikolai's throat, settle my arms around his waist, and give him what I can—comfort, understanding, and love.

It might be my imagination, but the rock beneath me softens some as Misha discusses an update he's received from a Brigadier called Valkov and how he's stamping out B4K and containing the situation in Miami until Nikolai returns home.

Despite his grief, the brutal underworld he exists in continues turning on its axis.

It's then I recognize what I can give him... a soft place to land when everything turns on its head.

43

CASSIE

A MAN CALLED Iosif Arsenyev is waiting for us when we arrive.

He's the one who tells us how Dmitri was shot. Who shares what's going down in the city as we traverse its boundaries and head for the Everglades.

Our first stop isn't a hospital like I assumed it'd be.

No, *Nav* is.

That's where Dmitri's hooked up to a million tubes and wires in a hospital room that I've never seen before.

That the estate has a medical wing is indicative of how frequently it's needed, I guess.

Nikolai takes one look at Dmitri, closes his eyes a second to bank the sorrow within, and then, he's back to being ice cold.

I'll never forget my father's bizarre mannerisms. Well, bizarre to an American. He could be so cold. So rigid. He could stare at me like I was nothing to him.

Then, he'd kiss my forehead while holding my face. He'd hug me tighter than anyone ever had until Niko. If I'd been a boy, he'd have done that too.

Russians are affectionate in ways that Americans aren't.

When I saw there was a separate course at college for Russian psychology, I'd known why—I'd had a lifetime of lessons from my papa.

So when Nikolai presses a kiss to Dmitri's forehead, it's so reminiscent of my childhood that it hurts my heart.

What breaks it, though, is when he murmurs, "Rest, my son, until we can meet again. I lov—"

Before he can finish the sentence, that's when all hell breaks loose.

Dmitri codes.

Like he was waiting for a final farewell from his papa, the alarms on the systems and machines bleat to life, and, from out of nowhere, a full team runs in and a nurse shepherds us out—not Grigoriy.

He's too busy trying to save Dmitri's life.

I didn't even know they had that many healthcare providers on staff, but they do, and suddenly, I'm glad they do because the look of agony on Nikolai's face almost brings me to my knees.

But the pain gets locked out. He shuts down, his expression becoming glacial as the alarms finally stop, but Grigoriy doesn't head out to explain things to Nikolai. Not like he would if everything is okay.

God, is he going to die?

He can't… can he?

I close my eyes at the stupid thought.

Of course, he can.

Better people than a Russian mobster die every day of the damn week.

My heart starts to pound as the strangest realization curls through me—Dmitri is family.

I don't want him to go. I don't want him to leave Nikolai.

When there's still no news, Nikolai sits heavily at my side. I know he's shut me out because he doesn't reach for me, doesn't even grab my hand and entwine our fingers.

And I don't care.

The ice doesn't bother me, not when I know it'll melt for me alone.

Moving to sit on his lap, I bury my face in his throat and cry. As I sob against him, slowly but surely, I can feel him start to defrost.

Then, finally, his arms cup my waist and he hauls me into him. Tighter than ever. So tight it hurts, but it hurts *good*.

That's when a door opens.

Both our heads whip around so fast on our hunt for the doctor, it's a small wonder we don't knock into each other. That's when we see Grigoriy.

His expression doesn't bode well.

Grim.

Dark.

Austere.

"No," I choke out, trembling in Nikolai's arms.

His hands clamp down, hard enough to bruise. Normally, those types of marks originate in pleasure, because he never hurts me.

His break in control tells me he's come to the same conclusion as I have.

"He can't be dead," Misha rasps, his voice hoarse.

Grigoriy rubs his eyes. "We almost lost him. Twice."

"Almost?" I whisper, hope hurting me more than Harvey ever could.

Beneath me, Nikolai is practically vibrating with it too.

"We had to induce a coma. There's a lot of damage, Pakhan." Grigoriy swallows, his nerves seeping through. "You need to prepare yourself for the worst."

If I thought Nikolai turned to ice before, now his rage is set. When Grigoriy escapes his boss's fury, making a swift retreat to the hospital room, the flames licking around Nikolai don't burn me as he presses a soft kiss to my cheek then shuffles me onto the seat where I was originally.

"Boris is bringing Rundel to *Nav*. The alligators will eat well tonight," he signs.

Surprised, I frown at him. "What does that have to do with anything?"

He doesn't answer.

"Where are you going?" I ask when he stands. "You can't just leave."

He stares at me, his ire surging around him like a visceral entity, leaving phantom shadows flicking over his face as he urges four anger-soaked, fury-bitten, wrath-filled words from his throat: "Dmitri will be avenged."

"He doesn't need that," I argue, suddenly terrified that he'll do something... crazy.

Fuck, who am I kidding?

Nikolai *is* crazy!

When I reach for him, he snags my hand in his and presses a kiss to the tips of my fingers before he lets go to sign, "I'll be back soon."

"Your son needs you," I cry desperately as he turns away.

His shoulders stiffen but he doesn't listen.

God damn him.

As he steps toward the door, Misha nods briskly at me. Igor too. And I'm alone again. Until Niko returns to the doorway and hovers in place, staring at me with such pain etched into his features that it hurts me like it's my own.

"Be with him. For me," he signs.

It's the plea in his eyes that has my lips trembling until I firm them. "I will."

He nods, relief easing into his expression before it disappears. Any and all softness blinks out of existence, leaving the Pakhan behind, not my Nikolai.

Because he *is* mine.

And, like he always says, I'm *his*.

Which means I'm the boss of Grigoriy too.

So when Nikolai heads out, revenge on his mind, I don't stick around in the outer waiting room. I get to my feet and return to Dmitri's ward.

The nurses frown at me, but Grigoriy doesn't say anything as he peers at me over a clipboard so they don't either.

Instead, I find a seat and I wait and watch them tend to Nikolai's son.

Later, when they've gone, after Grigoriy explains what the

upcoming hours will look like, Semion and Sergei move into place as my guards, and, ignoring them, I lean forward and squeeze his hand.

"They're so sure you're going to die, Dmitri. Are you? Or are you going to prove them wrong? I think you should. If you don't, you'll break your father's heart. If that happens, I'm not sure Miami will survive the night…"

Then, I settle in for a vigil, trying not to think about the last time I'd done this… with my mother at my papa's bedside.

I can only hope for Nikolai's sake that this has a better ending.

44

NIKOLAI

Finished Symphony - Hybrid

"YOU'RE SURE this is all of it?"

"This is their neighborhood," Igor snaps at Misha in affront while I just stare around the area.

"Seems stupid to me," Misha mutters. "Why do they all live together?"

"Strength in numbers. Like you don't live on the compound in NYC? Hell, *we* have subdivisions too."

Misha gusts out a heavy breath but doesn't argue with the truth. "There are no other pockets?"

"That's impossible to say. This is where the majority of their pushers live. Even Linton resides here."

"Do they have kids?"

"Last intel said they have baby mommas, but none are living here."

"That's weird. Why?"

"Because Linton won't allow it."

"How the fuck does he stop men from living with their women?"

"Threatens to kill the kids." Igor snorts. "It's a successful deterrent. We've looked into Linton before and his dad was the leader of MA$$. You remember them?"

Misha frowns. "Not really."

"Figured you might. They were here when you were a kid. Anyway, he was twelve when Indigo Cartel soldiers bust into his house and killed his dad. He got shot in the fray."

"You're saying he has a conscience where kids are concerned?" Misha mocks.

Igor shrugs. "Yup. Handy for us. Means we can burn this place down and the only fuckers who'll get hurt are the ones who deserve it." To me, his tone turns deferential as he asks, "You ready, Pakhan?"

His question breaks into the silent movie that I've had playing on repeat in my head since I saw the security footage of Dmitri's attack.

Like I was there, I can see the moment B4K tore into one of our office buildings.

Ram-raiding the storefront, they'd leaped out with SMGs and had sprayed the area with bullets, killing three men in the collision and one in the shooting.

Two B4K had sneaked into the main office where Dmitri was. Because my son never fucking listened to me, he'd had that godawful death metal music he enjoyed piped into his ears while he worked.

One second, Dmitri's head was bowed over the books. The next, the door exploded inwards.

He hit the panic button—that's why he lived long enough for me to say goodbye to him.

Then, he was shot.

The image of that will live with me until the day I fucking die.

A bullet speared him in the chest, blood spurting and soaring from the intensity, while another got him in the gut.

The gunfight was tough to watch, but it was seeing my boy, my *kid,* hide his agony, plow on through the pain and what had to be a sense of hopelessness that was worse.

My son—the fighter.

When Dmitri had gone for his gun, even managing to let off a bullet that hit one of the bastards in the shoulder, the other asshole pistol-whipped him.

As Dmitri sagged into unconsciousness, they'd found the strongbox behind the desk.

Another piece of shit had come in to help and within ten minutes, the safe had been removed and B4K was on their way.

Brigadiers have been in turf wars all night.

Miami is burning. I can see it from this distance despite the city being under lockdown.

But no fires blaze here.

Until now, we've had an accord—homes are off-limits.

Yet, as those images flicker on repeat behind my eyes, any accord between us is broken.

First, Pavel.

Now, Dmitri.

The likely progression is that B4K will target Cassiopeia next seeing as it's an open rodeo on the people I fucking care about.

I can feel the nerves in my face twitching as my brain tries and fails to deal with the emotions I'm experiencing.

Mostly, it's shame. Guilt.

I should have done this sooner.

Back a mortally wounded animal into a corner and it'll bite.

Shoot it in the head, the risk is gone…

"You're sure they're here?"

Igor grunts. "The police escorted them from the ER after Karl blew their HQ up. Linton's got minor burns. Couple had to stay in the hospital overnight."

"The cops are dirty?" Misha demands.

Igor shrugs. "Ivan was watching and got their badge numbers. Not a priority tonight."

He's right. But still, we need to know how many—

"How many of the upper rankers are here?" Misha asks, the question so reminiscent of Dmitri that it's like a knife to the gut.

Before Dmitri, Misha used to interpret for me.

Fuck.

My boy.

My fucking boy.

"I'd say seventy percent are on-site."

"Why aren't they out fighting?" Misha pesters.

"Linton runs his ship differently. The top ranks don't get their hands dirty like our Pakhan and Brigadiers do."

Igor's pride in that is obvious and it's the trigger I need.

Whether this will decimate them entirely or just kill Linton, I'm happy so long as that fucker dies tonight.

Sucking in a breath, resolve set, I give Igor and Misha a brisk nod.

The time for talking is done.

Storming over to the pickup truck that's loaded with gas canisters, I jump into the driver's seat.

Reversing out of the neighborhood, I ride along the street so that I can pull a U-turn. That's when I hit the accelerator and barrel toward their subdivision.

Halfway down the road, I shove the door open and throw myself onto the street. I know I broke my arm in the fall, so I hold it to my side as I get the hell out of there.

When a barrage of bullets from my men follow the truck once I'm safely on the ground, the explosion hits. It lifts me from the pavement and sends me flying.

I know the landing will be brutal.

But not as much as that explosion was.

As I soar through the air, there's a smile on my face, though.

Vengeance *should* be painful, and it *will* hurt, but at least Linton won't survive the night.

45

NIKOLAI

"YOU'RE A LUCKY MOTHERFUCKER."

That has me groaning.

"Yeah, I know you're hurting, but you'd be hurting a lot fucking worse if you hadn't landed in that swimming pool. We overestimated the blast. You're lucky these gangbangers are bougie."

Misha's dry tone has me squinting up at him as I finally dare to open my eyes.

"Bougie?" I try to sign, but, *blyad*, my hands.

Something's sprained. Maybe even goddamn broken.

Misha shakes his head. "And you wonder where Maxim gets his batshit crazy ideas from."

"Could. Have. Stopped. Me."

He snorts, but his eyes widen at the fact that I've spoken.

With the current state of my hands, I had no choice.

"He also inherited your obstinacy," he muses. "No way of changing your mind once it's set. It isn't like I can complain. Not when that was so effective."

"Worked?"

"*Da.* No bodies have been recovered yet according to the police radio—the blast's still burning. Miami won't forget tonight," he states, tone laced with satisfaction.

"If Linton survived…"

"He won't survive for long." Misha pats my shoulder. "We're on our way to *Nav*. Brace yourself."

"For?" I rasp, fearing the worst.

"When Cassiopeia sees you, you'll regret surviving. I saw her give you shit back at *Nav* earlier. I reckon you need to brace yourself for her reaction."

I'm too exhausted to deal with the silent question lacing the words, and I'm in too much fucking pain to even care.

I owe him no explanations. Not in this, not in anything.

Ten minutes later, when Igor and Misha help me into the hospital room, I learn what he means.

Not only that Dmitri lives still—thank God—but that Cassiopeia can communicate with bats when she hurls herself at me, her hands patting me down, making things hurt worse than they did originally.

It's worth it.

Each pat, each shout and screech is indicative of a solid truth—*she loves me.*

No 'think' about it.

And I wouldn't change that for anything.

"What the hell are you trying to do to me? Turn me fucking gray? Look at the state of you!" she shrieks. "How did this happen? Are you trying to break my heart?"

It's the last question that has me snagging her fingers in my damaged ones and pressing a kiss to her knuckles.

"Never, *solnyshko,* never."

Her tension doesn't abate, but Misha's does.

Visibly so.

Enough that I notice it even though Cassie's reaction to my injuries takes up almost all of my attention.

"Be lucky that you look like death or I'd go for your balls," she growls, apparently unappeased. "And don't even think about sex until you're out of that cast."

The louder she gets, however, the more her feelings for me shine through, and the happier my soul is.

My *solnyshko*.

She burns the brightest when all around me, the darkness takes over.

46

CASSIE

MY TEMPER HASN'T LESSENED when Nikolai's arm is set in a cast or after he groans as Grigoriy resets his dislocated shoulder or after his three broken fingers are taped up with splints.

The fact that he came in drenched keyed me into the fact that he was lucky to not be *more* injured. A pool had spared him from the worst, but that's not exactly reassuring.

Seated between Dmitri and Nikolai in the two-bed ward, I listen to Misha and Igor discuss the aftermath of the last few days' events.

The Krestniy Otets, the Bratva head, will have Nikolai on his shit list and the city is going to want answers for a massive gas explosion. Never mind the turf wars that sprang up overnight where the Bratva vanquished their enemy.

Hence the lockdown.

News reports say the fires will rage for days and the lockdown might too in an attempt to stop the looting and rioting.

They discuss heading to New York, where things aren't as *hot* right now, literally and figuratively, but after assuring me that he's okay despite the injuries, he's been silent until that suggestion.

"*Nav* is my—" He snarls when signing with broken fingers hurts, making it impossible to continue. It takes a few tries for him to rumble,

"*Nav* is home, Misha." Pain and self-directed annoyance spread over his face as in half-ASL and half-broken speech, he communicates, "I won't move us to New York unless it becomes necessary."

Us.

My lips purse.

Especially when he's saying the words for me, even if they're directed at Misha.

I huff.

"I thought you were from New Jersey?" Misha asks me.

"I am."

"So, wouldn't you be better off up there?" he inquires, his tone...

Huh.

He wants me to help him out.

Yeah, *no.*

I peer at my nails.

Registering that I'm a lost cause, Misha heaves a sigh. "You have to come to New York, Nikolai. When you went to Moskva, when you saved Maxim, you made a fucking choice. There are repercussions—"

"Of course there are," he growls, the words tight. I can hear the strain in them. Feel it *in* him. He's tired. Hurting. Grieving though Dmitri still lives. And talking is making it all much worse. "But those repercussions don't end in New York." Pushing through the pain, he signs, "If you think Maxim didn't start something that *I'm* going to have to fucking finish, you're an idiot."

Affronted, Misha sputters, "What do you mean?"

"Survival means taking the entirety of the US, not just New York City." His jaw works as he flicks a look at Dmitri. "He said it himself. The US is new. Younger. It's the Pakhans who rule it on the Bratva's behalf." Voice still hoarse, still broken, he slowly grates out, "If we want to live to see tomorrow, then this is only the beginning."

His words send a shiver rushing down my spine.

When Nikolai's cell phone screen flashes on, he snatches it from the nightstand with a glower at his brother, then he grits his teeth once he's read the message.

"Who was it?" Misha demands.

"Pavel. He heard about—"

A knock sounds at the door before he can continue. When a man pops his head into the room, Nikolai sits up with a grunt, his gaze expectant.

"He's here, Pakhan."

Amid this chaos, we still know what that means.

An effervescent welter of excitement floods me, which is, to be honest, obscene.

But I've been forced to leave my home, ran out of my state, divorced from my family, hunted and stalked and abused. Kidnapped.

I said it to Misha on the plane—I'm a survivor.

But that's no longer enough for me—it's time to thrive.

And that's when I come to a decision, one that shocks even me. "I don't want to see him."

Nikolai frowns. "I thought—"

I shake my head. "He's my abuser, but I'm not his. I don't need to fall to his level to erase him from my life."

His frown darkens but slowly, he nods.

Which is when I understand how far we've come as an odd couple —he doesn't force the issue. Simply accepts that I know what's best for me.

To the stranger, he asks, "Did you bring Cassiopeia's belongings, Boris?"

"*Da*, Pakhan."

"Take them to our suite."

Boris nods. "And Rundel?"

"Take him to the alligators."

"You don't want to oversee—"

Before Boris can finish, and seeing Nikolai start to get up from the bed, I grab his good hand and perch on his bedside so he can't get past me without having to lean on his bad arm.

"Nikolai's fine here. He doesn't need to oversee the trash being disposed of."

Nikolai growls, "Cassiopeia!"

I scowl at him.

What I want to scream is, 'You threw yourself out of a truck tonight, Nikolai. You were tossed into the air because of a gas explosion! The least you can do is stay in bed while the doctor continues to monitor you.'

But Grigoriy just walked in.

Semion guards us in one corner while Sergei hovers in another.

So, instead, I say, "You need to be here. For Dmitri. Harvey is a part of our past."

"Next you'll be saying we should let him go so he can live his life to the fullest," he grumbles, but he doesn't try to get up again.

"I'm not that generous," I snipe.

Misha shoots me a measured glance, but I ignore him until he murmurs, "The night that you contacted Savannah, she was terrified for you. Enough that she got her husband to call in a favor with the Russian Bratva to save you.

"Closure comes in many guises," he finishes.

"What's that supposed to mean?" I demand, nonplussed by the philosophical tone when he's only been suspicious and catty around me thus far.

"Leave her alone, Misha," Nikolai snaps. "Or I'll shut your mouth for you."

"If I don't want to see my ex being eaten alive by Vasily then that's my prerogative," I agree.

"You're being given an opportunity that few in your position ever have," Misha chides.

"To witness a brutal murder?"

"To have the man who made you plead for your life plead for his."

I don't want those words to resonate but they do.

The truth washes through me with a cleansing force that shakes my earlier resolve and pounds it to dust.

I turn to face Nikolai, who seems to sense the shift in my stance because he assures me, "Whatever you want to do, we can do, Cassiopeia."

"I don't want to see him die."

That's the truth.

I don't.

I mean, *I did.* But that was before Moscow.

As the plane taxied away and 'parked' in a hangar, I managed to catch enough of the ensuing 'battle' to feed my nightmares for a lifetime.

I never thought anything could be more terrifying than being tied to a bed and drugged, of meaty fists pounding into me like I was dough. Or those initial days with Niko, where I hadn't known if up was down.

But seeing Nikolai under fire? Watching a gunfight unfold in front of me and men being shot down?

Nothing could be more terrifying than that.

Harvey Rundel *is* my past.

Somehow, my future is crazier than the level of shit he heaped at my door.

I don't need to ask for new nightmares, which is undoubtedly what'd happen if I watched Harvey become alligator chow.

"But?" Niko prods.

For a moment, I'm unsure how to answer. Then, Misha's words echo in my head.

Closure comes in many guises.

They're powerful words, more fitting on an episode of *Maury* than from a Bratva foot soldier.

"I want to talk to him," I reply slowly, tasting each word as I utter them.

Though he frowns, he assures me, "Whatever you need."

I glance at Misha. "Thank you."

He hitches a shoulder. "My woman has issues with something that happened to her when she was younger. Issues that would have been resolved with closure. I'd hate for you to throw away your chance at gaining it."

That's surprisingly kind for a man who called me a gold digger yesterday. Today. Hell, *tomorrow*? I don't even know what time it is or the day either.

As I get to my feet, I can't help but look at Dmitri. He's so still that it's unnerving. The nurses did something to his hair to stop it from falling messily into his face like it usually does, and it makes him look young. So young. *Too* young for this.

"You don't have to come, Nikolai," I tell him gently. "You need to be here. Just in case."

In what I'm starting to consider his signature move, he raises my hand to his mouth and kisses my knuckles. "Where you are, I am."

"No—"

"Dmitri would have it no other way."

"He's right. Dmitri wouldn't," Misha agrees, but I can see his own worry swallow him whole as he looks upon the younger man.

The tubes… The wires…

We see them on TV all the time, but nothing prepares us for encountering them when they're on someone we love.

"W-We can wait until he wakes up," I argue weakly. *Because he'd better.*

His thumb rubs over my ring finger. "Needs my ring."

"Maybe I don't want to be your wife," I counter. "Especially without being asked."

His smile is somber, loaded with the remnants of the past forty-eight hours. Then, as casually as telling me the date, he takes my breath away and forever steals my heart by murmuring in my ear, that broken voice of his sending shockwaves down my spine:

"Would you settle for being my everything?"

47

NIKOLAI

The Kill - Thirty Seconds To Mars

I'M NOT twenty-two anymore and my body declares that with every step we take toward the alligator enclosure.

Cassiopeia placed my arm over her shoulder—whether that's for comfort or for me to lean on her, I'm not sure yet. Still, I appreciate the support even if I don't put any weight on her.

Her soft curves against my hard lines are more affection than I've ever had, and I can only be grateful that she's here. That she's mine. That she said she'll stand by my side forever.

Because a lifetime isn't enough.

Still, the pain clamoring its way through my body comes almost as a relief because I prefer the physical pain to the emotional agony that's coming.

Grigoriy says hope isn't lost, but I translate that as every breath Dmitri takes is borrowed.

Grigoriy doesn't want to anger me.

Which means he's downplaying Dmitri's situation.

She's right—we could have waited. Should have. But I've never been good at saying goodbye.

Especially not to Dmitri.

Never to him.

How the fuck am I supposed to be Pakhan without him?

He's my Sovietnik, but he's so much more.

How the fuck am I supposed to be *Nikolai* without Dmitri when he helped turn me into the man standing here today?

How am I supposed to be Nikolai if I'm a father without his son?

I imagined returning to the US and celebrating Fyodor's death by drinking vodka, eating blinis and caviar, and watching him sing karaoke songs out of tune in *Nav's* bar while wearing that fucking signet ring I brought for him, rejoicing in the fact that old bastard no longer pollutes the Earth.

I never imagined *this*.

Retaliation and revenge—they're watchwords of a mobster's life. Now, they're not just biting me in the ass, they're tearing at my fucking soul.

With grief a heavy burden on my shoulders, one that makes each step harder to take, we walk into the backrooms of the enclosure.

The alligators pretty much roam around the swamps because I don't believe in caging wild animals. They come here for regular feeds when they're feeling too lazy to hunt and because one of my favorites, Zub, before she died in a hunting accident, came here to birth another generation.

For whatever reason, that made this place a haven for her hatchlings who choose to make this their home too.

Zub died and in memorial, I used her skin for the shoulder holster housing the knife that killed the man who hunted her.

Full circle.

Things have a habit of doing that around me.

"Cassie!" When Rundel spies her through bruised and blackened eyes, he starts sobbing with relief. "Cassie, help me!" He shoots me a desperate look. "You have to make them listen!"

She freezes at his demand, hunches in on herself beneath my arm.

It will never stop devastating me seeing her do this—reacting like prey. The predator in me should respond to her weakness, but it doesn't.

Because it recognizes its mate?

Perhaps.

I can feel her quiver. Her fear is a visceral thing tainting the air.

My temper surges.

Not at her, *for* her.

This bastard reduced her to this. Never again.

"Why should I do anything to help you?"

That she's found her voice is reassuring. Mirroring her earlier actions, I squeeze her shoulder in both comfort and support. I want her to know she's not alone anymore. She has me.

Always.

"Cassie, for God's sake. You have to! The Russians—"

"You made me a target for the Albanians!" she snarls, her soft tenor suddenly being replaced with vitriol. Only, a second later, she's back to being quietly spoken. "You're here because of me, Harvey. Why would I help you when Nikolai brought you to me?"

"You bitch! How could you do this?" he screeches.

"Months in a psychiatric ward, only fuck knows how many nights spent in the hospital because of *you*, and you ask me how *I* can do this to *you*? The answer, Harvey, is easily.

"I'm glad you're here. I'm glad because I can say goodbye to you. I'm glad because I can watch you die and know that you can't hurt me anymore, and do you know what?" She sucks in a breath. "That feels really good. No more running like a frightened mouse. No more staying in shitty motels to escape you and diving from job to job to make ends meet. No more poverty.

"No more avoiding my family, no more being alienated from everyone who matters to me.

"I wanted to be a journalist, Harvey. I wanted to write the news, and instead, you drew me away from everything that mattered to me. Even then, you resented it. You resented that I brought in more money than you, and instead of being grateful, you made me pay for it.

"Well, it's your turn to pay, Harvey. It's your turn to suffer, and I want you to know that it's happening because of me. Because someone better than you loves me enough to let me have this moment."

"No one could ever love you, you fat cow," Rundel snarls, but that's as far as he gets.

Surging forward, ignoring the rattle of bones that have been shaken after the day's events, I kick his chair so that he falls flat on his back. As he splutters in reaction, Boris passes me something.

Staring down at the baggy in my hand, I peer at him in question and he answers, "RED."

My eyes flare wide, then I shake my head.

Two pills.

Harvey Rundel hasn't changed.

Still seeking an erection.

But these little red pills crafted by the Sicilians in New York are a lot different than the blue ones...

Delighted by the prospect of making his death more miserable, I empty the baggy into my palm.

Boris, reading between the lines, punches Rundel until he's moaning, head rocking dully against the ground, then he pinches his nostrils to force the bastard's mouth open.

Dropping the pills inside, I wait for him to swallow then snag a handkerchief from my pocket and shove it between his teeth. That's when Boris passes me a roll of duct tape.

As we tape Rundel's mouth closed, I grab my knife from my holster and I slice two Xs in his cheeks.

As his blood pours free and he pleads with eyes that showed my woman no mercy, I rumble, "Your foolishness is my gain, Rundel. You treated her like an animal, and I'll treat her like a queen." It's unlike me to make big speeches, not when each word feels like it slips from vocal cords wrapped in barbed wire, but this is a special occasion so I dig in the metaphorical knife. "You can die knowing that she'll live on and find happiness with another man. I'm sure that'll hurt but not as much as what's about to happen to you."

As he struggles, screaming against his gag, Boris hauls the chair toward the gates which open up behind him.

"Any alligators in the enclosure?"

"None at the moment."

I grunt.

The smell of blood will bring them quickly enough.

Boris drags Rundel out onto the shores of the swamp. Quickly, he rushes back into the enclosure, and the gates close behind him.

Cassiopeia hasn't moved since I left her side.

Gingerly, feeling every fucking ache in my body as if it's an echo, I return to her.

She nestles into me, hiding her face in my chest, whispering, "I loved him once."

I think about those red pills—the debt he incurred to get them because they're not cheap, what he intended on doing with them...

But I keep her in the dark.

She's been tainted by Rundel enough.

"Then he's the idiot for being given that gift and for throwing it away." It's getting easier to talk to her, but I still sound like I've been chewing glass. As I smooth my good hand down her spine, I rasp slowly, "I hope you know I'll never be that stupid."

She blows out a breath that spreads warmth over my chest. I'm sure she's thinking about the things that Harvey undoubtedly promised her in the past, promises he ultimately broke, but she makes no mention of that, merely nuzzles her face into my shirt and whispers, almost so low that I don't hear her, "I believe you."

It's only because she loves me, because she has faith in me, because she *trusts* me, that she can believe me, and that means more than a declaration of love—it means everything.

"Vasily will eat well tonight," I promise, knowing that I'm only able to speak those words because of her.

Before she came into my life, broken fingers or not, silence would have kept me in its cage.

She stiffens a touch then whispers, "I should meet him. I could tell Dmitri judged me when I said I hadn't."

Though inside, I tense at his name, I rumble, "Only because Vasily is special."

In my arms, she squirms. "Why?"

"He is Zub's son. Her first hatchling."

Cassiopeia sucks in a breath. "Oh."

I nuzzle my nose over her temple where her scent is sweetest. "You can meet him another time."

When he isn't busy with a Harvey Rundel-shaped appetizer, entrée, and dessert.

48

NIKOLAI
THE FOLLOWING AFTERNOON

BUSINESS IS the last thing on my mind, but today's gathering is more important than I'm comfortable with.

The outcome...

Blyad, everything rests on this meeting.

As my Brigadiers settle into their seats around the board table, I watch them with an intensity they're not used to.

It takes their triumphant posturing down a notch, but that wasn't my intention.

Instead, I'm checking for potential weak spots.

For men who'll flee when I tell them what's about to happen—the lay of the land is about to shift toward the west.

I'm just not sure who'll survive the cull because anyone who walks out of here won't get far.

That's why Igor's standing in one corner, Semion the other. Men who've already *shown* me where their fealty lies.

When the Brigadiers are seated, I stand.

Neither Pavel nor Dmitri are here, and it's my first meeting as Pakhan without one or both in attendance.

It isn't lonely at the top, but fuck if communicating won't be hard.

As my men stare at me, the first thing I declare is, "You honor me with your loyalty."

They're used to my silence.

My words, however, have them gaping at me.

Not the content of my short statement, just the fact I uttered it out loud.

Then, when that feat resonates, like a wave around the table, each soldier bares their throat to me—almost two dozen Oskals submitting to their Pakhan.

A solid start to the proceedings.

"Last night, you held this city in my stead." This time, I sign. It fucking hurts, but I won't be able to manage the whole meeting otherwise. "You will be rewarded, but first..." I press my good fist to my chest. "Thank you."

From their wide eyes, you'd think I was cursing at them, but slowly, when they realize I truly am grateful, they relax some.

Antonin Valkov even rumbles, "We'd have held the state for you if need be, Pakhan."

Iosif Arsenyev concurs, "The fucking country." He slams his fist against his knee. "Wouldn't we, men?"

Each Brigadier slaps the flat of their hand to the table in agreement.

Letting the ramifications of their backing hit home, it sinks in that the Krestniy Otets is fucked.

Taking a seat, some of my tension easing now I know which way the wind blows, I ask, "What's the damage?"

"Ten of our men are dead," Yuri Morozov answers.

My mouth tightens. "Married? With families?"

Nods come from the different Brigadiers who commanded them.

"See that their widows and children never go hungry. As for their funerals, coordinate with Igor and I will attend the services."

That comes as a surprise to them, but it shouldn't.

Those men fought for *me*. That will never go without compensation.

"What about B4K?"

Igor slips from the back wall and states, "We killed more of the

B4K leadership than anticipated in the offensive on their subdivision, Pakhan.

"The death toll is still rolling in. My police informant says the morgues are overflowing with their members."

"Linton's gone?" Iosif queries.

I nod. "Nothing more than ashes now."

Antonin sneers, "As he deserves. We dealt with the rest and those who escaped have fled with their tails between their legs."

"B4K is obliterated," Yuri growls. "Next, we have to deal with the Indigo Cartel. Smirnov lost his seat as Pakhan for allowing the cartel and that piece of shit gang to flourish in the city. Florida is *ours*."

Though I bow my head in agreement, I merely state, "We have bigger problems than a cartel, men."

Iosif blinks. "We heard about Moskva, Pakhan."

"Couldn't *not* hear about it," Yuri agrees.

"I'm glad that Turgenev's dead," Antonin mutters.

"Me too," mumbles Leonin Ovechkin. "Is it true you sliced his throat, Pakhan?"

"It's certainly not a lie." I heave a sigh when my voice locks and sign instead, "I'm an enemy of the Krestniy Otets."

"He's sided too many times with the Kuznetsovs for my comfort," Iosif comments. "His men are fucking animals. They play spy games. That's not what the Bratva is about. At least, it shouldn't be. I don't have stars inked on my knees so I'll bow before a bastard like Kuznetsov."

Yuri, a man with *six* daughters, grouses, "He hasn't been my Krestniy Otets since he tried to force that girl of his to marry when she was fifteen. Pig."

"What's your game plan, Pakhan?" Antonin asks.

My jaw works. "You follow me into the darkness, men?"

"*You* are our Pakhan," Yuri states. "The Krestniy Otets only grows fat on our earnings while *you* cover the increase in his tithe. You had my loyalty from the first day you took control of Florida, Pakhan.

"I know I'm not the only one who'd prefer a leader who hurls himself into warfare, who attends the funerals of his fallen, who cares for their dependents, than one who sits on his ass in Moskva."

"Now's the time to leave," I caution. "There's a war coming."

Iosif's chair scrapes back as he gets to his feet. He doesn't head for the door, however. Instead, it's his turn to slam his fist into his chest. "You are my Pakhan."

When the rest of my Brigadiers follow suit, leaving me the only man seated, I rasp, "The Krestniy Otets doesn't know what he's unleashed."

Antonin smirks. "He will soon enough."

CHAPTER FORTY-NINE

Nikolai Veles,

Your mutiny will not be tolerated.

You will stand down as leader of the Bratva in Florida.

You are officially an enemy of the Krestniy Otets.

May your death be painful and may your loved ones suffer in your stead.

50

CASSIE

DMITRI OUTLIVES HARVEY.

Boris said he stopped hearing my ex's strangled cries an hour after we left him outside the enclosure, but Harvey's death is a blip on the horizon in comparison to Dmitri's status.

He doesn't die, but he's still in a medically induced coma.

I'm hoping it's one of those daytime TV comas because, in the coming week, Nikolai's devastation is heartbreaking to watch.

He's quiet—and trust me, for a mute, that's saying something.

He's somber—more than before.

The only consolation is that I figured he'd pull away, but he hasn't.

Of course, the consolation comes with the caveat that he's more obsessive than before. Something to do with a note from Moscow.

The relief is unreal when they start to bring Dmitri out of the coma. Before he wakes up properly, however, the Krestniy Otets puts a wrench in our plans by sending two men to off Maxim while he's still in a hospital bed.

That's why we're heading to New York two days later.

Dmitri is okay—quiet, not speaking, battered, bruised, covered in bandages, but alive.

Thank fuck.

As a result, Nikolai feels he can leave Miami to handle the situation in New York.

I'm included in the 'fun' because unless Nikolai's got his eyes on me, he's not happy.

Which is how I learned there are cameras in our bedroom.

Now, *I'm* not happy.

Since I refuse to talk to him, it's been an awkward flight.

It also made me miss Dmitri because I've just started to realize how great of a go-between he was with a skill for breaking the ice and smoothing over sour situations.

And creating sour situations is a grade-A skill of my man.

No wonder Nikolai gained as much power as he did the last couple years—good cop, bad cop. Tried and tested. Dmitri was there to smooth over the path that Nikolai demolished and together, they ruled Florida's underworld.

I dread to think what could have happened if Dmitri *had* been lost to us.

With only twenty minutes remaining in the flight, Nikolai rubs his nose against my throat.

I sniff then tilt my face away.

"*Solnyshko*," he rumbles, that broken voice of his less gravelly than usual because he's had to start talking thanks to his many fractures and Dmitri's absence.

Not that he says a lot.

But for Niko, it's the equivalent of a sermon.

"What?"

"I have to keep my promise," he tries to appease.

"And you think someone's going to hide in our locked bedroom?" I twist on his knee to glower at him. "Are there cameras in the bathroom?"

He blinks. "No."

Because of the hesitation, I grind out, "If I discover there are, I'll cut you with Zub."

It's hard to be mad at him when most of his stories are heartbreaking—like how he lost his favorite alligator to a hunter and named the knife after her so he can keep the holster close to him for protection —but I'm angry enough this time to dismiss all that.

Especially when my threat has him smirking at me.

With another man, it'd be because he doesn't believe me capable of it.

But not Niko. No, he knows that I'd take his favorite knife and thrust it in his face.

"If you did that, *solnyshko*, there'd be repercussions."

Repercussions that come in the form of the erection that's made an appearance beneath my ass.

I roll my eyes. "Niko, this isn't sexual. It's my privacy! You've already stolen most of it from me. I think I should be allowed at least *one* personal area. Otherwise, it'll drive me crazy."

"I want to keep you safe," he says, and the pain that leaches into those words has me blowing out a breath.

Not only because that's the promise he's made to me time and time again, one he backed up with a team of guards who follow me around like shadows, but because Dmitri *wasn't* safe and he's taken on the full blame for that.

Sagging against him, I mutter, "I understand in the other rooms. I mean, that's how you saved me from Pavlivshev." A fact I'd learned during our argument. "But not our bedroom." I bite my lip. "Or my office."

"Your office?"

I nod, determined not to concede defeat. "Yes. I want an office. I used to have a blog before I left NYC, and I'm not going to continue with it, but I-I can't just sit around waiting for you to entertain me with your dick—"

"Why not?"

"—so I think I'm going to diversify," I continue, ignoring his interruption and waving my notepad at him. "I've been making plans."

"About what?"

"You'll laugh."

Niko frowns at me. "Me?"

Well, he has a point. That's a big ask for him. But...

"Yeah."

That has his frown darkening. "Why would I laugh?"

"Because I don't have..." I release another breath, annoying myself with my anxiety. "I was thinking about doing a cookbook."

"'Doing a cookbook,'" he repeats, then something slithers into his eyes. Something I don't trust. "You can have an office. Do you want a test kitchen too?"

"A test kitchen?" I ask warily. I mean, I do want one, but Niko, I've come to realize, is a born negotiator.

A nod.

"No cameras," I retort, diving into bartering mode. "Apart from one above the door to whichever hallway it leads onto."

"Agreed." He nods again. "I'll have—" His eyes close. Pain makes his already stark features bleaker so I know he was going to say 'Dmitri.' "—Igor arrange it. It can be done by the time we're back in Florida."

I already knew that money talks, but living that truth is insane.

We're supposed to be away for five days. Which means I'll have a full-fledged kitchen setup in *five* days.

Crazy.

"I want color options," I bargain.

He nods. "Of course."

I'm not entirely sure why he looks so satisfied, but hell, I just got a test kitchen out of it.

"We can make a studio too. For you to photograph the food. With your blog, you can use..."

And that's how, over the next twenty minutes, Nikolai has agreed to set aside an office, a studio, *and* a test kitchen on the second floor.

He's also confirmed that he'll use his contacts to get me a publishing deal which, to be honest, doesn't feel too much like nepotism because, with my blog and social media accounts, I think I'd have been a shoo-in for a publishing contract anyway.

It's only when we land and we're driving into the city that I realize what just happened.

I grab his uninjured hand. "By the time we're back home if you can make me a test kitchen and a photo studio, then you can have those cameras removed from the bedroom."

He thought I'd forget—*the cheeky shit!*

A soft gleam appears in his eyes. "Is there nothing I can put past you, *solnyshko?*"

Sure, there's plenty. But I still tip up my chin. "Nothing, *radnoy.* Nothing."

His nose crinkles. "Russian lessons, too."

I pout. "I learned that for you."

His smile is slow burn hell on my body. "*Meelyi*," he corrects. "That means loved one. *Radnoy* you would use with your father."

Well, that explains why Mom never used that on Papa.

Frickin' Dmitri—he was the one who taught me that.

"Ah, understood. *Meelyi.*"

He coaches me on the correct pronunciation, but his smile has twisted into a grin as I finally perfect it.

He graces me with a kiss in celebration then, against my lips, murmurs, "While I'm busy with my brothers…" He hands me a black Amex. "You will need clothes and things for this new endeavor of yours."

I smirk at the card. "You trust me with this?"

"I trust you with my life, *solnyshko.*"

That has my smirk dying as I ask, "Why? I could run away tomorrow."

I'm surprised when not a single flash of anger blasts into his expression. But his voice is deeper than usual as he rasps, "You would break my soul if you did, but I don't think you will. Around me, you are an Oskal. Predator, not prey." He kisses my knuckles. "Around me, you are the woman you were born to be."

He's right.

His love isn't a cage. It's a safe space. A place where I can be me. Where the woman I should always have been is celebrated. *Revered.*

"If I ran, would you hunt me down?" I question, but I already know the answer.

He hesitates, and I can see the fight *in* him, then he says, "I am not Harvey Rundel."

That in and of itself is a promise.

I twist our hands around so that this time, I can kiss his knuckles. "You're right, and *that* is why I won't run."

51

TEXT CHAT

Cassie: Hey! It's me. Cassie. I have a new number.

Savannah: HOLY. FORKING. SHITBALLS. CASSIE!!!

Cassie: Happy to hear from me?

Savannah: YOU KNOW IT. My God, I'm so glad you're okay!

Cassie: I'm better than okay. In fact, I'm gonna be in NYC soon. Want to meet up?

Savannah: You're coming to NYC?! I thought you were going to Canada! WHAT. THE. FUCK. IS. GOING. ON?!

Cassie: Jeez, enough of the caps. PlEaSe.

Savannah: Don't sass the original sasser! Now, you tell me what's going on!

Cassie: Harvey's not a problem anymore. :)

Savannah: Not a problem…?

Cassie: Uh huh. Anyway, tomorrow?
Shopping? The city? What do you say?

Savannah: I say there's too much you're
keeping from me.

Cassie: But… shopping? We both know
you're a shopaholic. Doubt that's changed.

Savannah: It's rude to use someone's
weakness against them.

Cassie: Lol. I mean, you're not wrong.

Savannah: I know I'm not. I rarely am.

Cassie: Bighead.

Savannah: ;)

Savannah: But sure. Tomorrow. Meet at Ellie's
Bakery?

Cassie: God, the last time I was there…

Savannah: I know, honey. That was when we
met for the first time in years.

Cassie: And Harvey had beaten me the night
before.

Cassie: Wow. That's… unnerving. In a
good way.

Savannah: We don't have to meet there?

Cassie: No. I like the symbolism of it. I'll get
Niko to drop me off.

Savannah: Niko? Who the fuck's Niko?

Cassie: Nikolai Veles.

Savannah: That sounds Russian.

Cassie: Probably because it is. He's my partner. :)

Savannah: Your partner? I don't hear from you in literal decades and when I do, you're in a relationship, unafraid of returning to the city, and aren't worried Harvey's chasing after you?

Cassie: Decades?! Hardly.

Cassie: Run a search on his name. I'm sure you'll figure out what happened.

Cassie: Anyway, tomorrow at 11?

Savannah: Sure. Now, don't disturb me. I have Google searches to run.

52

MISHA

FOR THE PAST TEN YEARS, I've anticipated chaos whenever Maxim and Nikolai share the same breathing space, but today's different.

Somber.

I suppose that's what happens when you're in limbo like we are.

Nikolai, much as he always does, walks into the room as if he owns it. Doesn't matter where he is or on whose turf he's standing, he just has that presence—a tsar in the flesh. His magnetic draw sucked me in when I was a child, sucked Maxim in too. Never mind the dozens of orphans who found their way to us over the years.

But it's not for me or Maxim that those same kids helped us out in Moskva—that was for Nikolai.

That was and is and forever will be his power.

The craziest thing of all? He doesn't even know he has it.

He strides over to Maxim, leans down, and kisses him on the forehead.

Maxim doesn't pull away.

My first clue that nothing will be the same today.

"*Brat moy*," he greets, voice gruff.

Brother mine.

Maxim grabs Niko's good hand—another shock. "Any news on Dmitri?"

"He's awake. That's all that we can ask for at the moment. And you? Are you better? Did the intruders injure you?"

He grimaces. "They didn't. But I'm still in pain from what happened in Moskva. I could use more time, but I have to maintain control. Misha's helping." He doesn't say that Kirill and Tima are as much use as *samovars* made out of chocolate.

"Who broke in and attacked?"

"Pushkin and Barkov."

"They're dead?"

Because I had fun with the men who thought they could harm my brother, I grin. "Of course."

Nikolai rolls his eyes. "Your poor girlfriend."

"I'm not into breath play with anyone other than enemies."

"Good to know," is my oldest brother's droll retort. "Are Pushkin and Barkov the traitors in your ranks that you've been seeking?"

"We hope there aren't anymore." Maxim rubs the back of his neck. "Is it true that you started that mess with the Albanians?"

Nikolai's smile is slow to form but when it does, it's clear that he had his hands all over that situation.

Shaking my head, I ask, "Why?"

His focus is stern. "Why not?"

"They're not our enemies," I point out.

"Neither are they allies. They wanted something that belonged to me."

"Enough said," Maxim inserts, which is a miracle in itself.

Normally, I'm the referee between the pair of them, not the other way around.

At my sniff, Nikolai ignores me and pins Maxim with a glance. "What the fuck were you thinking? Setting off explosions on Kuznetsov turf? We barely got out of there alive."

"It was worth it," Maxim mumbles.

"Worth burning bridges for? I doubt it," Nikolai snarls.

"Burning bridges?" he scoffs. "Like you did when you executed Turgenev?"

Though Nikolai grunts, he pins me with a look.

"What? You didn't think he deserved to hear the good news? We all have a reason to hate that fucker."

Groaning, Maxim sits up as he asks, "Have you heard of a hacker called Lodestar, Nikolai?"

Our older brother stills. "Everyone has heard of her."

"She went missing and I tried to find her at her last location." Maxim stabs a finger at Nikolai. "*That* is why I did it. Because she will owe me a favor, and that is the kind of favor every man wants. Especially when she's up to her eyeballs in the Irish Mob too."

Nikolai studies Maxim for long enough that I half expect Maxim to explode in temper, but instead, he asks, "How did you get involved with Lodestar?"

"That's my business," Maxim counters. "All anyone needs to know is that she owes me now. Twice over."

I don't rat Maxim out by telling Nikolai that no one has heard from Star Sullivan, aka Lodestar, in months.

"Who was on the team you used at Petrovsky Palace?"

"Does it matter?" Maxim dismisses. "They were allies."

Unsure why he's keeping the names close to his chest, I demur, "He wouldn't lie about that, Niko."

He'd better fucking not.

"What's your next move?" Nikolai demands, but that he's changed the subject means another miracle has happened—he's giving Maxim the benefit of the doubt instead of giving him shit for making bad decisions.

Maxim grimaces at that question because he's in more pain than he's letting on, but there *has* to be a next move—he must maintain control of the city and he can't do that from a hospital bed.

Even if he shouldn't be walking around for another month.

It's a 'kill or be killed' world, and we were lucky that the men we had on guard the other night were loyal. Any hint of sympathy to the Krestniy Otets in them and he'd be dead.

When he sucks in a breath, I can see his broken ribs still pain him, but he answers, "In the eyes of New York's underworld, I'm the de facto leader of The Forgotten Boys."

"That's cemented into place?"

"I attended a Summit with the other leaders. The three factions don't care who runs Russian turf. There's been enough gang warfare on the streets for them to want things to be business as usual. As long as I can assure that, I doubt we'll have any problems."

"And *can* you assure that?"

I clear my throat. "There's little loyalty left with Moskva among the men."

"How do you know that for certain?"

"Choices."

Maxim snorts at my brisk retort. "Return to Moskva or we'll kill your family."

I shrug. "It worked. The few who support that asshole fled."

"Fled to other territories that back the Krestniy Otets," Maxim counters with a tired sigh. "It was heavy-handed but it *did* work. Momentarily."

Nikolai frowns. "How many men did you lose?"

"Less than a dozen."

His brows lift as he comments, "Not many."

"*Da.*" His surprise is annoying. "I told you Maxim has earned their loyalty. You didn't believe me?"

"It's not that I didn't believe you; it's that you bought that loyalty. Anyone with a large bank account can come in and steal it out from under you."

"It's morphed by this point. Gossip from Moskva isn't good. And with Turgenev gone, there's going to be a power struggle for the role of Sovietnik."

"How did Dmitri take the news?" I ask.

Niko doesn't smile like I thought he would. There's no relish in his tone as he states, "He didn't react."

I blow out a breath into the sudden silence that falls between us.

Dmitri might be awake but if he doesn't rejoice in his sperm donor's death then…

Jesus Christ, I don't even want to think what that means.

Dmitri is the little brother that Maxim and I didn't particularly want. I think we can both admit that we were jealous when Nikolai gathered him into the gaggle of boys he saved from the streets after Maxim found him sobbing behind an overflowing trash can and brought him home.

Now, it's different.

He's family.

Whether he knows it or not, that's Nikolai.

He collects people. Not in a bad way, just in a *way*.

It could be his silence that lures people to his side, or it could be his strength.

That magnetism is something we need.

Desperately.

Grimly, Maxim changes the subject: "Has the Krestniy Otets retaliated against you, Niko?"

"Aside from this," he says, tossing a letter at us both. "Not yet."

'Yet' is the operative word.

It will come.

It always does.

Fatigue settles in my bones.

This life is exhausting but in all honesty, society is not a good place whether you survive in the underworld or above ground, and it's draining with or without my ties to the Russian Mob.

My girlfriend isn't a part of the criminal underworld.

She's the daughter of a rock god, yet she was kidnapped and *hurt*.

My mouth tightens at the memories of her nightmares last night. Unlike Cassiopeia, there is no closure for Aspen.

"The Krestniy Otets is in a difficult position," Maxim murmurs, breaking into my thoughts as he hands me the letter from our one-time leader. "You killed his Sovietnik and brought me back to the US, *but* you're the one who has the stronghold in the US South. You have the loyalties of one of the largest Bratva brotherhoods in the States, and you have alliances with almost every Pakhan here too.

"Then, there's the fact that Miami is still reeling from what happened with B4K. That was an undeniable show of strength, which will echo for years. He can huff and puff as much as he wants, but he has to know you're not going to be easy to take down."

Niko concedes that with a nod.

"You obliterated them all?" I ask.

"There's only a handful remaining. After they licked their wounds, they fled to the West Coast."

"That's the kind of power the K.O. should be frightened of."

Niko hums. "Perhaps. We won't have heard the end of him, though. That would be too easy."

"You have to make a choice, Nikolai," I tell him softly as I watch him sit back in the armchair beside Maxim's bed. He grimaces when his shoulder connects with the backrest.

The image of him flying through the fucking air as that gas explosion lifted him off the ground will stick with me for a lifetime.

As will the relief that followed when he landed in a goddamn swimming pool like something from the National Lampoon movies I used to watch with Dmitri when he was growing up.

"There is no choice to be made, Misha," is his cool and maddeningly calm retort.

I share a look with Maxim.

It speaks to how blank Nikolai's expression is that he's impossible to read.

"And what choice is that?" Maxim muses, his voice low.

Both of us know the truth—without Nikolai's support, we're dead men walking.

Might not be today, might not even be next year, but it'd happen.

Nikolai peers between us. "That you have to ask is irritating." His mouth tightens as he smooths his fingers over his suit jacket. "There was only ever one answer and I gave that to you when you were a small boy and I agreed to let you call me 'brother.'

"But I refuse to relocate to New York so we will have to take the entirety of the East Coast. Perhaps the States because I won't live here. It's too fucking cold."

That has Maxim blinking, but he sits up straighter than before, glee overtaking his fatigue from his injuries. "They forgot us once," he rumbles.

The energy in the room is infectious, enough that I rasp, "They'll never forget us again."

"We won't be silenced. *The Forgotten Boys.*" Nikolai nods but his lips twist as he releases—

No fucking way.

Was that a *laugh?*

Sure, it was bitter. But that *was* goddamn laughter.

While Maxim and I gape at one another in bewilderment, Nikolai is utterly unaware of how a sound we haven't heard in decades affects us as he tips his chin down and calmly, stalwartly, *ruthlessly* declares, "It's time to show Moskva who owns the States, *nyet?*"

53

MAXIM

THE SOUND of Nikolai's laughter haunts me even after he's left my apartment. Even after Misha has gone to sniff around his Z-list girl-friend. Even after I'm left alone to deal with my injuries.

I can't regret them, not when what I did was *right,* but fuck, what the hell have I started?

I triggered a war with my own men when I only meant to save—

"What does it matter?" I ask no one.

Grimacing with pain as I scrub a hand over my face, I lower my arm to the counter and try not to tense up as it makes the discomfort from the myriad cuts, bruises, burns, broken bones, and GSWs worse.

Unfortunately, as I do, I catch a look at my face in the vanity mirror.

I'm already covered in scars so the extras on my body can't spoil what was ruined when I was a child.

Still…

Every year, I'm turning into more of a fucking monster than I was before.

Grabbing the shit I need to clean up, I grit my teeth once I dab alcohol onto the raw wounds and then pat antibiotic cream on top after the area is dry. Wrapping it up again, I heave a sigh when that's finally done then shift on to the next one.

And the next one.

And the next.

When I'm finished, each future scar stinging with the echoing burn of the alcohol, I curl my hands around the cool marble counter and inhale then exhale deeply to relieve the discomfort.

Eyes narrowed as I stare at my reflection, the light of my cell's screen switching on draws my attention.

From this distance, I read the text:

> LHD Courier: Package Delivered.
>
> LHD Courier: Handed to and signed for by Eoghan O'Donnelly.

That has my lips tightening in annoyance.

Will my gift end up with Victoria Vasov, my future bride? Or will it be confiscated by her brother-in-law, the Irish Mobster, O'Donnelly?

As I withdraw a bottle of aspirin from the medicine cabinet, I mutter to myself, "Only time will tell."

54

CASSIE

"CASSIE!"

"What?" I retort innocently, grinning when Savannah rolls her eyes at me, making me grateful for the company and that she'd been able to fit me in today with only an evening's notice.

"That cost forty grand."

"He said I could buy whatever I wanted," is my logic.

Sure, Niko meant clothes, but I have clothes. He bought them for me. I need the specialist camera equipment more than I need another dress.

She huffs. "This isn't the shopping trip I expected."

"It's more fun?" I nudge her arm. "We can head to a clothes store after I pick a desk, seeing as I haven't thanked you for saving my butt yet."

Her lips form a pout. "I'm not certain there's much to thank me for when I got you tied up with the Russian Mob."

"Harvey's gone," I assure her. "That's a gift in itself. And that gift only came to pass because of Nikolai. Ergo, you."

"When you texted me about... everything last night, I looked into him. Deeper than a Google search, let's put it that way."

I expected no less.

"You know who he is, right?"

That was a multifaceted question. "I mean, yes."

"They call him 'Mute.'"

"Knew that." I'd overheard Dmitri calling him it once. *Mockingly.*

"They say he doesn't talk."

"Well, he didn't. He does now. Ish."

"What?"

"He kind of had to start. He doesn't say much but it's better than it was. And you can tell it hurts him."

She frowns. "Hurts him?"

"I don't really understand it but when he speaks, it's like he's in pain."

I can tell that doesn't fit the image she'd painted of him, but it doesn't stop her from asking, "You know he kills people for a living?"

"Excuse you? Who, pray tell, are you married to?" Though she rolls her eyes, I snort. "Managed to figure that out, Savannah. Why are you warning me off him? I don't think Aidan is any better."

"Yeah, but I like that about him. I don't want him to be better. I love that he's..." Her eyes turn dreamy. "...feral."

I nudge her again. "Before I lose you to the world of fantasy, can we get this conversation over with so I can go and choose a desk?"

She harrumphs. "I'm just saying, I enjoy that about my husband. You're not like me."

"No, I'm not," I agree. "There's only one Savannah Daniels."

"Savannah O'Donnelly," she corrects with a grin.

I think about my father for a moment, then about what Nikolai said to me on the plane.

"I'm not saying he's Christian Grey, Savannah, but I think Niko is pretty perfect for me. Just like Aidan is for you."

Her brows lift but she asks, "As long as you're sure?"

"I am."

"And if you need him to be killed, then I have a great in with a mob boss, you hear me?"

"You're a better friend than I deserve, Savannah."

She sighs but winks at me. "Story of my life."

When the cell phone Nikolai bought me yesterday buzzes with a notification, I frown as very few people even know I now possess one.

Despite having a million guards on me, Nikolai couldn't deal with me leaving his side without being able to get in touch.

Funny how that'd have felt like a chain around my neck with Harvey.

With Nikolai, on the other hand, it's a reminder of what I am to him, of who *he* is to the world.

> Unknown: Nikolai gave me your number this morning. I assume he wants us to be friends?

> Unknown: This is Maria. Pavel's wife.

My frown deepens.

"What is it?" Savannah asks.

"It's this woman… She's the wife of Niko's third-in-command."

"What does she want?"

"To be friends."

She snorts. "You look like she asked you to eat rotten eggs."

That has me blinking. "I guess I'm just not used to making friends anymore."

"Now's the time to start. If she's the wife of someone high up the ranks and has been for a while, it'd be good to get her on your side."

"Why?"

"Because she'll know things you don't, things you might need to learn if you intend on being with Nikolai for a long time." She tilts her head to the side. "*Do* you intend on staying with him…?"

The words *forever and a day* whisper through my mind.

I just clear my throat and nod.

She hums. "Then, make friends. Better than making enemies."

"True. I guess I'm out of the habit, you know?"

"That bastard. How did Rundel die again?" she queries, a curious look in her eye.

"Painfully," I chirp, knowing she was guessing that was why Harvey isn't a problem anymore.

At my confirmation, a smile beams from her. "Fabulous!" She wafts a hand at me. "Go on, answer her."

"God, you're bossy."

That has her preening. "Aidan says that's his favorite part about me. After my ass." She stills. "Or was it my tits?"

"I don't want to know," I groan as I type out:

> Me: Hey there. Nice to hear from you :)

> Maria: Nice? I'm not nice. That's the first thing you should learn about me.

> Maria: Myata has flown the nest BTW.

"Who's Myata?" Savannah asks over my shoulder, reading the messages when they come in.

"This woman who told everyone she was engaged to Nikolai."

"Good thing she's gone seeing as he belongs to you."

I like that turn of phrase more than I want to admit.

> Me: Oh, that's good news, I guess?

> Maria: The best. You've already got half the women in the Bratva sniffing around Nikolai. One down is better for you.

> Maria: Plus, he cut her out in the most humiliating way imaginable so that should stop the ovaries from getting ideas above their stations.

> Maria: I'll help you keep him. Come to my store when you get back, da? We'll find you clothes to keep him on his toes.

> Me: Store?

> Maria: Niko says you got your toga from the gala there.

Oh.

That store.

"She owns a clothing store?"

"Trust you to be interested in that, Savannah," I tease, but a smile flirts on my lips. "And yes, she does. Apparently. Well, I don't know if she owns it. Nikolai kind of reappropriated this dressmaker's place."

"Reappropriated?" Savannah asks carefully. "Why do I think there's a story you're not telling me here?"

"The proprietor called me fat, so he threw her out." *And fed her to Vasily.* "Seems like he's given the business to Maria."

She blinks at me. "He seriously did that?"

I blush. "He did."

"Okay, I love him, then. That's the kind of whacko shit Aidan would do for me." She sighs. "Don't you just adore these assholes who'll burn the world to the ground at your feet for you?"

That has me gaping at her. "I mean, I guess?"

"There's no *guessing* about it. Reply to her. You need her on your side, stat, if she can hook you up with clothes too. No offense, honey, but you tend to dress like a nun."

Though I roll my eyes, I tap out:

> Me: That sounds great. Maybe we can go for coffee when we return to Miami?

> Maria: Haha. If you think Nikolai will let you out of the house for coffee in Miami, you're mistaken. But I have nice Lamborghini now. I come to you, da?

> Me: Da.

My cheeks flush when Savannah snorts.

> Me: I mean, yes.

> Me: Talk soon.

"We've started reserving a hotel room."

I frown at Savannah. "Who has? You and Aidan?"

I'm not sure I even want to know. Savannah is the queen of over-sharing. Doesn't matter that our friendship has been on hiatus for a decade, she dove right back in as if we'd been BFFs for years.

"No. My sisters-in-law and I. We get together in the hotel room and that keeps the men from worrying and we have some non-penis time."

My lips twitch. "Sounds like an idea. Nikolai's really worried about me."

Consistently.

Constantly.

Ceaselessly.

It'd be suffocating if I didn't understand *why*.

After what I saw on that Moscow airfield, I get it.

"Well, they have a reason to worry about us, don't they?" she asks, but it's rhetorical.

I guess if anyone understands, it's her. Aidan's the head of the Irish Mob and Nikolai's the head of the Russians.

We're their weaknesses.

Comfortingly, like she knows where my mind tripped, she curves her arm around my shoulders. "Come on, let's go buy you crazy expensive office furniture then we can head to my favorite shoe store and I'll show you some heels that'll drive Niko wild. He deserves it for getting rid of Rundel and for sorting that bitch out for calling you fat. What a cunt."

My smile morphs into a grin. "Sounds like a plan."

55

NIKOLAI

"IT'S a pleasure to meet you, O'Donnelly."

Aidan flicks a look between Cassiopeia and me and then his wife. Slowly, he holds out his hand for me to shake. When his fingers tighten around mine, I don't let the pissing contest bother me or my fractured fingers.

Especially when we're in his home—an apartment in one of the largest skyscrapers in the city, one from their billion-dollar front Acuig Corp.

Surprisingly, it's not the penthouse, but the space is cavernous for all that.

"You hurt her, I'll hurt you."

The warning doesn't set my teeth on edge because he means it, and my Cassiopeia deserves nothing less.

"Aidan," Savannah hisses, nudging him in the side as she clutches at his hand. She disarms me by not chiding him for his incendiary words but, instead, by leaning onto tiptoe and kissing his cheek. "I'll thank you for that later."

Cassiopeia snorts at my bewildered stare. "You get used to their PDAs. I barely spent any time here and knew to approach any room, closed door or otherwise, with caution."

Savannah, still curled into her husband's side, beams at me. "Aidan's only saying what I'm thinking. He'll go the mob route, but I'll just figure out how to send anthrax to you."

"I'd trust her on that score. She's more than capable of procuring it," O'Donnelly demurs, finally relinquishing his hold on my hand.

Knowing that I'm expected to speak, as always, I'm cautious with my words. "I appreciate the protection you offer her. As unnecessary as it might be."

O'Donnelly grunts. "Never thought I'd be hosting a Bratva Pakhan in my home after the last one canceled our dinner party."

"You have Cassie to thank for that," Savannah muses, eying her. "Didn't know she had it in her."

Cassiopeia snorts, unoffended. "Yes, you were always the crazy one in college. I was the smart, sensible one."

"You weren't so sensible today when you dropped forty grand on that camera setup." Savannah winks at me. "She's got expensive tastes. I taught her well."

I slide my arm around Cassiopeia's shoulders. "Whatever she needs, she can have."

O'Donnelly grunts. "What she *needs*," he drawls, "is a dead husband. Is that asshole dealt with? You didn't see the damage after he'd beat the fuck out of her."

My eyes narrow with remembered fury. "He's dead. And I made sure it hurt."

O'Donnelly smirks at me. "Misha told me that you have alligators… Is that true?"

Misha shared such things with the Irish? I'll have to beat the fuck out of him the next time I see him. "You know my brother well?" is my response.

"Not well, but from dinners with Savannah's family," he concurs.

"I have an alligator sanctuary, yes."

"Interesting. Easy way to get rid of the evidence."

I tip my chin up, neither confirming nor denying that, then offer, "I thank you for giving Cassiopeia a safe place to stay."

"You don't have to thank him. You didn't even know me back then," she mutters, her cheeks blooming with heat.

I can't stop myself from cupping one and swiping my thumb along the blossoming red that's trickling down her throat. "No, I didn't know you back then, but you were still mine. He protected you, kept you safe for me until I came in to take over, and for that, I owe him."

Something flickers in her eyes, but when she licks her lips, I know she needed to hear those words.

"A token?" Aidan muses, his interest clear before Savannah drops his arm and this time, she doesn't squeeze him and kiss him—she tuts.

"No, Aidan. No token. She's my friend. No favors. She needed help and we gave it to her." With a huff, she snags Cassiopeia's hand then, in a snit, declares, "Men!" and drags my woman away to the kitchen.

As I watch her go, amused by the hapless shrug she shoots me, I murmur, "Regardless, the offer remains, O'Donnelly."

"No, she's right. It was the least we could do." His gaze locks on mine when I cast him a surprised glance. "What's going on with Maxim Lyanov, Veles?"

"Officially, I don't care but Misha won't say a fucking word. I know he's stopped being Bratva and has started being a Forgotten Boy or whatever the fuck that is."

"Your intel is correct. However, I'm no longer Bratva either."

He eyes me up and down. "You're as old as me which makes you too long in the tooth to be any kind of 'boy.'"

My smile morphs, darkens. "You were raised in New York City with a silver spoon between those orthodontic-set teeth in a school that the children of senators attended, O'Donnelly. I was bred on the streets, lost to society, and forgotten by everyone other than the family I collected for myself.

"You can take the child off the streets, but you can't take the streets out of the child."

O'Donnelly tensed at my initial retort, but slowly, he nods. Then, he holds out his hand again. "Truce?"

I shake it.

This time, there's no pissing match.

"Truce."

56

CASSIE

A Little Bit Yours - JP Saxe

"MOM," I rasp as the door opens to reveal Dema Turgenev, whose arms immediately fling wide to embrace me.

This visit was unexpected, to the point that I didn't know I was on the way here until Nikolai warned me during the ride over.

He promised me that she wanted to see me, and how she holds me in her arms is all the confirmation I need.

When she hugs me, embracing me as fiercely as I need to be embraced, I don't even try to withhold my sob of relief.

Like he senses my inner turmoil, Nikolai's hand settles on my lower back. Warm. Affectionate. A reminder—*he's there*. Not intruding, just a whisper of safety that lets me settle deeper into my mom's bear hug.

As I squeeze her in return, she rocks me, muttering, "I let you down, Cassie. I'm so sorry. I didn't even know Harvey was…" She swallows. "I just didn't like him. Didn't approve. And when you married him so soon after your father's death, I got angry. Bitter.

"I let distance come between us when I should never have allowed that to happen." She swipes at her tear-stained cheeks. "I didn't even know he was hurting you until Nikolai contacted me. I'm so ashamed—"

"Stop it," I order, finally able to get a word in edgewise. "Please. There's no need. I hid it from everyone."

"You'd never have been able to hide it from me. Not if I hadn't been—"

"Grieving? You'd lost Papa, Mom. You were reeling. We both were." I close my eyes. "I don't know why I let him persuade me to get married so soon after his death. It felt right. I was lost, and I was sure it'd help me find myself again but he used my grief against me. Isolated me even more. I was stupid—"

Behind me, Nikolai releases a hiss. "Stop it. You were not."

Mom flickers a look at him, but she doesn't comment. Just pulls back to study me, then she lets go of my waist so that she can cup my cheeks. "It's not stupid to love someone. It's not stupid to let yourself be vulnerable with them. They're the stupid ones for taking that love and weaponizing it.

"I just wish I'd known. I could have done something—"

"I wouldn't have let you," I mumble. "He had me under his thumb."

"I didn't even know you were missing."

"How could you?" I appease, her despairing tone soothing something raw inside me.

I've missed her.

She cups my chin. "I will do better by you from now on, child. Do you hear me?"

I smile at her. "I'm not a child, Mom."

"You'll always be my baby. That's why I'm angry at myself. I should never have..." Her eyes flicker shut. "Your father would have been so mad at me for letting such distance come between us. He'd be ashamed of me."

"He shouldn't have left us," I counter, still irrationally annoyed that he *did* dare to leave us.

Papa was always our referee so, without him, it was natural that we'd flounder.

A soft laugh barks from her. "You're right. He shouldn't have." With her grip still on my chin, she tilts my head to the side. "You look good. Better than good. Beautiful. Happy."

When she presses a kiss to my forehead, it reminds me so much of my father's patented move that more tears prick my eyes.

"I *am* happy." It's nuts but that doesn't stop it from being the truth. I really am. "I'm safe. He can't get to me anymore. Nikolai saw to that."

"He's dead?" She doesn't aim that strange question at me—she aims it at Niko. "Well?"

The expectant tone has my eyes widening.

"Yes, I know who you are," she retorts, aiming the words at Niko, whose expression isn't as blank as usual—he's taken aback too. "Is that bastard dead or do you not deserve my daughter either, '*Mute*?'"

'Mute?!'

"Mom! You can't say things like—"

"He passed away, yes," Niko interrupts me, angling his head to the side.

Mom shoots him a wide grin, eyes sparkling with delight. "Good!" Then, she encourages me over the threshold and tugs on Nikolai's good hand too. "I made tea. How your father took it."

The Russian way.

"Mom," I mutter, tone wary as she slams the door closed. "How do you know who Nikolai is?"

She doesn't answer, just continues dragging us toward the kitchen where there's a spread that takes me back to my childhood.

There's Keemun black tea infused with orange and served with jam for sweetness, cookies on one side and crackers with ham and cheese on the other. She's gone all out—fresh blinis surrounded by a bowl of sour cream, with small dishes of red and black caviar on a bed of ice. That's all for Niko because she knows I hate fish roe.

There's my father's favorite, Medovik cake, and Bird's Milk cake, too.

Smiling, I inform Niko, "She's trying to impress you."

"He returned my daughter to me," Mom declares, tone stout as she hustles Niko into the chair where my father sat—at the head—then, she glances between us as she plants herself at the packed kitchen table while she drains boiling water from the *samovar* into a small teapot. "That's worth baking for."

Though I slip into my seat, I ask again, "How do you know who Nikolai is, Mom? How do you know people call him 'Mute?'" In fact... "What do you know about Dad's time in Russia?"

I hadn't even thought about broaching this topic of conversation today, not on our first meeting in years, but I have more questions than ever thanks to her bloodthirsty interrogation.

Exactly *who* are my parents?

I gasp as a thought occurs to me. "You're not Russian as well, are you?"

Mom snorts. "No. I'm not, thank you very much. American born and bred."

"Sleeper agent?" Niko rumbles, but his question makes me tense.

"No. I hate Russia. Hate the Kremlin. Hate everything Russian-shaped apart from my husband. And," she mumbles, her tone begrudging, "you if you *did* deal with the bastard who hurt my baby."

Is this conversation actually happening?

While I'm gaping at her, Niko confirms, "He's dealt with."

Mom sniffs. "Good. I'd like to say I told you so about Harvey, honey, but I won't—"

"You technically just did," I grumble.

Ignoring me, Mom serves us tea and passes out the dishes. "I'm just a standard American who fell in love with an ex-spy. It's not how the romance books make it look," she says dryly, but there's a wistfulness to her tone that tells me how little she regrets her choices.

My mom and dad loved each other.

I know, categorically, that was why I'd married Harvey—I'd been chasing that love.

Hunting something so pure it was borderline mythological in how it bound two people together so intrinsically, it was soul deep.

I'd always been a daddy's girl, but when we'd lost him, I'd practically lost her. Her grief had led to depression, and Mom at rock bottom had been, in a word, *mean*.

The memories are tough, but not as tough as living back then.

Nikolai's hand slides across my shoulders and he curves his arm around me.

He couldn't have known where my mind took me, but I'm not surprised that he's found an excuse to touch me.

Touch is his love language.

Because yes, he does love me.

I can feel it.

With every beat of his heart and mine, I know ours chime to the same song...

Just like my mom and dad.

Biting my lip as I turn into him, I rasp, "Dad worked for the Kremlin?"

"Before the USSR crumbled, yes. He liked to say that he was smart and got out in '85 but he was injured in a job. That was when he lost his hearing. We met a year later." She blinks. "He was a good man, darling. Don't ever question—"

"I don't," I state, cutting her off. "He was my papa. You don't have to excuse what he did."

When I tip up my chin, obstinacy rattling through me, she purses her lips at me then studies Nikolai. "I suppose it's a good thing you're short-sighted when it comes to those you love."

The words should hurt because of Harvey, but I know she doesn't mean it that way.

"Nikolai is a good man."

"He's Bratva."

"Yes," I agree, "he is. And he's the first person to love me unconditionally since I lost Papa."

She tenses, accepting the sting I'd intended to cause her, but bows her head in agreement. "I deserved that."

"You did, but I won't make a habit out of it. I didn't come here to throw insults. I want to be friends, Mom. I want to know you again. I've missed you, and when I was on my own, I didn't dare come to you because I knew Harvey would—" Just the thought of what he could have done has me swallowing.

"I sleep with a shotgun. I'd like to have seen him try to get past me," she says with a sniff.

"You can put the shotgun away," Nikolai drawls as he picks up his glass of tea contained within the old-fashioned *podstakannik* and takes a sip. "This is good," he says appreciatively.

Mom's smile is smug. "It's how Peshnya liked it best."

Niko's brows lower but he drains the cup and silently returns it to Mom for her to refill. "You have guards on you."

Mom pauses mid-refill. "They're your men?"

"They are. I'm surprised you noticed them."

"Peshnya made me paranoid," she mumbles, but her hand is shaking so she rests it on the table which is where I lace my fingers with hers. "When they didn't approach me..." She sags. "God, I thought it was the Kremlin. After everything that happened in Moscow recently, I wasn't sure if they thought..."

"We all know Peshnya's dead," Niko assures her.

She grunts then tugs my fingers tighter into her grip. Her smile is brighter, even though I can see how shaken she is with her relief. "Don't think I don't know you've changed the subject." Her expression turns expectant. "So, are you going to tell me how that son of a bitch died, or do I have to drag it out of you?"

57

NIKOLAI

Let Me Go - Maverick Sabre

"YOU KILLED HIM, but that doesn't mean you're worthy of her."

It comes as no shock to me that she takes that stance once Cassiopeia heads to the bathroom.

"I agree," I tell her, not for the first time glancing around the very ordinary, very tired kitchen.

Peshnya had a reputation that is far too large for a house this small.

Everyone wondered where he went before the USSR collapsed. It seems Warren County was his hideaway of choice, in a tiny two-story townhouse with a garden larger than the property itself.

Perhaps she can sense my confusion about her home because she keeps scowling at me, even as she placed me at the head of the table earlier.

I begin to see where Cassiopeia got her contrary ways from— they're inherited.

With narrowed eyes as she serves more tea, tea that I half expect to get tossed in my lap, Dema inquires, "Why isn't she wearing your ring?"

"Because I had to kill him, first, and secondly, I needed your permission seeing as her father is no longer with us."

"Smooth, very smooth." Her mouth tightens as she lifts her teacup to take a sip of the incredibly strong brew.

If I hadn't known she'd been married to a Russian, that alone would have confirmed it.

"She didn't know who her father was but when did you find out?"

She eyes me over the cup. "A year after we married."

"Do you mind if I ask how?"

"I got shot by one of his old... colleagues. Lost our first baby. I nearly left him."

"He chose to tell you everything?"

"Almost everything. By that time, he'd retired from his work. My husband was a lot older than I was." She studies me. "I already lost my daughter once to a bastard who tried to destroy her. Your rep makes Harvey look like a puppy dog."

"I would never hurt her. I only want what's best for her."

The question is, how does she even know what my rep is?

"I'm sure Harvey would have said the same thing at one point."

I concede that with a nod then pick up a blini. "I'm a murderer. I've killed hundreds, Dema. Will kill hundreds more before I die." I hitch a shoulder as I use the mother-of-pearl spoon to drop beads of caviar onto the homemade pancake. "I'm not a good man but I'm better than Harvey. Her safety will always be my priority."

"And what if she needs to be protected from you?"

"That will never happen."

"If it does?" she persists.

Studying her, and seeing the intensity behind the question, I grace her with my full attention. "Do you know what an Oskal is?"

Her sniff is disparaging. "Of course I do."

"I've seen your daughter around Rundel. I've seen her when she's cornered—she reacts like prey. With me, she does not because she knows, deep in her being, that I will never hurt her. That she is safe with me. I can offer no assurance other than that." I pause. "When I found her, he'd tied her to a bed and had drugged her. The moment I set eyes on her, I knew what she was to me."

"What?"

"My little sun," I say simply. "I lead a dark life, something you're already aware of if you know *who* 'Mute' is and *what* 'Mute' has done, but she brings light to those shadows."

"Life is long. Marriage makes it seem even longer—"

"It will never be long enough. Not with her at my side." I purse my lips. "How did Peshnya keep you safe after that first attack?"

Dema doesn't blink at the change of subject, but neither does she pick it up. Instead, she requests, "I expect your vow that if Cassie—"

"Cassiopeia," I correct.

"I call her Cassie. That name was her father's idea. Not mine. Obsessed with the stars he was," she says on a huff. "*Anyway,* if Cassie ever wants to leave you, I want you to promise that you'll let her go."

"My word might mean nothing," I point out.

"Perhaps, but I have ways of making you comply."

That has my brows arching. "Ways?"

"Jeremy Beech."

Suddenly, this woman stops being my future mother-in-law and she becomes a threat.

Despite the situation, I grin at her. Slowly.

If she knows what an Oskal is, then I'm sure she also knows she's looking at the human version of one.

"It's been a long time since I heard that name," I drawl.

"Twelve years?" she prods. "Twelve years since you killed a US senator and never got arrested for it."

That job was how I became Brigadier.

Slowly, I nod. "And we have an agreement. We didn't need it, but I understand that you've already been assured and lied to by her ex-husband that she was safe with him."

Her eyes narrow even further. "I'm glad we understand each other. After I die, I'll leave the evidence with her so that she can escape if she wants."

"That's only fair." It'll never be necessary, but I *can* empathize.

I also understand that Dema, with her fussy kitchen overdecorated with clashing florals and pig ornaments dotted on every surface, is not to be underestimated.

"How did you know about Beech?"

"When those men showed up, I started snooping through my husband's things."

His things?

Spying my confusion, she gets to her feet. "Come with me." Hesitating, she says, "I don't trust the Bratva."

"I don't blame you."

"But you're not the Bratva anymore, are you?"

I catch her gaze with my own. "I'm not, but you could trust me anyway. Cassiopeia will only know safety as my woman."

"That's a promise you *can't* keep. Not in this world you live in." She startles me by patting my shoulder. "But this old heart appreciates the reassurance. Come with me. It's worth it."

Still studying her, *still*, I'll admit, impressed, I follow her as she leads me to a door off the kitchen.

As we head toward a basement I didn't realize she had, I find there's another door with a bare lightbulb swinging above it.

"You asked me how Peshnya kept us safe," she says flatly.

It isn't the first time she's called him that, but it's the first time I feel comfortable enough with her to ask, "You actually called him Peshnya?" Cassiopeia had told me as much but hearing it is rather surreal.

She hitches a shoulder. "It became a term of endearment."

"You know what it means?"

Her grin is cold. "Ice pick. His weapon of choice."

My eyes widen.

Blyad, it's no wonder my woman turns into an Oskal around me—it truly is in her bones.

Dema unlocks the door to reveal a room that is lined with filing cabinets. Each row makes a solid wall, creating a passageway within the tight confines of the basement.

It's almost like a labyrinth.

I can't help but wonder where the Minotaur's hiding down here.

"Peshnya ran from the USSR before its collapse and he collected information on the right people to keep us safe when the Kremlin wouldn't leave him alone," Dema informs me. "You heard of someone called Bear?"

I shake my head. Then, it clicks. "The right people meaning the Bratva?"

She dips her chin. "I know what you're capable of. Know what the Bratva is capable of too. But I told you so already."

Something flickers in my mind, but I just demur, "I will *never* hurt her."

Dema doesn't respond to that, just says, "I've been reading up on your situation, Nikolai. My daughter's safety lies with you—"

"You can't trust everything you read in the papers." That 'something' which fluttered in my mind crops up again. "Or on blogs."

"*Your* safety was compromised when you killed Fyodor Turgenev," she states, ignoring me entirely and holding out a hand that encompasses the room. "Take whatever you need to ensure her protection. It's yours.

"Now, I'm going to spend some time with my daughter and leave you to deal with business."

She starts to leave, but I stop her by gracing her with an offer I didn't expect to make, "I have a large estate in Florida with plenty of room and an expansive garden. You are always welcome to visit."

That has her shooting me a grin, one that beams from her—once again, I'm reminded of her daughter. "I accept that invitation. We already lost too much time. I won't lose anymore."

Curious, I clear my throat. "Turgenev—was your husband related to Fyodor?"

"Second cousins. He'd have approved of you killing him. He always said his family were a bunch of assholes."

I dip my chin but ask, "How did he die? It says 'accidental death' on his death certificate."

Her hand tightens into a fist at her side. "He was dying of cancer and took pills to speed up the process. Cassie… doesn't know any of that. She thinks he never recovered from a heart attack."

Remorse hits me and all I can think to say is, "I apologize for intruding on your grief." It's obvious that she feels the pain of his loss as if it happened yesterday and not close to two decades ago.

"I appreciate that."

"Who's Bear?"

She hitches a shoulder. "Friend of my husband. Worked on this with him. Thought you might have known him."

When she makes to leave, I don't stop her, but only as her steps fade into silence do I start pulling open drawers.

As I flick through the files, I smile to myself. Old the information might be, but that doesn't stop it from being very, very pertinent.

"*Solnyshko*," I whisper, feeling the heat of her light even in this basement, shadowed by the crimes of my brothers.

Some things, I recognize, are fated.

My meeting Cassiopeia Turgenev was one such event.

The future is not as secure as I'd like it to be for her, but there is one solid truth that I will live my life by until the day I die—she *is* my little sun.

My Persephone.

And this Hades will never let anyone, man or God or her mother, steal her from me, and her father just made sure that will never happen.

CHAPTER FIFTY-EIGHT

I told you so...

BLOG

And you heard it here first, boys and girls, Çela, the leader of the Albanian Mob in Kentucky, is officially no longer on this mortal coil.

Rumors abound in Lexington of the circumstances behind his death, but until the autopsy is completed, we won't know for certain.

It's clear that this time, Çela lost the war.

I'll be watching to see if Adrianu Kadare finds his place at the top of the tree or if someone steals it from him.

If Kadare *does* take over, then Kentucky, you're not ready for what's about to hit you.

That's a promise.

59

TEXT CHAT

Nikolai: Was that you?

Troy: :)

Nikolai: How's it feel to be free of him?

Troy: Better than you can even imagine.

Nikolai: You want Kadare as a leader?

Troy: I don't care. Feel free to meddle…

Nikolai: I will. But you still owe me a token.

Troy: I don't forget my favors.

Nikolai: Until we talk again…

Troy: Until then.

60

TEXT CHAT

Ilya: Did he go through with it?

Dmitri: Da.

Dmitri: He's off the market for real.

Ilya: All the pussies will cry.

Ilya: Never thought I'd see the day that the great Nikolai Veles would get hitched.

Dmitri: If you say so.

Dmitri: Why are you messaging me anyway?

Ilya: We're family, aren't we?

Dmitri: My family's in the States.

Ilya: Don't burn bridges, kid. Not when your side of the world could go up in flames tomorrow.

Dmitri: I'll let Nikolai know you said that.

Ilya: Snitch all you want.

Ilya: When it boils down to it, we're on the same side.

Dmitri: What side's that?

Ilya: I see what game you're playing, kid… I'll bite.

Ilya: We both want the same man dead, don't we?

61

CASSIE
LATER THAT SAME YEAR

Daylight - David Kushner

WHEN NIKOLAI PINS me to the wall, I don't argue.

His hands hold mine overhead, and his face nuzzles deep into my throat as he kisses me there before nipping the tender flesh.

I can feel his teeth scraping and know he's marking me. I hope the bruise lingers. I love seeing them, love trailing my fingers over the visual reminders of his need for me.

Because he knows of my fascination, he places open-mouthed kisses on my throat then moves down, down, not stopping until he's on his knees in front of me. One foot he angles on his shoulder, spreading my thighs, and then he's there.

Feasting on me as I stand, tongue flickering over my clit, suckling me, sliding a finger in deep before thrusting another inside my pussy and pumping them into me.

Rocking my hips, pressing my sex into his face, I fight his control over my orgasm by increasing his pace, sliding my hands into his hair to grip a firm hold of him.

I've earned this.

He growls against my clit, the vibrations sending sparks through me that have me yelping in response. A deep groan swiftly follows as he takes me higher but, uncaring about my hold on his hair, he jerks away, slams to his feet, then hauls me up, grabbing both my thighs and drawing them around his waist.

When I realize his cock is out of his fly, I moan as he slides into me —this time, not his fingers, but his dick. My nails scrape over his scalp as he fills me, inch by glorious inch until gravity does the rest and I'm overfull with him.

Even after months together, and after weeks spent with a broken arm, fractured fingers, and a dislocated shoulder, speech isn't comfortable for him. He communicates through groans and growls, his voice no longer lost but not exactly found.

So, when he rumbles something in my ear, something in Russian when he's usually quiet, a soft whimper escapes me after he nips my earlobe.

I'm still shit at Russian, private lessons or not, and he knows that— the tease.

I gasp in his ear, "What did you just say?"

I recognized *solnyshko* but not much else, and when he pumps faster into me, my query fades because all that matters is he. Does. Not. Stop.

With a mewl as his hand tunnels between us so he can find my clit, I rear against him, back arching as he takes me there. Higher, harder. Deeper, faster.

My face crumples as I soar through the orgasm, melting and burning and exploding—

"Nikolai!" I sob as he takes me through the first climax, growling more words in my ear, words I can't understand in this state.

I don't bother trying.

Then, I feel him explode inside me, but he doesn't stop. His cum drenches me. He's so deep that I can feel him butting up against my cervix and the bittersweet pleasure/pain is so excruciatingly good, it has lights flickering at the edges of my vision.

Then, he wreaks further devastation on his poor wife… He coats my clit with his cum as he continues to rub the center of my pleasure, not stopping until I bite his shoulder. Until I sob again. Until I clench around him, not wanting to let go of him, not wanting him to leave me.

The next thing I know, I'm not against the wall. I'm in our bed and he's looming over me, studying me as if I'm the most precious thing in the world to him.

I might be coming in a close second in the future, but that's a demotion I can handle…

His eyes burn with heat as if he didn't just take me moments ago, as if his cum isn't pooling between my thighs.

"There was a time when this painting was the only sunlight in my life," he rumbles, making me angle my head back on the pillow to flick a glance at the Clyfford Still above the bed. "I would give it away plus everything else I own to keep you at my side, *solnyshko*."

"Aren't you lucky I come for free?" I tease, leaning up to press a kiss to the corner of his lips.

He grunts then starts to move, ultimately laying his head on my belly, muttering, "I never imagined you'd give me the sun as well as the stars, *solnyshko.*"

Stroking my hands through his hair, I smile. "Only fitting seeing as you gave me the moon."

A moon I didn't think I'd be gifted with—not at my age, not with my problems.

A soft breath escapes him, then he continues on his way down, down, down.

As he studies my pussy, a pussy that he shaved this morning, and watches his cum trickle out of me, making a mess on the sheets beneath us, he states grimly, "If you faint again, I'll kill Grigoriy."

That has me huffing as I lean on my elbows. "Hey, no murder in bed. I told you that already."

"He hid this secret from me," he signs before his tongue flickers out so that he can circle my sensitive clit.

I shudder as I watch him.

There's something animalistic about watching him eat his own cum and it'll never not annihilate me.

I spread my legs because, again, I deserve this—fainting wasn't fun, and the landing was worse. Thank God for the million guards I have or I could have really hurt myself.

Not that I share that fact with Niko—I'll have a detail of two million by tomorrow.

"Only because I didn't want to get your hopes up," I mumble, eyes turning dazed as he goes to town on me.

"No secrets, Cassiopeia," he chides, speaking the words this time.

"Like you 'forgot' to tell me about getting Oborin and Yolkin—" The Pakhans of Arizona and Chicago who were now *Shukhers*—leaders in The Forgotten Boys. "—on board?"

He grumbles and I feel the soft vibration against my pussy.

"Like you 'forgot' to tell me that Dmitri and I are cousins?"

He grumbles some more then has me crying out when he leaves, but he's soon back between my thighs and his wunderdick is sliding through my folds.

When his tongue teases mine and I taste us both, he continues rocking his hips, nudging my clit with every thrust until release sparks through me.

Fire slaloms through my veins, lighting me up from the inside out as pleasure overtakes my senses. Throughout it all, he doesn't relent on the kiss—stealing my air which intensifies my orgasm.

My entire being quivering in reaction, it takes a while for me to come back, for the earth to be beneath my feet once more, and when it does, when he knows I've returned to him, he murmurs, "No business or family talk in bed."

I roll my eyes and, hoarsely, joke, "I think I prefer it when you're silent."

Humor lights up his face—an expression that I know I'm privileged to see.

Cupping his chin with one hand, I trail my other over his cheekbone.

Right here, in this bed, is my entire world. My future too. *Our* future.

And he made it all possible.

Every day, he safeguards us. Every day, he shields us from Moscow's wrath.

The red tide is changing.

The Bratva foothold in the States is shifting, morphing, turning toward us rather than against us. A feat he works tirelessly to ensure— all for our future.

My eyes close. The joy I'm feeling is too much for me to contain.

Even my mother, who moved in with us last week, can't deny that Nikolai doesn't just *tell* me he loves me—he shows me.

Every goddamn day.

When he presses a kiss to my temple, I sigh as I cuddle into him.

"How was Savannah?"

I grin a little at the wariness in his tone. Still, it's a relationship I know he's trying to cultivate because it's a struggle for me to make friends. So far, Savannah and Maria are the only women, outside of my mom, whom I talk to on the regular.

Trust... it's not easy for either of us. Hell, I don't even trust the staff at *Nav.*

While resolved, the situation with the Albanians made me paranoid, so I prefer to stay in my office, cooking up recipes rather than trying to play nice with a bunch of bitches who envy the man I get into bed with.

That's probably why I have one cookbook with a publisher's editorial team already and another in the works that'll be a collaborative project with my mom.

"She's fine."

"That woman is never fine. She's a drama queen."

I hitch a shoulder, unable to deny it. "She told me some interesting news."

He tenses. "I don't want to know if it's from her."

My lips twitch. "It wasn't sex-related."

"Thank God for that. I'm no prude but she shares far too much with you," he mutters disapprovingly, which only makes me chuckle as I press a kiss to his cheek. "What's the news then?"

"You know Lodestar is her kind of sister?" I pause. "And her sister-in-law, I guess. Well, almost. When she gets married to Conor O'Donnelly—"

He starts stroking my hair. "I know what you mean, yes, *solnyshko*."

"Sorry," I mumble. "I'm still learning the ropes with her family. There are so many of them."

"You never have to apologize to me," he disregards. "Especially as I know you only took an interest in the O'Donnellys because I asked you to."

I'd happened, one day, to tell him about a woman called Lodestar who was practically Savannah's sister—in the same way that Maxim and Misha were his brothers—after Savannah had spent the entire day bitching about Lodestar's inability to check all the TikToks she sent her.

Because I could empathize with Lodestar's dilemma as Savannah sent a ridiculous amount of videos to me too, I'd shared the tale with Nikolai.

When he'd told me that Maxim had only gotten us all into this mess because of a woman called Lodestar, not exactly a common name, I didn't think it stretched the bounds of my friendship with Savannah to keep a close eye on that situation...

Especially when this Lodestar owed Maxim a favor.

I'd come to learn the importance of favors in this world—they ran deep.

"What did you learn?" he asks, his tone bland, but I know him too well.

The blander his tone, the more curious he is.

"Apparently, a man called Anton Kuznetsov died yesterday."

He tenses. "Really?"

"Yes, really. Who is he?"

"A man whose name we never utter in Russia."

I snort. "Like Bloody Mary?"

"Only worse." He presses a kiss to my temple. "Why did she tell you?"

"She didn't mean to. She got all awkward and quickly changed the subject." I cuddle into him. "That's why I thought you'd want to know."

"Good call, *solnyshko*," he praises. "Interesting that his death hasn't made the news yet."

"He's powerful enough to make the news?" I ask, surprised.

"*Da*," he rumbles, and his drifting into Russian merely punctuates Kuznetsov's power.

Not particularly interested, I shrug. "They're probably keeping a lid on it then. Maybe until his family can make a statement?"

"Perhaps." He graces me with another kiss on the temple. "Did you see that link I sent you today?"

I grimace. "Yes." Misha's girlfriend Aspen had just gone viral thanks to her and her twin swimming with sharks. "I still don't think it's fair for you and Maxim to try and break them up. What were you even doing on Instagram anyway?"

He shoots me a dour look. "I wasn't the one who found it."

"I quite like the idea of you scrolling through videos for fun…"

His expression grows impossibly dour*er*. "Maxim sent it to me."

"You should just let them be. You're happy. Why isn't Misha allowed to be happy too?"

"He can be happy. With a woman who isn't making a name for herself as a celebrity Z-lister. It's not as if she flies under the radar."

I huff. "Meanie."

His lips curve as he nuzzles his nose against mine. "Vasily's spawn were hatched today."

My nose crinkles. "Congratulations?"

"Thank you," he teases, chuckling.

"I still don't know how you figured out they're his kids."

"Breeding program," he says simply. "Looks like we'll be going through the joys of early fatherhood together."

"So long as you don't eat your hatchling…"

"I won't," he drawls.

"Zub's line continues," I say softly.

This time, his smile is genuine with his joy.

Having met Vasily, I'm not sure how to be joyful about more alligators being in our backyard, but hey, we all have our quirks, don't we?

"Grigoriy gave me some good news today, by the way."

"About Dmitri?" I ask excitedly, tipping onto my side to stare at him.

"He's ready to stop physio."

Relief beams through me. "That's fantastic news!"

Dmitri has had a rough passage back to good health so that's wonderful to hear.

"I'm sure the added incentive worked as motivation."

My smile is knowing. "I wonder why."

He taps his finger on the end of my nose before signing, "It was needlessly dangerous for Sofia to escape to the US to see him."

"You say that, but if her presence is helping him…"

He doesn't have to say or sign a word for me to feel his relief too.

That Dmitri will get to meet his baby brother was one of the first things I thought of when I received confirmation of my pregnancy.

I blame my hormones for the tears in my eyes, the tears that choke me up much as they did when I had that thought initially.

And it's ridiculous, so off-topic that it's nuts, but I can't go a minute longer without telling him the one solid truth, the only thing that makes sense to me in the craziness that is our life together: "I love you, my *Aides*."

A soft chuckle rushes from him at the nickname, one that he earned when my Russian tutor told me the story of *Aides* and his *Persefóna*, but amusement aside, the words come from his soul as he intones, "And I love you, my *Persefóna*. Always."

I believe him.

For forever and a day.

Meant To Be - Bebe Rexha, Florida Georgia Line

Stay tuned for Dmitri and Sofia's story—BANISHED...

AUTHOR NOTE

DARLINGS,

I hope you fell for Nikolai and both love and envy his Persephone.
;)

When I said this was a retelling, I actually borrowed from Greek mythology and Slavic paganism!

Hades and Persephone are from the Greek myths.

In their story, Persephone lives with her mother, Demeter, in a world of perpetual summer. One day, Persephone is kidnapped by Hades and is trapped there. While Demeter searched for her, her grief led to the first winter. Persephone knew that eating or drinking anything from the Underworld would imprison her there forever. Demeter demanded her daughter's return and Hades complied, but he offered her one final thing to eat—a ripe pomegranate of which Persephone ate six seeds.

Upon her return to her mother, the earth experienced its first spring.

Yet, each of those pomegranate seeds represented a month. For six months of the year, Persephone would return to the Underworld to be with Hades, and winter would come to the earth. In spring, she would return to her mother, and spring would ensue.

So, I twisted that myth with Slavic ones because I'm cheeky like that!

Nav is their Underworld, and Veles is their Hades.

There is a myth that Hades once cheated on Persephone with a Naiad called Minthe. Persephone, learning of this, turned her forevermore into the mint we eat today. Myata is the Russian word for mint! :D But, of course, *our* Hades would never cheat on his *solnyshko*. And our Hades doesn't have to return his Persephone to her mother, he just brought the mother to his Underworld. :P

Anyway, I hope you enjoyed their story!

So, a few things:

- We first meet Cassiopeia in FILTHY KING, which just so happens to be Aidan and Savannah O'Donnelly's second book. Their love story begins in FILTHY HOT.
- Please know that I do not believe that ANYONE who is neurodivergent or on the spectrum is a freak. However, in Russia, things are not as cut and dry as they are for us. Autism is not easily recognized/diagnosed, and people with it aren't treated in the manner they deserve. To be frank, I don't think even in *our* society, people on the spectrum are treated how they deserve to be treated. This world could use more kindness, period.
- When **SILENCED** reaches 500 reviews, head to my Diva reader group for a bonus scene! www.facebook.com/groups/SerenaAkeroydsDivas
- If you enjoyed SILENCED and are new to my universe, then flip the page and find the full reading order for a world where the Irish Mob, a Jersey MC, and the Sicilian Mafia reign over New York with The Forgotten Boys.

Much love,
Serena
xo

SERENA'S MAFIA/MOB/MC UNIVERSE

THE FIVE POINTS' MOB READING ORDER WITH THE FIVE POINTS' MOB, A DARK & DIRTY SINNERS' MC, & VALENTINIS...

FILTHY
FILTHY SINNER
NYX
LINK
FILTHY RICH
SIN
STEEL
FILTHY DARK
CRUZ
MAVERICK
FILTHY SEX
HAWK
FILTHY HOT
STORM

THE DON
THE LADY
FILTHY SECRET
REX
RACHEL
FILTHY KING
REVELATION BOOK ONE
REVELATION BOOK TWO
FILTHY LIES
FILTHY TRUTH

RUSSIAN MAFIA
Adjacent to the universe, but can be read as a standalone
SILENCED
BANISHED - Coming Soon

FREE BOOK!

Don't forget to grab your free e-Book!
Secrets & Lies is now free!

Meg's love life was missing a spark until she discovered her need to be dominated. When her fiancé shared the same kink, she thought all her birthdays had come at once, and then she came to learn their relationship was one big fat lie.

Gabe has loved Meg for years, watching her from afar, and always wishing he'd been the one to date her first and not his brother. When he has the chance to have Meg in his bed—even better, tied to it—it's an opportunity he can't refuse.

With disastrous consequences.

Can Gabe make Meg realize she's the one woman he's always wanted? But once secrets and lies have wormed their way into a relationship, is it impossible to establish the firm base of trust needed between lovers, and more importantly, between sub and Sir…?

This story features orgasm control in a BDSM setting.
Secrets & Lies is now free!

CONNECT WITH SERENA

ABOUT THE AUTHOR

I'm a romance novelaholic and I won't touch a book unless I know there's a happy ending. This addiction is what made me craft stories that suit my voracious need for raunchy romance. I love twists and unexpected turns, and my novels all contain sexy guys, dark humor, and hot AF love scenes.

I write MF, menage, and reverse harem (also known as why choose romance,) in both contemporary and paranormal. Some of my stories are darker than others, but I can promise you one thing, you will always get the happy ending your heart needs!

Made in the USA
Monee, IL
16 June 2023

35945148R00246